BENEATH LONDON

ALSO BY JAMES P. BLAYLOCK
AND AVAILABLE FROM TITAN BOOKS

Homunculus
Lord Kelvin's Machine
The Aylesford Skull

JAMES P. BLAYLOCK

BENEATH LONDON

TITAN BOOKS

Beneath London
Print edition ISBN: 9781783292608
Electronic edition ISBN: 9781783292615

Published by Titan Books
A division of Titan Publishing Group Ltd
144 Southwark Street, London SE1 0UP

First edition: June 2015

1 3 5 7 9 10 8 6 4 2

This is a work of fiction. Names, places and incidents are either products of the author's imagination or used fictitiously. Any resemblance to actual persons, living or dead (except for satirical purposes), is entirely coincidental.

James P. Blaylock asserts the moral right to be identified as the author of this work.

A CIP catalogue record for this title is available from the British Library.

Printed and bound in the United States.

Did you enjoy this book? We love to hear from our readers.
Please email us at readerfeedback@titanemail.com or write to us at
Reader Feedback at the above address.

To receive advance information, news, competitions, and exclusive offers online,
please sign up for the Titan newsletter on our website.

WWW.TITANBOOKS.COM

As ever, this book is for Viki

And for John and Danny, best of all possible sons

"Men do not change, they unmask themselves."

MADAME DE STAEL

PROLOGUE
THE DARK REALM

The distances that stretched away on three sides of the great cavern lay in perpetual half-darkness, with absolute darkness above, the invisible ceiling of the cavern supported by limestone columns as big around as forest oaks. Now and then Beaumont could discern the pale tips of stalactites overhead, conical shadows standing out against the darkness. He could hear the sound of ambitious bats skittering about, which meant that night was falling in the surface world. The ruins of a stone wall built in a long-forgotten time were just visible to the southeast, according to the compass that Beaumont carried in his pocket.

The track he followed ascended to a secret passage on Hampstead Heath very near the Highgate Ponds. It was a four-hour journey, and he intended to complete it before the moon rose over London. He rarely had need of a torch to find his way topside, although he carried one of his own making beneath his oilskin cloak, which he wore against the wet of the upper reaches where the underground London Rivers, the Tyburn and the Westbourne and the Fleet, leaked through their brick-and-mortar floor and through the cracks and crevices in the limestone below, forming other nameless rivers in the world beneath.

Behind him stood the stone dwelling to which his father had added a stick-and-thatch roof many years ago, the thatch well preserved in the dry air in this part of the underworld. The structure itself, which his father had called simply "the hut", was built of stone blocks and was ancient beyond measure. Minutes ago it had been cheerful with lamplight. Beaumont had a plentiful supply of lamp oil in the hut, as well as food – jerk meat and salt pork and dried peas, and there was sometimes a feral pig to shoot, although no way to keep the meat fresh. It had to be butchered and hauled topside. It was a mistake to leave a pig carcass close by and so invite unwanted guests out of the darkness. He had seen the leviathan itself not far from this very spot when he was a lad, an immense reptile four fathoms in length with teeth around its snout like the tines of a harrow. Today he had left his rifle in the hovel, wrapped in oilcloth, along with several torches. He had no safe place to stow it topside, and no reason to carry it topside in any event.

The ground stretching away roundabout him glowed with a pale green luminosity now, reminding Beaumont of the wings of the moths that swarmed around gas lamps late at night in London alleys – "toad light", Beaumont's father had called the glow when he had first allowed Beaumont to accompany him to the underworld. The "toads" were in fact mushrooms, some of enormous girth and as tall as a grown man – much taller than Beaumont, who was a dwarf – although these monsters grew only in the deep, nether regions. The older, dried-out toads burned well and were plentiful enough for warmth and cooking both.

Those toads that were living glowed with an inner light,

brighter on the rare occasions that they were freshly fed with meat, dim and small if they subsisted on the wet muck of the cavern floor. Fields of smaller toads grew in the shallows of the subterranean ponds where Beaumont sometimes fished. These were the brightest of the lot, dining on blind cavefish that swarmed in the depths. When he was a child, his father had told him that the toads were nasty-minded pookies, fashioned by elves at midnight, but Beaumont didn't hold with elves. He had never seen one, neither in the underworld nor topside, and he had no reason to believe what he hadn't seen with his own eyes.

After an hour of steady travel he entered a bright patch of toads, where he could check his pocket watch, which he had pinched from an old gent in Borough Market. It was past eight o'clock in the morning on the surface. He was weary of the darkness and the silence, which he had endured for three days now. He saw nearby a pool of water glowing with toad light. A misty cascade fell into it from the darkness above, geysering up in the center and casting out a circle of small waves. Despite his weariness, Beaumont stepped across the muddy fringe of the pool to look within – to do some fishing, as he thought of it, although not for the swimming variety of fish.

He had always been a lucky fisherman, as had his father been, finding castaway treasures that had fallen from the underground rivers and sewers that lay in the floor of the world above. There had been gold and silver rings aplenty, some with jewels, and all manner of coins, including crown and half-crown pieces and enough gold guineas to fill a leather bag, which was buried in the hut under rocks for safe keeping.

He took out a torch and used the stick end to shift the stones, and saw straightaway a fused ball of coins the size of a large orange.

He waded out into the water and picked it up, then quickly waded back out again and shook the water from his oiled boots. Crouching by the edge of the pool, he broke up the ball of coins against a rock, swirling mud and debris from them, and carefully collecting them again from the bottom. He counted them as he did so: one hundred and forty-two Spanish doubloons. That they had come to this place was uncommonly strange: birds of a feather, mayhaps, the way they were gathered together. But they were clearly meant for Beaumont to find and no one else, which he knew absolutely because he had found them.

He stowed them away and set out again, moving upward along a muddy game trail that had been trodden flat by feral pigs, some of them prodigiously large, judging from their hoof-prints. But these prints were old enough. They didn't signify. And pigs were a noisy lot that stank; they wouldn't take him unawares.

Just as he was telling himself this, he saw the impression of a boot-print, half trodden out by the passing of the pigs. He stood still, unsettled in his mind. Rarely had he seen such a thing before, not this far beneath, not unless it was a print of his own boot, which this was not. He tried to recall how long had it been since he had taken this particular way to the surface – two years, perhaps. He moved on slowly, peering at the ground until he found a print of the toe of the boot, almost too faint to make out in the dim light, for the nearest cluster of toads was now a good way ahead of him. He had to be certain, however, of the thing that he feared – he was surprised to feel his heart beating so – and so he removed his cape and drew a torch out of his bundle, lighting the beeswax-soaked rope with a lucifer match and shading his eyes from the brightness.

The shallow print was plain in the light of the torch – a hobnailed boot, the nails forming the five outer points of a pentagram and the five inner crossings. Beaumont quenched the torch in a shallow pool before moving on again as silently as he could, anxious now to make his way toward the surface, and not at all anxious to meet the man whose boot had left its mark in the mud – a man whom he had believed to be dead.

He rounded a bend in the path, but stopped at the sight of a man who reclined on an enormous clump of vibrantly luminescent toads, his flesh and hair and beard aglow with the moth-green hue. The stalks had affixed themselves to him, his right hand and forearm deeply imbedded in the pale sponge. A broad, fungal cap had crept down over his forehead, although his face was still clear of it, and would remain so, for the toads would allow him to breathe.

Beaumont had seen pigs kept alive thus, wounded pigs that had stumbled in among the toads and were imprisoned by them, sustained for years, perhaps forever. He could see the slow heaving of the man's chest as he drew air into his lungs. His fob-chain was still secure in the pocket of the vest, stained green-black from fungal secretions, the fabric of the vest half rotted away where the chain was pinned to it by what looked to be a ruby stud, although the stone was more black than red in the strange light. A yard away from the imprisoned figure sat the telltale shoe, its hobnailed pentagram visible on the sole.

Was the man asleep? Or was this a mere semblance of sleep, a wakeful death? Perhaps it would be a kindness to shoot him, although he owed the man no kindness. It wasn't in Beaumont to kill a man, however, even this man, who was already as good as dead. But certainly it made no sense to leave such a man in possession of a pocket watch and chain. He stepped as close as he needed to and hooked the stick-end of the torch beneath the fob-chain. With a careful circular motion he turned three loops of chain around the stick, lifting the watch out of its pocket.

"Father Time lives topside, your honor," he said in a low voice. "He has no influence here below." And with that he jerked the barrel upward and away, snatching the watch out of the vest pocket and tearing the chain stud away from the vest.

In that moment the eyes of the captive fluttered open, glowing green and unnaturally wide, a look of terror within them, but without, thank God, any hint of recognition.

ONE

MR. TREADWELL AND MR. SNIPS

"Only the two maps, Mr. Lewis? And very tentative maps, I must say. They were apparently drawn by someone with only a modest knowledge of the underworld. This is a meager offering, sir, scarcely worth our time."

Mr. Treadwell, the man who had spoken, wore a smile on his face – a smile that was habitual with him, as if he were in a constant state of subtle amusement. He was a large man with a trim white beard, dressed in brown tweed and with a comfortable look about him. He spoke in a light-hearted, easy tone, though his voice did not at all put Mr. Lewis at ease. Mr. Lewis, a small, pale man with the face of ferret and a tubercular cough, was rarely at ease, although never so ill at ease as he was just now. There was nothing artificial in Mr. Treadwell's manner, and so Mr. Lewis was utterly incapable of reading him.

"As you can see," Mr. Treadwell continued, "I brought one of my associates along today. You can call him Mr. Snips – or not, as you see fit. People have called him worse things, certainly." Mr. Snips apparently saw nothing funny in the quip, for he stared in a bored way in the direction of Admiralty Arch. Mr. Snips's hair was receding, and he wore a small toupee inexpertly glued on, something that was apparent now in the freshening wind. It might have been comical on anyone else.

They sat, the three of them, on metal chairs around a small table in front of Bates's Coffee House in what had recently been the Spring Gardens, although it was now an area with islands of lawn and occasional small trees. The day was cool, autumn leaves skittering past on the pavement before lifting into the air and whirling away. Behind them stood the Metropolitan Board of Works building with its Palladian façade, people going in and coming out through the high entry door that had been eccentrically fixed into the front corner of the building. Mr. Lewis, who was employed by the Board of Works, looked from one to the other of the two men, his own countenance slowly taking on an appearance of desperation in the extended silence.

"Snips is a whimsical name, Mr. Lewis, don't you agree?"

"No, sir. I mean to say... whimsical, sir?"

"You have no grudge against whimsy, I hope."

"No, Mr. Treadwell, I do assure you." He nodded at the alleged Mr. Snips, affecting a smile, and said, "I wish you a good morning, Mr. Snips." The man turned his head slowly to look in Mr. Lewis's direction, but his eyes held no expression at all and were apparently fixed on some distant object behind Mr. Lewis's chair, as if Mr. Lewis were invisible.

"Mr. Snips, allow me to present Mr. Lewis of the Board of Works, adjutant to the Minister of Rivers and Sewers," Mr. Treadwell said. "I very much hoped that Mr. Lewis would find the gumption to make a bold stroke on our behalf after taking our earnest money and then betraying us to our meddling friend James Harrow. It was Mr. Lewis who provided Harrow with the ancient bird recovered from the sink-hole by a common tosher, a wonderfully preserved bird alleged to be aglow with an interesting variety of luminous fungus moss. And now Harrow is anxious to lead an expedition into the unknown realm beneath our city, there to discover we know not what, to our great dismay. But we cannot allow that to come to pass, can we Mr. Snips?"

"No, Mr. Treadwell, we cannot. We *will* not."

"Mr. Lewis has thought to do penance for his sin by providing us with the odd map, such as you see here, but his efforts are less than enthusiastic. I have it on good authority that Harrow was given a set of first-rate maps, nothing like these mere sketches. His were *secret* maps, apparently, unavailable to the public – the public being your humble servant." He pursed his lips and shook his head, apparently far from satisfied. "What do you say to that, Mr. Snips?"

"What do I *say* to it, Mr. Treadwell?" He regarded Mr. Lewis sharply now, as if memorizing his features. "I don't *say* a thing. I *ask*, rather: does this man have any family to speak of?"

"Oh my, yes," Mr. Treadwell said. "Seven children and a loving wife. They dwell in lodgings off Lambeth Road that are surprisingly smart, well beyond Mr. Lewis's station, one would think. The Board of Works, however, provides wonderful opportunities to better one's station with very little effort, you see. In this case the betterment was offered up by Dr. Harrow and a wealthy friend of Harrow's by the name of Gilbert Frobisher, who has been very much in the news recently. Gilbert Frobisher has a deep purse, Mr. Snips, and he has allowed our friend Mr. Lewis to dip into it with an open hand. Mr. Lewis, understandably, has taken a special interest in their desires and very little interest in ours."

"Then I suggest that we have Mr. Lewis draw straws, here and now, to choose who gets his thumbs lopped off, oldest or youngest child."

Mr. Treadwell looked appropriately shocked to hear this. He held his upturned palms out before Mr. Lewis in a gesture of helplessness. "I'm afraid that Mr. Snips is a desperate rogue, Mr. Lewis, when the fit is upon him. I'm deeply appalled by his bloodthirsty suggestion."

"The two maps was all I could reproduce in the moment, Mr. Treadwell," Mr. Lewis said in a strained voice. "It would take a mort of time to have the Board's maps copied out fair, and a solid reason for asking it, too, them being secret. This makes four maps in all, sir, this past month, which amounts to very nearly the agreed upon number."

"Very *nearly* the agreed upon number, do you say? That's scarcely mathematical, sir. If your banker used such a phrase, you'd be in the right of it to take him to task. But none of us are bankers, thank heavens. Our hearts are not bound in triple brass like the men in the counting houses. Now sir, something has occurred to me that might satisfy Mr. Snips." He patted his coat pocket, nodded brightly, and drew out a piece of paper. "I'll tell you what it is, Mr. Lewis, as plainly as I can manage. Dr. Harrow's expedition is to be limited to three men and three men only. You see their names written down here, and I'll warrant that you recognize all three. Two of them are, of course, Gilbert Frobisher and James Harrow. The third is a Professor Langdon St. Ives, one of Mr. Frobisher's particular friends. Those three and no others are to be allowed permission to set out on this expedition. It is my wish that you limit the size of the expedition at the *very* last moment. Do I make myself quite clear? The area exposed by the sink-hole will be closed to any but these three men."

"But Mr. Frobisher has asked permission for a round dozen to accompany him and Dr. Harrow, sir, aside from Professor St. Ives – porters, learned coves from the university, a photographer from the *Times*, even Harrow's sister. I cannot see how I can ..."

"Oh, I can see it quite clearly, Mr. Lewis, and I can see the result if my wishes are ignored. A photographer from the *Times*, do you say? And carrying first-rate maps? Heaven help us. We cannot countenance such a thing, can we Mr. Snips?"

"No, sir. Not for an instant."

"Here is the way of it, Mr. Lewis. Permission to any but these three must be denied in the eleventh hour, as you value your children's thumbs. Mr. Snips is unfortunately handy with his pruning-shears, which he keeps carefully honed. Come now, Mr. Lewis! I beg you not to disfigure your features in that antic manner. Keep it in your mind that if you fail us, you fail your family. I'll thank you to have the four remaining maps in our hands by Tuesday. If you cannot have them copied out in a thoroughgoing manner, then fetch us the original articles – those that you haven't already passed on to Harrow. Feign ignorance when the time comes to explain to your superiors why they are missing. You are apparently practiced at the art of prevarication. You'll keep us informed, of course, as regards the Harrow expedition."

Mr. Treadwell nodded meaningfully in Mr. Snips's direction now, and Mr. Lewis swiveled his head in a mechanical way to follow his gaze, his face a rictus of fear. Mr. Snips had opened his shirt at the neck in order to reveal a curious necklace – a strand of wire upon which were strung a round dozen withered thumbs.

* * *

A short time after sending Mr. Lewis back to work, Mr. Treadwell and Mr. Snips leaned against a wooden railing above the Thames and looked down into the void opened by the Great Sink-Hole, as the *Times* referred to it. From their vantage point they could see little of the cave that reportedly led away beneath Upper Thames Street, but they could easily make out the remnants of the fallen buildings and the rubble of broken pavement that lay mired thirty feet below.

An army of men was active along the river: shipwrights, carpenters, masons, and laborers taking hurried advantage of the waning tide, and, in the case of the laborers, of the Crown's offer of ten shillings a day for ten hours work, many of the men working double shifts to gain the one-crown bonus. A bulwark of posts had been sunk into the Thames mud in a great half circle around the hole. The posts were fitted with strake upon strake of good English oak. The pitch tubs were smoking hot, the heaps of oakum ready for the caulking mallets. A portable crane on a barge belched steam and noise as it placed enormous boulders at the upriver end of the hole in order to convince the Thames to flow around it rather than sloshing into it when the tide rose again.

"Poor Mr. Lewis," Mr. Treadwell said, although *Treadwell* was not in fact his name, nor was *Snips* the name of the man who accompanied him. "He doesn't much like the look of a severed thumb."

"Not many men do, I've found."

"You're in the right of it there. It's a persuasive argument. What did Mr. Franklin say? 'An ounce of prevention is worth a pound of cure,' if I remember correctly. I find Mr. Franklin a sad bore with his maxims. What do you think of him?"

"I don't know him, unless you mean Sidney Franklin, the prizefighter. I knew him when he was tap-boy at the Lamb and Kid near Newgate. He was a good lad, but had his eye gouged out and his back broke in his bout with Digby Rugger. That put an end to his capers in the ring. He died a beggar."

"I suspect that we're referring to different Franklins. But speaking of pugilists, I'm not entirely fond of your new mate, Mr. Bingham. He's weak, deceptive, and deeply stupid. By 'weak' I refer to his mind, of course."

"His fists have come in handy a time or two. I can keep him on the straight and narrow."

"Can you now? I'll hold you to that. When you go into Kent a week from now, watch him carefully. If he becomes a hazard to navigation, sink him. You'll collect his portion of the profit if you do. The decision is yours to make, although I advise you to consider it thoroughly."

"What if this Professor St. Ives won't play cricket?"

"He will. Harrow's expedition will draw him into London. St. Ives put paid to Narbondo's capers with Lord Moorgate, which cost several of us a pretty penny, and he's a neighbor of the Laswell woman, who, as you know, mustn't be allowed to interfere with our goals, but at the same time St. Ives must not be harmed. I have use for him. I do not resent St. Ives for his efforts, mind you. He's a do-gooder, widely known as an honorable man, which is his chief weakness. That being said, we had best not underestimate his considerable intellect and his penchant for what is commonly called heroics. No, sir. St. Ives can be a right dangerous opponent, although also being a humble man he does not characterize himself that way, which has led others into stupidities, Ignacio Narbondo among them. I repeat that he must not be harmed. As my agent you'll avoid stupidities as you value your life."

TWO

A GOLDEN AFTERNOON

It was a rare autumn day in Aylesford, Kent, the year 1884, a cloudless blue sky in November after a long week of Indian summer, the warm breeze stirring the lace curtains through the open casement. Langdon St. Ives sat in his easy chair with his feet on a cushioned footstool, his copy of the *Times* open on his lap: more news of the vast sink-hole that had collapsed a section of the Victoria Embankment several weeks past, swallowing shops and houses near Blackfriars Bridge.

The collapse had occurred very near the site of the destroyed Cathedral of the Oxford Martyrs, a debacle that had almost cost St. Ives his life a little over a year ago, not to mention the lives of his wife Alice and his son Eddie. The Metropolitan Board of Works had managed to dam the river edge of the sink-hole, stopping the Thames from emptying into it at high tide, and planned to stuff it full of asphalt, sand, and gravel at the first opportunity.

St. Ives gazed out of the window into the far distance where a line of tall beech trees stood along the edge of Boxley Woods.

Among the native trees stood copper beeches that must have been planted in a distant age, given their great size, and the air was clear enough today so that St. Ives could see the distinctly purple foliage, still hanging on. He contemplated the turning of the seasons, trying to prevent his mind from straying to the possibility that his own part in the destruction of the Cathedral had caused a subterranean shift that had ultimately resulted in the collapse of the Embankment. Perhaps the two events were simply coincidental, he thought. Surely they were. Despite his momentary uneasiness, however, the fair weather pleased him, and the mild breeze was like a tonic.

The dormant hops fields in the near distance made a stark contrast to the fields that had flourished with vivid green plants in midsummer. Small hillocks of soil covered the rhizomes and stubs of last year's vines now, all very tidy and ready for cold weather. The dead vines had been burned, and the buds dried in the oast house and delivered to Mr. Laporte, the brewer in Wrotham Heath. Hasbro, St. Ives's long-time friend and factotum, although by now more friend than anything else, had driven away in the wagon half an hour past to collect the several kegs of ale that St. Ives had negotiated in partial payment for the hops. Hasbro's return would add a celebratory air to the already perfect afternoon.

A portion of the fields had been enriched experimentally with elephant dung, of which they had a fair quantity. Dr. Johnson, their resident Indian elephant, had been a birthday gift from his wife Alice a little over a year ago, and had proved to be an amiable creature, quickly becoming a member of the family and setting up a strong bond with Hodge the cat, with whom it often took a ramble. Finn Conrad, the fifteen-year-old boy who lived in a cottage on the property, was at the moment teaching the elephant to turn a capstan that opened a broad panel in the roof of the barn. Now and then cries of "Ho, Johnson!" and "Heave away, sir!" drifted in through the windows, along with the ratcheting sound of the mechanism that opened and closed the panel.

The dirigible that St. Ives had at one time intended to levitate through the open barn roof had been destroyed beyond repair when he had deliberately sailed the craft through the glass lid of the doomed Cathedral of the Oxford Martyrs, of which nothing now remained – neither of the Cathedral nor the dirigible. That had occurred a year ago last spring, shortly before the coming of the elephant, and the expense of another dirigible was too great to be considered. St. Ives had purchased a hot air balloon in its stead, soon to be delivered, which would make both the elephant and the moveable barn roof eminently sensible.

"I believe I've got it," Alice said, looking up from her work. She was dressed in duck trousers and a blouse of the same linen, the cloth having been washed with stones until it was soft and pliable. She was tall – very nearly six feet in her stockings – with long black hair, haphazardly arranged. She showed him a tied fly, which she held by the hook, the fly glowing in sunlight through the window. "It's a spring dun fly. What do you think of it?"

"It's a glorious thing. If I were a fish I'd swallow it right down, regardless of the season." Alice looked remarkably attractive in the linen garments, which she wore only around the house – her lounging garb, she called it. His lounging garb was an orchid-embroidered Bohemian morning coat, purple velvet, very exotic, but far past the fashion and worn to a perilous extent, the once-plush nap long ago scoured off at the elbows. "What is the wing feather?" he asked.

She regarded the fly with a happy look on her face. "It's from a starling, darling – young, before the feather darkens. There's blue, yellow, and brown in it – you can see the colors if you look closely – and primrose-colored silk wound around the body of the fly, with a strand of yellow over the shaft of the hook. I'm afraid it's too gay by half, but I'm fond of it as an ornament."

Alice was particularly cheerful today, and the joy she took in tying the flies brought out her natural beauty, despite the magnifying goggles that she wore for close work, which made her eyes appear to be uncommonly large. She was rarely unhappy, thank goodness, for she had a formidable temper when she was offended, especially on someone else's behalf, St. Ives's included. She had, in fact, bashed a man in the back of the head with a three-inch-thick oak plank some four years past when she saw that St. Ives was threatened. He rather liked the idea of being married to a woman who could beat him to pieces if she chose to, which she would not, the two of them still being very much in love. He had never been attracted to the hothouse lily sort of woman recommended by Charles Dickens (nor had Mr. Dickens been, apparently).

"Is that your Uncle Walton's notion of a trout fly, then?" St. Ives asked. Izaak Walton, famous among fishermen, was Alice's two-centuries-removed uncle. Her Aunt Agatha Walton had been a keen fisherwoman and amateur naturalist. Alice had inherited her passion for fishing from Aunt Agatha, along with her aunt's house and property when the old woman had died two years ago. The fish inhabiting the River Medway, not two hundred yards from their front door, had no doubt celebrated when they heard that Aunt Agatha, their old enemy, had passed away. Now they dwelt in fear of Alice.

"No, it's not Uncle Walton's," she said turning back to her desk and picking up a book that had been propped open with a glass paperweight. *Practical Fly Fishing* the book was titled. "I ordered it from Murphy's catalogue, along with this batch of feathers, hooks, silk, and wire. It's alleged to be irresistible to a trout."

"The *book*, do you mean? It must make tolerably soggy reading, although perhaps it's all one to a fish."

She removed the goggles and gave him a look of feigned exasperation, but she couldn't maintain it, and her smile returned to her face.

"You're… irresistible yourself today," St. Ives said to her. "We might repair to the bedroom for a nap, if we find ourselves… sleepy." Their children, Eddie and Cleo, had been taken to Scarborough to stay for a week with Alice's grandmother, old Mrs. Tippetts. Mrs. Langley, who was the St. Ives's housekeeper, cook, and nanny, had gone along with them, being great good friends with Grandmother Tippetts. The house was quiet, in other words, and the empty afternoon stretched before them.

"A *nap*?" Alice asked. "Are you making love to me? You must be, because you've lapsed into euphemism. Make your meaning plain, for goodness' sake. In what sense am I irresistible? I'm wearing linen trousers, after all, that are stained with paint and glue, and my hair appears to have been pinned up by a madwoman. Is it my wit alone that attracts you?"

"Only obscurely," St. Ives said. "It's the magnifying goggles that make my heart race. You have the eyes of a frog when you wear them. You know that I'm partial to frogs."

"I do know that, although I make an effort not to let it worry me, nor am I persuaded by flattery. Is it too early in the day for a glass of cold shrub? We'll take it upstairs, perhaps, in order to add to the general dissipation, if I've puzzled out your intentions correctly."

"Yes. I mean to say that you've puzzled them out. And it's not at all too early for anything having to do with dissipation. I'll mix a pitcher at once." He stood up and walked toward the kitchen, hearing in that moment someone coming up the porch steps, and through the front window he saw that it was the postman, who, when he opened the door, gave him two letters and a copy of *Cornhill Magazine*. He set aside the magazine for Finn Conrad. One of the letters – from Scarborough – was addressed to Alice, and turned out to announce that everyone had arrived safely and that the seaside weather was satisfactory. The other was from their absurdly wealthy friend Gilbert Frobisher, a retired steel magnate and captain of industry who had recently endowed the avian wing of the British Museum's Natural History building: the Bird Wing, as Gilbert referred to it at every opportunity, always happy to laugh at his own witticism. Gilbert was good company, generous to a fault, and his happy laughter often set others to laughing, which made him value his own humor all the more highly.

St. Ives sat down on the footstool and slit the envelope open with his penknife. "A missive from Gilbert Frobisher," he told Alice.

"The answer is no," Alice said. "You know I'm tremendously fond of Gilbert, but if he intends to lure you away from me again, I'll take a very dim view of it. I'm already taking a dim view of it, and I have no idea of the contents of the letter. Surely he doesn't have another excursion planned. The man is mad with doing things, and he seems to have no alternative but to involve his friends. That's the consequence of retiring from more useful work."

"Not at all. He's just himself returned from his second voyage to the Caribbean," St. Ives said to her, "and he's written to say that someone has found a fully preserved great auk in the cavern left by the sink-hole along the Thames."

"That's worth the three-penny stamp, surely."

"You're correct in that regard. The great auk has been extinct for forty years, last seen in Iceland, I believe. Bones and feathers wouldn't have excited anyone beyond a murmur, although it's moderately strange that it was living a subterranean existence. A preserved bird is something else indeed, Alice." St. Ives read further, and then said, "There's some fungal quality to the whole thing that mystifies Gilbert and his friend Dr. James Harrow from the museum. Harrow is quite a learned man, an ornithologist, you know, and a brilliant paleontologist. I run into him now and then at the Bayswater Club. Gilbert wonders whether I might come into the city to take a look at Harrow's auk, given that I published that monograph on Paleolithic avifauna and have a passion for mushrooms and their ilk. He's got permission from the Board of Works to explore the sink-hole cavern along with Harrow. There's little time to lose, because the Board of Works is anxious to begin the job of filling the hole and restoring the Embankment, which is currently in perilous condition."

"Of course you must join them, Langdon, but surely not *today*, not on a day that we've marked as our own?"

"Not at all. We'll make our foray on Tuesday, and so we must be in London on Monday. You're to come along, he says, if you're amenable. Gilbert has already talked to William Billson at the Half Toad, and has booked our usual room for a week."

"If Gilbert is anxious that we come into London then so am I, and it's a perfect time for a holiday, what with the children being away. At the moment, however, there are shortbread biscuits in the crock by the sink that might go well with that pitcher of shrub."

But they were once again interrupted by a clatter from the front of the house. St. Ives looked out to see a rising dust cloud thrown up by the wheels of a chaise driven by a heavy woman in a flamboyant scarlet garment and with a shocking lot of red hair. It was their neighbor, Harriet Laswell – more commonly known as Mother Laswell – from Hereafter Farm, a quarter of a mile away to the west. She had a deep understanding of the paranormal and occasionally held séances for the citizens of Aylesford if they had a pressing desire to chat with someone from beyond the pale.

St. Ives rejected the idea of trying to hide. Alice frowned on that sort of thing, and it was too late anyway: Mother Laswell, climbing the veranda stairs, had apparently spotted him through the window. He swung the door open and invited her in, seeing in her face that she was troubled. The afternoon at once became sensibly less empty, and when he felt the breeze through the open door it struck him that something had come into the day that struck a false note – a chill beneath the superficial balminess. He saw that clouds were moving in from the north like an invading army, promising a change in the weather.

THREE
ELYSIUM ASYLUM

The madhouse and surgical hospital called Elysium Asylum, owned and operated by Dr. Benson Peavy, lay on Wimpole Street near the corner of New Cavendish Street. It was a large house built of gray stone on a deep property half hidden by ancient trees and greenery, and with an expansive lawn on which the more sober-minded lunatics could be seen playing croquet on warm afternoons. A high, spiked, wrought iron fence surrounded the property, its gates kept locked at all hours. The gatehouse was occupied from early morning until nine o'clock at night, and no one entered the grounds without passing the gatekeeper, who used a speaking tube to summon one of the staff to attend to the occasional visitor.

Many of the occupants were thoroughly deranged, dwelling in so-called "quiet rooms," with double glass in the windows and the walls filled with oakum to dampen noise. Even so, passersby could hear occasional shrieks and incoherent snatches of feral human speech from within the depths of the asylum. The keeping of mad patients in private hospitals was a lucrative business, particularly if a patient's family was interested in the inflicted person's welfare and comfort, and so the hospital also contained a number of "day rooms," which were nicely outfitted – bright rooms with paintings on the walls and sunlight through windows, barred only for the safety of the patients. Visitors came to the asylum now and then to commune with a loved one or in order to see whether a family member, not quite right in the head, might be housed in the aptly named hospital. At those times, selected lunatics, usually drugged with laudanum, could be shifted into the very pleasant day rooms for observation.

Dr. Peavy's operating theater stood in the depths of the house, hidden and locked away in a vast cellar. In it, the unwanted and unidentified were trepanned, flayed, dismembered (sometimes while fully conscious) and otherwise experimented on in the name of science. It was visited upon invitation by the sort of men, and occasionally women, who were willing to pay a considerable sum either to be enlightened or entertained.

Today there was but one man in the audience, a man whom some knew as Treadwell and others as Klingheimer, and who in fact had possessed a number of names over the decades. He had been watching and listening with a keen avidity these past two hours. He had no idea of being entertained by what he saw: he was largely indifferent to the process, but he had a deep interest in the outcome. At present there was a lengthening silence in the operating theater, which was worrisome to him.

Inside the surgery a man sat bound with leather restraints into a heavy chair that was fastened to the tiles beneath it. A disk of skull some four inches in diameter lay on the table beside him, along with the bloody trephine that had sawn out the disk. From the brain visible within the patient's opened head, gold wires coiled away, affixed with tiny thumb screws to similar wires protruding from the head of a well-conducted asylum resident named Willis Pule, who sat in a separate chair alongside.

Pule suffered no restraints, and his head was un-trepanned. There were small holes drilled into his skull, however, through which wires had been inserted into his brain many months previously. The tiny wounds had healed, and the wires, now permanent, were usually invisible in his hair, when he wasn't wandering through the mind of another human being, some of those minds being frighteningly chaotic and obscure. Pule's insanity was transient, and at present he was very nearly rational, and had been free to wander the asylum without restraint for the past months, earning his keep as a subject in benign experiments. Today Pule was a mind reader, uttering aloud the thoughts that traveled along the golden wires issuing from the exposed brain of the man next to him.

Mr. Klingheimer watched Dr. Peavy's face through a pair of purple-tinted goggles, which revealed a layered aura of colored light roundabout his head. Klingheimer "read" the glow and shimmer and hue of the aura. Anger had just come into the aura in a red wash, which quite likely meant that the patient's mind had gone silent or else that he was dead. Peavy himself was insane, it seemed to Klingheimer, for his fond regard for the pain and misery of others had no rational ends. As a child he had no doubt tortured small animals, and in that way he was still a child. His particular insanity shone as an ochre band of light around his forehead, a sickly color like an unhealed wound. To Mr. Klingheimer's mind, Peavy wore the face of a man who would one day be murdered or hanged.

The doctor was no doubt a savant, however – a keen student

of the electronic stimulation of the brain. He had endeavored for years to transfer thought from the mind of one being into the mind of another, lately with great success. He had carefully mapped and measured various parts of the cortex, plumbing depths, seeking out regions of memory and speech, and what he believed to be the seat of psychic experience. His electronic equipment, contained within a wheeled box built of wood, leather, and brass, and covered with glowing dials and switches, generated carefully measured electrical currents, as well as registering cortical impulses. The Elysium Asylum, along with Mr. Klingheimer's wealth, allowed Peavy a measure of medical freedom impossible elsewhere. He wisely distributed his income among foreign banks and kept cash money, passports, and other documents ready to hand in the event that he was forced to flee on short notice.

Peavy's utter lack of scruples made him quite valuable to Mr. Klingheimer, as did Peavy's love of money – a simple, predictable motivation. Klingheimer himself was largely indifferent to money, however, perhaps because he already possessed it in vast quantities. He sometimes wondered whether that indifference would disappear if he were suddenly made a pauper. He believed that it would not, for he was entirely satisfied with the perspicacity of his own mind. Mr. Klingheimer had no "feelings" to use the popular term – no sympathies as such, except for a mild admiration of genius in others and a fervent wish to possess what lay within their minds in order to expand his own. His intention was quite simply to appropriate others' genius, to pirate it away with the help of Benson Peavy and his machinery.

A spray of sparks erupted from the electronic machinery, and there was the smell of burnt dura mater on the air, which reminded Mr. Klingheimer that he hadn't eaten breakfast this morning. The aura roundabout the patient strapped into the chair faded and winked out. Mr. Klingheimer removed the goggles, put them away securely in the pocket of his coat, and asked, "Has our patient succumbed, Dr. Peavy?"

"Perhaps. Tell us what Mr. Simmons is contemplating, Pule."

"He's gone silent," Pule said.

"He's dead then?" Klingheimer asked.

"It's meaningless if he is," Peavy told him, "but, yes, stony dead, I should think. The experiment was immensely revealing, and the man is inarguably happier in his present state."

"Given that one day I'll be in a similar position, I don't share your definition of 'happier.'"

"You'll be sitting in the other chair, Mr. Klingheimer. Nothing at all similar about the position." Peavy unhooked the dead man's neck restraint, and the body slumped forward, revealing that the neck and back were awash with blood. "It was merely the trepanning that did it," Peavy said. "The man bled to death. I severed a small artery, which I attempted to clamp off. It leaked rather copiously, however. His family is traveling in the south of France. By the time they've returned he'll be disposed of."

"What about you, Mr. Pule?" Klingheimer asked. "How are you feeling? Did the man's death unnerve you in any sense? Did you *feel* the death?"

"No. He went missing. One moment he was thinking of his child, who drowned, and the next the curtain fell and his mind went dark." Pule's face, pock-marked and gaunt, glowed a strange shade of green, the result of a diet of luminous fungi.

"How strict is Mr. Pule's diet, Dr. Peavy?"

"He eats fungus for dinner and supper. Stewed, raw, juiced, boiled, and roasted. His blood appears to be about a quarter fungal soup, if you grasp my meaning. He's never been fitter – apparently growing younger by the day, if I'm not mistaken."

"I'm relieved to hear it. That at least is going well. Have we another willing subject for the trephine, then?"

"In fact we do," Peavy said. "But we'll need more subjects soon. Few of the patients are expendable without arousing suspicion."

"We shall find more subjects for you, then. Suspicion is the great bug-bear to men like us, indeed it is. The streets are alive with superfluous humanity, however, easily plucked from the pavement and beneath the notice of their fellow men, alas."

Mr. Klingheimer rose from his seat now. He was tall, some three inches above six feet, and he appeared at a hasty glance to be sixty or perhaps even seventy years old. His carriage was that of a much younger man, however, and he possessed obvious strength and vigor. His own skin had a green pallor to it, although it was not as pronounced as that of Willis Pule. His smile was very nearly perpetual – an evident mask to his acquaintances (for he had no friends).

"I wonder if you'd fancy a holiday, Dr. Peavy – a little jaunt into Kent, at most overnight, but more likely a single long day. I require your considerable skills. I believe you'd find it good sport, and profitable, too. I can guarantee you a head or two, immensely interesting heads, at no risk whatsoever."

~ FOUR ~

THE PAWNBROKER'S

The yellow glow of the gas lamps hissing along Peach Alley was obscured by fog, the narrow alley angling down toward the river from Lower Thames Street, very near Billingsgate Market and to the west of the Custom House. The alley resided in nearly perpetual shadow, light falling directly upon it for an hour before and after noon or on cloudless nights when the moon hovered for a brief period right above the looming buildings. Even in high summer there wasn't enough sun to dry up the damp filth that stood in runnels between the cobbles. The air was heavy with the constant reek of fish from the market and, at low tide, of river muck from the Thames, which flowed some sixty feet beyond the dead end of the alley. The tops of ghostly masts moving along the river were just visible beyond the roof of the Goat and Cabbage Public House.

Beaumont the Dwarf stood outside a pawnbroker's shop near the mouth of the alley. He carried four pocket watches in his leather purse, three of which he had liberated from their owners, most recently from Dr. Ignacio Narbondo, who was unlikely to miss it, now that he dwelt among the toads. The chain that had come with the watch was silver, the ruby genuine. Beaumont had hidden the ruby and chain away, part of the treasure that he was hoarding against old age, when he was past work and his fingers were no longer nimble. The fourth watch was no longer a watch, because he had turned it into a simple automata. Its bulbous case was very like the round carapace of an insect. He had painted it with many coats of black lacquer and then laid on fiery red daubs, the exact shape and color of a four-spot lady beetle, although many times the size. Its jointed, wire legs made little swimming motions when it was wound by means of twisting the head, and it could walk an erratic line across the floor, its head turning from side to side until it wound itself down. He had no idea of trying to sell the object, which he had built merely to pass the time, and because the watch inside the case wasn't worth repairing.

Beaumont wore an old beaver hat that he had purchased from a hatter in a Piccadilly shop some ten years ago, when he was gainfully employed as a watchmaker. He had remarkably nimble fingers and a sharp eye, but he had come down in the world since those days, his last situation being employment as a coach driver for Dr. Narbondo, which he had liked well enough, being partial to horses. The beaver hat added a foot to his height, making him something over four feet tall. A complementary beard of the same length and shape mirrored the hat in a startling, topsy-turvy way, so that his wrinkled face seemed to peer out from the center of a hairy, elongated egg. At the moment he was down on his luck, having lost his position as coachman a year ago and not having found steady employment since. Now he was compelled to earn a hard living by the quickness of his hand, and he dwelt in squalid lodgings in Limehouse, which was better than sleeping on a filthy porch in a damp and stinking alley such as this.

The pawnbroker had been recommended to him as being "discreet." The shop was unlicensed, given the absence of the usual golden balls on the sign, which meant that there would be no questions put to him when he displayed the watches, all three of which were of fairly high quality. Treasures of the meanest sort lay beyond the shop window: chipped china cups, foreign coins, dusty glassware, a hodgepodge of bric-a-brac, and a basket of severed porcelain dolls' heads – awful things with staring eyes.

Shoes lay heaped in bins inside the shop, and an array of petticoats, gowns, shawls, and old coats hung from wooden rods affixed to the ceiling. The store was apparently empty of customers, and the shopkeeper was attentive to his work. Beaumont's eyes returned to the clutter of items in the window, where there lay a nine-key, four-part German flute with ivory and silver filigree, the fine-grained wood polished to a luster by handling. He stared longingly at it, having pawned his own flute, not as nice as this one, some months back. German flutes were neither rare nor expensive, even to a person of modest means, but he couldn't afford the flute no matter what he was offered for the watches, which represented several days' careful labor. He had been hungry and cold so often these past months that he had become like the ant in the fable: for every shilling he spent, he put two away for tomorrow, even if it meant that on two-shilling days he went hungry. Still and all, he had eaten his fill of bread and cheese just now in Rodway's Coffee House, meat being too dear, and so hunger was a remote worry.

He heard the rattle and squeak of loose wheels now, and looking up toward Lower Thames Street, he saw a costermonger wheeling a hot potato cart in his direction, compelling him to step up onto the shop's stoop among a litter of ironmongery in order to let the cart pass. "Watch your poke in that there shop," the boy said to him without looking up. Beaumont was tempted to stop him, to buy a potato that he didn't want, but he stepped noiselessly into the shop instead, seeing that the shopkeeper's back was turned. He leaned in toward the broad window-sill, his hand darted out, and he grasped the flute lightly, flipping it round and thrusting it up the sleeve of his coat, and then letting it slide back down into a pocket sewn on the inside of the sleeve for just such a purpose. The flute lay there snug and safe by the time the shopkeeper, a surly-looking dark man in a leathern apron, with the face of a dried French prune turned and looked at him with evident disapproval.

"I've got these time pieces, Squire," Beaumont said to him, and he drew the watches out of his purse, lining them up in a neat row on the counter. Lying beneath the dirty glass was an array of costume jewelry, virtually all of it pinchbeck rubbish, and a half-dozen decorated snuff boxes. No doubt the proprietor kept the real wares somewhere else, another shop, perhaps.

The man grunted by way of reply when he saw the watches. He picked up the best of the three and snapped it open, looking at the interior of the cover, which was unfortunately engraved with its owner's initials. Shaking his head doubtfully, he examined the other two. "How does a villain of your size come by *three* silver pocket watches?" he asked. "Half a watch would do the likes of you, I should think."

"My old grandfather died yesterday," Beaumont told him. "That's how I came by them. They were his."

"What was his name, then? Old Scratch, I don't doubt."

"Bartholomew Compton, your honor, of Dove Court in the Seven Dials. He was uncommon fond of knowing the time of day, and used the one watch to check the accuracy of the other two."

"And yet the one watch is engraved with another man's initials –
an ef and a zed. That's mighty curious – suspicious some might say."

"Not at all, sir. He couldn't read nor write. It's the great pity of
the world, for he would have been a great man, else."

The shop door opened just then and a squalid, thin woman
who was losing her hair in patches came in wearing a worn
cotton gown raveled at the neck and sleeves. A tiny, fair-haired
girl trailed at her heels, her eyes on the floor. Both of them had
seen hard times. The woman held a lidless iron pot containing a
striped bonnet forty years old if it was a day. The stripes might
have been red once, but now were the color of dried blood, and yet
were scarcely distinguishable against the dirty white of the rest of
the bonnet, which had evidently been trodden flat and then batted
back into shape and fixed with glue and water. She pushed past
Beaumont and endeavored to set the heavy pot on the counter.

"Put it on the floor, Mrs. Billings," the shopkeeper told her,
"and wait your turn. And I don't want the bonnet today, ma'am,
any more than I wanted it last week or the week before. There's
not a living soul in London would want the bonnet, nor a corpse
neither, which is apparently who's been wearing it."

Looking at Beaumont, he said, "Four crowns for the three of
'em. The engraving's spoilt the best of the three, without Mr. Filby
Zounds comes in to claim it. You won't get more elsewhere, but you
might get taken up for theft, and you knew that very thing when
you walked into my shop. Take the money or leave it, Dwarf. It's all
one to me." He set four coins on the counter, and without waiting
for an answer he swept the watches into a box, which he placed in
a drawer, turning to stare silently at Beaumont, who looked at the
coins for a moment before picking them up. He had been swindled,

but that was the way of things. And the swindle meant that he was quits for the flute, which meant that his conscience was clear.

He pocketed the coins, hearing a wet sort of noise behind him. Mrs. Billings was weeping, her narrow hand pressed to her forehead to hide her eyes. Beaumont said, "Don't weep, my lady. I'll buy the bonnet if you'll part with it." She looked up, suspicion in her eyes until she saw the silver coin in his hand. She plucked it from his palm before he changed his mind, holding it in her fist and wiping her eyes with her knuckles.

"Thank you for your great kindness, sir," she said, handing him the bonnet. "You're a small man with a large heart, not like some I could name, whose hearts are shriveled like an apple john left in the barrel." She gave the pawnbroker a hard look, and he either laughed or snorted, it was difficult to say.

Beaumont was indifferent to the man now, although he had a high regard for Mrs. Billings, who had said a kind thing to him, which was rare. Cuffs and insults were more usual, as they no doubt were for her and her daughter. He touched his fingers to his forehead by way of a salute and held out the lady beetle automata to the small girl, twisting the head twice, meaning to give it to her. It walked straight off his palm, landing on its back on the floorboards, its legs gyrating, a grinding noise coming from within it. The girl shrieked and clung to her mother, who slapped her on the side of the head. Beaumont picked up the bug and hurried out into the foggy afternoon, berating himself for frightening the girl. Certainly he hadn't meant to. He felt the German flute tapping against his forearm, and that went some distance toward easing his mind. He was glad that he had pinched it.

There sounded the rattle and creak of the costermonger's cart again, and that very item once again materialized out of the fog, bearing down on him from the opposite direction. "*Hot* potatoes!" the boy shouted. "*Hot* roasters!" The afternoon had grown even colder, and Beaumont drew three pennies out of his pocket and handed them to the boy, who gave him a potato wrapped in a triangle of damp newsprint.

"No rot in this one, sir, and twice the size of the others. Prime King Edwards. Nothing but the best. And I'm to give you this," he said, taking a printed sheet of foolscap out of his pocket and handing it to him – a handbill of some sort, of which the boy apparently had a quantity. Beaumont put the potato into the pocket of his coat and then looked at the handbill to see what it advertised – General Clinky's Raree Show, perhaps, the bearer of the handbill to receive a tuppeny discount at the ticket window.

But it wasn't any such thing. This was more interesting by far. The legend across the top read, "Have you seen this man?" and below that there was a middling good sketch of the upper body of a demonic-looking gent who was evidently a hunchback, with short, straight hair and canny eyes. Beaumont stared at it in growing disbelief. "I *do*," he whispered in answer to the query. And then, without reading the rest of it, he tucked it away in his coat.

The boy was off again, shouting "*Red* hot potatoes!", very shortly leaving the alley and disappearing into the fog-shrouded traffic of Lower Thames Street. Mrs. Billings and her daughter came out through the door of the shop and hurried away, leaving the door standing open. The proprietor stood just inside, watching Beaumont with evident distaste.

Beaumont realized that the bonnet was still tucked under his arm, and so he pitched it through the open door and said cheerfully, "Bugger off, old cock." He thumbed his nose at the man, removed the potato from his pocket, unwrapped it and bit off the top, wishing that he had a shaker of salt.

He walked along the alley to the Goat and Cabbage, pushing through the door and buying a pint of plain before sitting down in the corner to finish his potato in peace. He thought about how the boy had warned him to watch his poke, although he had no call to do so. He was a good boy, not a blackguard like some, but civil, and he had given Beaumont a vastly interesting piece of paper. There was something right with things today – not luck, maybe, for to call it luck might kill it – but the world spinning plumb and true for the moment, and out of the spinning had come opportunity. Who knew what it would bring to a man who didn't ask for more than he deserved?

The Goat was nearly full, several of the patrons weeping drunk and one man was sitting on the floor, his back against the wall, his eyes closed and his mouth open and wheezing. Most were dressed in greasy coats and caps that stank of fish. There was the smell of gin and spilled beer and fried oysters and a general human fug. One of the hot potato boy's handbills lay on the adjacent table, three glasses sitting atop it, the three men surrounding it hunched over and talking to each other in low voices. They were useless, mean, hateful men with low habits. Beaumont could smell it on them – the stink of poisonous thoughts, nothing to recommend them but their ugly faces.

One of the three stared back at him, a heavy man with a red beard, and Beaumont averted his eyes so as not to further summon the man's attention – attention generally coming to no good when one is a dwarf. He heard one of them say, "…a goddamn leprechaun, or I'm a codfish." Another of them said, "I say we stuff him into a bag and make him give up his gold. Either that or throw him in the river, the little frog."

Beaumont swallowed the last of his potato and drank off half his beer. Perhaps he was mistaken about the quality of the afternoon. He raised his right hand and patted the top of his beaver hat, feeling the flute slide out of its pocket and up his sleeve, and when he dropped his arm along the chair leg, the flute slipped neatly into his fingers. He left it there, easy to hand.

"He's deaf, the sodding little pip," one of them said in a voice meant to carry. "What do you keep in that there hat? Thumbelina, no doubt."

Ignoring the laughter that followed this witticism, Beaumont unfolded his own handbill in order to study it. The artist had got the eyes just right, as well as the slope of the shoulders and the cape tied at the throat. Beaumont indeed knew the man – Dr. Ignacio Narbondo, for whom he had been employed for a number of months prior to Narbondo falling headfirst into the bottomless pit that had opened in the marble floor of the Cathedral of the Oxford Martyrs. There was a twenty-pound reward for knowledge of his whereabouts, the bill said. Beaumont possessed that knowledge. The address at the bottom of the handbill read, "12 Lazarus Walk," near the Temple – a posh address, if his memory served.

A shadow fell across the table, and Beaumont looked up to see the red-bearded man standing over him, tottering drunk, although dangerous enough. He had a nasty leer on his face, and he put out his hand and slowly pushed Beaumont's beaver hat off his head, and then took Beaumont's nose between his knuckles, pinched it, and gave it a vicious twist, causing great mirth among his friends.

The moment he released it, Beaumont tucked the handbill into his coat, flipped the flute around in his hand, gripped it tightly, and drove it into the man's throat. He turned away at the same moment, snatching up his hat and running toward the door, hearing the gagging sounds behind him, but not looking back until he was halfway down the alley, pounding along toward the street, where he could easily lose the three of them if they chose to follow. The fog was so thick now that he couldn't say for sure whether they *had* followed, but it would hide him more easily than it would hide the three of them, and he turned down Lower Thames Street toward London Bridge and the address of the house where he might collect his reward, if he knew enough to satisfy them. He listened for the sounds of pursuing footsteps, of which there were none.

FIVE

MOTHER LASWELL'S REQUEST

"This shrub goes down gratefully," Mother Laswell said when they were situated around the kitchen table over a plate of shortbread biscuits, and bowls of jam, clotted cream, and lemon curd. So far she hadn't revealed the reason for her visit, but had kept up a stream of small conversation – avoidance, it seemed to St. Ives. "The shrub syrup is made from cherries and oranges, if I'm not mistaken – a very fanciful syrup," she said.

"Blood oranges," Alice said. "Hasbro brought them back from London a week ago. It's perhaps even better with brandy at Christmastime, but rum seemed to be more seaworthy on a warm afternoon."

"I'm in complete agreement," Mother Laswell said, affecting a smile that quickly faded. She spooned up jam and then cream, decorating her shortbread with it before taking a bite and chewing it attentively. "These biscuits are perhaps Mrs. Langley's work?"

"Yes, indeed. Mrs. Langley is a prodigy with biscuits," Alice said. "The shrub syrup is hers also. It was her grandmother's concoction originally. I wish I had half her powers in the kitchen."

"And she no doubt wishes she had half your beauty. I know I do, although there was a time when I could look into a mirror without flinching."

"You've no reason to flinch when you look in the mirror," Alice told her. "Your face has more character than any five women together. If I were a painter, I'd make a study of it."

"I wish that were true," Mother Laswell said. "I'm an old, foolish woman, is what I am, who has made a mort of mistakes in the past that keep coming round like a bad penny." She set her half-eaten biscuit on her plate and sat back in her chair, fingering the large glass beads in her necklace – various images of the human eye, some of them eerily authentic. They waited for her to go on, but her attention had strayed to a painting on the wall – two orang-utangs standing in the branches of an enormous, vine-draped jungle tree, watching an alligator walking along the beaten path below. "What a wonderfully whimsical picture," she said after a moment. "The apes are very like angels, watching the world from the heights, with no reason to fear the leviathan. We earthbound mortals, however…"

She looked out the window and thought for a moment. "I value your friendship – the both of you," she said. "It seems unnatural to bring one's troubles into the home of people one esteems."

"On the contrary," Alice said to her, laying her hand on Mother Laswell's arm, "it would be unnatural not to. We haven't forgotten that you rescued Eddie and returned him to us when he was in trouble, and we *won't* forget it, either."

"Alice is correct," St. Ives said. "We're heavily in your debt, although that puts it coarsely. Please speak your mind."

"I will," she said, "God between us and all harm. I very much fear that something dreadful has come to pass, and I'm here to ask a favor of the two of you."

"We're at your service," St. Ives said to her.

"Then you might go along with me in the wagon, a half hour up the road. I'm mortally afraid that there's something amiss with a friend of mine, and I'm compelled to call upon her. Bill isn't back from Maidstone yet, where he's keen to see a man about sheep, and the boy Simonides is too young. I don't want to go alone, Professor."

"Then you've come to the right shop. Where to, ma'am?"

"There's a cottage in Boxley Woods, where my friend Sarah Wright dwells. I have a clear foreboding that all is not well with her. She is known to be a witch, you see, and has suffered for it, as is the lot in life of those who can see what most people cannot."

"I've heard the name," Alice said. "Aunt Agatha spoke of Sarah Wright from time to time."

"Your Aunt Agatha consulted her. I know it for a fact, as did other women, generally in secret. Agatha Walton strolled to her house in the light of day, however. I'm happy to be able to say so. Children threw sticks at Sarah when she came into the village, and reviled her as a witch, so in time she stopped coming and was largely forgotten. There's a beaten path from her cottage in the wood to Hereafter Farm, however, and I've carried meat and greens and black bread to Sarah Wright for many, many years. She was a hermit, you might say, although she was good company when she had something to say, and she harmed no one."

She stopped then, a painful look on her face. "I mustn't say 'was.' From time to time the more daring children in the village, hearing rumors of the witch, make forays into Boxley Woods to look at her. At Hereafter we've seen them sneaking along the path, but since Bill came to the farm they've mostly stayed away, because he won't allow them to cut their capers. It was this very morning, however, Bill being gone off to Maidstone, that I saw three boys running back along the path toward the village as if the Devil were after them. Seeing those boys put ideas into my head." She paused for a moment and then said, "I believe that you've both met Clara," she said, "the blind girl who lives at the Farm?"

"The girl who sees with her outstretched elbow, as I recall," St. Ives said, careful to keep his tone clear of any suspicion of doubt. He had seen the girl's powers, which at the time he suspected of being a clever parlor trick. He had few such suspicions now, nor did he have any notion of explaining the phenomenon, which was beyond his ken. The scientist in him knew that there was an explanation somewhere, but the other part of him wasn't as sure.

"Indeed. Clara is Sarah Wright's daughter. She came to live at the farm when she was eight years old. She was understandably withdrawn, and Sarah rightly believed that the girl wanted company, although Sarah herself did not want company, and Clara had come to fear the woods. I like to think that Clara has thrived at Hereafter, and you can understand that I'm unwilling to allow her to come to harm. In any event, Clara also saw the frightened boys, and fell into a swoon. It was Clara's… condition that convinced me to come to you. Clara sees what many of the rest of us cannot see. I fairly dread looking into the cottage alone because of what the girl saw, or rather sensed. Perhaps I'm simply being foolish. Indeed, I pray that I am."

"I'll just take myself in hand," Alice said. "I'll fetch your coat from upstairs, Langdon. The weather is changing. Give me two minutes, and I'm with you." She rose and hurried away up the stairs.

St. Ives took up his pen and wrote a note to Hasbro, asking him to bring the chaise around to Hereafter Farm and to wait for them there, and then he took Alice's double-barreled fowling piece from the wall and slipped four shells into his trouser pocket, before compelling himself to sit back down at the table. He was anxious to see this through in order to be back about his business.

"Sarah Wright granted me a particular service once, Professor, for which I owe her a great deal, although it's nothing I can speak of here, and nothing that I would willingly make public. I was mortally certain that our secret was safe, but if it is not, if someone has..." She struggled to her feet when she saw Alice descending the stairs, and the three of them went out beneath the afternoon sky, her sentence left unfinished.

Mother Laswell drove the wagon, the three of them sitting together tightly on the seat. St. Ives's shillelagh, which served him as a weapon and walking stick both, lay on the bed of the wagon along with Alice's fowling piece. He had no idea of taking the women along to Sarah Wright's cottage until he had seen it for himself, or of leaving them defenseless in the chaise. He had raised the issue as soon as they had started out, and neither woman had protested, Alice agreeing immediately to remain with Mother Laswell.

His mind turned on Boxley Woods now, which he had regarded through the window not an hour past. He had tramped through it on two previous occasions, searching out mushrooms for Mrs. Langley, but he had never traveled deeply enough into it to see the cottage where Sarah Wright lived. Now the wood lay a hundred yards in front of them, the copper beeches at the outer edge, and the upper branches of the old forest towering one hundred and fifty feet above the ground. Had it been the purple color in the beeches that had attracted his attention earlier today, or had his attention been attracted by something else? By a presentiment, say. It was a novel idea – one that he would have laughed into oblivion fourteen months ago, before he had met Mother Laswell and got caught up in her desperate affairs, which had turned out to be his own.

The wagon entered the wood and fell into shadow. The vast trunks of the beeches were green with moss along the woodland floor, although gray above, the sparse leaves a hodgepodge of browns, reds, and yellows. There was almost no undergrowth – far too much shade – and the beech saplings were puny and starved for sunlight. Mosses and lichens covered the rocks that lay along the roadway, with here and there a patch of grass when a break in the foliage above let in a ray of sun. Mushrooms grew up through the litter of leaves and rotted wood on the ground – blewits were particularly plentiful, and oyster mushrooms on fallen limbs. St. Ives promised himself that he would return in the next week or so with a basket. The family would make a day of it.

But the pleasant idea disappeared from his mind as quickly as it had entered, replaced by a sense of indefinite dread, which increased as they drove deeper into the trees. He wondered whether his mind had been infected by Mother Laswell's sense of foreboding, or whether the foreboding had some authentic existence. The wind gusted, and leaves fell from overhead and skittered along the dirt track, which had narrowed.

A fork appeared in the road ahead, the track on the right being hidden by leaf-covered grass, as if no one had passed that way since summer had ended. Mother Laswell turned down along the path less traveled, and soon the trees closed in on either side, and she reined in the horses on a clear, grassy patch of ground.

St. Ives climbed down, handed Alice the fowling piece, and set off down the footpath, coming in sight of the cottage within a few minutes. The plank door stood open. He paused, hiding himself behind a tree trunk, listening to the wind through the branches, but hearing little else. Nothing moved. There was no smoke from the chimney of the slate-roofed cottage, which was built of stone and with windows of old bull's-eye glass. He listened hard for sounds from within, and looked for an indication of someone lurking, but there was nothing visible, neither a wagon nor a horse. He stepped from his hiding place, crossing a board that lay over a deep, still brook, and he saw that a wagon track ran away west from the clearing where the cabin lay – the road past Hereafter Farm, no doubt. A white chicken hurried out through the open door now and ran off around the side of the house.

He stopped just outside the open door, listening again to the silence, and then peered in past the low lintel. There was the unmistakable smell of a dead body on the warm air, and he could hear the buzzing of flies. The interior of the cottage – one room, very nearly square, and with a wooden floor – was dark, and it took him a moment to see that someone sat on a chair by the hearth, unmoving. It was a corpse, headless – a woman, no doubt Sarah Wright. Her gown was soaked with blood, and she was tied into the chair. There were several turns of rope about her body.

He took in the rest of the room before going in: a tall cupboard set into a recess in the wall, the contents strewn on the floor – dishes, books, cooking implements. The cupboard itself had been pulled away so that the intruder could see behind it. The bed stood on its side, the torn mattress on the ground spilling out feathers. A loom near the hearth had been broken to pieces, a half-woven rug in the frame. Floorboards had been prised up, exposing the packed dirt beneath.

Someone had pulled the place apart searching for something. Quite possibly they had murdered Sarah Wright because she wouldn't give it up – the secret, perhaps, that Mother Laswell had mentioned, although to murder her in this horrific fashion... There was a necessary room in the corner, with a door that stood open, the small closet clearly empty.

St. Ives looked carefully around himself at the trees that stretched away on all sides. The place had a lonesome air to it. A pair of squirrels scampered along beside the stream now and up the trunk of a beech, chattering to each other, and a rooster strode out from behind a pile of firewood and stood looking at him. He stepped into the interior of the cottage, where he set his shillelagh against the corner of the wall by the door. He saw now that holes had been dug into the dirt beneath sections of torn up floorboards. Had they found what they were looking for, he wondered, and he walked across to view the body, his eyes growing used to the dim light. From the charnel house smell it was likely that she had been murdered yesterday, the village boys discovering her this morning.

A bunched square of cloth lay on the floor, which he picked up and held to his nose, immediately smelling the residue of chloroform, although it had dried by now. Whoever had committed the atrocity had done Sarah Wright the service of deadening her senses. Possibly she had simply been murdered with the chemical, although the ghastly quantity of spilled blood argued that her heart had pumped it out unto the very last moments. The incision appeared to be remarkably neat to him – the work of someone who was familiar with the use of a scalpel and saw.

There was a rattling outside now – the sound of a wagon drawing up, having come along the road from the west. St. Ives stepped to the door and retrieved his shillelagh, before looking out at the wagon, and recognizing the driver – Dr. Lamont Pullman, the coroner, along with the village constable, a pleasant but slow-witted man named Brooke. With a deep sense of relief St. Ives went out under the now cloudy sky to meet the two men, leaving the door open as he had found it.

≈ SIX ≈

BEAUMONT'S REWARD

The several houses that lined Lazarus Walk were large, many-roomed structures from the last age, with multiple chimneys and lamp-lit geminate windows glowing through the fog. Beaumont looked into the courtyard of number 12, through a broad, scrolled-iron gate between the high walls of granite stones that separated the immense house from the rest of London. It was a half-timbered mansion with colored glass in the downstairs windows. Many years ago someone had bled money to build it.

There was no gatekeeper to be seen. A gold-painted Berlin carriage, very old and very elegant, stood on the cobbles near the arched front door, its two patient horses waiting in front of a large carriage house, lanterns lit within. A man – the driver, perhaps – came out of the carriage house now and stood smoking a pipe, the reek of burning tobacco mingling with the fog. He was a narrow man, his legs needlessly long – *The Duke of Limbs*, Beaumont thought. He wore a red bowler hat with a low dome. Beaumont waved the handbill at the man, who stared at him with a look of disapproval on his face. A crowd of laughing people jostled Beaumont, shoving him against the iron bars of the gate, one of them knocking his hat askew and laughing as he did it. The chin ribbon saved it before it fell.

"Be off with you, dwarf!" the gangly driver shouted at him, but Beaumont held up the handbill again and pointed at the picture drawn on it. The man considered him for another moment before stepping across to the gate and said, "State your business, then."

"I'm here to lay claim to my reward, your honor: twenty pounds, it says here on this bill, as you can see right enough."

"Tell me what you know, then, and I'll fetch your money. If it's worthless to Mr. Klingheimer I'll fetch you a kick in the arse."

"I'll fetch my own reward from Mr. Klingheimer, if you please, sire," Beaumont said. "It'll spend better in my hands than it will in yours. The man you see here, I was his coachman, the same situation as you, I don't doubt. A black Landau coach, which I cleaned and polished and cared for the horses. I was ostler and driver both for near on a year."

"And where is he now, this master of yours?"

"Under my hat, which is where he'll stay."

"Tell me what the man did, then. What line of work?"

"All manner of evil more than aught else. Viversuction, poisons, resurrection. I had nought to do with any of that. It weren't in my line. I mostly minded his horses' business, not his."

"Go around back, then," the man said, "down the lane there. If it's twaddle you're peddling, you'll regret it." He nodded up the road, where there was no doubt a cut-through. "The red door, first you come to. Don't bang the knocker. Mrs. Skink will open it in due time." He turned away and walked back into the coaching house, disappearing within.

Beaumont considered what he would reveal as he walked along the narrow bit of pavement toward the red door, which he could see now through the wisps of fog blowing past, hiding and then disclosing things. He realized that he had little to say to anyone that he had not already said, except that the man they sought had gone to damnation, a prisoner of the toads. They would pay little for news about someone who was as good as dead. Beaumont would brass it out, though, to see what came of it – a farthing for his trouble, perhaps, which was twice better than half a farthing.

He waited as he had been told, standing several paces back from the stoop, removing his hat and holding it in the crook of his arm. The door was standing open at present, a greengrocer handing crates of vegetables through it to someone unseen in the shadows. The grocer went away in the direction of the river pushing his now-empty cart, and the door swung shut. Beaumont looked up at a bank of long windows that led out onto a narrow balcony along the third floor and at the ledges and heavy moldings that decorated the wall beneath it – foot and handholds enough for a person leaving by one of the windows. He had never been happy playing the ape, not since he was a boy, but he still considered houses as places from which a person might find it necessary to leave in considerable haste.

There was a clatter from within now, what sounded like a bolt banging open before the door was drawn back by a withered housemaid with a scraggle of hair and a long green gown with a tattered hem – Mrs. Skink, no doubt. Two men pushed out past her. Both of them stared at Beaumont for a moment, one of them with apparent ill intent, before they walked slowly in the wake of the grocer. The one who had given him the stink-eye was as bad a man as Beaumont could recollect, known along the river as

Cobble, and was in the smothering lay, which paid well – better than the resurrection men were paid, the smothered corpses being still fresh and warm. Cobble had brought two of them to Narbondo one dark night at the old Shade House in the Cliffe Marsh near Egypt Bay.

Beaumont noticed that Mrs. Skink was regarding him now, as if taking his measure. He bowed to her when she gestured him forward, and walked into the dim light inside. He smelled cooking odors and heard the noise of the nearby kitchen, and he watched as the woman shut the door. There was a Chubb lock with a twist latch set into the door a foot from the top. The latch clicked shut when the door stopped against the jamb, which meant it was always locked unless the lock was fixed open. She lowered a heavy bar across the door and padlocked the bar into place. What did *that* signify, he wondered, a door with locks meant both to keep the outside out and the inside in? – and him inside now.

He saw that there was a closet in the wall with a black curtain across it, the curtain half open at the moment. Inside the closet stood a bed and a chair, the bedclothes tossed in a heap – Mrs. Skink's cupboard, she being always on duty. The gaoler, he thought. He didn't like the look of her, nor she of him, apparently. And there was something in the air of the house that wasn't right – a smell of physic, perhaps, beneath the cooking odors, or the smell of death coming up through the floorboards. It was more than a mere *smell* – fresh ghosts, more like, troubled and unhappy. It was a house, he thought, that wanted to be burnt to the ground. He wondered now whether it was the sight of the man Cobble that had played on his mind, but his wondering was interrupted when the gangly man with the red hat appeared and said, "Come along, then."

They set out along a hallway toward a flight of stairs. Beaumont looked back and saw Mrs. Skink hide the padlock key inside a pitcher-pot that sat on a shelf near the door. A blind mouse could find it, which meant that they hadn't had any troubles with blind mice, so to speak. She sat down on a stool against the wall, crossed her arms, and bowed her head as if to sleep.

There was a maze of narrow corridors at the top of the stairs, and he memorized the left- and right- hand turns, noting the look of things in case he needed to find his way back out in a hurry. Dealing with the door locks would take some doing, especially since he mayn't be tall enough to reach the pitcher that held the key to the padlock, nor the latch on the uppermost lock. He could use the doorkeeper's stool, perhaps, which would make a handy weapon in a pinch.

At the top of the stairs lay another hallway, this one broad and paneled, brightened with electric-lamps suspended from the ceiling and with rich, Turkey carpet running along the floor. Heavily framed portraits lined the walls on either side, dark and dim with age. A door opened ahead of them, apparently of its own accord, and red hat ushered him into a large room, scattered with upholstered chairs and settees and wooden tables. It at first appeared to be empty of people, but then Beaumont saw that a large man in shirtsleeves sat at a desk along the far wall, writing with a quill pen. The door closed silently behind him, red hat having gone out like a ghost. It seemed as if the man at the desk – Mr. Klingheimer himself, no doubt – was unaware of his presence, which was an awkward business. Best to wait him out.

As ever, Beaumont glanced around quickly for something small that he might nick, the owners of the house being not likely to suffer if a loose item or two found its way into his pocket. A crystal paperweight with a garden of glass flowers inside caught his eye on a nearby console table, shining in the light of an Argand lamp. French crystal, no doubt. Heavy, but in that regard useful as a weapon or for beating out a window – or a man's skull – if there were trouble. He picked the orb up, slipped it into his coat pocket and pinned it with his elbow, watching the back of Mr. Klingheimer's head the entire time.

"That's a lovely bauble, isn't it?" Mr. Klingheimer said in a cheerful voice, without looking up from his work. "It was given to me by a woman who I remember fondly, dead now, alas."

Beaumont bowed, removed the crystal ball from his pocket, polished it on his cuff, and set it down again on the console table. He glanced again at the closed door, wondering whether it, too, was bolted on the outside. He could play the flute caper again, as he had in the Goat and Cabbage, but it was one thing to strike a no-account piss-maker in a low pothouse, and another to strike a rich man in his mansion. And in any event, gaffing Mr. Klingheimer in the throat wouldn't unlock doors. Beaumont would be brought to heel, and that would be the end of it.

The man rose from the desk and walked toward him. He was a stout man, and tall, a second cousin to Father Christmas, with a clipped white beard and lengthy white hair with a curl to it, his tweed trousers held up with braces. His collar was loosened, and there was a spray of ink on his shirt. Beaumont wished that he hadn't played the fool with the piece of crystal, for there was something about the man that belied the smile – something that made the hair on the back of Beaumont's head creep, although there was nothing to account for it in the way he looked or spoke, which was pleasant enough.

The man pointed toward a round, upholstered chair of the sort a woman might sit upon to make up her face. "Take a seat, Mr....?"

"Zounds, your honor, Filby Zounds of Dove Court in the Seven Dials." He sat down, his feet not reaching the floor. The man before him remained standing, looming over him like a giant. "Do I have the honor of speaking to Mr. Klingheimer?" Beaumont asked.

"Indeed you do, Mr. Zounds. Sit very still for a moment, if you would. I need to have a look at you." With that the man drew a pair of goggles from his coat pocket – round glass lenses, heavily smoked, with sturdy black rims and a leather band stitched around the rims to keep out the light. He put the goggles on his face and stared fixedly at the lamp on the console table for a long minute, and then he peered at Beaumont, canting his head this way and that before removing the goggles.

"There we have it," he said. "Do you wonder at all what I saw through these very interesting lenses?"

"Aye," Beaumont told him. Beaumont wasn't fond of games, and this was surely a game, although perhaps a deadly serious game.

"I saw into your mind, sir, which occupies the space within your skull, but which is very much like a lamp. These ingenious goggles allow me to perceive the glow of that lamp. What I saw before me was a man who tells what he believes to be true – such as he understands it to be, I mean to say, which can be a dangerous business for the truth teller, to be sure. But turnabout is fair play, as they say. Take a squint through them, Mr. Zounds, and tell me what you see of *me*, after first gazing at the lamp here on the table for the count of sixty."

He handed Beaumont the goggles, and Beaumont put them on, not altogether happily. Through the lenses the room glowed in shades of purple and violet, although those parts of it that were not directly illuminated were now in deep shadow. He stared at the Argand lamp and then regarded Mr. Klingheimer through the lenses, seeing a shadowy ring form around the man's head like a ring around the moon, except dark as coal dust, so that it was very much like looking into a black pit with a head staring out of it. Beaumont removed the spectacles and handed them back to Mr. Klingheimer, happy to be rid of them.

"What did you see, Mr. Zounds?" Mr. Klingheimer asked.

"Naught but shadow, your honor. Perhaps I haven't the knack of it."

Mr. Klingheimer regarded him for a long moment and then smiled more broadly. "Perhaps," he said, and he returned the goggles to his pocket. "Now, sir, I'm told that you were employed by the man named Narbondo, who is known to be a bloody-minded villain."

"That's the honest truth, your honor, both them things. I was in his service, so to say, for a year, roundaboutly speaking. I drove his Landau coach."

Mr. Klingheimer squinted at him in a new way for a moment, canting his head. "*Of course*," he said. "I *know* you! I do indeed. Narbondo's coachman! Tell me, sir, as a test – where in London did he dwell at the time that you drove his coach? It was there that I got a glimpse of you, although I'm reasonably certain that you did not see me."

"Angel Alley, your honor, the rooms atop the wall. Roundabout Flower and Dean Street."

"Right you are. Tell me, then, under what circumstances did you lose your situation? For pocketing the odd bauble, perhaps?"

"No, sir," Beaumont said. "We parted company when the Doctor pitched into a hole in the ground and went out of the world, or better to say into it."

"*Pitched* into a hole, do you say? Within the lamented Cathedral, was it?"

"I seen him depart, sire, head-foremost, sir, through the crack in the floor right before the walls began to come down in earnest."

"You're not certain he's dead, then? You didn't see his corpse?"

"No, your honor," Beaumont said, truthfully enough. "He had the lives of a cat, did the Doctor, which perhaps he hadn't used up. For aught I know he's alive as you or me, mayhaps having come up topside again and starting fresh, and everyone thinking he's copped it. He weren't well liked." He watched Mr. Klingheimer's face, wondering whether he'd seen through the lie – half a lie, really.

But Mr. Klingheimer nodded and stroked his beard with a long-fingered hand. "How might he do that, Mr. Zounds? *Come up topside*, as you put it? That implies you have some knowledge of an *underside*, shall we say? A world beneath."

"We might say it, sir, and not give it the lie. The Doctor was up and down both from time to time, and me along with him. He wanted a guide, do you see, and I know of some places that are right difficult to find."

"In the underworld?"

"Aye, sir, so to say. The land beneath."

"And how did you find your way there? It's not well known, I believe."

"My old dad showed me when I was a boy. He went down a-hunting of wild pigs and took me along often enough. There was good shooting in them days."

"How far did you travel underground, you and your father?"

"Only after pigs and what other game we could find. If you mean me alone, then to the Margate Caves, your honor, although mayhaps I dreamt it. Clear under the Thames, howsomever, and that often enough." Beaumont saw a faint look of surprise come over Mr. Klingheimer's face, and just as quickly disappear.

"And you acquainted Narbondo with this *route*, shall we say? Your father's route beneath the Thames or out Margate way?"

"Some of it, when he asked it of me, but not so far as Margate nor so deep as the lower reaches. He had no real notion of what lies beneath, do you see, nor had my old dad in his day. I found such places in my own way."

It came to Beaumont that he was saying too much. There was something in Mr. Klingheimer that drew it out of a person. "I forgot half of what I knew in the years since my old dad went to the knackery," he said for good measure, although it rang false as soon as it was out of his mouth. He looked at Mr. Klingheimer's round face, but couldn't read anything into it, much like looking into the face of the clock on the wall.

"I see," Mr. Klingheimer said. "Well, well. You're a fortunate man, both to be rid of the likes of Dr. Narbondo and for coming to me. I'm told you have a copy of the handbill drawn up by the printer."

Beaumont took it from his coat and held it out, and at that same moment Mr. Klingheimer drew two ten-pound Bank of England notes from his pocket and handed them to Beaumont. "You've convinced me, Mr. Zounds," he said, "although it would be of more use to us if you knew whether Narbondo was dead or alive."

"Alas, sir. If I knew for certain I would say it. I heartily wish him dead, but wishes don't fill an empty belly, as my old dad used to say when he was a-hunting pigs." He slipped the banknotes into his coat. Mr. Klingheimer wanted something more from him, of that Beaumont was certain. But did he mean to get it by main force, or to pay for it? There was something bent in the man, as false as a weeping crocodile. He wore a mask upon his face, so to speak, and Beaumont thought of the black orb that he had seen through the goggles. He had seen such men before – men like Narbondo, with darkness in them – and had a fear of them.

"Perhaps we can do further business, Mr. Zounds," Mr. Klingheimer said finally, looking hard all the while into Beaumont's eyes. "I would very much like to know more specifically the routes that your father traveled when he went a-hunting for pig. Where did he enter? On Hampstead Heath? Along where the Westbourne rises near Highgate Ponds, perhaps, near the old manse? Is that where you would enter if you were to lead my men to where Narbondo had fallen into the pit?"

Beaumont considered the question for a long moment before he spoke. Mr. Klingheimer knew a thing or two, and no doubt about it. A lie wouldn't do. "I won't say no, sire, but Hampstead Heath ain't sensible-like for the descent, being at a considerable distance. There's a more likely passage in Deans Court, tolerable close to where the Doctor was swallowed up. His corpse is either a-moldering down there this very moment or it ain't, and if it ain't then he ain't dead, unless the pigs have ate him. They're a brazen lot, the pigs. The gate in Deans Court is locked tight, howsomever."

"It happens that I know the gatekeeper, Mr. Zounds. Locked gates flee before us, I am happy to say."

"Still and all," Beaumont said, "a man's finding the way once he's in the Fleet tunnel is a puzzler, sir, without a guide. There's iron ladders and stone chimneys to navigate, like going down a well, with skulls and dry bones lying thick in places – lost travelers, so to say. There ain't no map of them reaches – none that I know but that what's in my head."

"I'm fully persuaded of it, Mr. Zounds."

"And then, you see, if the Doctor is found and we must bring him out, it'll be on the Heath or not at all, and only after dark when nosey parker's abed, for there's no returning by Deans Court hauling a burden, not with them shafts and ladders to climb."

"Quite so. The Heath it is on the return trip. Capital plan. Let me ask you one last thing, Mr. Zounds, another test, you might say, so consider your answer carefully. Now… it must be precious dark below the ground."

"Parts of it is."

"You brought lanterns along, then, you and your old dad?"

"That we did, for when we had need of them. Torches, mainly."

"But you did not always have need? Why not, then?"

"Because of the toads, sir. The witch-light toads. We hunted by toad light, your honor, for lantern light would warn the pigs we was nigh."

"You call them toads, but you mean fungus, no doubt. Toadstools, if you will. Describe them, please."

"Aye, fungus-moss, toadstools, pookies. Like vast great blood suckers, they are, if they get hold of you. Bigger'n the likes of me, some of them, when you're deep beneath the world."

Mr. Klingheimer nodded and stroked his beard again. "Have you seen them bigger than the likes of *me* as well, the toads, as you call them?"

"Oh, aye, maybe just, if you know where to look, now and then a right forest of them. Fat stalks with round lids on top that a man might sit upon, if they didn't smell like horse-shit, begging your honor's pardon."

"You amaze me, Mr. Zounds. You're a small man with an outsized knowledge of some tolerably arcane things. Did you inform your previous employer about the great fungi?"

"No, your honor. He didn't ask."

"Ah! Well then I'm glad that I *did* ask, and I'm pleased to make you an offer that I believe you'll not despise. There's another twenty pounds for you if you show us a 'right forest of these toads,' as you put it so poetically – paid down tomorrow morning at dawn when we set out. Twenty more if we find Narbondo's corpse. Forty if we find the living man. That's a mort of money, Mr. Zounds, all in a heap. I can't say fairer than that. If you serve me well on the morrow, then you will have passed the third test and will have found another situation into the bargain. You can fetch your belongings from your quarters in the Seven Dials and be quit of that neighborhood forever. I very much hope that suits you."

Beaumont put two fingers to his hat and bowed at the waist. "It suits me down to the ground, your honor," he said.

His luck was in, just as he had hoped not an hour past when the potato boy had given him the handbill. He could disappear out of Mr. Klingheimer's world when he chose to, he told himself, whenever the man played him false, and he could shut the gate behind him with a peck of gunpowder.

SEVEN
HEREAFTER FARM

The old ragstone house, which had stood at the center of Hereafter Farm for over a century, had a blue-gray cast to the stone. The traces of blue heightened in wet weather until they were very like the color of a robin's egg. The red tiles of the roof were stained a deep, autumnal brown. St. Ives, Alice, and Mother Laswell sat in the parlor on upholstered chairs, looking out through a French window at a glasshouse some distance away, the shadow of vegetation visible within. The fine weather had quite disappeared, and the sky was dark with clouds.

A barn stood nearby, the top half of its Dutch door open and the gray mule Ned Ludd standing just inside, assessing the wide world with a satisfied face. Clara Wright stood beside him, stroking his neck. The mule was reputed to be astonishingly intelligent, had learnt his letters up to T by now. When he had the entire alphabet he would be taught to spell, all of this under Clara's tutelage.

At Mother Laswell's insistence St. Ives had been compelled to reveal the cause of Sarah Wright's death before she would leave the wood, but the revelations were more mystifying to her than revealing. The hole in the floor had been evidently troubling. She had made him describe what he saw in particular detail, and then had shaken her head and said, "They didn't find it." She took it no further, and St. Ives refrained from asking what it was they didn't find and how she knew. When they had arrived at Hereafter Farm, Mother Laswell had conveyed the sad news to Clara – although only that which needed to be conveyed – but Clara had merely nodded. Clearly she was already aware of her mother's death, and in fact revealed to Mother Laswell the exact moment on the previous day when it came into her mind that her mother had breathed her last.

Mother Laswell poured tea into their cups now, and passed around the milk and sugar, then sat back in her chair. "Clara lost her sight when she was seven years old," she told them. "Shortly thereafter Sarah Wright expelled her husband – the scoundrel Clemson Wright – from the cottage. It was… very bad. He beat Sarah, do you see? And he took the money that she had laid by – that she had received from her own mother. He never returned, thank heaven. Clara came to live here some few months later, nearly eight years ago now."

"Was the loss of Clara's eyesight organic in nature?" St. Ives asked Mother Laswell. "Did it advance over time?"

"It was quite sudden, in fact."

"Is it *psychical* in nature, then?"

She shrugged, as if the question was not vital. "*Hysterical*, do you mean? It's an unhappy word, Professor. Will it surprise you to know that I corresponded with Monsieur Charcot himself on just that subject? Have you heard the name, sir?"

"A prominent physician in France, although with some tolerably modern notions."

"My good friend Mabel Morningstar had met the man. He was a friend of Mabel's late husband. Charcot suggested that I convey Clara to Paris for a course of hypnotic therapy. We were to be prepared to stay for some time. Clara refused to go, and neither Sarah nor I insisted. Half of me believed that Charcot was a charlatan, you see – another Mesmer, if you will, who intended to publicize Clara's misfortune in order to promote himself."

"Indeed," St. Ives said, "I believe that the jury is still out on that subject, ma'am, although Charcot's work has borne interesting fruit. I have no business playing the grand inquisitor, but may I ask whether Clemson Wright misused the girl?"

"There you have it," Mother Laswell said.

"Ah. And now this terrible business." St. Ives shook his head and stared into his teacup, as if reading the leaves.

"And yet Clara possesses a strength of spirit that I envy," Mother Laswell said. "Sometimes I feel like a weakling when I'm in her presence."

Alice looked out through the dark afternoon and saw that Clara was still in the lamp-lit barn, feeding an apple to the mule. It astonished her that children could undergo such hardships and still have any happiness in them. Mother Laswell poured more tea into their cups. She looked worn out, and not merely from the day's tribulations, Alice thought, but from early years of trouble and pain – a wicked, murderous husband of her own, and a son who was worse. Both dead now, and the world better off without them. Their malicious ghosts still haunted her life, however.

"Shall I tell you something that will surprise you?" Mother Laswell asked, breaking the silence.

"By all means," St. Ives said.

"I'll reveal to you that Clara is a hydroscope of enormous power. Her ability to sense the presence of underground water and of dead things buried near it is quite remarkable."

"Do you mean that she's mastered the art of the divining rod?" Alice asked.

"No, Alice. I mean that Clara *is* the divining rod – a human hydroscope. She falls into fits if she stands above underground water, even very deep beneath the earth. She begins to spin, and can't help herself. She'll seize if she's not forcibly moved away."

"I'll tell you truthfully," St. Ives said, "that I'm skeptical of wands and hydroscopes having the power to find buried human bodies or treasures or suchlike. The notion was exploded long ago."

"You would not be skeptical if you'd witnessed Clara entering a cemetery, Professor. In truth we keep her very nearly a prisoner at Hereafter Farm, for the ground beneath her can become a living nightmare if she's not careful. Her mother fashioned a pair of shoes soled with sheet lead for her, which diminishes the effect, but the girl is unhappy wearing them. The shoes diminish her powers, you see, and her second sight fades because of the layer of lead that separates her from the earth. When one has second sight in abundance but is lacking in eyesight, one is loath to lose one's powers and be left impaired. At times she wards off such threats by reciting rhyme or running through the alphabet in strange sequences that she has invented. Sarah taught her a poem by Mr. Lear – 'The Jumblies' – making certain that she had it word for word despite its being nonsense, or perhaps because of it. They used the poem to call each other – telepathically, to use the modern term. Those who know the art scarcely need to name it."

"Clara is an interesting girl, to be sure," St. Ives said. "I don't wonder that you wanted to keep her out of the hands of Monsieur Charcot or anyone else who wanted to make a study of her."

"Then you can perhaps understand that I must know what Dr. Pullman discovered in regard to Sarah Wright, but that I very much want to remain out of the way, if you take my meaning, and Clara also."

"Certainly," St. Ives said. "You seem to be carrying a great weight, Mother; you needn't bear it alone. There's no greater burden than secret knowledge."

"You're in the right of it there. To put it plainly, I fear that my dead husband is the source of this evil. When I first spoke of him to you I refused to utter his name, which was an abomination to me. But our doings in London and in the marsh a year ago left me a changed woman, and his name no longer has any power over me. He was born Maurice De Salles. Now you two know his name, in case you hear it again. When they hanged him for practicing vivisection and for the murder of children I wrote that name on a slip of paper and buried it in the dung heap, in order to be done with it. I haven't used the name since. It has become imperative, however, that I know whether his… whether Maurice De Salles's legacy, so to speak, is at work here."

"Your dead husband's legacy is not your own legacy, Mother, whatever his name is," Alice told her. "And the man has been dead as a stone for a good many years."

"So he has, after a fashion. But what he _knew_ hasn't died with him, Alice, nor ever will, apparently, and it attracts those who want the knowledge for their own ends. I told you something about him, Professor, when we first met on that dark night after poor Mary Eastman was slaughtered in the graveyard, but I left much out, because it didn't signify. I believe it signifies now. After my husband was hanged, they buried his body at the crossroads down from the old bridge in order to maze the body, and a stake was driven through the body to fix it in place."

"Surely that sort of thing was given up in the last century," Alice said.

"Not in special cases, ma'am, I do assure you, and his was a special case. Worse than you can easily believe. The body still lies there today, pinned in place, but not in the state in which it was first buried. I have no desire to offend you with what I reveal, but I'm afraid I must reveal it. The night after the burial, when the dirt in the grave was still loose, it was opened in the dark of night and the head was taken. The grave was closed again, the soil tamped flat and swept clean, and so it's remained. The road was metaled some years since, but thank God the body was deep enough to lie undisturbed. The desecration of the body was done at my request, and I'll tell you plainly that I would do it again without a qualm."

Alice had covered her mouth with her hand and stared at Mother Laswell now in simple surprise. "Why on earth?" she asked. "It must have been terrible."

"It was ... necessary, ma'am."

"In certain European countries," St. Ives said, saving Mother Laswell the effort, "it is still quite common to cut out the heart or remove the head of a condemned murderer, divide the body into pieces, and bury the pieces near running water, so that the stream will bear away fragments of the spirit. According to popular thought, the body must be separated into parts in order to confound the ghost, just as the several paths that merge at a crossroads confounds it, disallowing it from returning home. The law takes a dim view of the practice, but the law takes a dim view of many notions that innocent, well-meaning people are entirely dedicated to, although they mightn't speak of it."

"Just so," Mother Laswell said. "The law has an understanding of the world that has little to do with things of the spirit. I recall you telling me that you saw strange things yourself when the Cathedral was besieged, Alice – things that were beyond your ken?"

"Yes," Alice said. "You're perfectly correct. I find once again that I've led a moderately sheltered life in some ways."

"Be happy that you were allowed to. I wish to heaven that I had. As I said, however, I contrived to have the head removed. I myself did not take an active part, although I watched through a pair of opera glasses from a high window in the Chequers Inn, where I had put up during my husband's trial, being in fear of staying at home alone. I saw little beyond moving shadows, for it was a fortunately dark night, but my conspirators worked swiftly. The gravediggers were the two men who had buried the body that very morning. Mr. Sarney, the butcher, who owed me a debt, cut through the neck of the corpse to take the head. Sarney died not long after, and the two gravediggers kept mum, being culpable themselves and well paid for their work. One of them passed away long years ago, but the other was alive until a week past.

"He became sexton in his time at St. Peter and Paul's, and I came to know him quite well. He was ninety years of age, old Mr. Peattie, and it was thought that he passed away in his sleep, but I have my doubts. There was one other person who stood by me, and that was Sarah Wright. It was she who boxed up the head of Maurice De Salles and buried it as a favor to me, laying counterfeit coins on the eyes and stuffing the lead box with mistletoe and dipping it in layers of wax. I have no idea where it lies, or, God help us, where it lay, if indeed she buried it beneath the floorboards of her own cottage, which I very much doubt that she would have. We never spoke of it after, lest we call up spirits."

Mother Laswell paused. She pursed her lips and shook her head, as if to rid her mind of the recollection. "Sarah Wright was murdered," she said, "because someone wanted something of her. She was quite penniless. She had nothing to give them aside from knowledge. When you speak to Dr. Pullman, Professor, you would do me a favor to say nothing of what I've revealed to you just now, although you could mention my name innocently enough. I don't ask you to lie, but I must know if the head of Maurice de Salles was recovered from the cottage."

"I have nothing against an honorable lie, Mother, or a convenient fiction."

"Nor have I," Alice said. "We're entirely with you, and we'll do anything that can be done for Clara."

Langdon poured the rest of his tea down his throat and looked at his pocket watch. Alice knew that he was counting the minutes, waiting for Hasbro's arrival. Dr. Pullman and the Constable had passed by on the road some time ago, the body lying in the back of the wagon, covered in a shroud, and Langdon had spoken to them briefly, agreeing to pay a visit to Dr. Pullman's residence at the very first opportunity.

Now three ragamuffin children, two girls and a small boy, orphans taken in by Mother Laswell, walked into the room along with Clara Wright, the two girls holding Clara's hands. Clara was quite pretty despite the sad look on her face. She wore smoked spectacles and a pair of thin stockings, but no shoes. Alice had found her sightless eyes disconcerting in the past, which struck her now as a shameful weakness.

The children gawked for a moment at Alice and then ran giggling toward the door to the kitchen, the little boy ducking past the girls and endeavoring to squeeze through the doorway first. The taller of the girls snatched the collar of his shirt and dragged him back, calling him a cauliflower-head, and the three disappeared into the kitchen, shouting abuse at each other with a happy vigor.

Clara curtsied and then cocked her right arm around so that her hand rested on her left shoulder, the crook of her elbow pointing straight out before her. As if "seeing" that Mother Laswell sat in the chair six steps away to the left, she walked in an uninhibited manner in that direction and put her hand on the old woman's shoulder. Mother Laswell covered Clara's hand with her own.

Alice, hoping that Clara would recognize her voice, said, "It's good to see you again, Clara, although I wish it were under other circumstances." It occurred to her immediately that her phrasing wanted improvement, although no amount of improvement would make mere words say anything useful. Clara turned toward Alice and acknowledged her statement with a nod of her head, and then sat down in a chair next to Mother Laswell. Mother had told Alice that Clara rarely spoke except in her sleep, sometimes laughing aloud, which seemed to Alice to be both hopeful and troubling in equal measure.

There was the sound of a vehicle coming up the drive now, and, as if put off by the thought of visitors, Clara followed her elbow out of the room, turning away down the hall.

St. Ives rose and went to the window. "It's Hasbro," he said, plucking his coat and hat from the hooks by the door. "With haste there's the chance we'll return before dark."

EIGHT

THE BROKEN LENS

The way to Dr. Pullman's house, with its morgue in the rear yard, led along the River Medway for a time, the water brown and high with the season and the tide, and then through the village, approaching the Chequers Inn over the very same road beneath which Mother Laswell's murderous husband lay buried, his headless body long rotted away, but his memory still alive. Hasbro drove the chaise, and St. Ives looked up at the old inn, seeing what must be the window through which Mother Laswell, a comparatively young woman at the time, had watched the grisly business of the taking of the head. He was quite sure that she recalled that dark night all too perfectly, and that it haunted her dreams. The ghosts that remain in one's memory, St. Ives had often found, are not often easy to lay.

They drove out across the old bridge now, the open sky above them dark with clouds, the fine weather a thing of the past. The air smelled of rain, calling up in St. Ives's mind happily empty childhood days. He untied the lashings that secured the folding hood and raised it over their heads, and none too soon, for the rain began to fall in earnest when Hasbro turned up the road toward Dr. Pullman's house, past occasional cottages that stood among bare orchards and fallow fields. Most of the cottages had small gardens, already showing the shoots of broad beans and onions and winter lettuce. There was something beautiful in autumn rain and in the autumn countryside, something that he had forgotten when the remnant of summer had appeared this morning and beguiled him.

"It's a philosophical sort of day," St. Ives said to Hasbro, raising his voice in order to be heard above the clatter and jingle of the cart and horse.

"Indeed it is," Hasbro said. "It's a philosophical season to my mind, a regretful season, just the opposite of spring. If it weren't for Christmas, there'd be little joy in it, although there's comfort in home and hearth when the air outside is full of flying snow."

"I find myself somewhat gladdened by the changing season, which is apparent on such a day as this. If the world is turning toward winter, it is turning toward summer at one and the same time. There's something to be said for looking ahead, at least in moderation."

English oaks grew on either side of the road now, their nearly leafless canopies closing overhead, but blocking little of the rain. They came out under the sky again at the edge of Dr. Pullman's property. The man himself, wearing a stained medical coat, sat on a bench on the veranda, watching the rain. He had a glass in his hand, and he raised it in a gesture of recognition when he saw who was coming along in the chaise.

St. Ives knew Pullman well enough, had visited on several occasions in the year and a half since he and Alice had moved to Aylesford, he and Pullman dissecting a gibbon ape that had died of apoplexy on one occasion. Pullman was much the superior anatomist, which was edifying for St. Ives, who valued the gaining of ready-to-hand knowledge. The ape's body had been obtained from Mr. Marchand, a former zookeeper who lived in Maidstone and who still kept a variety of exotic animals on his considerable property. It had been Mr. Marchand who had sold Johnson the elephant to Alice.

Pullman rose and stepped down the several stairs, greeting them cheerlessly. "Will you take a glass of whiskey?" he asked, holding up his own glass again by way of illustration after leading them under the cover of the veranda and out of the rain.

Both men declined, and St. Ives said, "We're here on an errand for Mother Laswell of Hereafter Farm. You know her, I believe. I'm afraid that she's sadly distressed by the death of her friend."

"Indeed I do know her. A very sensible, capable woman despite her eccentricities. I have no idea of her ghosts and fairies, but her struggle against what the poet referred to as 'black, satanic mills' has my entire sympathy. I assume you mean that she's anxious about the particulars of the death."

"Yes. I hope there's something we can tell her that would be comforting, even in a small way."

"There is not," Dr. Pullman said. "It was foul murder of the most unnatural, cold-blooded variety. I've never seen anything like it, a senseless, unimaginable horror. "

"When did it occur?" St. Ives asked.

"Yesterday, in the morning to my mind."

"What motive would a murderer have to kill an innocent woman in such a manner?" Hasbro asked. "Do you suspect a madman?"

"I'm not at all certain that I distinguish between murderous madmen and other varieties of murderer. From my point of view, cold, thoughtful murder is madness in any case, whether it be temporary madness or permanent. I can tell you, however, that if this man was literally insane – given that the fiend was a man and not a woman – he was also a skilled surgeon."

He set his glass down on the little deal table next to the bench and said, "You won't relish what you are about to see, if you choose to see it, but it's the only way to convey the nature of the thing. But you already know that, Professor."

"My knowledge is superficial, Doctor. We're very keen to understand what sort of monster walks among us."

Dr. Pullman ushered them into his modestly furnished home, which smelled of pipe tobacco, formaldehyde, and cooking grease. The wooden floors were covered with braid rugs, the place almost empty of needless decoration, but cluttered with shelves and shelves of books, many with Latin titles. Anatomical drawings papered the leftover wall space, and a wired-together human skeleton hung from a coat-rack in the corner, the hook behind it bearing an umbrella and a bowler hat.

The stove was lit in the small kitchen, the oven door standing open, no doubt in order to heat the house now that autumn had truly descended upon them. There was a broken disk of Stilton cheese atop a plate on the oil-cloth covered table, next to which a dead pelican shared a breadboard with half a loaf of bread, the bird's breast cut open and its wings pinned back.

"I've been anatomizing over my lunch," Dr. Pullman said. "One finds curious things in the bellies of sea birds."

Without expounding on the matter, he led them out of the back door, down the stoop, and back out into the rain. They hunched across a patch of weedy grass to a stone building with a slate roof. A ladder leaned against the side of the building. On the ground below, a heap of broken slates lay piled beside a bucket that was black with tar, the brush stuck in it. Inside the operating room, however, there was a sense of organization and cleanliness: plaster walls with wooden cabinetry along the length of the room, drawers both large and small, framed anatomical depictions, jars containing various human organs and fetal animals. At one end of the room, beneath a window that let in afternoon light, was a broad basin with water taps above. The room reeked of carbolic acid. Mingling with the chemical odor was the smell of death, the summer-like heat earlier in the day having hastened the process of decay within the body that lay covered in a stained sheet upon the operating table. Dr. Pullman raised the end of the sheet and drew it from the corpse of Sarah Wright, folding it across the dead woman's shoulders.

"Even though the murderer evidently meant to kill her, he removed her head after subduing her with chloroform," Dr. Pullman said. "He wanted an unconscious but living patient. Lord knows why. The result, as you know, was a bloody mess.

"A skilled surgeon, you say?" St. Ives asked.

"A surgeon's assistant might have committed the atrocity, although competent, surely, and willing to take great care with scalpel and saw. As you can see, the flesh has been neatly incised and the spine divided between the third and fourth vertebrae. The carotid and cervical arteries were severed last, to my mind, in order to put off certain death until the last moment. The body, of course, pumped out a tremendous amount of blood in its final seconds."

"There is certainly more to be discovered," Hasbro said. "The motivation could not have been mere deviltry. This is too systematic, too careful."

"Indeed," Pullman said. "There has been a spate of murders in London recently that involved surgeries – adrenal and pineal glands taken, brains entirely removed from the skull. Heads removed in much this same matter. London is full of vagabonds and orphans whom no one would miss, and such crimes are rarely solved. So this murder is not untypical, gentlemen, except that in this case the murderer traveled into Aylesford and thence into the heart of Boxley Woods in order to find a cottage that few even know exists."

"Just so," said St. Ives. "It was clear that the cottage had been thoroughly investigated – furniture upended, cupboards emptied onto the floor, floorboards prised up, holes dug in the ground beneath. Evidently there was something else they were searching for. Was there no evidence that they'd found it? Constable Brooke is looking into the mystery, I take it."

"In his usual… careful manner, yes. In the cottage he found a great deal as regards the crime, but very little as regards the criminal."

"Does he have any idea what might have been found beneath the floorboards, then?"

"He does not. He would have told me if he had. Perhaps the fiends found what they were looking for and took it with them, along with the poor woman's head."

St. Ives was abruptly conscious that rain was drumming against the slates of the roof, and he found that he was sick of the smell of carbolic and decaying flesh. He considered revealing Mother Laswell's fears about her long-dead husband to Pullman, and of the man's head being taken, but he rejected the idea. She had asked to remain in the shadows, and in the shadows she would remain. "Can you discern any similarity between the death of Sarah Wright," he asked, "and that of the old sexton who passed away some few days ago?"

"Yes," Pullman said. "Now you've hit upon something odd."

He drew the sheet over the corpse, and they walked out onto the covered stoop and into fresh air, the rain falling on three sides of them like a curtain. "The ingestion of henbane was common to both of them," he said. "The smell of it was upon Sexton Peattie's mouth and in a glass that had a small amount of gin in it. It was the probable cause of the old man's death, although there was no autopsy, he being upward of ninety years old. I thought it odd, however, until I discovered in my reading that henbane is in fact steeped in various liquors as a flavoring, which satisfied me at the time that his death was at worst accidental, or that he was a self-murderer, which is no concern of mine."

"But you discovered that Sarah Wright had been dosed with it also," Hasbro said, "and your opinion changed?"

"I detected it in a teacup sitting on the windowsill in her cottage. The strong tea left in the bottom of the cup masked the smell somewhat. If I hadn't been thinking of the Sexton, I would not have remarked upon it. It is now my suspicion that someone wanted something similar from both Sarah Wright and Sexton Peattie – information – and that they used a heavy decoction of henbane to promote truth telling. It's quite possible that they succeeded with Sexton Peattie, who sent them into the wood where they treated Sarah Wright in a similar manner. Perhaps she resisted when they compelled her to drink the poisoned tea. A certain amount of it had splashed over her clothing."

"Perhaps they found nothing beneath the floorboards," Hasbro said, "and so tried to compel her to say where the thing was hidden."

"Perhaps," said Pullman, "although I'm not happy with assumptions. There was one other odd thing, gentlemen. I found this lying on the floor some distance from the body. It lay hidden by a broken section of floorboard." He reached into his vest pocket and took out a flat piece of thin glass, round on the unbroken edge – evidently a piece of a lens of some sort. "Look through it," he said, handing it to St. Ives, who held it up to the sky.

"Distinctly purple," St. Ives said. "A twilight purple, if you will." He handed it to Hasbro, who also peered through it.

"It's quite dark," Hasbro said. "It would inconvenience a person to wear them."

"That it would," Dr. Pullman said, "if in fact that person were walking about. I believe, however, that I know what such goggles are meant to do, although their existence on the floor of the cabin makes not a jot of sense to me. Have you heard of the work of Walter John Kilner, Professor? He's a medical electrician at St. Thomas' Hospital, Lambeth?"

"No, sir," said St. Ives. "I know very little of so-called medical electricity, and what I do know, I don't much like."

"Nor do I. Kilner is an old friend, however. We were in school together. I last saw him a year ago when I was in London. He was busy fabricating goggles with chemically coated lenses much like this."

"For what purpose?" St. Ives asked.

"His work at the hospital has led him into the study of the human aura – light energy, if you will. We all emit invisible light, strange as it sounds, and Walter Kilner was hard at work to develop a way to make that light visible and to determine what it portends – sickness or health, perhaps, or a disordered state of the nerves."

"And you believe this to be a fragment of one of Kilner's lenses?" St. Ives asked. "Surely you do not suspect him of the crime?"

"Yes to the first question and no to the second," Pullman said. "It's unthinkable that Walter John Kilner could have committed such a crime. I'd sooner suspect my own mother. I believe, however, that the murderer, or perhaps the murderer's accomplice, possessed a pair of Walter Kilner's aura goggles, so to call them, and that they were broken in the struggle. His work is very new, and such lenses must be tremendously rare. Why they were brought to Sarah Wright's cottage I can't say."

"Yet another mystery," Hasbro said. "Here's something practical, although gruesome: if the villain wanted to keep the head fresh, Doctor, how would he go about it? Ice?"

"Ice or perhaps refined brandy in a large receptacle. Ice would make more sense, to be certain. The trick would be to keep the ice from melting – particularly difficult given yesterday's fine weather. It could be done, however, if there were a sensible way to store it. If they knew in advance what they were after, it would have been simple to come prepared, ghastly as it sounds. But I'm weary of these speculations. I very much hope that this fiend is caught, gentlemen, and that I have nothing further to do with his depredations. You may keep that piece of lens if you fancy it, Professor. I have no use for it."

"It's not... *evidence*, then? Constable Brooke has no interest in it?"

"Constable Brooke was confounded by it. He's a good man, as you know, but this sort of oddment is beyond his ken. Walter Kilner would be the man to ask if you happened to find yourself in Lambeth, but I'd lay odds on his being equally confounded."

NINE

"Another cup of tea?" Mother Laswell asked Alice.

"A half cup, perhaps," Alice said. "Unless you find my curiosity offensive, Mother, I'd like to ask one last question about Clara."

"I can't imagine you offending anyone," Mother Laswell said.

"She seems to have extraordinary abilities. I mean that in the old sense of the word, not merely rare or unusual – her seeing with her elbow, for instance."

"Yes, and certainly she has – or had – an extramundane ability to communicate with her mother, although that is not uncommon in children. Her powers, I believe, are prodigious. She keeps them to herself, however, and I don't press her. She came to Hereafter Farm a year after she was stricken with blindness, unable to bear living in the forest any longer. We had no idea that her presence here was anything other than temporary. I visited Sarah one afternoon, alone. Sarah asked me to give Clara a small owl, carved from chalk and painted, a mere trinket that had been purchased in a seaside shop in earlier, better days. When I returned to Hereafter, Clara met me at the stile on the meadow. She asked did I have it? I asked her what she meant, thinking that I did indeed have it, but that she could not possibly know. 'The owl,' she said. And so I gave it to her, and she went off quite joyfully."

"You're *certain* she could not have known?"

"She could not – not in the sense you mean. And yet she *did* know. That was the first of many such incidents. You'd be quite amazed."

Through the window Alice saw a man appear in the Dutch door beside the mule; apparently he had come in through the front of the barn in the wagon. She recognized him just as Mother Laswell said, "It's Bill," and stood up out of her chair. Mother heaved a loud sigh and began to weep, perhaps with relief. "We're all right now," she said. "Bill's home."

Bill Kraken, betrothed to Mother Laswell and an old friend to the St. Ives family, was tall and lean, his skin worn like old leather, baked for years in the Australian sun on a sheep farm after he had been transported for smuggling, and hammered by being out in all weather during his time on the London streets selling pea-pods and sleeping rough. His hair seemed to be permanently laid over, as if there were a stiff wind blowing. He scratched the mule behind the ear and whispered something to it, and then he ducked through the rain and up onto the veranda, disappearing from view.

"I'll just step into the kitchen and speak to Bill," Alice said, moving toward the kitchen door. It would be better for her to bear the news in order to spare Mother Laswell, who was already in a sad taking. The boy who had been called a cauliflower head stood on a stool at the kitchen counter, expertly shelling walnuts on a stone slab, cracking them open with one whack of a hefty wooden rod and putting the perfect halves into a wide-mouthed, stoneware jar. The girls were nowhere to be seen.

The boy had apparently just said something to Kraken, who stood stock-still in his damp coat, his face both disturbed and baffled. "Is it true what the boy is going on about?" he asked Alice. "That's why you've come along to the farm on such a day as this?"

"Yes, Bill," she said.

"I know what's what," the boy said, breaking another walnut. He put the two halves into his mouth and chewed on them, holding the wooden rod up as if it were an illustration. "It's Clara's mum what's dead, sir, like I said. I heard it from John Peters, who saw her with his own eyes this very morning, a-sitting there without a head at all. Someone had did for her."

"Clap a stopper over it, Tommy," Kraken told him. "Talk like that ain't genteel."

"It's what I heard from John Peters, sir. It's what he seen. It was him as told Constable Brooke."

"And now you've told us, Tommy," Alice said to the boy. "But Mr. Kraken is correct. Clara doesn't want to hear any such coarse talk."

"Yes, ma'am," Tommy said.

"Then be off with you," Kraken told him. "Take a heap of them nuts with you. Keep your gob stuffed with 'em till you learn how to speak like a Christian."

"Yes, sir," Tommy said, scooping up a handful from the open jar and shuffling out onto the veranda, where the girls were evidently playing.

Alice could hear a top strike the deck and then the clatter of pins being knocked down.

"Langdon and Hasbro have gone into the village to speak to Dr. Pullman," she said.

Kraken nodded. "The Professor will see things right. But it's too late for me to be of any use. There's naught to do now that Sarah Wright's dead. I shouldn't have gone into Maidstone. I shouldn't have gone off over a few sheep, ancient sheep, too – a fool's errand. Look what come of it."

"Nonsense, Bill," Alice told him. "The crime quite likely occurred yesterday, in the middle of Boxley Woods, before you left for Maidstone. The lot of us were within half a mile of Sarah Wright's cottage at the time. There's nothing you nor anyone else could have done to prevent it."

"Mayhaps," he said. "Still and all…" He was silent for a moment and then said, "I'll look in on Mother. She'll have took it hard."

Alice followed him into the parlor, wishing now that Langdon and Hasbro were still here, if only to lend a semblance of order to the chaos of murder and its aftermath.

Kraken put his arm around Mother Laswell's shoulder, hugging her awkwardly. She clutched his hand and said, "I'm all right now you've come home, Bill." Kraken sighed heavily, his sigh catching in his throat. Alice felt like an interloper, but reminded herself that her own emotions were trivial.

Needing very badly to be useful, she walked back into the kitchen and set about cracking walnuts, working proficiently and steadily, until the sound of a coach sent her to the window, relief flowing through her – Langdon and Hasbro, perhaps, returning more quickly than she could have hoped. But she was wrong. It was a black brougham with white flourishes painted on it and brass headlights, carrying two men, both of them wearing the uniform of the London Metropolitan Police.

One of the policemen was tall and dignified – an affection of dignity, perhaps – with a Roman nose, heavy eyebrows, and a wide mustache. The other, driving the horses, was heavy, short, and unfortunately ugly, his face having taken a beating on more than one occasion and his teeth snaggled. He had a snide, knowing look in his small, close-set eyes. His uniform fit him like a sausage casing and he wore a beard of sparse, straight bristles. The dark scowl on his face made him appear to be a hard man, but perhaps that wasn't surprising, Alice thought, given his work.

"Bill!" Alice called, but he was already on his way, opening the door at the first knock and letting the men into the house, the shorter man carrying a leather valise.

"You must be Harriet Laswell, ma'am," the taller of the two said to Alice. "Detective Shadwell of the Metropolitan Police and Sergeant Bingham, at your service."

"*I* am Harriet Laswell, gentlemen," Mother Laswell said, having come in from the parlor. "This is Alice St. Ives, our neighbor."

"Ma'am," Shadwell said, bowing in Alice's direction and regarding her with particular attention.

Alice stood aside in order to allow Mother Laswell to pass. Then she moved back into the doorway. She was aware that Clara stood behind her, wanting to listen, perhaps, but not to be seen.

"We scarcely expected that the London police would take an interest in the case," Mother Laswell said. "I *assume* you've come about the murder of Sarah Wright."

"Yes, we have. London in fact takes a *very* deep interest in the woman's murder, and in the wellbeing of her daughter, who lives here with you, if I'm not mistaken."

"She does indeed, Detective. Have you consulted with Constable Brooke at all? We know very little of the circumstances of the crime."

"Constable Brooke was very helpful in his small way, but I'm afraid that the implications in the case require the full attention of the Metropolitan Police. The local constabulary is at a sad loss to puzzle things out."

"God help us," Mother Laswell said. "Let me introduce Bill Kraken to you, Detective. Mr. Kraken and I are to be wed at Christmas. And I'll point out that Alice's husband is the illustrious Langdon St. Ives. Professor St. Ives is a highly regarded member of the Royal Society. You can speak freely in this company."

"Indeed," Detective Shadwell said, nodding at Bill Kraken and bowing to Alice again. "We won't consume much of your time. If you could instruct the girl Clara to pack a bag while we talk, we'll consume even less of it. We must return post haste to London with the girl in our custody."

St. Ives and Hasbro traveled beneath swiftly moving clouds, the rain having diminished to a spewy irritation rather than a proper downpour. Hasbro turned up Farthing Lane to the icehouse at the end, a wooden structure with 'Cromie's Wenham Ice' painted on the boards above a depiction of a sweating ice block clamped in a pair of tongs. A wagon stood outside the open door, where two men loaded blocks of ice onto the bed, one heaving the blocks and the other, aboard the wagon, tossing straw onto the ice and packing it in. St. Ives and Hasbro found Mr. Cromie, a hearty-looking old man, in his office, his foot in a pail of hot water.

"It's the gout," Cromie said to them. "The change of the weather does it. Every time. Sets it off like a squib. There's nothing for it but a hot soak and the doing of as little as possible, a sport at which I excel. Only complication is that I can't quit and rest." He burst into laughter, a loud "Ha ha!", the violence of it jolting his leg. He recoiled in pain and his face drained of color. "I'm a danger to myself, gentlemen," he wheezed. "What can I help you with? Building an Eskimo hut, perhaps?"

"Something much simpler, Mr. Cromie," St. Ives said. "My name is Langdon St. Ives, and this is my particular friend Hasbro. My wife and I have recently occupied the house and grounds owned by the late Agatha Walton, my wife's aunt."

"Have you now? A game old woman, Miss Walton. I was sorry when she passed away. I can see that you haven't come to Mr. Cromie's icehouse accompanied by your friend with a singular name merely to purchase ice. Why *have* you come?"

"Can you tell us whether a man, or two men, stopped in yesterday, midday or thereabouts, to purchase ice?" St. Ives asked. "Probably strangers in these parts."

"Indeed they did not, sir, neither one of them nor two. There were three of them, in point of fact. Why do you ask?"

"Constable Brooke is interested in them – *three*, do you say?"

"That's right, a rum cove in a yellow coat, what they call a seaside coat these days. A bruiser, I said to myself. Face hammered in the ring. He stayed in the wagon, so I didn't get a look at him except through the window. There were two who came in to purchase a small quantity of ice. One of them was a gent from the cut of his jib. Fringe beard, well dressed. Newmarket coat despite the weather. Pair of spectacles with a heavy black frame. Hair to his shoulders. Foreign cove, I said to myself, Mediterranean, mayhaps, and I found I was correct when he spoke. 'I want *eese*,' says he. I knew what he meant, of course, but I made him say it three times as a lark. Didn't like him. Not a bit. Pretentious as an owl. The other was an average-sized man, looked to be a swell. The foreigner called him 'doctor' once, and the fellow didn't like it a bit. Dark hair. Blue eyes with a scar directly beneath the left – a close call, no doubt. A great one with the women, I should think. Scotchman, says I to myself, but with most of the burr civilized out of him."

"Can you guess the age of either of them?" Hasbro asked.

"Forty-odd for the foreign cove, thirty-odd for the other, although mayhaps older for him as well. Boyish face with those blue eyes. The foreign cove ordered the ice."

"Anything odd about the purchase?" Hasbro asked.

"*Odd*, do you say? Well, sir. Odd enough, I suppose. He packed a box with ice, chiseled to fit just so. Size of a large hatbox, wood, but tinned inside. Smaller box inside that, tinned. Paid us to chip out the slabs, do you see? They must fit tight, he says to us, all the way around. Off they went, direction of Wrotham Heath when they got to the end of the lane, London bound, perhaps."

"Were you curious about the purchase?" Hasbro asked. "Strange business wasn't it – these tinned boxes?"

"Not a bit curious, truth to tell. I mind my business. Not like some gents I could name, who mind Mr. Cromie's business as well as their own. Enlighten me, if you will. What the devil does the Constable care about men buying ice?"

"Perhaps nothing," St. Ives said.

"And yet he sent you two to Cromie's icehouse to carry out an inquisition? Thumbscrews in your pocket, I dare say? Stretch poor Mr. Cromie on the rack?"

"Not a bit of it," St. Ives said. "It's a simple business. A grave was robbed at Boxley Abbey, but the corpse would scarcely fit into a hatbox, even a large one. We've come on a fool's errand, it seems. Thank you for your time, Mr. Cromie."

Mr. Cromie looked at them blankly for a moment and then

shrugged, apparently satisfied with the explanation. Hasbro did him the favor of refreshing his hot water bucket from a large kettle swathed in an over-sized tea cozy, and they left him soaking. Outside, the ice wagon was gone, the world empty of people.

They turned up the lane, back into Aylesford proper, bound for Hereafter Farm. St. Ives thought hard about what he would tell Mother Laswell – *how* he would tell it, which he had to do. There was nothing in any of it that would ease her fears.

"**P**ack a bag?" Kraken asked Detective Shadwell. "You ain't thinking of taking Clara to London town?"

Sergeant Bingham helped himself to a pair of walnuts, cracking them easily in his hand and eating the pieces, not saying a word, although the smirk on his face was evident to Alice. Kraken was livid with rage and surprise, and she was happy that he stood behind Bingham, out of sight, and hadn't noticed the trespass with the walnuts. None of them needed more trouble than they already had.

"We're not *thinking* of doing anything, my man," Detective Shadwell said to him. "We have orders to take the girl into custody for her own safety. She's in mortal danger. We've been led to believe that she's a savant, *touched* by the hand of God, if you will, and there are those that would make use of her."

"Who told you such a thing, sir?" asked Mother Laswell.

"Your own Constable Brooke and the girl's father, ma'am. We're tolerably certain that Mrs. Wright's murder was due to her… calling, which the girl shares."

"Her *father*? Clemson Wright? That *husk* of a man? What

business does he have saying anything at all about Clara? To the best of my knowledge he hasn't seen the girl since he was driven away many years ago, nor has Clara seen him. He's a viper, sir. An eater of dung." Mother Laswell had drawn herself up as if ready to explode. Alice took her arm to quiet her, or to hold her back if necessary.

"I fully believe you ma'am," the detective said, "but be that as it may, he *is* the girl's father. He has certain rights under the law, and the law is indifferent to his character unless he runs afoul of the law, which he has not."

Alice saw that Kraken had picked up the heavy piece of wooden rod from the kitchen counter and was gripping it hard, his face set. Neither of the two policemen were paying any attention to him at the moment, thank God. Alice stared meaningfully at Bill, and when she caught his eye, he looked abashed. Kraken's transportation to Australia had ended when he stowed away on a ship returning to England. He had managed to leave the ship on its way up the Thames, hiding himself in the Thames Marshes where he found employment tending sheep, until by chance he fell in with Harriet Laswell, and his life was on an even keel again after many years of rough seas. He could scarcely afford to be taken up for striking a policeman or for anything else, not unless he wanted to be hanged. He laid the rod back in its place now, but the unhappy state of his mind was clear to Alice.

"The girl is safe at Hereafter Farm, sir," Mother Laswell said, "safer than she is with the likes of Clemson Wright."

"I regret to say, ma'am, once again, that I am under orders. Miss Wright's father has laid claim to her for the sole purpose of protecting her. I'll reveal that several days ago he was approached by a man who offered to purchase the girl."

"*Purchase* her?" Mother Laswell said. "As if she were a *slave*?"

"Just so, and for a considerable sum. Wright was incensed, of course, by the very idea of it, as are all of us. He dismissed the man with hard words, but it started him thinking about his daughter, and about his duty to her. This very morning that same man came to him again in Thwaites's Coffee House, and told him that Sarah Wright was dead, and that he should think hard about the girl, who was *not* dead. Once again he offered money, but it amounted to three pennies, which he dropped into the cup out of which Wright was drinking his coffee. It was clearly a threat, do you see. If money would not move Clemson Wright, then there were surer means.

"Wright understood them to be deadly serious, and he asked the man for a day to consider how to accomplish the task, for he knew that the girl Clara would likely spurn him, and he needed time to puzzle out what to do. The man agreed. Clemson Wright came straight to us, in fear for his own life and the life of his daughter. Fortune, however, was with us. Constable Brooke had just ten minutes earlier reported the murder of Sarah Wright by telegraph. Sergeant Bingham and I were in the coach bound for Aylesford as soon as the story was out of Wright's mouth."

"And we mean to be back in London by supper time," Sergeant Bingham put in. "You lot can take that to the bank. Stand aside now and let us do our job and there won't be trouble." He picked up his valise at that point, opened it, and blithely removed a straight-jacket. "We've heard that the girl is given to fits."

Detective Shadwell shrugged. "It's unfortunate," he said, looking straight at Kraken now as if taking particular notice of his face, which was petrified with fury. "Sergeant Bingham is anxious to do his duty, once he knows what it is. He's tenacious in that regard."

"The girl ain't in no condition to do nowt," Kraken said. "What I say is that you two servants of the people fetch Constable Brooke and bring him back along to Hereafter. We'll wait for him and for the Professor, too, who is right now looking into this business out at Dr. Pullman's. Professor St. Ives will get to the bottom of it quick enough – see if he don't. There ain't no tearing hurry. Not now there ain't. The girl won't be murdered while Bill Kraken is with her. And god-*damn* your supper," he said to Sergeant Bingham. "Them chin whiskers look like they was shaved off the arse end of a Berkshire hog. Put that damned filthy garment back in that there bag or by God I'll hang you with it."

"Watch yourself, cully," Sergeant Bingham warned, shaking his head.

Detective Shadwell held up a restraining hand. "Take the pot off the boil, gentlemen!"

"*Yes*, Bill," Mother Laswell. "For heaven's sake do as he says. For *my* sake, Bill. We all want what's best for Clara."

A change came over Kraken, who slumped a bit, shook his head tiredly, and said, "I'll fix up Clara's bag," his words evidently surprising Mother Laswell as much as they surprised Alice. "Right is right," he said, "and legal is legal. I lost my head, gents. We can follow along into London on the train first thing in the morning and see that Clara's treated fair."

"That's eminently sensible," Detective Shadwell said to him. "I thank you for your cooperation, sir. We'll get this sorted out, I assure you. Clemson Wright might be a viper, but he'll lead us to this criminal gang, whom we believe to have perpetrated a string of murders and mutilations. We'll see justice done for the girl and for her mother."

"Aye," said Kraken. "That we will. Fetch in the squeakers," he said to Mother Laswell. "They won't ken what's happening. Get 'em out of the way."

He pushed through to the doorway into the parlor, Alice stepping back into the parlor herself to allow him to pass. It came to her that she had been occupying doorways most of the afternoon, watching but doing little or nothing to help. She saw Kraken whisper into Clara's ear now, the girl immediately walking across the room, sighting as ever over the crook in her bent elbow. She opened one of the French windows and stepped out. The rain was nothing but a light mist now, but the ground was muddy, and the wind blew in through the open casement.

Alice crossed the room to close the window, watching as Clara lifted her skirt with her free hand and hurried across to the door in the side of the barn, where Ned Ludd the mule again stood guard. Ned turned to follow Clara into the darkness when she let herself in. The entire business was puzzling, but when she looked for Bill Kraken he had disappeared down the hallway, deeper into the house. She returned to the kitchen, wishing to heaven that Langdon would arrive.

Mother Laswell was herding the children in through the kitchen door just then, past Alice and away up the hall, leaving Alice alone with the two men. Detective Shadwell gazed at her silently, his face blank, while Sergeant Bingham helped himself to another handful of walnuts, winking at Alice as he did so, a look of plain lust on his face. She responded by staring hard back at him until he looked away. Neither of the men was worth the price of yesterday's newspaper as far as she could see. Sergeant Bingham was a mere thug, and Detective Shadwell nothing but a hollow-headed mouthpiece. The Metropolitan Police must be a sorry lot if these two were representative samples.

"I've fetched the bag," Kraken shouted from behind her, but when he strode past into the kitchen he was carrying a rifle at port arms. "A bag of *cartridge*, I mean to say. This here's a *Henry* rifle," he said, swinging it downward and pointing it between the two. "You gents is just leaving, and you ain't a-taking Clara Wright. If Constable Brooke says we're to take Clara into London, then so be it, we'll do as he says, but she ain't a-going with the likes of you. And you can take *that* to the bank, you whoreson bastards!"

Sergeant Bingham reached into his coat, and Kraken aimed the rifle at his face and took a step forward as if to drive the barrel through the man's eye.

"Stand down, Sergeant!" Detective Shadwell said. "And you take that rifle out of here, Mr. Kraken. You're confounded in your mind by this turn of events. I would be, too, perhaps. But you're treading on…"

"I'm a-going to tread on you two humbugs, Mr. Shat-well. See if I don't. Let's take this out into the yard, gents, the three of us and Mr. Henry. Mother Laswell don't allow no gunfire in the confines of the house. So if I've got to shoot you two down like dogs, it had best be outside under the sky where you can bleed into the dirt."

"Be reasonable, sir…!"

"Get out!" Kraken yelled at Shadwell in a voice fit to carry in a hailstorm, and the two men turned and went out, Kraken following, muttering to himself.

"Keep your temper, Bill!" Alice said to his back – uselessly, since he had already lost it. Then she saw that Bingham had left his valise, so she picked it up, crammed the straitjacket into it, and walked to the kitchen door, which stood open. The valise suddenly infuriated her, and she felt a great liking for Bill Kraken, who was at risk of undoing himself. The two policemen had already climbed into their brougham, both of them blustering at Kraken and uttering threats. He still had the rifle up, sighting down the barrel.

Alice pitched the valise through the kitchen door just as Sergeant Bingham hied-up the horses and made a turn in the yard between the house and the barn. Kraken, evidently caught up in a desire to shoot something, fired repeatedly into the valise, making the bag hop and skitter, and then stood and watched the brougham as it drove away down the lane in the direction of Aylesford.

St. Ives was still considering his duty to Mother Laswell, when, halfway along the lane to the farm, he heard the unmistakable sound of gunfire. Moments later a brougham passed, necessarily close by and clipping along. One man sat inside, the other drove, both of them dressed in police uniforms, which, given the nearby gunfire, was a curious business, or so it seemed to St. Ives. The man within the brougham looked hard at St. Ives, as they passed, his face in shadow, but he glanced away when he perceived that St. Ives was returning his gaze.

TEN

LEAVING FOR LONDON

"**M**other informed me when I visited this morning," Alice said, "that Bill is ready to take Clara into the marshes if the two men return today. He won't give the girl up, nor will Mother." Alice tilted a cheval glass and looked into it, pinning up her hair.

St. Ives nodded. "Quite right, too, for Bill's own sake as well as Clara's. That caper with the rifle was unwise, although it was effective. I hope they consider my suggestion that they spend a quiet month or two in the north." He had a small pile of clothing laid out on the bed, and his large portmanteau open next to it. Sunlight shone through the windows, and the weather was fair again, but could no longer be mistaken for summer. "Two shirts should do the trick, I believe."

"*Two* shirts?" she said. "We'll be in London the better part of a week, Langdon. You're descending into a pit in the earth that's filthy with Thames mud. *Four* shirts is more to the point, and put in your sack coat and a topcoat."

"Of course," St. Ives said. "Sack coat and topcoat it is, and the

Monticello boots, I think. I've scarcely worn them since Tubby brought them back from Connecticut. Their soles are made of vulcanized rubber, a wonderful purchase on slick pavement." He sat thinking for a moment and then said, "I honor Bill Kraken immensely, you know, for his tenacity, but he's on thin ice here, Alice – if in fact the two men in the brougham were on the up and up."

"Indeed. But *were* they? I wondered at the time how they knew that Clara Wright had *fits*, as they put it. They had just come down from London, after all. I wonder how did this doubtful band of murderers determine that Clemson Wright was Sarah Wright's husband? Wright is a common name."

"Perhaps Clemson Wright's involvement is a mere invention."

"I'm inclined to believe that it might be," Alice said, "although we mustn't make unwarranted assumptions about Shadwell and Bingham, especially if Bill Kraken is in the room. He's easily provoked."

"Invariably against provocative people, however, which is certainly a virtue of some variety, as well as a great danger."

"In any event, Bill and Mother have decided to do as you suggest," Alice said. "She has a friend in Yorkshire, a very secluded residence in the West Riding, where they can remain hidden from all and sundry. The sooner they leave the better, I told them, and they agreed to leave this very day."

"Was there no hint of an accent in the taller of the two men – this man Shadwell? Fringe whiskers, perhaps? A pince-nez? A Mediterranean cast to him? Spoke foreign, perhaps?"

"Not a bit of it."

"I saw him briefly when we passed on the road, although he was in shadow. It was obvious that he looked very intently at me, as if taking particular notice, almost as if he knew me, although I'm fairly certain I've never seen the man in my life."

"Bill revealed that you were looking into the murder, I'm afraid, and that your return was imminent. That must have attracted his attention, and he wanted to know what sort of interloper you appeared to be."

"Conceivably," St. Ives said, moving toward the window. "Look here, Alice. Here's Finn Conrad coming along atop Dr. Johnson, reading a book. I believe he's returning from Hereafter Farm, or that Johnson is returning from Hereafter Farm, bearing Finn. He told me that he meant to offer his condolences to Clara today."

Alice stood up and joined him, the two of them watching as Finn swung along, gnawing on a cylinder of Dr. Johnson's sugar cane. "Finn is a highly romantic lad, you know," Alice said, "and I don't refer to his literary tastes."

"*Finn?* He's rough and ready, perhaps, and can do anything he sets his mind to, but *romantic*? Why do you say so?"

"Women have an eye for that sort of thing. He's been across to see Clara more than once, you know; any makeshift errand will provide him with an excuse."

"To see *Clara*? I'm astonished, Alice. No, I put that wrongly. But one wouldn't have thought… I mean to say that I simply had no idea of it. A woman has an eye for such things, do you say? What does your woman's eye say about me? Am *I* romantic, then?"

"Certainly you are, dear, when your mind isn't taken up with sink holes and Paleolithic avifauna. Just yesterday you complimented me by saying that I looked like a frog. That's worthy of a sonnet, surely. Finn is almost certainly sweet on Clara. He's *sensitive*, or so Mother Laswell tells me – uncommonly so. He might easily perceive that Clara is fond of him, that she sees things within him that aren't visible on the surface. You'll admit that we often love the creatures that love us, human beings included. It's no great mystery. Mother told me that Clara can see evidence of it in Finn's 'golden halo,' as she calls it."

"The boy sports a golden halo? I'm baffled by this sort of talk, Alice. It conveys very little meaning to my mind. But if Mother Laswell says that it's true, then so be it, golden halo or no golden halo. I've doubted her before and I've turned out to be a fool. I now possess what might be called a variegated skepticism."

"It's mother's belief that we all have such a thing – an aura, she calls it."

"Does she now? An 'aura'? What else did she have to say about it?"

"Only that Clara can see them, as could her mother, although the rest of us cannot."

"Is that so?" St. Ives asked, as they watched Finn ride out of sight, heading toward the barn. A boy on horseback appeared now, trotting up from the road along the pleached wisteria alley, clearly visible beneath the leafless vines. He was a telegraph messenger from the look of his coat and cap.

"Hasbro will receive the message," St. Ives said. "I'd best see to my packing before you accuse me of being a slow-belly."

Very shortly a bell chimed, and St. Ives stepped to a speaking tube on the wall and listened at it for a moment. "Ten minutes," he said into the mouthpiece. "I'll fetch it down." To Alice he said, "We haven't a moment to lose. Gilbert will meet us at Cannon Street Station at six o'clock, along with James Harrow, who will bring the celebrated great auk for us to see. Apparently Gilbert has his own jolly surprise for us."

"My bags are already on the veranda, Mr. Slow-belly," Alice told him, looking into the mirror one last time in order to arrange a black straw bonnet on her head. There was a spray of dried flowers sewn to the band of her bonnet, pinned with the spring dun fly that she had tied yesterday. "Finn's bag is there, too. I told him that we would take it along with us so that he was unencumbered when he followed along tomorrow." After a moment she said, "You seem pensive. Are you worried that we're shirking an obligation to Mother Laswell and Bill by rushing off to London?"

"Perhaps, although I very much hope not," St. Ives said. "And by staying at home we would shirk an obligation to Gilbert and to science, although those are perhaps obligations of a lower order. I'm persuaded, however, that Mother Laswell and Bill will do what's best for Clara, and in any event we'll be back from our little London journey many weeks before they return from Yorkshire."

Finn Conrad, holding Hodge the cat, cheerfully waved the chaise down the wisteria alley, mud flying from under the wheels. He put Hodge onto the ground, and the two of them set out toward the barn in order to feed and water Dr. Johnson, and to muck out his pen, which Finn did daily. Johnson, a very particular sort of elephant, liked clean quarters, as did Finn, who neatened up his own cottage every morning, shaking out the rugs and sweeping the floor. Hodge disappeared once they were in the barn – looking for mice, no doubt – and Finn set about hauling the dung and dirty straw out in a barrow to the heap fifty yards distant, running the barrow along over the path as quickly as he dared. Three weeks ago he had overturned the barrow, gone straight over the handles, and landed in the muck, and the accident was still fresh in his memory, although he had managed to wash it out of his clothing.

It was just past two o'clock, and the fish in Hampton Brook would be growing hungry in another hour or so. Alice had taught him to tie his own flies, and he had invented three new varieties and was anxious to give them a trial. In the barn he filled the five-hundred-gallon tank from a standing pipe, and then shoveled apples, carrots, cabbages, sugar canes, and dried hops into the enormous food bin while Johnson watched him with a keen eye, snuffling at the back of Finn's neck with his trunk. The elephant was deeply greedy, and mustn't be allowed to grow hungry. A hungry elephant was an unhappy elephant.

He filled a second, smaller bin with buns and loaves – yesterday's wares from the baker in town. Johnson dearly loved a bun. The baker's lad made daily deliveries, as did the greengrocer, who obtained the sugar cane from London once a week, shipped in from the West Indies, and bales of peanuts when he could get them. The carrots, apples, cabbages, and other fruits and vegetables were grown right there on the farm by Mr. Binger, a brilliant gardener, who had taught Finn about irrigation, fertilizer, and how to prune the roses and apple and cherry trees in late winter. Mr. Binger had gone into Aylesford to dine with his sister today, as he did every Sunday afternoon, and wouldn't be home until some time in the evening.

"All laid along, as you can see," Finn said to Johnson, handing him an apple, which Johnson took delicately with his trunk. Hodge came out of the shadows with a rat in his teeth now, and Finn left them to their respective dinners, heading back across the lawn toward his cottage to fetch his fishing pole and creel and his copy of *Black Bess*, the story of Dick Turpin the highwayman and his gallant horse. Finn dearly loved a horse story, and to his mind Black Bess was the true hero of the tale. It was no mystery that the book's title was the name of the horse. He took a pocket-sized notebook out of the drawer in his desk, and a piece of sharpened pencil some four inches long, just in case he found it necessary to write something down.

It wouldn't be a bad thing, he thought, to fish his way to Hereafter Farm, arriving in time to see the family off, which would give him an opportunity to say goodbye to Clara again. He sat down on the side of his bed and thought about not seeing Clara during the time she'd be away. He was surprised at the degree of longing that welled up within him, and he wished that he had a gift for her – something to remember him by. She had given him the copy of *Black Bess*, had put it in his hands herself. It was plain bad luck that he had finally come to know Clara just when she was going away.

It came into his mind that he could make her a gift of an owl that he had carved with his oyster knife, and he fetched it now and put it into the creel, along with the two sandwiches and the bottle of ginger beer that were already stowed there. It was a middling good copy of the screech owl that lived in the hollow tree behind his cottage, and was the sort of thing that Clara could see with her hands, so to say. When she returned they could take a ride together atop Johnson and visit the owl in his tree. He pictured it: Clara perhaps allowing him to hold her hand, her happiness with the gift, the owl in the tree looking down at them, screeching once or twice in order to amuse her.

Eating a sandwich and reading his book as he went along, the creel hanging around his neck and arm, he followed the path that he had traveled just an hour ago on Dr. Johnson's back. He veered off the path toward the wood that stretched along the south edge of Hereafter Farm and made up a good deal of its acreage. The brook ran through the middle of the wood, falling for a time through a wide ravine that was rocky and sometimes steep, but with shady pools and broad shallows that were often full of trout. It meandered out over the sheep's meadow, where there was a gate through the hedge and a path that led to the farm's oast house. He could easily fish his way to the farm's back door before Clara was off to catch the eight o'clock train, and with time to spare.

ELEVEN

UPSIDE DOWN

"It's like a holiday," Mother Laswell said, speaking to Clara, but trying to convince herself. "We'll do nothing but read novels and take the air. I've packed *Nickleby* and *Pickwick* and also a copy of Mrs. Gaskell's *Lois the Witch*. I looked into it a year ago but was distracted and never finished it."

Clara nodded, although whether happily or merely out of politeness it was hard to say. She was most often silent – always silent in company – and more so at the moment, Mother Laswell knew, for her mind was on her mother's death. Best to let her be. It would be some time before any of them saw Hereafter Farm again, and Mother Laswell neatened the room now, intending to leave it just so. There was bad luck in leaving an untidy house. This afternoon they would take the post chaise south to Tunbridge Wells and then a train north through the night into Yorkshire. That had been Bill's idea of a ruse – heading south before running north. They had a basket of Alice's pasties and a bag of their own apples along with cheese and biscuits for the four of them to eat along the way. Young Simonides was traveling with them. It might put the boy in some peril, but it might just as likely remove him from peril. There was no saying.

The world was upside down, it seemed to Mother Laswell as she stepped out through the French window and walked toward the barn. In such times as these one had to trust to prayer and dead reckoning when navigating, for the stars were often hidden from sight. The valise that the man Bingham had brought along yesterday lay in the mud against the barn wall like a dead thing, shot to pieces. She'd had Mr. Tully burn the straitjacket on the rubbish heap yesterday evening.

She picked the valise up now, looking at the compartments inside, and saw that it contained nothing apparently of value. There was a flat cloth bag with what appeared to be a set of false eyebrows and what might have been a stage mustache inside, much crimped from being smashed into the bottom of the bag. There were several sheets of paper also, wrinkled and stained as if with coffee or tea. She pulled them out, flattened them, and saw that they were handbills.

She stared at the picture depicted on the bills, confusion in her mind. It was a clear sketch of a man whom she recognized as her own son, Dr. Ignacio Narbondo – not his given name – dead this past year and more, something she thanked God for, although it was no doubt sinful. She had last seen him in London, in his lair in the rookery near Flower and Dean Street. There she had attempted to shoot him with a pistol in order to remove his shadow from the light of the world.

She had failed, and perhaps the failure had preserved her own sanity, and anyway he was dead within a few days. The handbill offered a reward for information of his whereabouts. There was an address listed, but it meant nothing to her. St. Ives had told her that Narbondo had fallen into a cleft in the floor of the Cathedral of the Oxford Martyrs when it had been destroyed. Alice had confirmed it. Mother Laswell needed no more proof than that. She wondered, however, whether her dead son was of interest to someone who had taken against him for some other reason – someone ignorant of his death.

What was particularly troubling to her was that the handbills were in this particular valise. Given his criminal past, the Metropolitan Police might easily want news of Narbondo if they were unaware that he was dead. The only coincidence, really, the only disturbing thing, was that the handbills had ended up at Hereafter Farm. She wished that the Professor were handy. He would shine some light on the mystery. But he was not, and she would see neither him nor Alice again for some time.

She folded two of the handbills up small. And then, from a pocket in her gown, she removed the cloth purse in which she kept their traveling money, and she put the papers into it. She had no desire to keep her son's likeness close, but the whole business was simply too curious. She would show it to Bill when they had a moment to themselves. She put the other objects into the otherwise empty valise, walked around behind the barn, and pitched it onto the prunings that Mr. Tully was burning, watching as he pushed them around with a hay-fork. Finally she walked back into the house, where Clara still sat in her chair, wearing her darkened glasses and lead-soled shoes. Her face was a complete cipher. Mother Laswell could not tell whether she was happy to leave Aylesford for a time, or whether it was all one to her. The girl was uncannily stoic.

Mrs. Tully, the gardener's wife, passed by hurriedly on her

way into the kitchen where she was cooking supper. She and Mr. Tully would stay behind to look after the children. As far as the two of them knew, Mother Laswell and Bill were traveling down to Tunbridge Wells for a long stay with an old friend, a friend who did not in fact exist. Mother Laswell had written out the location of the friend's imaginary cottage on a piece of paper so that anyone who came calling would be able to find her there, if only they could find the cottage, which they could not, it being imaginary – a dead end.

"Ten minutes, and we'll be off to Aylesford to catch the coach," she said to Clara, who nodded again. Mother Laswell walked down the hall and into her bedroom, where there stood a little-used door letting out to the side of the house. Bill had just minutes ago gone outside to water the pots of begonias that Alice had given them in the summer. They were in an area favored with afternoon sun and were fairly safe from the depredations of the children's games, although not quite so safe from whitefly and grubs. Mr. Tully had promised to spray them with soap. *So many things to fret about*, she thought, *when one goes away on holiday*. Something she hadn't done, really, since she'd gone into London a year and a half ago, and that had been no holiday.

She swung the door open and stepped out onto the small wooden porch in order to tell Bill that all was packed and ready. He lay face down on the ground, however, his arms thrown out in front of him as if he were attempting to fly. There was a bloody gash on the side of his head, pooling on the flagstones next to his ear. In her surprise it took Mother Laswell a moment to see it. She stepped down and hurried forward, crying out Bill's name and hauling her kerchief out of her bodice.

A hand grabbed her wrist then – a man's hand – and she was jolted to a stop. Another hand covered her mouth as the man stepped behind her, and in that moment she knew that she had been a fool, that Bill had been knocked on the head.

Murderers, she thought, and she heaved herself sideways in a vain effort to throw her attacker off balance. She saw his hat fly off, but he held on tightly, so she bit down hard on his fingers, hearing him curse, and then she kicked backward with the heel of her shoe and connected with his leg, although feebly, for she wore only a pair of cloth list slippers. The man pinched her nostrils closed now, and very quickly she was suffocating. He pulled her backward, clipping the back of her knees, so that she sat down hard, and then pulled her own kerchief from her hand, yanked it between her teeth, and tied it off. She made an effort to climb to her feet, but her tormenter pushed his boot into her side and tumbled her over, and then stepped over her and bound her wrists with a length of rope. It was Detective Shadwell.

Of course it was, she thought miserably. She had sensed that he was a bad man, but to their undoing she had ignored her instincts. Shadwell's face was altered, however: his nose smaller, his mustache gone, his eyebrows narrower, his hair receded halfway up his head. It was his eyes that gave him away. He picked up his hat, a jaunty, green-felt affair, and put it onto his head.

Mother Laswell cursed herself for her stupidity. Alice had advised her to leave at once for Yorkshire, but she had dallied, foolishly trying to put things in order before their journey, and now…

The other one, Bingham, came out through the open door at that moment, leading Clara. He closed the door behind him. He carried Clara's jacket folded neatly over his arm, her bag in his hand. It came into Mother Laswell's mind that there was no reason for them to take the girl's bag if they meant to murder her as they had murdered her mother, which they surely had. Shadwell pulled

Mother Laswell to her feet, and straightaway he led the way into the trees along a little game trail and out of sight of the house. He held onto the end of the rope that bound Mother Laswell's wrists, the rest of the rope coiled in his hand. Clara followed, her hand on Mother Laswell's shoulder. That was good. With luck they would think that Clara was helplessly blind, although she would have precious little chance of eluding them if she bolted. She must wait for her chance. She remembered Bill now, who might be either alive or dead. She prayed that he was alive, and that he would come to his senses and…

And what? Bill could have no idea where they had gone. No one had seen the two men arrive, evidently, nor had anyone seen the lot of them leave. She stumbled on a tree root and very nearly fell, but Shadwell, whatever his name actually was, pulled on the rope and held her up, and once again she trudged on, more helpless even than poor Clara. Low sunlight shone through the trees, which were mostly bare now that November was upon them. The trail led toward the back of the farm – she knew its course well enough – past the oast house, which many years ago had been the site of her dead husband's laboratory, although it had burned when Mother Laswell herself had lit it afire while attempting to put an end to her husband's experiments into vivisection, the last of which had been perpetrated on the body of their own son. Would that she had burned it ten years earlier, she thought. Would that she had murdered the man in his sleep.

They skirted the sheep pastures, entering the woods at the point where the brook flowed out onto the meadow. There the ground became uneven, the path edging around boulders and beneath fallen branches. Mother Laswell's slippers weren't made for rough walking, and the handkerchief pulling at her mouth was increasingly painful now, her mouth dry. She tried her wrists against the rope, but to no avail.

After a weary time they stopped, perfectly hidden from the world. The stream formed a wide pool here, with sandy banks on both sides that ran along for fifty feet or so. Come the winter rains the stream would drown the banks, and then it would be midsummer before they reappeared. A beech tree rose straight skyward on the outer edge of the bank, which was cut away by the moving water. Shadwell led Mother Laswell to the tree and bound her to it, taking several turns around her body with the rope before tying it off.

"I told you to cut another fathom of line, Dick," Bingham said. "She's as broad as she is tall."

"We'll melt the fat off her right enough before we're through," Shadwell said, and he stepped behind a heap of boulders and dry limbs and pulled out a shovel with a long iron blade, spearing it into the sandy soil and pressing it home with his boot. He withdrew two faggots of wood from the hiding place now and set them at Mother Laswell's feet, and then gathered sun-dried brush and leaves, tucking them in and around the bundles. "That should do," he said. "When the fire gets hot, the tree will go up like a torch and she'll roast fore and aft, the witch."

Clara had begun to moan, softly, rocking forward and back, and putting aside her terror. Mother Laswell wondered what it was that had set her off. The meaning of the bundles of wood and Shadwell's bloody-minded comment were clear enough to a sighted person, but Clara couldn't see the bundles without the aid of her elbow. It was something else that she sensed, something buried beneath the bank, perhaps. Despite her lead-soled shoes, she felt it.

Mother Laswell was certain she knew just what it was. The two men had searched for it beneath the floorboards of Sarah Wright's cottage, but hadn't found it. In the end she had told them. She closed her eyes and focused her mind. There was nothing she could do to save Clara or herself. Sarah Wright had been compelled to reveal her secret, and whatever she had revealed was understood by Shadwell to be true. Nothing Mother Laswell said – even if she could speak – would convince them otherwise. The head was buried under the streambed, and the two men meant to unearth it. Clara was their lodestar.

She realized that she was breathing shallow and fast, and was growing light-headed. She would fall if it weren't for the rope binding her to the tree. She closed her eyes to calm herself, picturing the clear water of the pond on the farm where she had lived as a girl, the waterweeds growing in the depths, the silver fish darting about, appearing and disappearing, glinting in the sunlight. Her breathing slowed, and her head cleared, and she opened her eyes to witness what was coming to pass.

"Do you hear me, Clara dear?" Shadwell said now. "I'm right certain you're not deaf. We mean for you to find what's hidden beneath the stream, what your mother buried with her own two hands – a dead man's living head, if such a thing can be imagined. So remove those iron shoes and walk about the shore, girl. Your old mum told us what was buried here before she passed into Hell, and I can tell you that she was happy enough to go. The fat woman will travel that same road, girl, unless you do as we ask. We mean to burn her alive, you see, but only if you're troublesome. You can save her life if you have a mind to, and your own life into the bargain."

"Hear him, girl!" Bingham said. "The fat woman will flame up quicker nor a bum's rush, her flesh being unctuous and so much of it. The Smithfield witches ain't in it." He set Clara's jacket and bag on dry ground and brushed his hands together.

Clara cried out, as if to stop their threatening talk. She shuffled her shoes from her feet and stepped bare-foot along the sand. She angled toward the edge of the brook until she felt the cold water with her bare foot. Then she stepped away again, moving toward the trees now, to a point very near Mother Laswell, some several feet above the river. Abruptly she stopped, and slowly she began to spin in place, her hands thrown skyward, her head back. Her smoked spectacles flew off her face as she spun faster, her mouth open, hair flying. Now she staggered and fell, landing in shallow water on her hands and knees, her dress billowing around her.

Bingham fetched her spectacles and then dragged her back onto the bank, where she lay in a patch of sunlight. Where her feet had augured into the bank, Shadwell began to dig, pitching sand and mud and debris to either side. Bingham watched him, taking his ease now. Clara was racked with trembling, her hands pressed over her ears and her eyes clamped shut.

"Lend a *hand*, Mr. Bingham, if you don't mind," Shadwell said, holding out the shovel and wiping sweat from his forehead with his sleeve.

"Easy, Dick," Bingham said, taking the shovel and stepping down into the hole. "I'm as willin' as the next man to do my part, now that we're close to the prize." He began to dig, putting his back into it until the pit was widened and deepened. Shadwell watched with a keen anticipation. The blade struck something hard just at the point when subterranean water began bubbling up into the hole, turning the sand to a heavy slush. Bingham hurriedly jammed the blade beneath the object, whatever it was, but could get no purchase on it.

"Here, Mr. Bingham," Shadwell said, picking up a heavy stone from the bank and letting it drop into the hole. Bingham shoved the blade into the sand again and levered the shovel blade against the stone, prising the object out of the muck with a sucking noise – a black box, some twelve inches square and deep.

"The very object," Bingham said cheerily, handing the shovel to Shadwell. He swirled sand and mud from the surface of the box, wiping at it with the palm of his hand. "Heavy," he said, grinning like a dog. "Lead, it is, like the girl's shoes, covered in beeswax. Take a squint." He handed it to Shadwell, who took it by one of its leather handles, hefted it, and then set it down heavily.

"Worth a mint of money to the two of us," Shadwell said. "I congratulate you, Mr. Bingham. You'll live in style now, as you deserve." He held the spade with his right hand, and held his left out to Bingham, who grasped it and attempted to clamber out of the hole, which was heavy going. He was up to his knees in watery sand now, and the edge of the hole collapsed in front of him when he leaned his weight against it. He sprawled forward, his legs trapped in a dense gruel of muddy sand. Shadwell yanked his own hand away and clutched the handle of the spade tightly with both hands, drew it back, and shouted, "Goodbye, Mr. Bingham!" and smashed the flat of the spade onto the top of Bingham's head, driving him downward, and then smashing his head again and again as if he were sinking a tent stake.

Bingham covered his head with his hands and endeavored to pull himself free, but his feet were held tightly by what had become quicksand, the entire hole awash now. Shadwell knelt in front of him, soaking his own trousers to the knees, and brought the spade up over his head, Bingham raising his hands to ward it off. The spade knifed downward, the blade severing two of Bingham's fingers and tearing into the flesh of his neck. Bingham screamed, falling forward and sucking up sand and water. He threw his head back, drowning now.

Mother Laswell shut her eyes and turned away from the horror, listening to the sound of the blade hacking against flesh and bone. Finally all was silent, and when she opened her eyes again, Bingham's corpse lay face downward, afloat in the collapsed hole, his legs buried in the heavy sand, red blood swirling away downstream. The shovel lay on the bank near where Shadwell was fitting Clara's shoes back onto her feet and her spectacles onto her face. He stood up now and approached Mother Laswell, carrying the leaden box and holding Clara by the wrist.

"I'm told that the item in this box is the severed head of your late, esteemed husband, ma'am. If his head could speak, I don't doubt but what he would have a wild tale to tell. But he cannot speak, no better than you can. One day perhaps he will." He picked up Clara's jacket and bag, the box tucked under his arm.

Mother Laswell kept her face dead calm and looked into his eyes. He could easily murder her, bound as she was, but she was damned if he'd steal what little dignity she had left.

"I find that I cannot set you afire after all, more's the pity, for I've drowned my lucifer matches in my scuffle with the late Mr. Bingham, and aside from that we promised the girl that we would allow you to live if she did as she was told, and so we will. Or *I* will, at least, Mr. Bingham being indisposed. I'm compelled to leave you here in your present thankful state, however, and I fear you'll be less thankful tomorrow, perhaps, than you are at present, and even moreso the day after that – diminishing returns, one might say. Perhaps you'll come to consider your own foolishness. If only you'd given the girl to us yesterday …"

He shook his head sadly. "But you did not. I'll look after Clara, you can be certain of that, ma'am. I leave it to my employer to decide her fate. I'm desolated to say it, but I can make no assurances regarding the girl's future. That will depend upon her compliance. Adieu, ma'am."

Mother Laswell worked to keep her mind from running off course as she chewed on the fabric of the handkerchief, trying to gnaw through it, watching as Shadwell led Clara up the path toward the farm, guiding her gently along as if he had a vast concern for her welfare. The girl did not so much as cry out now. *Good*, Mother Laswell thought. Clara had gumption. She was a cipher to the likes of Shadwell, and that might be the small bit of hope in this affair, which wasn't finished by any means, not while she had any life left in her.

The thought seemed to mock her, however, as time passed. The thin roll of cotton cloth was unyielding, turning between her dry teeth, and she worked to wet it, grinding away at it long after the two of them had disappeared from sight and sound.

TWELVE

MISS BRACKEN

The train entered Cannon Street Station amid a shriek of air brakes and clouds of roiling steam. Alice looked out of the window at the crowds of people hurrying to and fro with what seemed to her to be a celebratory air, although no doubt it was her own high spirits that she felt. She had first stepped out into Cannon Street Station as a young woman, looking up in awed disbelief at the immense glass and iron arch that roofed the station, nearly seven hundred feet in length, the immensity of the place quite taking her breath away. At the time she was accompanying her Aunt Agatha Walton to a meeting of the Royal Society, where her aunt was to read a paper upon the curiosities of salmon scales.

Alice had found herself seated very near a young man who was rather handsome in a craggy way, and who turned out to be a scientific-minded student of Richard Owen, the famous naturalist, an acquaintance of Aunt Agatha's. The young man's name was Langdon St. Ives. She thought now of his question earlier that day – whether he was a romantic creature at all. His idea of wooing her had involved squiring her to lectures from time to time, and once, under the supervision of Aunt Agatha, to the Kent Downs where they had dug ancient seashells out of a sandstone cliff. After a time, Alice had begun to feel unhappily like a mere occasional companion. It was Aunt Agatha's advice, however, that she should encourage St. Ives to pursue his natural enthusiasms, which he was likely to do in any event, and to wait until the time was right.

Shortly thereafter he had gone off to Edinburgh, to the university. They had written to each other sporadically, but his wanderlust often led him to out-of-the-way-corners of the natural world, at which times he disappeared out of her life, and in time she found herself being wooed by a man named Benson Winn, who had inherited an estate and an income in Abbey Wood. He was cheerfully pleasant and handsome, and with an enviable tenor voice, a member of no fewer than three choirs. Alice was twenty-four years old at the time, not ancient, but not anxious to live alone, as did Aunt Agatha, who was utterly and happily self-reliant.

And then one afternoon, home from Edinburgh and from his travels, St. Ives had come round to her home in Plumstead without warning, carrying nets and large collecting jars. He was searching out juvenile crested newts in marsh ponds and wanted company. St. Ives had the idea of making a study of them and then returning them to their ponds the following month, in time for their metamorphosis into adult newts. Alice was fond of newts, especially crested newts, which she had kept as pets when she was a girl.

Carrying a picnic basket, they went out into the Plumstead Marsh to a pond that Alice knew, where they found four exotic-looking specimens along with snails and tadpoles to fatten them up on. The two of them were watching the newts paddle about among the waterweeds in their glass containers, the afternoon warm and empty, silent but for the sound of birds and the light breeze whispering through the trees, when Alice decided that the time was as right as it would ever be and kissed him – a shockingly bold kiss – which led to more of the same, much more. The following day she had made her apologies to Mr. Winn. Things had worked out very nicely indeed, and all of it due to newts.

They descended to the platform now and straightaway caught sight of Tubby and Gilbert Frobisher swarming along toward them, looking happy and thoroughly overfed. Gilbert's double-breasted dinner coat bore silver buttons the size of half crown coins that glittered against the black satin. Tubby, who cared little for fashion, wore a brown flannel coat and checked trousers, very large examples of their type. Weighed together, Tubby and his uncle would tip the scale at well over thirty stone, but they had a hale and hearty look about them, as if they would happily beat the stuffing out of Satan himself.

Holding onto Gilbert's arm was a fair-haired woman of perhaps thirty years of age, buxom and markedly short. She wore a hat with what was evidently a small crow secured to the side of it with an immensely long hatpin. A ball of polished amber was affixed to the end of it. The bird, its wings half spread, appeared to be launching itself into the air. It was an eccentric hat to be sure, although so was her own hat, Alice thought, decorated with the spring dun fly.

"Allow me to introduce Miss Cecilia Bracken," Gilbert said to them. "Cissy, these are my great good friends, Langdon St. Ives, his wife Alice, and the inimitable Hasbro, which is just what his friends call him."

Miss Bracken curtsied like a schoolgirl. "Charmed to meet

you, Mr. Inimitable," she said to Hasbro, and then she favored St. Ives with what could only be called the glad eye – a startlingly lascivious look – and then a quick glance in Alice's direction, giving her an up and down inspection.

Tubby, Alice noticed now, was looking away, his demeanor one of suspicion, disgust, and impatience, among other things. "Cecilia… made herself *known* to my uncle in Jamaica," he said. "It was the most miraculous thing…"

"Indeed it was," Gilbert said to St. Ives, cutting Tubby off short. "I told you about my own Miss Bracken, I believe, directly after our trial with the great octopus."

"The love of your youth, as I recall – Miss Bracken, I mean to say. Did you locate her?"

"She passed away some years ago, alas, but Cissy is that good woman's daughter – Miss Bracken's Miss Bracken, if you will. It was my undeserved fortune to find *her* – an astonishing turn of fate. Born and raised in Kingston, she was, and would still be there if Tubby and I hadn't brought her back to London." He gazed at Miss Bracken with evident pride.

"And how do you find England?" St. Ives asked her.

"Colder than a sailor's arse," she said, and then laughed out loud, as did Gilbert, who put his arm around her shoulders.

"Jesus, Mary, and Joseph," Tubby muttered. "She's familiar with *that* particular item." He noticed that Alice had apparently heard him, and he muttered, "My apologies, ma'am," although without evident regret.

Miss Bracken looked hard at Alice now and said, "Is that not a fly on your hat, ma'am – a fisherman's fly, I mean to say. Surely it is." She smiled broadly. "We're fish and fowl, you and I, ha ha!" She reached up and waggled one of the crow's wings.

"Did you hear that, Tubby! Fish and fowl!" Gilbert said, enormously happy with the quip.

"My husband, who's dead now, thank Christ, fished for mullet in Bluefields with something like the same fly, tied up out of goat's hair – a black goat, although no blacker than his heart, I dare say."

"There's very little that you don't dare say," Tubby put in. "Tell them the woeful tale of your husband's demise, Miss Bracken."

"His throat was cut," she said flatly, staring at Tubby. "From ear to ear, and deep enough so that his head was dislodged." And then to all of them, she said, "No one confessed to the crime. I know I wouldn't have, but I'd give a guinea to the murderer if I happened upon him. He did me a service, if it was a man that done it. Like as not it was a woman, though. My husband was a right bastard who had done enough women wrong, just as he did me. He died the death he deserved."

"And yet you must have loved the man dearly when you were wed," Tubby said, shaking his head sympathetically. "*Were* the two of you wed, Miss Bracken?"

"We've hired a lad to see to your dunnage," Gilbert put in hastily, gesturing at a sad-looking boy in livery, the ill-fitting clothing apparently bought out of a rag stall near Tower Hill. "My coach is waiting with provisions aboard: Champagne, petit fours, and canapés – what the French call *amuse-bouche*, sweet and savory both, ha ha! That should forestall cannibalism until James Harrow arrives. He's anxious to descend into the cavern at high noon tomorrow. Perhaps he's waiting out on the road as we speak. He's bringing in a wagonload of supplies from Chiswick, where he lives with his sister. It's a crying shame that the lot of us cannot undertake this adventure together, but the Board of Works was adamant. They're a timid lot – afraid of another collapse and anxious to limit the carnage."

They found their way outside, their bags following along, where Gilbert's coach-and-four was waiting. His cockney driver, Boggs, was busy retying the complication of reins, one of which had apparently parted from the bit, and Gilbert hurried off forward to give him un-needed advice, Miss Bracken trailing along behind. Alice, Hasbro, St. Ives, and Tubby climbed into the commodious interior, their bags strapped on behind by the boy in livery.

"There it stands," St. Ives said, gesturing toward the Thames, where lay the rubble of a row of collapsed buildings some twenty running yards along the river side of Upper Thames Street.

The sink-hole itself was hidden by barricades put up by the Board of Works. Some short distance farther up the river, very near Swan Lane Pier, a fire burned in a heap of debris at the base of a set of stairs, and in the glow of the fire one could see the flaming wreck of a wagon that had somehow gone off the embankment near the upriver end of the sink-hole, evidently dangerous ground until repairs were complete.

"Gilbert and Miss Bracken are taking a stroll up the river, it would seem," Alice said, watching as the two of them made their way past the barricades. Boggs still worked with the reins, and James Harrow was still pending. Alice took a small round of bread with a paste of smoked salmon from an array of small tarts. She was determined not to eat more than four of them, since they would consume one of Henrietta Billson's vast suppers at the Half Toad within the hour.

"I could do with a hogshead of this Champagne," Tubby said, drinking off half a glass. "But I'm at the very brink of saying something that will make me sound like an ungrateful scrub, so I shall practice moderation."

"Not a bit of it," St. Ives told him. "Let me refill your glass.

You're among friends here. You don't have it in you to be a scrub of any variety."

"This *alleged* Miss Bracken…" he said, shaking his head darkly.

"You're not convinced that she's the daughter of Gilbert's lady friend of old, are you?" Alice asked.

"No," Tubby said. "I am not. I would lay five hundred pounds against it without a qualm. I have it on good authority that she was a common prostitute in and around Kingston, although Uncle Gilbert flew into a rage when I revealed it to him. He was apoplectic. I had to recant before his head exploded. And as for her husband, he *is* apparently dead, murdered, just as she makes him out to be, his throat slashed so deeply that his head hung from a bit of tendon. This false Miss Bracken was tried for the crime, in point of fact, but evidence was wanting and no one on the island had an interest in digging any up. She was found innocent for lack of an alternative, but it's good odds that she cut the man's throat."

"Gilbert spoke of Miss Bracken when we were in the Caribbean," St. Ives said, "the Miss Bracken of old. I don't mean to encourage gossip or idle speculation, but are we moderately assured that the current incarnation of Miss Bracken is not Gilbert's natural daughter? That there's no scandal, I mean to say."

"No," Tubby said, shaking his head. "No scandal, not in that regard. She's too young, for one thing, far too young, and Gilbert has reassured me that it's impossible, thank God."

"There are *two* Miss Brackens, then?" Alice asked.

"That's debatable," Tubby told her, "but my uncle believes that there *were* two, the first Miss Bracken allegedly being the second Miss Bracken's mother. Miss Bracken the elder – the *authentic* Miss Bracken – had allegedly married after she and my uncle parted ways thirty-five years ago, and this second Miss

Bracken is the alleged result of that union."

"And yet she bears her mother's surname?" Hasbro said. "How did that come to pass?"

"It seems as if the husband of the first Miss Bracken was a card-sharp," Tubby told them, "and was shot to death some two years after the daughter was born. This was a genteel crowd, you see. The first Miss Bracken despised her wicked husband and so retained her own name when she was widowed. When we were in Jamaica only a month ago, Uncle Gilbert happened upon the daughter, the second Miss Bracken, or so she claims, in a Kingston Tavern. And now, as you see, she rides about London in Uncle Gilbert's coach. To my mind she's a base deceiver. And that is the scrub-like notion that I threatened you with. Favor me with another glass of Champagne, if you will, Hasbro, so that I can wash the taste of this out of my mouth."

"But how can you *know* that?" Alice asked, holding out her own glass. "Perhaps both are authentic Miss Brackens."

"My uncle was searching for his lost love, the Miss Bracken of his youth. He busied himself making inquiries in and around Kingston, and like a fool I wished him good luck and went off to Montego Bay in order to fish for tunny, which are often the size of small cows in that part of the world. When I returned to Kingston at the end of the week, he threw this second Miss Bracken in my face. 'She's a great beauty,' he says to me, 'a rare goddess. It was the most wonderful chance occurrence,' he says – 'the kind of luck rarely seen outside the theater.' I was fully persuaded. As luck goes it was too good by half, and theatrical enough to make one sneer. I discovered that the old man had made no effort whatsoever to be discreet in his search, but had advertised his aims to everyone who would listen to him, and the result is that whereas I caught nary a tunny, he caught this… this land shark, who leapt bodily into his net. And now he's brought her back to England entirely against my wishes, not that I expect my own uncle to pay heed to my wishes. But he intends to *marry* her, for God's sake." Tubby shook his head regretfully. "I should have kept close by him in Kingston," he said. "I would have sent her packing, by God."

"Might *you* say something to dissuade Gilbert, Langdon?" Alice asked. "Tubby is quite possibly right. It would be easy for a man of Gilbert's wealth and disposition to find Miss Brackens under every stone. I'm surprised he didn't return with a harem."

The coach joggled as Boggs climbed up onto his seat now, and Alice glanced out the window, searching for Gilbert along the river, and saw that he and Miss Bracken were just then topping the stairs above the still-burning debris, apparently returning from their tour of the debacle.

"I cannot," St. Ives said. "Not in so many words. I'm sorry to say that, Tubby, but as you well know, Gilbert is a juggernaut once he's made his mind up. And it's *his* mind to make up, after all. Unless he is clearly threatened, his affairs are entirely his own to mishandle."

"You're in the right of it, of course," Tubby said, "but in this case your being right is cold comfort."

Alice was fond of Tubby Frobisher. Indeed, Langdon owed the man his life twice over, most recently in a brawl in the rookery around Flower and Dean Street, where Tubby had allegedly brought down a man with a pistol who was an ace away from making Alice a widow. He was a good friend in every sense of the word. His Uncle Gilbert's fortune had grown like a honeysuckle vine over the years, and Gilbert was currently wealthier than the Queen. Tubby would inherit a fortune when his uncle died, and so it was naturally difficult for him to make an issue of Gilbert's enthusiasms. It would not do to appear to be grasping, but he would be understandably loath to let the Miss Brackens of the world deceive his uncle.

"It *is* possible, Tubby, that you're simply mistaken," Alice said.

"Perhaps," Tubby said darkly. "The guilty flee when no man pursueth, as the scriptures tell us. I'll keep a weather eye on Miss Bracken. If she flees, I'll happily let her go to the devil."

The coach door swung open now, and Gilbert looked in at them wide-eyed and pale. Miss Bracken peered past him, authentically upset, it seemed to Alice. Gilbert was holding a tan felt top-hat, battered nearly flat and splashed with blood.

"That's James Harrow's wagon burning along the river," Gilbert said in a tired voice. "It went off the embankment at the edge of the sink-hole, and his paraffin lanterns smashed and set the wagon aflame. His horse is drowned in the Thames, as is much of his equipment."

"What of Harrow?" St. Ives asked.

"Dead. Stone dead." He held the hat out by way of illustration. "The police informed me that he was kicked in the head by his horse in the melee. They've taken the body to a dead house."

THIRTEEN

NED LUDD

Finn lost the first of his flies almost at once. He had tied it on badly, and the fish had taken it away without so much as breaking the line. He tied on the second fly, giving it a yank to tighten the knot and making his way around a rocky outcropping to a shady pool with a fast-moving riffle that was happily clear of low-hanging boughs. He cast his line, whipped out another length of it, and hooked a fish before he had time to think, the trout darting nobly back and forth through the shallow water half a dozen times before throwing the hook and escaping. Despite his near-luck, Finn decided to move on. He had spent too much time reading, and he ran the risk of being late.

There was an exposed bit of shoreline some distance farther downstream, indented with animal prints – badger and fox, for certain, and what might be the tiny paw prints of a hedgehog. All of them had come down out of the forest along a narrow path. Finn followed it, working his way downhill, the stream tumbling over rocks away to his left now. He stopped short and listened when he heard someone calling out – a woman's voice.

He set out at a run when he heard it again – a cry for help, and no doubt about it. He came out on level ground, picking his way around a tumble of rocks and finding himself on a flat run of shoreline along a wide pool. A man, bloody and half buried in the pool, swayed in the current face down. On the opposite shore stood Mother Laswell herself, tied to a tree, deadwood heaped around her feet, a shovel lying nearby.

It was a confounding sight, but inarguable. He held onto his creel with his free hand and took a run at a line of half-submerged rocks, leaping out to catch the edge of the first one with his toe, bounding off of it even as it shifted beneath his weight. He danced across the stream dry-shod until his final leap, when he splashed ankle-deep into the cold water. He cast down his pole and creel and took out the oyster knife that he had carried since his days on the river, an Irish knife with a short blade, sharp on both edges. He tried to listen to the rush of words tumbling from Mother Laswell's mouth as he flung the brush and bundles of wood away, but he made out little of what she was saying.

"Hold up, ma'am," he said to her, cutting her bonds with his knife. "You're all right now."

Mother Laswell staggered to the brook, drank out of a cupped hand where the water tumbled over a clean stone, and then sat on a nearby boulder breathing hard, her hands on her knees.

"It's Clara," she gasped. "The man Shadwell has taken her into London, the one who murdered her mother, the false policeman. That's his own partner there in the stream, whom he betrayed and murdered."

"Yes, ma'am," Finn said. "I'm bound for London myself, and might as well leave now as tomorrow. I'm ready this very moment.

The man Shadwell, what's his appearance?"

"We'd best talk as we move along," she said, standing up, pausing to catch her balance, and then hurrying away down the shore, leaving Finn to pick up his fishing pole and creel and follow. She told him the story of Sarah Wright's murder and the coming of Shadwell and Bingham in the black brougham, disguised as Metropolitan Police, some of which Finn already knew, and about Bill Kraken being wounded, maybe worse. "This man Shadwell is a human monster, Finn. Don't let him near you. Use all your cleverness, but do not engage the man. He's a murderer, but with a convincing tongue about him, like a serpent. Clara is safe from him for the moment because he means to put her to use, but you're not safe, Finn, no more than his partner was safe."

Her gait had slowed considerably, and she hobbled along now, the soles torn out of her slippers. Finn looked at the stile in the distance, the farm out of sight beyond. Speed was essential if he wanted to catch up with Clara and Shadwell on the London road, and he was in a tearing hurry to be away. "I'll do just as you say, ma'am. Are you all right, though? Not injured?"

"Tired and defeated, Finn, but not injured. Shadwell doesn't know you, and that's your main strength. Don't show your hand or..."

"Yes, ma'am, and you're to bear in mind that the Professor and Alice are in London along with Hasbro, or will be in due time, and it'll be strange if they don't lend a hand as well."

"Yes. I'd forgotten. My wits are astray, Finn. Warn the Professor that Shadwell was disguised. He is a hook-nosed man who wore a toupee when first we saw him, but today half his head is bald as an egg on top, although he's wearing a flat-topped felt hat, green in color, which would..."

"Forgive me ma'am, but I must run ahead if I'm to be of any service to anyone."

"Wait, Finn! You'll want money in London. Do you have any?"

"No, ma'am," he said, and she drew out the purse that she had put away for their Yorkshire journey, now never to be made.

"Spend what you need," she told him, drawing out half the currency and assorted coins. "And this handbill, Finn," she said, sliding one of the several folded copies into the purse, "if nothing serves, and you're all to seek, there's an address on it. It might come to nothing, but the men were carrying a quantity of them, as if they had something to do with it."

He stuffed the purse into his pocket without looking into it. "Thank you, ma'am," he said, walking away from her backwards, not wanting to be impolite, but thinking of Clara still, the girl's face clear in his mind. He would do whatever was needed to find her – that he knew – but he was burning daylight, and Clara was further along the London road with every passing moment.

Mother Laswell waved him on, shouting, "Don't stint!" And then, "Take the chaise, Finn! Shadwell will be driving a coach or so we must assume, a black brougham with a white squiggle. Send the doctor back to Hereafter if you find him at home!"

Finn was halfway to the stile now, waving his fishing pole in the air to acknowledge her final shouted entreaty. He went through the gate in the hedge and loped up past the oast house and into the woods along the path to the farm, where he saw spilled blood and broken flowerpots on the paving stones near the back door. He set his pole against the wall – he would want his creel – and he knocked hard on the door. He opened it without waiting and shouted a greeting before walking in, where he found Mr. and Mrs. Tully standing next to the day-bed in the parlor. Kraken lay on his side, breathing heavily, his eyes shut. Finn begged their pardon for his hurry and ask Mr. Tully about the chaise.

But there was no chaise. Simonides had already taken it to fetch the doctor. The boy had gone off half an hour ago, Mr. Tully said, when Bill Kraken had staggered into the house and collapsed. It would be another half hour before the boy's return, and who knew how long it would take him if the doctor were away from home? They feared for Mother Laswell and Clara, Mrs. Tully put in, to which Finn replied that Mother Laswell was quite all right, and would be here soon, but what about the wagon – could he borrow the wagon? It was no living good to anyone at the moment, Mr. Tully told him. This morning a wheel had seen fit to separate from its axle and fling itself into a stone, breaking two spokes, and wasn't yet repaired. Two hours would put it right, if Finn could lend a hand.

Out the window the evening gloom was descending. Real night was half an hour away, and Mother Laswell would arrive shortly with more advice for him, very good advice, no doubt, but…

"Is there a saddle for Ned Ludd?" Finn asked, and as soon as Mr. Tully said, "Oh, aye," and began to nod, Finn set out for the barn, through the French window, happy to see through the open top half of the Dutch door that a lantern was lit within. "Where are you taking him?" Mr. Tully called after him.

"London!" Finn shouted back, and didn't wait to hear the reply.

There stood the wagon, with the wheel off but supported by blocks. The broken spokes lay on the ground, the new spokes waiting to be knocked into the hub. There were three saddles on a rail, and Finn looked at each carefully. A mule saddle hadn't much rocker, a mule being flatter in the withers than a horse. Having ridden all sorts, from zebras to camels to elephants, he quickly found it and hoisted it off the rail. He draped a blanket over the creature, stroking his cheek and whispering into his ear. He had cared for mules during his days in Duffy's Circus, and he had a way with them and their stubborn notions. Keeping them happy was the salient thing.

Dr. Johnson came into his mind as he was saddling the mule, specifically that he was making ready to abandon the elephant. He wished he hadn't said out loud that he would top off Johnson's food bins in the morning, because he was certain that the elephant not only had a long memory, but that he understood human talk fairly well, especially as regards food. He hoped that Mr. Binger would look in on him as soon as he returned.

Finn filled a bag with oats now, collected a nosebag, checked to see that the saddle was cinched tight, and walked Ned Ludd to the swing-gate that barred the open barn door. The mule stood looking out into the dusk when Finn drew the gate back, and for a moment Finn thought that he would refuse to leave the barn. But it wasn't so. As soon as Finn was settled into the saddle, Ned Ludd set out at a steady pace, as if he knew that they hadn't any time to waste, and within minutes Hereafter Farm had disappeared behind them. They soon passed through the village and came out onto the London road, where a sign told him that it was six miles into Wrotham Heath. Finn felt the freedom of it, of the open space fore and aft and to either side, and of having no one to answer to but himself and his duty to Clara.

The missing chaise from Hereafter soon hurried past in the opposite direction, Simonides driving, apparently having come from Doctor Pullman's house. The Doctor and Constable Brooke rattled along behind in the Constable's wagon. Simonides looked at Finn in surprise as they passed each other, and Finn shouted, "It's Clara!" although the message would not convey any meaning either to Simonides or Constable Brooke until they had reached Hereafter and heard the story from Mother Laswell. Finn wondered briefly whether he should return to the farm in order to borrow the chaise, but he would lose most of an hour doing so, and in any event he couldn't abide further waiting.

Clara returned to his mind now that he was settled and moving and had time to think. She was quite the most beautiful girl he had known, and he was certain that she fancied him – at least a little bit, he thought, not wanting to press his luck. He thought then of what had been done to her mother – what he had been told by Tommy earlier today at Hereafter – but he set the thought aside.

There wasn't room enough in his mind for that sort of darkness, which took up an outsized amount of space and cast its pall over common sense and muddled the immediate present. And as for the immediate present, Finn wished that he'd had time to bring a warmer coat. It would be a cold night, and his right shoe was still damp from plunging into the stream. Then he remembered that he had an unknown quantity of Mother Laswell's money in his pocket, although unless he happened upon a coat for sale, little good it would do him now. Better to have yesterday's newspaper to stuff under his shirt against the wind.

In due time the moon rose above the trees, for which he was thankful; several times now a coach or chaise had driven past, and only one of them – the mail coach – with headlights. He wanted to see and be seen, not edged off into the canal that ran alongside the road. Ned Ludd was happy with the canal, however, having stopped to drink deeply from it a short time back. If the villain Shadwell were driving a chaise or the brougham that he had driven yesterday, surely the vehicle would carry him and Clara into London long before Finn would arrive, and then the both of them would simply disappear into the great city. Finn would seek out the Professor at the Half Toad, as they had planned, but he would arrive in a state of shameful ignorance, merely a bearer of bad tidings. And of course there was no certainty that Shadwell and Clara were ahead of him at all, no certainty that they were bound for London, now that he thought of it.

His mind ran uselessly on various uncertainties until he recalled something his mother had once told him: "With enough ifs one could put all Paris in a bottle." And so he compelled himself to put the ifs aside. His destination was London until the destination changed for good reason. But what then? He would discover it in due time as was always the case, for good or ill.

He fed Ned Ludd oats out of the nosebag when they arrived in Wrotham Heath, where he bought a meat pie for himself at the Queen's Rest. Sitting beneath the gaslight that illuminated the road in front of the inn, he opened the purse that Mother Laswell had given him, feeling the weight of the several coins and looking through the banknotes, which would have seen him through six months back in the days when he was living hard. He unfolded the paper that was slid in among the banknotes and was startled to see that the likeness of Dr. Narbondo was drawn upon it.

This was very puzzling indeed – something he could not have anticipated even if he had put his mind to it. Mother Laswell had told him that a quantity of the handbills had belonged to the men who had taken Clara, and that had an ominous air, implying secret connections, perhaps real wickedness. The address was near the Temple. He knew the area well enough, grand houses, which made this all the more puzzling. What did a rich man want with the likes of Dr. Narbondo? All the money in the world, however, could not resurrect Narbondo from where he had gone, so it was all one.

An hour later Finn was well out into the countryside, with a line of trees on either side. Pastures stretched away in the moonlight, visible now and then through the trees. He came to the peak of a hill and saw that a farmhouse lay off to the right-hand side. It was brightly lit, comfortable looking, with smoke rising from the chimney. The sight of it made him aware of the lonesome night and of the long odds against him. He bent forward to have an encouraging chat with Ned Ludd, reminding him of their sacred duty to Clara. The mule's ears twitched, as if he were attending to every word. A mule had no concern with hopelessness, thank God.

A lantern appeared a hundred yards ahead, someone just then coming around a bend in the road – a boy, Finn saw after a moment, about his own age, holding the lantern out in front of him so as to illuminate as much of the road as possible. The light showed his face clearly, and Finn saw that he carried a brace of rabbits and had a rifle tilted against his shoulder. He also wore a heavy wool coat.

"Hello to you," Finn said, reining the mule in when they drew abreast.

"Hello to you, too, friend," the boy said. "Are you off to the races, then?" He wore a smile on his face, as if he thought that Ned Ludd looked droll, or more likely that Finn looked droll, riding upon the mule.

"Aye, racing into London," Finn said. "Dinner, is it, that you've got there? Are you from the farmhouse, then?" Finn saw that the boy's coat, although heavy, was worn ragged in places, and was stained with what might have been blood – his hunting coat, no doubt.

"Yes and yes," the boy said. "And you?"

"From Aylesford. Can I ask you whether you saw a coach driven by a man in a green felt hat, a low, flat topper. If he wore no hat then he was bald atop. A girl might have been with him, riding inside, a blind girl with smoked spectacles."

"I did, an hour back along the road, with its lamps lit, which is how I know it was your man. It was the girl caught my eye, looking out through the window. The coach lamp lit her face, do you see? She wore the spectacles like you said, although she looked square at me and pressed her elbow to the window, so I don't know as she was blind. I couldn't see her eyes through the spectacles."

"An hour, do you say? Moving right along?"

"Aye. You'll not catch them between here and London, not astride a mule you won't, unless she can run like a thoroughbred. If you'd like supper, come along with me. You'll travel snug on a full stomach."

"There's nothing in life I'd like better, but I cannot. But it'll be right cold before dawn, and if you'd part with your coat, I'd pay you double for it."

"Would you now? How much?"

"Would a crown do it?"

"It would," said the boy, and he divested himself of the coat and handed it up to Finn, who took out his purse and found the coin, which he handed over before pulling on the coat and putting his purse away inside it. "Good luck to you, then," the boy said, going on his way.

Finn set out again at a settled, steady pace, grateful for the coat. Now he knew where he stood. Catching up with the coach was impossible, unless it stopped along the way, which was unlikely. Perhaps it had put in at the Queen's Rest for a time, which would explain how it had been hereabouts so recently. He must pin his hopes on the address near the river, and if that came to nothing, then he would do what came next, which was unavoidable – what came next was what one always did.

He let his mind wander as it would, and he looked up now and then at the moon in order to calculate the passing of time. He held further conversations with Ned Ludd, who listened with great interest. For a time he fell asleep, awakening and catching himself as he was falling out of the saddle, and realizing that he was on top of a hill, and that there were the scattered lights of a great city ahead. Greenwich, he thought, and the Thames twinkling beyond, tall ships moving downriver with the tide. Ned Ludd had found his own way while Finn slept, like Black Bess when she carried Dick Turpin two hundred miles from London to York in a single long night.

Gray Ned, he thought, *An Heroic Mule*. A mule could certainly be made heroic in a poem. He had never tried his hand at poetry, and so it was high time that he did. As a test he undertook to find a rhyme for "Clara," which seemed easy enough. But nothing came to him at first except *Sarah*, which, being her mother's name, would not do. *Sahara*, he thought with some satisfaction – the great desert wasteland. But what would Clara be doing in the Arabian Desert, after all? Would she need rescuing?

He thought of George of Merrie England, astride the horse Bayard, riding into Egypt, and considered Finn Conrad, astride Gray Ned, riding into London Town to slay the dragon Shadwell. He tried his hand again at rhyming – dragon, flagon, wagon – saying sentences out loud in order to keep Ned Ludd amused. And so the time passed, Finn trying to fix the better flourishes in his mind so that he could recall them later when circumstances lent themselves more readily to writing in his notebook.

It was still well before dawn when he passed beyond Greenwich, traveling now among a growing throng of people going into London, many with full carts and wagons, bound for Covent Garden or Brick

Lane or Portobello Road. When the western sky was pale and the stars faint, he rode along Borough High Street, past the church of St. George the Martyr, to which he tipped his cap. He turned into the courtyard of the George Inn where there worked a stableman that he knew, an ancient Welshman named Arwyn who had been stableman in Duffy's Circus, shortly before the death of Finn's mother, when Finn had left the circus for good and all.

There was a fire burning cheerfully in the yard, where he found Arwyn dressing the leather seat of a hearse, the red-trimmed black paint glowing in the firelight. "Well, Finn, you've come into London again," Arwyn said to him. "Last I heard you was oystering with Square Davey."

"I'm in Aylesford now, living among good people. I've got an elephant to care for."

"I've always liked an elephant," Arwyn said, "when they was treated right."

"Strange carriage," Finn said. "Is Death putting up at the George?"

"So to say, but at St. George Church up the way. I put a polish on it before the day starts. Who is this fellow, now?"

"Ned Ludd. He'd have been the favorite of Duffy's Circus, Arwyn. A better mule never drew breath. Can you keep him for two days?"

"That I can. Put your money away, Finn."

Finn shook Arwyn's hand, and assured Ned that he would return for him. As the mule was led away toward the stable, Finn pitched the handbill that he carried into the flames. It wouldn't do to be caught with such a thing about his person. He went into the inn, and ten minutes later set out across London Bridge, eating a breakfast of bread and cheese out of his hand.

FOURTEEN

THE VIEW FROM THE RIVER

"There it lies – Aladdin's cave," Gilbert Frobisher said to St. Ives, the two of them standing atop a makeshift staging platform over the dried mud and rock of the sink-hole. The debris from the collapse – building rubble, rock, and mud that had flowed in from the Thames – ran steeply downward from where they stood. St. Ives could make out broken furniture, shattered lumber, pieces of brick wall and chimney – a disaster that could not be put right, but must simply be buried and forgotten. A set of stairs leading to a wooden causeway angled out over the debris, the causeway extending thirty feet farther.

Rearing up behind the two men stood the shoring along the Thames, oaken beams six-inches thick affixed to deeply sunk posts, the river swirling past beyond. The tide was making, and rills of water ran out from between the planks, so the platform was dank and slippery. The odor of the place was indescribable – fetid water, wet lumber, and the rising smell of the bodies that would remain interred beneath the amalgam of sand, crushed rock, and tar that would very soon fill the hole. The quarried granite pavers of the restored embankment would serve as gravestones.

Due to the death of James Harrow, the Board of Works had foreshortened their expedition. They were to be in and out in six hours. St. Ives and Gilbert Frobisher would carry their own gear in knapsacks, enough for an afternoon jaunt, but not for real scientific work. A lantern hanging on a post at the end of the causeway illuminated Tubby Frobisher and Hasbro, who had shuttled out the last of the gear – a Ruhmkorff lamp with its attendant induction coil and battery, compasses, a coil of rope, and other odds and ends chosen hastily from the mass of equipment that Gilbert had hoped to take along. The lamp, with its delicate Geissler tube, was packed away in a basket and padded on all sides by pine needles stuffed into cloth bags. St. Ives's multifarious knapsack contained the induction coil and battery together, which filled the central pocket. It was surrounded by further pockets that were accessible from the outside – some of them coated with India rubber to serve as collecting bags – so that he could add or remove what he needed without disturbing the machinery within.

St. Ives heartily wished that Tubby and Hasbro were going along, for although he had a high regard for Gilbert Frobisher as a generous, decent man, it had to be admitted that Gilbert was getting on in years and was sometimes dangerously spontaneous. He weighed something in the vicinity of eighteen stone and was easily winded. Early this morning Gilbert had been warned by a Mr. Lewis – his 'agent' inside the Board of Works – that the Board was threatening to disallow the expedition altogether, what with the unfortunate death of poor Harrow. There were rumblings of disapproval from James MacNaghten Hogg himself, the Board's Chairman, who was sensitive to any hint of scandal or misjudgment after recent accusations of corruption. The sink-hole had taken a mort of lives, and the expedition had an ill-fated air to it. Lewis had suggested that they set out early in order to avoid being done out of their adventure entirely if they waited.

"If the sun would rise above these infernal clouds," Gilbert said, removing his pith helmet and wiping his brow with his kerchief, "you could make out what appears to be the very slightly arched roof of a small gallery down and to the left, far down the slope – a natural gallery, I believe, narrow at the opening. It was there that the auk was discovered, remarkably preserved and couched in a bed of foul-smelling fungi that had affixed themselves to the creature, perhaps slowly devouring it, or so Harrow speculated when Lewis gave him the creature. What lies beyond that dark portal, no man knows, although the two of us soon will, by God."

"The fungus must have been devouring the auk very slowly," St. Ives said, "unless the bird had recently died, which would mean, of course, that the auk isn't extinct at all, but was somehow living happily underground. The bird was not recovered, then, after Harrow's debacle?"

"No, sir. Like as not it's far down the Thames. I mourn the loss of that bird, I can tell you, and of course the loss of the man."

"Was there anything... *amiss* when they found his body?"

Gilbert looked askance at him. "Amiss?" he asked. "Why, the man's brains were dashed out, or so I was told. The imprint of the horse's shoe was visible on his forehead. That's amiss enough for most of us, I should think."

"Did the police allude to any sign that he might have been misused, I mean to say, any deviltry? You say that the body had already been removed?"

"*Deviltry?*" Gilbert gave him a long look now, evidently not having considered the idea. "If you're suggesting murder…?" He shook his head. "The body had been taken away, like I said, and so I can confirm nothing. The police had no suspicion of foul play, however, unless they were keeping it to themselves. No, sir, it doesn't stand to reason. Harrow had no enemies. It's a simple business to my mind. The fates played James Harrow a fiendish trick on the very eve of what would have been his greatest adventure."

"Indeed they did," St. Ives said. "Let's pray that they are kinder to us."

"Here's our sunlight now! Do you see it, the mouth of the gallery?"

"I do," said St. Ives. He could just make it out – impossible to say what lay beyond. Still and all, the dark archway was full of promise and mystery, and St. Ives found that he was abruptly as anxious as Gilbert to be underway. It would be a damned shame if they were cheated of their chance through no fault of their own.

Tubby and Hasbro loomed up alongside them now, having ascended the stairs, Tubby looking anxious. "I wonder if this is a good idea, Uncle," he said. "I'm leery of the two of you going down into the darkness alone. If one of you is injured, there's damn-all that the other can do to get the injured man out."

"In that case the uninjured man will hurry topside in order to summon help from the two of you," Gilbert said. "This is a grand opportunity, Tubby. Its like will never come again in my lifetime. Surely you don't begrudge me this chance?"

"Of course not, Uncle. I…"

"Then let us hear no more about it," Gilbert said in a rising passion. "You've been curiously insistent on nurse-maiding me, Tubby, for reasons that are clear to me. If you want to do me a *real* service, join Miss Bracken aboard my yacht and make friends with her. She's likely to be your aunt one day, you know – Aunt Cecilia. Have you considered that?"

Tubby was apparently struck dumb by the statement. Before he could answer, a trio of noisy gulls landed on the bulwark behind them, perched for a moment, and then flew straight through the sink-hole and into the mouth of the cavern, caught in the sunlight for a moment before they disappeared in the darkness beyond, off on their own expedition. St. Ives shook hands with Hasbro and then turned away and headed down into the darkness, Hasbro going off in the other direction, leaving the two Frobishers alone.

St. Ives heard Tubby remonstrating with his uncle now, angry and placating in equal measure. He closed his ears to their exchange. It was none of his business, he told himself, but he was aware that there was a brother's keeper element to it that gnawed at him, as well as the problem of the troubled state of Gilbert's mind. Gilbert was an excitable man, much at odds within himself when he was upset, which might further complicate their trek underground. Better, he thought, that he was going on alone.

The landing at the end of the wooden causeway lay beyond most of the collapsed rubble, and from that vantage point St. Ives had a clear view of the fairly steep, uneven ground that they would traverse on their way to reach their immediate goal. Two more gulls flew past on a cool wind off the river, one of them defecating copiously on the shoulder of his coat before flying into the cave – a good omen, if one believed in omens. He slipped his knapsack onto his back, slung the coil of rope over his soiled shoulder, and hung the basket containing the Ruhmkorff lamp from the crook of his elbow. He looked back up the pier, where Tubby and Gilbert had finally parted company, the old man walking slowly down into the darkness as if under a great weight.

* * *

Gilbert Frobisher's steam yacht, the whimsically named *Hedge-pig*, was a Scottish-built, side-wheeled craft that he had brought down from Dundee to its moorings in Eastbourne two years past. It was now anchored fore and aft along the Thames shore, a biscuit-toss from the great sink-hole. The yacht was a lavish affair, sixty feet long and built for idle pleasure, most of the deck being a saloon and galley, with sleeping quarters below. Alice stood under a party-colored awning, the long saloon shielding her from the south wind that had recently arisen. It was a cold wind that promised rain.

The tide was at its peak, and she had a high, clear view over the bulwark of stone and wood that dammed the edge of the collapse. From that elevated vantage point Alice could see into the reaches of the dark void itself. She watched Langdon and Gilbert apparently chatting, pointing out marvels. Alice felt strangely distant from her husband, regarding him through opera glasses, which made the entire undertaking seem like a piece of theater.

The notion of the women remaining aboard the yacht was Gilbert's idea – very festive, a view of the proceedings without mud and turmoil. Alice would just as soon explore the sink-hole cavern along with her husband, taking James Harrow's place. But it wasn't to be. She was plagued by an indeterminate but ominous dread that had settled in her chest last night when they'd heard of Harrow's unfortunate accident. The smell of the bodies buried in the sink-hole added to the weight of her doubts. The feeling of dread wasn't entirely rational, of course, but the knowledge didn't dissipate it in the least.

Barlow, Gilbert's butler, came out through the saloon door

carrying a silver platter and a cylindrical silver coffee pot. The coffee had been roasted and ground that very morning by Madame Leseur, Gilbert's French cook, whom Gilbert took along with him on his travels, Gilbert being a slave to his stomach. Barlow poured the coffee into a large china cup decorated with the Frobisher crest: two bright stars above a rampant hedgehog, a flailing red devil in its teeth. Alice took the coffee gratefully, foregoing sugar or milk, and went back to her post. Tubby and Hasbro had just disappeared into the sink-hole carrying knapsacks and a coil of rope.

She saw now that a man was crouching among the boulders some few feet above the river, partially hidden by the stone bulwark thrown up in the first days after the collapse. He had a sneaking air to him. She wondered how long he had been there. She had been so intent upon watching Gilbert and Langdon that she had seen little of what was going on roundabout them.

The man crept closer now, as if anxious to see into the cavern itself, but equally anxious not to be seen. He was a small man with a narrow, weasely face, what she could see of it, and he wore a uniform of some sort. It came to her that he might be a man from the Board of Works, although what he meant by hovering about in such a way was a puzzle.

Alice suddenly wished that she had company, another pair of eyes, so to speak. Miss Bracken sat in the saloon, out of the weather, and Alice turned toward the window, raising her hand to knock on the glass in order to summon her, but at just that moment she was shocked to see the woman slip three silver coffee spoons into her embroidered bag, which she instantly clasped shut.

It was a recklessly bold theft, for Barlow would certainly discover that the spoons were missing. Except that Barlow might easily be constrained from telling Gilbert, especially given Gilbert's open sparring with Tubby on the issue of Miss Bracken. The woman knew very well what she could get away with. What was the point of stealing Gilbert's spoons, however – mere trifles – if she anticipated marrying the man? Perhaps she did not anticipate any such thing. Perhaps what she wanted was a free passage to London, a bag of stolen silver, and an opportunity to disappear.

Alice turned toward the sink-hole once again and looked through the glasses. Hasbro and Tubby had come topside, and Langdon was making his way down into the darkness, very quickly passing out of sight, still some few yards from the lantern light at the end of the dock. Gilbert and Tubby appeared to be carrying on an impassioned argument. After a moment Tubby threw up his hands and walked away. But he paused suddenly, turned, and grasped his uncle's shoulder as if to bid him farewell. Gilbert, however, shrugged away and followed along behind Langdon without looking back. The whole business was both sad and troubling, and Alice's feelings of general unhappiness increased.

The lurking man along the bank had climbed up toward the top of the embankment by now, perhaps to get a better view of the two men below. He bent over, meddling with something hidden within the rocks. *Who are you?* Alice whispered, hearing Miss Bracken come out through the saloon door now, having donned her bird hat. Alice beckoned to her, but just as she called Miss Bracken's attention to the lurking man there was the sound of a muffled explosion, and the man scurried away across the rocks.

For a moment all was still, and then, as Alice watched in horror, the roof of the cavern slowly collapsed. A great heap of stone and embankment and barricades fell like a piecemeal curtain, blowing a shower of dust and debris out of the void.

Miss Bracken screamed, but Alice's throat was closed, her

breath stopped. It began to rain at that moment, wind-driven rain, and the dust quickly cleared away. The dark cavity that had been there only a moment ago was gone, the Thames swirling in through a breach in the wall, lapping against what was now a hillock of broken stone. Tubby and Hasbro climbed down over it, evidently searching fruitlessly for some passage into the interior. Unable to look away from the disaster, Alice watched through the opera glasses until rainwater obscured the lenses.

"Where is Mr. Frobisher?" Miss Bracken asked in a small voice, the wet blackbird leaning over her ear. "I don't mean that Tubby. Where is Gilbert? Where is my Gilbert?"

A double crack of thunder sounded, and the rain redoubled.

"Gone," Alice said to her. "Both of them are gone."

And upon hearing these words Miss Bracken fell to the wet deck in a faint, her hat tumbling off, the rain beating down. Alice looked for the lurking man again, but he was nowhere to be seen.

FIFTEEN

BENEATH LONDON

When St. Ives came to his senses he lay sprawled on his back in what at first appeared to be a meadow of glowing clover, but in fact was thick with some variety of mushroom. There was the smell of a filthy horse stable in the air, and he felt the plants beneath him moving like sandworms in a seabed. He sat up, unhappy with this and with the pain in his side – a bruised rib, maybe cracked.

He set about moving his hands, arms, legs, and neck in order to take stock of his injuries, discovering in so doing that he had lost his pith helmet. He remembered being cast bodily from the end of the pier as if slammed hard from behind. He had landed upon his feet, toppled forward, and had instantly begun to run, gravity helping him along. The ground was too steep for running, however, and he retained the sensation of hurtling along wildly for a distance, his legs flailing, unable to control his forward flight. He had tumbled for a time, desperately clutching the strap of his knapsack, which he was not clutching now. When he had been knocked unconscious and how far he had fallen he couldn't say.

He wasn't paralyzed, at least. His extremities were functional, his hands opening and closing, his fingers active, his toes working inside his boots. His head throbbed with pain, and he discovered a swelling above his right ear, where his hair was matted with blood, but he could discover no dizziness, nor any indication of a cracked skull. He wasn't apparently still bleeding from the head wound, which was poulticed with a clot of bloody dirt. His injuries were nothing desperate, he told himself – the aches and pains, say, of a man who had been beaten or had fallen off a horse, the sort of thing that he had experienced often enough in the past.

He ordered his mind in an attempt to recall what had happened. The sound of grinding and cracking had filled his ears, the all-pervasive rumble of the earth moving. He had been but half conscious of the noise as he had wind-milled forward and then tumbled down the steep incline. But just before that he had looked back toward Gilbert, and he was certain that there had been a flash of light. He could picture Gilbert being suddenly and sharply illuminated. The sound of an explosion would quickly have been consumed by the indistinct cacophony of the cave-in, the world falling in upon itself. What had Alice seen from where she stood on the deck of Gilbert's yacht? He had waved to her a few minutes earlier, before joining Gilbert on the staging platform. Alice no doubt wondered if he was dead.

He abandoned that line of thinking and thought again of James Harrow being kicked by his horse, and of the strangely variable actions of the Metropolitan Board of Works, in particular their declining opinion of the exploration. Was there an unseen hand at work here? An old grudge, perhaps, playing itself out? Or, he wondered, were there powerful forces that meant to keep the subterranean world a secret for reasons of their own?

He caught sight of small movements on the ground roundabout him. He looked more carefully and saw that they were struggling insects in the grip of the fungi, which appeared for all the world to be consuming them, or perhaps paralyzing them with some variety of toxin. The mushrooms seemed to be a cousin of the blewit, although stinking and a phosphorescent shade of sickly green. They were stout, meaty things, despite their luminescence. Certainly they were nondescript: James Harrow's auk fungi. A hairy white spider the breadth of his hand struggled in a mushroom's grip, and the sight of it compelled him to stand. His dislike of spiders was both irrational and inarguable.

He made out the dark form of his knapsack now, very welcome indeed, lying on a glowing green carpet twenty feet away, and near it the basket containing the lamp. Its lid appeared to be securely fastened, its fall cushioned, perhaps, by the carpet of fungi. The coil of rope was nowhere to be seen. St. Ives found that he was steady enough on his feet, and so he trudged to where his knapsack lay, fetching up the basket first and unlatching it, removing the bag of stuffing and scrutinizing the lamp, which looked and felt whole, the Geissler tube evidently unbroken.

He set the basket down carefully and picked up the knapsack, drawing from an outside pocket his hand compass in its brass pill-box and putting it into his coat pocket. Then he drew out the wires snaking out of the induction coil before slipping his arms through the straps of the knapsack and hanging it onto his back, the wires draped over his shoulders. He sat down, holding the lamp securely in his lap. Squinting in the darkness and feeling the way of it with his fingers, he affixed the wires to the lamp. He turned the crank and the gas within the Geissler tube grew luminous, the glow increasing until it was a bright white, revealing the details of the world roundabout him. He hung the lamp around his neck, clipping the stiff metal harness at its base to his heavy leather belt in order to steady the lamp, and then very carefully rose to his feet.

"And Ruhmkorff divided the light from the darkness," he said aloud, looking around him to get the lay of the land, that which he could see. He calculated the angle of the rubble-covered hill in front of him – a fifteen percent gradient perhaps. It would be hard going if he tried to ascend straight up it, probably impossible, given that he would slide backward with every step. And if he fell and the lamp were damaged it would be very bad indeed. Still and all, in that direction – to the south lay the Thames, arguably the most sensible direction for him to travel if he meant to search for Gilbert.

He put his hands to either side of his mouth and shouted, "Hello!" and then listened for a reply, which came at once: the cry of a seagull, however, and not of a man. The bird swooped into view and landed nearby, drawn by the lamplight and perhaps his voice. "Good morning," he said to it, wondering whether it was the good luck bird that had honored him with a gift just a short time ago. He shouted again and then a third time, but there was no answer. His voice sounded strangely deadened, as if it carried no great distance at all.

He removed the compass from his pocket and opened the case. He knew that he was on the north side of the river, and unless the tumble had entirely turned him around, he was somewhere downriver from the sink-hole, although no great distance, certainly. As for searching for Gilbert, his best effort would be to shout at regular intervals, like a ship ringing a bell in heavy fog. He would travel west, he decided, rather than attempt a direct ascent, and do his best to keep track of the distance he traveled if he had any hope of finding his way back to the sink-hole by dead-reckoning.

The gull took wing now and disappeared in the darkness overhead. It would have a bird's-eye view of St. Ives in his bubble of light, but St. Ives would be blind to it unless it descended again. He suddenly felt tolerably conspicuous, as if spotlighted on a stage, and he was anxious to be moving. He set out across the hillside, leaving behind the field of mushrooms and taking his bearings often, shouting Gilbert's name when he did so. He shifted slightly downward with each sliding step, leaning into the slope in order to avoid falling. The traverse seemed to take a great deal of time, and it was impossible to tell exactly how far he had traveled, the lamp only shining so far into the darkness. The ground finally grew more stable, and was studded with immovable mineral formations, like sharply bent knees protruding from the sand: stalagmites in various stages of development.

Here the ground had little of the loose scree of the cave-in, and St. Ives began climbing upward and across it, making real progress. A forest of mature stalagmites slowly grew visible ahead of him, and he moved in among them, seeing here and there the conical tips of stalactites descending from above, hanging ghost-like in the dark void.

A movement in the gloom ahead brought him up short – a large creature of some sort, or a man crawling on his knees. For a moment he ceased breathing. The creature moved out from behind a stalagmite now, and he saw then that it was a brindle goat, which saw him as well and scurried off into the darkness, quickly disappearing.

Had he imagined it? Were his wits astray? It was useless to speculate, and in any event a goat was no less likely to be wandering about in the underworld than was an auk – considerably more likely, perhaps. It stood to reason that if a goat had found its way in, St. Ives could find his way out. Very soon, however, the way was blocked by an almost vertical wall of limestone, chalk-white in the lamplight. It was deeply fissured by little rills of water, and he was thankful for the rubber-soled Monticello boots, the wet limestone beneath his feet being dangerously slippery.

The wall, reaching into invisibility overhead, compelled him to travel even farther westward along a narrow track of stone that seemed to him to have been leveled and broadened in some past age. He could see what looked like the scars of picks or chisels – the work of enterprising Romans, or perhaps of a civilization even more ancient. He wished to God that Gilbert's man from the *Times* could have come along. Six good photographs would be utterly convincing. St. Ives's testimony, on the other hand, would be explained away as madness due to the lump on his head.

He rounded a bend and found himself on a narrow landing, looking down into a steep-walled defile cut by a waterfall that rushed along sixty feet below. Stone stairs led away downwards along the edge of the waterfall. They were unmistakable stairs, not a mere quirk of geology, some of them cut out of the solid limestone, some of them enlarged by cleverly placed cut stones so tightly fitted together that he could only just make out the joints in the nearest of them. The track that he had been following also led away upward, perhaps to the surface. He would have to choose: up or down.

Far below him he saw the illumination of a vast field of the strange mushrooms – very much the sort of light emitted from the female glow-worm or from within the bodies of luminescent squid. He drew out his brass, achromatic telescope, a finely crafted quadruple-tube instrument, which revealed a broadening-out of the canyon below him into a landscape of rectilinear shapes: gravestones or crypts, perhaps, or stone huts.

He peered at this phenomenon for some time, dumbfounded. He was convinced that he knew just where he was: somewhere beneath Blackfriars. He had seen these structures before – not something *similar*, but this very thing – when the ground had split open in the floor of the Cathedral of the Oxford Martyrs and Ignacio Narbondo had fallen to his doom. The fissure had revealed a clear view of the underworld that had closed again on the instant, and the brief image of it had been fixed in St. Ives's memory. As the months passed he had come to doubt what he had seen, for that long afternoon had been very like a dream. There was no doubting it now.

Moving slowly in deference to his ribs, he reached behind him and drew a canteen of water and a newspaper-wrapped packet of food from his knapsack. He sat down and leaned back against a dry section of the limestone wall and unwrapped a sandwich of ham, mustard, and pickled onions, realizing that he was both thirsty and famished. Presently the seagull appeared once again, alighting very nearby and looking greedily at the sandwich. The gull hopped closer, and St. Ives tore off a piece of crust and tossed it to the creature, who caught it neatly and gulped it down.

St. Ives considered the great cavern below. He might well have been eating his sandwich on the second or third level of a vast house with a section of floor removed. The steep passage between the levels had no doubt been carved out by the flow of water over countless eons, dissolving the limestone strata. The entire void beneath London had surely been excavated this same way: surface water from the many rivers and from endless seasons of rain trickling down through the limestone, patiently eating away solid rock. The wonder laid out beneath him was an open invitation complete with an accommodating stairway. It was clearly his scientific duty to consider this an opportunity rather than an inconvenience and to proceed deeper into the underworld.

He pitched a fragment of ham in the direction of the seagull and then reached for the smeared newspaper that lay on the ground beside him. The seagull snatched the ham out of the air and gobbled it down, and in the same moment it lunged at the newspaper, plucking it away and flapping its wings wildly, launching into the air and flying out of sight carrying its greasy prize. Seagulls were the thieves of the bird world, St. Ives thought, which, alas, entirely accounted for their temporary gestures of friendship.

He stood up, found that his balance was still sound and took one last look through the telescope. After hollering Gilbert's name and hearing no response, he started downward, counting the steps while idly considering the irrationality of ascribing human emotions to animals – the loyal dog, the inscrutable cat, the wise owl. Perhaps greed, he thought, was the essential foundation of human behavior as well. Perhaps love was merely biological in origin, and selflessness a mere illusion fabricated to put a good face on what was in fact self-serving. The idea didn't appeal to him, however, and his musings were interrupted when he saw, on a rock ledge some twelve feet below him, a black pistol with a fat barrel. It lay on a flat outcropping below the sheer edge of the staircase.

Here was yet another item that he had seen before. Narbondo had carried just such an unlikely and deadly weapon, which had fallen into the void moments before Narbondo had done the same. He considered the wisdom of attempting to retrieve it, but dismissed the idea as far too risky. Another dozen stairs farther along, the lamplight revealed a dark stain on the pale limestone. He stepped past it, down three more steps, then turned and knelt on the stone in order to get a better look at it. The stain was almost certainly blood, long dried. He couldn't think of an alternative explanation for it. He turned carefully, stood up, and resumed his descent, soon discovering more blood – what had been a considerable pool of it – and bloody boot-prints on the three steps below it. One of the boot prints very clearly revealed a pattern of hobnails that formed a pentagram.

There could be no question at all: Ignacio Narbondo, injured, had descended this flight of stairs a little over a year past. St. Ives was doubtful that the man had returned to the surface, for if he had he would have sought revenge against St. Ives and his family. Narbondo was scarcely human, motivated by a bloody-minded joy that he took in human suffering. St. Ives discovered that his scientific curiosity in the underworld had diminished now. That Narbondo might be alive – or the more optimistic possibility, that St. Ives might find the man's corpse – had become an unavoidable distraction.

Soon he came out onto the floor of the great cavern, which was sectioned off with high walls of limestone and pools of standing water. Patches of mushroom grew down into pools, illuminating the depths. There were enormous knee-high clumps that cast a substantial light, the air fetid with their odor. The geometric shapes that he had seen from above – stone ruins, perhaps – were hidden now, but were no far distance away. He stood for a moment tempted by them, but suppressed the temptation. If he found a way out to the surface world he could return to investigate the underworld more thoroughly, the Board of Works be damned. And if he could *not* find a way out, then he would become a denizen of this world and could investigate it at his leisure – or until he went mad, the fate of many maroons.

A clear path, much-traveled, imprinted with hoof-prints and what looked like the remnants of a boot-print, led away uphill toward the north-west, and St. Ives set out in that direction, moving at a steady pace. He considered what he knew of London's underground rivers, which were quite likely the source of the subterranean water that was now in evidence all around him. The Fleet, he knew, rose near Highgate Ponds on Hampstead Heath, and the Westbourne and the Tyburn very nearby in West Hampstead. He had been inside the tunnel through which the Westbourne flowed, and had seen the iron doors and ladders that led to tributary streams and sewer tunnels on yet lower levels.

As he moved along, he passed a number of pools filled with carpets of the glowing fungi, very apparently carnivorous, for they were often in the act of imprisoning both blind cave-fish and milky-white salamanders, all of their victims apparently alive or in stasis. He wondered whether the fungi lived in some state of symbiosis with the creatures they caught. If they did, the advantage was entirely with the fungi, for the trapped animals clearly suffered a variety of living death, whereas the fungi were quite monstrously alive. Floating duckweed grew in profusion in the light of the mushrooms, as if their luminescence was as potent as sunlight. The hoof-prints of goats and pigs were visible in the mud along the shore.

Spotting a black strip of fabric several feet from the path, he recognized it as the wide belt of the cassock that Narbondo had been wearing when he had entered the Cathedral, carrying the infernal device with which to blow them all to kingdom come. Some distance farther on he discovered the cassock itself, bloodstained, the dried gore visible against the black cloth. The man had apparently discarded encumbering garments as his strength gave out.

St. Ives traveled onward, into a country of ever-larger fungi, with caps as round and broad as pub tables. They dipped nearly to the ground, some of them, and glowed ever the more brightly when they were in possession of fresh meat, birds and bats for the most part, and the occasional rat. Again, most of the animals were still alive in some sense of the word, or at least had failed to decay. He entered a forest of head-high fungi with enormous trunks. The light emanating from them was quite bright – bright enough so that the light from his lamp was consumed by it. It seemed to him that the fungi bowed toward him as he passed, an uneasy thing to be sure, and he kept carefully to the depression trod into the soil by countless passing creatures over the years.

As an experiment, he touched a finger to the jade-colored gills of a large fungus, which immediately sucked at his skin like an anemone, the cap pulling backward as if in an attempt to draw him into the thicket. He jerked his hand away, a flap of luminous gill coming away with his finger, stuck tightly to his flesh, and he felt a tingling sensation, like oncoming paralysis. Hurriedly he scraped his hand on the metal fixture of the lamp where it attached to his belt, scrubbing the fungus from his skin before taking out a magnifying glass and studying the gills more carefully. He was surprised to see that they were lined with tiny suction cups or disk-like mouths – predatory creatures, to be sure.

A short distance farther on, he was stopped by a strange sight – a broad swath of fungi that had been severed very near the ground, cut out in a neat rectangular box-shape nearly a fathom or so on each side. St. Ives stood and stared at the phenomenon, contemplating what it meant. Narbondo's boot prints had been scarce along the trail, trodden out by the animals that had come and gone in his wake. Now there were a plethora of human footprints that obscured the animal prints, very recent, apparently: a party of men who had come down the trail from above. There were the indentations of wheels along with the boot-prints, as if they had brought along a cart on which to haul out their treasure, or so it seemed to St. Ives – a treasure of flesh and bone and luminous fungi.

SIXTEEN
FELL HOUSE

Beaumont's quarters were in the garret – the most commodious quarters that he had ever enjoyed – with a view looking out over the Temple and with easy access to the roof through gable windows. The room was often lit with sunlight, and the wind blew through the open casements, chasing away the reek of physic and death and pain that filled the lower levels of the house. Beaumont had climbed out through the window and sat on the roof at present, smoking his pipe and watching a bank of clouds approach from the south. He was safely out of the wind because of a broad brick chimney with half a dozen chimney pots. Pigeons and house sparrows stood or hopped roundabout, regarding him carefully, waiting for him to share more crumbs from the half-eaten loaf thrust into his vest. A particularly fat sparrow hopped up onto his shoulder and pecked away at the top of the loaf. Beaumont sat very still so as not to frighten it. He was fond of a forthright sparrow.

When it hopped away, he tapped out his pipe, put it into his pocket, and then tore up the rest of the bread and cast it out over the slates, watching the birds scrambling happily after it, others winging down from the sky. He played a tune on his flute, a melody he had contrived himself, and noted with satisfaction that the birds seemed to enjoy it, especially the pigeons, who stopped their incessant eating and watched him play. He bowed to his audience after a time and put the flute away in his coat, removing a leathern bag from another pocket and shaking it, listening to the cheerful clink of sovereigns inside.

He had converted Mr. Klingheimer's Bank of England notes to coins, having a liking for gold but very little for paper money, which rustled like insect wings and would burn to ashes if a fire were hungry for it. The sovereigns shared the bag with the Spanish doubloons and Narbondo's ruby stick-pin. This last he had thrust down into a short length of India rubber tubing to keep it safe. He thought of his treasure hidden below ground – enough to set him up in his carriage some day. He didn't mean to live alone, however. He was no hand with the ladies, alas – no kind of fisherman in that regard – and had suffered rebukes when he had been emboldened to speak to them. Some day, perhaps his luck would change there, too.

He put the thought aside and considered what Mr. Klingheimer would pay him for his services now that Narbondo was stowed away in his box. He had long ago decided to be beholden to no man, a rich man especially. His old father had told him to keep it in his mind that he was Beaumont the Dwarf, as was true of no other man on earth. Klingheimer had put him in charge of the toads and the heads, which was as good a situation as many he'd had over the years, although it meant working in the basement in the stinking dead air and in the midst of unhappiness. But how long would Klingheimer have need of him? A man like Klingheimer would take Beaumont's head from his shoulders just as easy as kiss-my-hand if he had need of it, and that would be the end of poor Beaumont.

What would his old father say to him about Mr. Klingheimer? "Watch your poke," like as not, just as the potato boy had uttered when Beaumont was down on his luck and at the mercy of the pawnbroker. That had been good advice – and even better advice when a man's luck was in – especially in a house full of villains like the house of Klingheimer.

He stowed his bag of coins in his coat and took out his pocket watch, the very same watch that he had sold to the pawnbroker in Peach Alley: the silver watch with an F and a Z engraved upon the case. Its return had cost him three of the four crowns he'd been given for the watches in the first place. It was evidently a good-luck watch, however, and he would keep it as long as he kept Mr. Filby Zounds as his name.

Holding onto his hat, he climbed in at the window, shutting it and hearing that it had latched. Then he went out and down the dark and narrow garret stairway to the top floor landing, where there were proper stairs, with great fat newel posts and a broad banister and oil lamps lit night and day, which he liked better than the electricity. Oil was something that a man could reason with. He saw a moving shadow rising toward him, now, and he stepped back up the garret stairs until he was out of sight. He removed his hat and crouched as low as he could manage in order to see who it was and where they were going.

He was surprised to see that it was a girl who came into sight first – a blind girl, apparently, who wore dark spectacles. Her face was expressionless, and her eyes, being hidden, told him nothing, but he sensed a deep unhappiness in her and a portion of fear and confusion. She was followed by the villain Shadwell, a rum-looking, hooknosed man with an unending forehead and evil features.

They turned away down a hall, and Beaumont was emboldened to creep farther downward in order to see where they went – not far, as it turned out. The man stopped before a framed painting that hung on the wall, pushed the painting aside, and removed a key hidden behind it, with which he unlocked a door. He made no effort at secrecy – because the girl was blind, perhaps, or because she would have no way to unlock the door from the inside, having no key of her own. He ushered the girl into the room, said something to her that Beaumont couldn't hear, and then laughed and shut the door and locked it again. Beaumont retreated quietly up the garret stairway, putting his hat on his head and preparing to descend once again as if he was just now coming down. When he returned to the landing, however, Shadwell was gone down himself, and the hallway was empty. Beaumont made his way to the painting on the wall and looked behind it – a simple recess in the plaster where the key lay safe as a baby.

Clara sat on the side of the bed, her hands in her lap, her mind full of images moving in darkness, her ears full of sound. She had come from Dr. Peavy's hospital that morning, and she was mortally tired. At the hospital she had met Mr. Klingheimer. He was old, was Mr. Klingheimer, very old, although he hid his age and his thoughts behind a mask. He had told her that he knew her quite well, although she did not know him. She would soon come to know him, he had said, and he had spoken of himself as her benevolent friend. He had taken her hand and pledged his troth to her in a brazen manner. It was quite the last thing that she expected when Shadwell had brought her to him. He had also told her that he would come to see her later in the evening when she was comfortably ensconced in his mansion. They had much to talk about, he had said.

The old house creaked and sighed. Doors opened and shut. There were footsteps on the floor above. There were many people on the floors below. She could sense them – a hive of evil, it seemed to her. She touched the crook of her arm, which was painful beneath the bandage where Dr. Peavy had put the heavy needle into her and had leaked Klingheimer's blood into her own veins.

She stilled her mind now and listened within herself, hearing the rush of blood in her ears, hearing her heart beating, searching for some sign that Mr. Klingheimer's blood had tainted her own, that his shadow lay within her. Impossibly, she felt her mother's presence roundabout instead, her mother's voice whispering to her, although the whispering was like the wind under the eaves, and she could not make out the meaning. Her mother was dead and gone, however. She could have no *presence*, no voice of any sort, not in this distant, closed-up place. And yet here it was, unmistakably.

Clara breathed deeply, smelling rain on the air creeping in through the window. The thought of rain brought her back to the present, and she contemplated the room that was her prison. There was the smell of apples on the air, and the closed-up, stale smell of dust and age. She stood up now and made her way around the room, starting at the door, which was locked. A small desk stood near the door, the surface marred with what must be years of use. Someone – a boy, she imagined – had cut his initials into the surface, a G and a B. She wondered what his name was, whether he was a prisoner, as she was, or perhaps a boy who used the desk under happier circumstances. She found her bag and set it on the desk.

There was a closet with a ring-pull to open it, the closet empty but for a blanket on a high shelf that smelled of damp wool and a chamber pot on the closet floor. Nearby stood a dresser with a heavy pitcher atop, full of water, and with a glass tumbler alongside the pitcher. She smelled the water before pouring some into the glass and drinking it. The apples, two of them, sat on a plate next to the pitcher. Should she eat one? It was doubtful that Mr. Klingheimer would bring her into London merely to poison her. Such a thing made no sense given Mr. Klingheimer's solicitations. She bit into an apple, which was quite good, and she went on around the room, feeling the high wainscot, the bit of carpet on the floor, the counterpane on the bed – a duvet, stuffed with feathers, the cover finely woven, satin. She lay down upon it.

When she and Shadwell had crossed the bridge, leaving Aylesford for London, she had been sitting alone in the coach, grieving for Mother Laswell. A clear image of Finn Conrad had come into her head. He had been reading the book she had given him, happy with the book and happy with her, and her heart had lifted – a tide of hopefulness flowing into her. In her vision Finn was sitting by a clear stream in which fish swam in the late afternoon sunlight. It was the very stream where Shadwell had compelled her to find the horrible box beneath the sand.

She knew it was the same stream, for she had seen it often enough when she was a girl – when she could see the world roundabout her, not the ghost of the world that she saw through the crook of her elbow. And then they had passed a boy walking on the side of the road, holding a lantern and carrying a brace of rabbits. In the light that briefly illuminated him, she had seen him quite clearly, her heart leaping at the thought that it was Finn, and that he had come for her. But the boy was not Finn, and he had quickly passed out of sight.

Now Finn's presence was in her mind once again, as was her mother's. She wondered if their presence was merely a craving – her wishes taking shape and color. And as she wondered about this, a flute started up, playing prettily, strangely at odds with the atmosphere of the old house. The music came down to her from above, where she had heard the footsteps earlier. There was a crack of thunder, and then another, as if the flute had called it down from the sky, and she heard the rain against the windowpanes, the sound of it lulling her to sleep.

Finn Conrad, pushing a cart of currant and meat puddings that he had bought entire from a costermonger on Fleet Street near the Old Bell Tavern, made his slow way along Whitefriars Street toward Lazarus Walk. He found number 12, giving it a glance through its broad, wrought-iron gate as he passed: a many-roomed mansion of four and five stories, with an abundance of ornate chimneys and gables. The vast front yard with its cobbled drive was empty of people from what he could see, and the door to a wide carriage house stood open. He made out an elegant Berlin carriage inside and a black brougham, complete with white squiggles on the footboard, as Mother Laswell had referred to the ornamentation.

He walked toward the end of the street now, past a paved path that ran up along the side of the house. Dozens of windows looked out from the high wall, some of them barred with decorative ironwork. He wondered what that meant – barred windows. Nothing good, to his thinking. He thought further, considering the foolishness of trying to gain entrance to a rich man's house and the likelihood of being taken up as a common thief and hung, as opposed to the shame of doing nothing at all to rescue Clara when he had his chance. He would rather die than miss his chance.

The barred windows argued that there had been prisoners within the house in the past, which meant that there might be a prisoner now. He looped back down a narrow byway, past a milliners and a tobacco shop and a chemist, and then, out of sight of the house, along Middle Temple Lane, and around to Whitefriars Street and Lazarus Walk again. "Currant and meat puddings, tuppeny each!" he shouted now and then for good measure, and stopped to sell two of them.

He drew up toward the big gate once again, which he saw was locked. He contemplated going over the wall – easy enough to do, but a risky business in broad daylight. He could see the sweep of the carriage drive and the front door now, and he stopped on the pavement, deciding to make his stand, as the soldier would say. It was a useful place to set up shop, at least until he was told to move on.

He hobbled the wheels of his cart and helped himself to one of the puddings, which was first rate. People passed along the pavement, the morning having come into its own, and Lazarus Walk being a short cut between Tudor Street and the Temple. Sales were brisk and it quickly seemed to Finn that he might recoup a measure of Mother Laswell's money, which he had squandered on the cart. Low clouds hurried across the sky on a south wind, however, and there was little doubt that it would rain soon. The street was increasingly empty of people. He was grateful for his coat and happy that the cart sported a wide umbrella that could be hoisted overhead, which, along with the wall behind him, would shelter him well enough from the rain.

A flurry of drops fell, and then a double crack of thunder opened the sky and the rain came down in earnest. Finn wafered himself between the cart and the wall, sheltered and dry enough for the moment beneath the umbrella. He wondered what to do next as he ate a second pudding and then a third, filling his belly against what might be a very long day. Setting up as a costermonger had seemed a good ruse an hour ago, but not as good now that he was threatened with a soaking.

The wind picked up, endeavoring to blow his umbrella into the next county, and he held tightly to it, gripping the pole in front of him as well as the fabric over his head and watching the slow approach of a covered van drawn by two horses. The van was a small wooden house on wheels with a flat, lean-to roof of tin. When it drew near he saw that a sign on the side read "Waltham's Goods and Parcels." The driver sat snug out of the rain beneath a canvas enclosure that was an extension of the walls and roof of the van. He was a long-legged man in a red bowler who looked overmuch like a spider, all elbows and knees. The horses drew to a stop, and the man jumped down, unlocked the gate with a key that he carried in his pocket, and swung the gate open – a strange business. He gave Finn a hard look, as if he would happily kick him into the street.

The man took his seat again in order to swing the wagon into the yard. As the van moved forward it seemed to Finn as if he would be offered no better chance than this. He must do something rash on Clara's behalf or nothing at all. "Death or glory," he muttered, seeing that the road was mostly empty of people.

Hidden by the van itself as it moved past him, he let go of his umbrella, which the wind immediately carried off, and he darted around behind, stepping up onto the footboard and grasping the latch of the wooden door, pulling it open and slipping through. Strangely, the floor beneath him slid forward two inches, and he caught himself before he fell. Then it stopped abruptly and rolled back, as if it were on wheels, which made not a bit of sense. He expected darkness, but it was not dark.

The interior, lighted with a pale green radiance, stank like a filthy stable, although it was a human animal that it housed: Doctor Narbondo himself, whom Finn had first met on a dark night in Aylesford a year and a half ago, and whom he had last seen falling into a fissure in the floor of the Cathedral of the Oxford Martyrs several days later. It was confounding to see him now, perched on what were apparently enormous, glowing mushrooms, which sat in a shallow metal box. Narbondo's eyelids were half open, although he stared at nothing at all.

Finn began to breathe again after the first shock, and seeing that Narbondo was apparently no threat. His right arm was held in the grip of the mushrooms, and the thick leaf of fungus growing over the top of his head was apparently attached to his scalp. The translucent green flesh of the fungus throbbed like a heartbeat, and he could see fluids moving within it.

Finn pressed himself against the door, fighting the urge to open it and leap out. He heard the horses champing and shuffling, the sound of the driver jumping to the ground, and then of the horses being led away. Silence followed, and he took the chance of opening the door a fraction and peering out. They were in the carriage house. He could see the black brougham, the high wall beyond it hung with tackle. A curtain of rain fell across the doorway, visible for only an instant, and then the door slid across, closing off the carriage house from the world outside and making flight impossible.

Finn eased the door shut and watched Narbondo, who shifted uneasily now, like a sleeper about to awaken. The fungi that imprisoned him shimmered, as if enlivened by his restlessness. The rim of a plate-sized mushroom cap stood near Finn's shoulder, and it very slowly shifted toward him now, as if sensing his presence, its outer perimeter wrinkling and rippling like a human lip. There were tiny suckers visible roundabout it, thousands of them, which expanded and contracted. Finn stepped back against the door, but something held his foot – the cap of a low mushroom that had settled over the toe of his shoe. He yanked his foot away, tearing off a crescent of green flesh, and a smell like a wet manure heap rose around him.

He took out his oyster knife and unsheathed it, wondering whether the monsters would try to defend themselves if he cut them – how quickly they might move. The piece that had torn away with his shoe still glowed. Voices sounded now, and Finn was surprised to feel the wagon rolling forward again, bouncing on its springs. It stopped with a muffled clank, having run up against something. He kept his eyes on the mushrooms, his knife in his right hand and his left hand on the door latch. The wagon lurched once again, and then there was the sound of a mechanism coming to life, and it felt for all the world as if they were moving downward.

Astonished at this, Finn peered out past the door again and saw that they were indeed descending along an illuminated wooden shaft. The interior of the van, evidently a wooden box, had been rolled onto a lift. Doctor Narbondo must dwell in this cabinet as if in a tomb, supported by the mushrooms and hidden away beneath the great house. The box settled on the ground now, and the sound of the lift motor died away. Finn considered various lies to explain what he was doing in the house, but could think of nothing better than to say he had climbed inside the van to get out of the rain.

Now there was the sound of turnbuckles or bolts being manipulated, and the entire wall began to fold in on itself, at the same time swinging outward and upward, a blood-red light filtering into the van to mingle with the green, so that everything was a sickly yellow.

Finn held the oyster knife behind his back now and flexed his knees, getting ready to jump, hearing an odd assortment of noises – the wheezing of a bellows, a bubbling sound like a cauldron on the boil, and the ticking of a great clock or pendulum. He considered his choices, which were few. He had cut someone only once with the knife, and he hadn't liked it, although it had saved his life. He would rather run, if given the chance.

There was a clatter overhead as the folded wall settled onto the roof of the box. Directly in front of him a dwarf was just then climbing down from a short stepladder. He wore an immense beard, a tall beaver hat that was an upside-down twin of the beard, and a stained leather apron. He stared in at Finn without any show of surprise. Then, in a strange, high voice – a voice that Finn had heard before – the dwarf asked, "Do you have a name, young roustabout?" The question was entirely matter-of-fact, neither angry nor surprised nor suspicious.

"Finn Conrad, sir," Finn said, climbing down to the floor and putting away his knife.

"*Finn*, is it? That's a good name, with something of a fish in it. I'm known far and wide as Beaumont the Dwarf, on account of my size. My mother was a French woman, bless her heart. In this house of villainy, howsomever, I go by the name of Mr. Filby Zounds."

"Might I call you Beaumont, then, or do you prefer Mr. Zounds?" It occurred to Finn that this was a monumentally unlikely encounter, and he wondered what the dwarf was playing at.

The dwarf stood for a long moment regarding him and then said, "You might call me Beaumont, but not in company. I *know* you, sir, and you know me. Think on it. You was a stowaway in the marsh all that time ago, in Narbondo's Landau coach, a-going out to Shade House. I glimpsed you when you clumb on behind and hid yourself there at St. Mary Hoo, and I saw you again when you fetched me my breakfast next morning. And you was the one as rode the great air-ship into the Cathedral and come down along a ladder made of rope as nimble as a gib cat. Aye, it was me who drove the Doctor's coach, do you see, and it was me a-playing of the organ when the Cathedral fell. I played the church to pieces, is what I did. The great organ was the jawbone that brought down the walls, Jericho come again. It was the 'Little Fugue' that done it. Do you recall it? You was there. You heard it, no doubt."

Finn was dumbstruck, but he managed to nod. Every word the dwarf said was true, although Finn knew nothing of the "Little Fugue." The entire business was mystifying, as was the dwarf's presence in this room. Finn had first seen him clearly near Angel Alley near George Yard, driving Dr. Narbondo's carriage. Finn had stowed away on the back of the carriage in London and had climbed off to limber his bones when they got to St. Mary Hoo in the marsh, just as the dwarf said. He had climbed aboard when they set out once again, thinking himself unseen, but he was wrong in that regard, and no doubt about it. The dwarf had seen him then but hadn't peached on him. Finn didn't know what to think about that. Certainly the dwarf showed no sign of hostility now, and Finn could sense hostility in a man even if it wasn't made plain. He felt as if he had found an old friend in a time of great need, except that the dwarf had no reason to show him any kindness.

He saw now that some few feet behind the dwarf stood several barber's basins brimming with bubbling green fluid along a wide stone bench bathed in red light. In two of the basins sat severed heads, a man and a woman, on neck-like trunks of glowing flesh. He realized that the "flesh" was a thick slice of mushroom stem, moored in the bubbling fluid. The man's eyes were open, his mouth working as if he were both chewing and trying to speak. The other, a woman, was evidently asleep, or was dead, although that was scarcely sensible.

It came into Finn's mind that the woman was perhaps Clara's mother. Probably it was. Tommy had told him that her head was gone, and he knew it was Shadwell who'd done it, and who had perhaps brought Clara to this very house. The woman's eyes moved now, shifting behind the close lids. Above hung a geometric maze of brass pipes, aerated fluid dripping through holes into the basins, bathing the mushrooms and the heads. There was a wheezing sound from behind the bench, the inhaling and exhaling of a round bladder the size of a moderate hippopotamus. It was depressed by an iron plate, which lifted off again when the bladder was squeezed flat, at which point the giant lung re-inflated, drawing in air. One of the sleeping heads – the woman – made an unhappy noise, something between a sigh and a groan. Her eyes blinked open and peered at Finn, who looked away from the ghastly sight.

"They're alive, do you see," Beaumont said, "although they're nought but heads. It's the toads what does the trick, and the green blood, which is from the toads as well. Now and then one of them says something, and you can just make it out if you listen right close, but it don't amount to nothing. They tell me there's a third head in that there lead crate standing yonder, which will be opened tonight and set onto a bed of toads. It's been a long time dead, although it's true that salt pork lasts a hundred years in the keg."

The dwarf took up a length of rubber hose that snaked out of a brass panel covered with dials and spigots and shoved it over the spout of a similar spigot set into the side of Narbondo's prison. He turned the handle and Finn heard the burbling noise of fluid swirling into the metal box that covered the floor.

"They'll keep like this for a tolerable long time," Beaumont said, "their brains a-working as ever, by way of the fungus blood. Mr. Klingheimer puts it into his own self, or so they say, and has lived past his earthly time. Mr. Klingheimer's rich as Creases, the Greek fellow."

"It's a great marvel," Finn said, "although the heads might have been happier when they had a body to go with them."

"Mr. Klingheimer wants the brain, but not the body. A brain don't cut up rough, you see. How did you come to be a-riding along of the Doctor?" He jerked his head toward Narbondo's box.

There was no useful falsehood, and so Finn told the truth. "I waited outside the gate and climbed in when the wagon drew up."

"What for, then? You don't have the face of a sneak-thief." He peered at Finn closely. "You've got a true face."

Finn looked into the eyes of the man who stood before him, who had the face of a gnome beneath the beard, but it held no apparent cunning, no deceit, nothing hidden. "A girl I know was kidnapped from Hereafter Farm, Aylesford," Finn said boldly. "I've come to fetch her back if she's in this house. They killed her mother before they took her. That's no doubt her mother's head there in the basin." He nodded at what he supposed to be the head of Sarah Wright.

Beaumont's face grew dark when he heard this. "The blind girl, is it?" he asked. "The one who just this morning come in with the scoundrel Shadwell?"

"Yes, sir," Finn said, his heart racing now. "It was like as not

Shadwell who murdered her mother. You've seen Clara, then?"

"Oh, aye. I've seen the girl, but she ain't seen me, by which I mean no disrespect. She oughtn't to be here. It's a fell house you've come into, Finn. There's things in this house to turn a man's stomach." He gestured toward the bubbling basins now by way of illustration. "These two weren't always heads, like you already said. They was *divested* of their bodies. But now it's my lot to keep the heads alive, so to say, which is the Christian thing to do."

Finn nodded. There was both sense and nonsense in what the dwarf said, maybe more sense than nonsense. "Where is Clara kept, then? Do you know?"

"Aye, away up on the fourth floor. It's me who lives in the attic above her. I saw the man a-locking her in, second door along from the stairs."

"Can we unlock that door?"

"We might, young sir, if no one's about. It's precious seldom, though, that no one's about in Mr. Klingheimer's house, it being watch and watch, day and night in this house, four hours on and then a new man to go around for another four. I had my turn for two days of it, but very soon they put me to this here business with the heads, me being handy and knowing something of the toads. In a word, if you're *seen*, Finn, you're like as not a dead man. Mr. Klinghcimer is a pleasant-looking old cove, but there's a right monster living beneath the skin and bone, and make no mistake."

"He's the chief, then? Mr. Klingheimer?"

Beaumont nodded.

"What if I want to go out again? How do I manage it?"

"The way you come in. There's other ways, maybe, but not unless you know where's the keys. Every door is locked from without, you see."

"And you know where's the keys?"

"Beaumont keeps his eyes open when it comes to business that ain't his own, looking out for his main chance, you might say. But he keeps what he knows under his hat till there's need of it. Mind this, though. I live up top, like I said, looking down on the back garden. I won't lock my door while you're in the house, but if they catch you, you don't know me, or else we're both dead."

In that moment there was the ringing of a bell, and Beaumont took Finn's arm and hauled him through a door into what was apparently a storeroom, for there were crates and bales piled high, sacks of flour, cases of wine – a dozen places to hide. Electric lamps illuminated the room, hanging on cords from the ceiling. In a trice the dwarf was gone without saying another word.

Finn, listening hard, heard a voice that said, "We're to hunt for a man down below, Zounds, and are to bring him back to Mr. Klingheimer. If he's dead we're to bring his head in a sack. Ten minutes from now at the red door. And mind you're there betimes. His majesty is in a rare old state. It's *our* heads that'll be in a sack if we don't look sharp, depend upon it."

"I'd pay a farthing to see his *majesty's* head in a sack," Beaumont said.

"Keep them thoughts to yourself, Zounds. This ain't Liberty Hall. Outside in ten minutes, then."

Finn heard the door shut, and immediately Beaumont returned. "Stay here, Finn," he said. "I'm a-going out with Arthur Bates. Keep hid. When I come back, I'll signal you thus," and with that he warbled out a blackbird's call, uncannily clear. Then he put his finger beside his nose and winked.

SEVENTEEN

THE GIPSY ENCAMPMENT

After a steep ascent, the tunnel through which St. Ives traveled took a hard right turning. Abruptly the walls were built of cut stone – not the stone that he had found in the ancient downward stairway earlier in his travels, but stones with heavily mortared joints, walls that were quite likely Medieval in origin. Given that he had been walking at a steady pace, checking his compass along the way, dead reckoning would have it that he was beneath north London, perhaps beneath Hampstead Heath itself, although admittedly the reckoning had been confounded by twistings and turnings and traveling uphill and down.

He came upon an arched doorway with its heavy door standing open on old bronze hinges that were set into the walls with massive bolts. A length of wood that pivoted on an iron rod pinned the door shut. Rubbing had grooved a quarter circle into the door where the wood had been shifted back and forth, and St. Ives opened it easily, moving it upward from where it lay against a second short rod. He pulled the door open, and realized that he had come to the end of his journey, or nearly so. The way beyond the door was level, a corridor that led to a short set of stairs. There were fairly fresh clots of dirt on the floor, crushed by the wheel of the cart.

What would be the point in taking out the dead Narbondo, St. Ives wondered as he walked along the corridor. But in that same vein, why take out the *living* Narbondo? To extract him from the grip of the fungi? Why? Not pity, for Narbondo had neither friends nor living family, aside from Mother Laswell, who had herself tried her best to shoot him when last she saw him, an infamous act only in theory. In truth there was no one alive who would be unhappy to see Narbondo dead.

The thought of Mother Laswell brought to mind the murder of Sarah Wright. Mother Laswell had feared that her own dead husband had been the source of this new trouble, and she had been worried that the man's severed head might have been dug up from beneath the floorboards of Sarah Wright's cottage in Boxley Woods. She supposed, in other words, that someone was actively searching for the head of Maurice De Salles, the stepfather and paternal uncle of Ignacio Narbondo – the same someone who had taken the head of Sarah Wright. And now someone had gone to a good deal of trouble to collect Narbondo into the bargain. The several acts might be coincidental, but it would be folly to assume so.

Who are you? he wondered, ascending now into a small antechamber, scattered with a lumber of ancient furniture: wooden pews, an altar, a cabinet with the door fallen from the hinges. On the cabinet shelves lay what appeared to be sacred vestments, neatly folded and put away many years since, and next to them a chalice covered by a chalice cloth that was more web than fabric, and a censer that hung from a dowel. He was in a priest's hole, of that there could be no doubt, a remnant of England's centuries-long war on Catholicism. He wondered how many priests had hidden here, and whether any of them had escaped into the underworld beyond the arched door. A stone stairs stood in the center of the room forming a landing on top. Above it a large trap-door was set into the ceiling, the wood dark and old but reinforced with iron cleats.

He climbed the stairs, set his knapsack and lamp on the landing, and knelt beneath the trap, putting his back against it and heaving it upward despite his protesting ribs. Dust and debris fell into his hair. He put his hand into the opening and felt the heavy, woven material of a carpet, perhaps weighted with furniture. He heaved on it again, standing as the trap swung upward, dragging the carpet with it, heavy, unseen objects tumbling. He yanked a corner of the carpet past his head, pushed his gear through the opening, and pulled himself through.

The room was apparently a secret chapel. Its ancient needlework carpet, framed in vines and blossoms, bore a coat of arms – that of a recusant family, no doubt, that had been threatened with persecution. The trap itself was built of two-inch-thick oak planks with a layer of cut stones fixed atop it, the stones so cleverly cut that the trap appeared to be part of the floor. The rest of the floor was scattered with chalky dirt, and he took a few minutes to sweep it into the cracks around the closed trap, completing the disguise before pulling the rug back over it and pinning it with the pews.

He hurried out of the room and along a corridor, smelling clean night air. Fairly soon he was compelled to turn to the right, where he very nearly stepped into a deep pit. He flailed his arm to catch himself, dropping the lamp into the pit where it smashed to pieces, the light going out. He stood for a moment, catching his breath, realizing that he could see without his lantern. Moonlight shone faintly from above. Some fifteen feet over his head, up a stone chimney, lay an iron grate with vines growing through it. Through the sparse, leafy branches he could see two stars in the night sky and the bright glow of the moon. On the floor of the pit below lay the shattered remains of his lamp, in the midst of which was a length of rope with a block tied to it. They had rigged tackle to hoist out the cart – easy enough to do if they had brought along lumber to crate it up.

A tall ladder was tilted against the far wall. He could just reach the ladder from where he stood at the edge of the pit, and he pulled it across so that it tilted against the wall beneath the grate. It would be easy enough to climb out through the grate and then heave the ladder back against the far wall in order to keep interlopers out. He stepped onto the ladder, pulled himself aboard, and climbed upward, seizing the grate and pushing it up and out. He clambered through, hauling himself to his feet, deciding to leave the ladder where it stood. He would want it when they returned to search for Gilbert.

After setting the grate carefully into its depression and ascertaining that he was alone, he walked up to the top of a nearby hill and into the shadows of a grove of trees. He thought that he knew where he was now, and he hoped he knew what he would find. Given the time of year, there was some chance that he had friends hereabouts, although they were gadabout friends, and might already have gone off to winter quarters somewhere. From the hilltop he looked down upon a meadow that contained two small ponds – Wood Pond and Thousand Pound Pond on the north end of the Heath. On the rise above Wood Pond stood a dozen gipsy caravans. A fire burned, throwing sparks into the sky, and many lanterns were lit, so that the scene was brightly illuminated. Men, women, and children were active on the green, the entire crowd apparently stowing gear into the caravans, evidently getting ready to move on. Their horses – two dozen of them – were tethered nearby.

He was certain he knew one of the caravans – that of the Loftus family, who had camped on the green at the farm in Aylesford just two months past, picking hops and working in the oast house, helping to dry the harvest. The wagon was bright red and with an arched green roof. St. Ives thought of it cheerfully as Christmas on wheels. The Spaniards Inn, where he and Alice had stayed for several nights some years back, was tolerably close by to the west. Alice, in fact, was certain that their son Eddie had been conceived at the Spaniards and St. Ives had no reason to doubt her. Both of them had a sentimental regard for the old inn as a consequence.

Overhead the clouds tore along, and now they covered the moon, so that he walked down the hill in darkness until he stepped into the firelight and in among the people, his happy eyes fixed on the red-painted caravan with its green roof and yellow under-carriage. He might have been a ghost, for no one acknowledged his presence aside from two small boys who gave him a strange look and moved away instead of asking for a coin or actively picking his pocket. There was the smell of turpentine in the air, and St. Ives saw that two young women were busy decorating the red spokes of the Loftus wagon in the light of paraffin lanterns. One of them was Theodosia Loftus, to whom he had once given an illustrated book of English garden birds. The girl was a fine artist in her own right, and had painted a beautifully rendered black and gold carp for Alice.

"Theodosia Loftus," he said, his voice coming out in an unintelligible croak. Both girls turned to look at him, the one who was not Theodosia leaping up with a shriek and hurrying away, carrying her paint pot. Theodosia, however, looked carefully at him, her face full of surprise and wonder, and then shouted, "It's the Professor!" She hurried toward him, taking his hand and leading him to a keg that stood at the front of the wagon. "Mother!" she shouted, and then said, "Sit down, sir," in a firm voice, compelling him to do so by hauling on his arm.

There was the sound of someone coming out of the wagon – Charity Loftus, the mother – who peered at St. Ives for a moment, said, "Just you sit still, Professor," and then to Theodosia, "A bucket of clean water." Charity disappeared, returning moments later with a glass filled with what turned out to be brandy and carrying folded pieces of cloth. The bucket arrived and she soaked the cloth in the water and began mopping his face. "Drink down that glass," she told him. "It'll restore the senses."

"Adamina took fright, sir, when she saw you," Theodosia said to him. "It looked like you'd been dug out of a grave. Were you beaten?"

"Beaten?" he asked, turning in her direction. "No. Not at all, I'm happy to say."

"Sit *still*, Professor, if you will," Charity Loftus said. "You're covered in bloody dirt, right down the back of your neck, and your poor shirt won't come clean no matter what's done to it." She paused long enough to peer into his face. "You've had your brain pan shaken. I can see it in your eyes. Does the head ache?"

"No, ma'am," St. Ives said, only a small lie. He realized that the entire side of his face must be covered in dried blood. He saw that he was filthy too, now that he looked at his hands in the lamplight. His clothing was streaked with dirt and white dust. He hadn't given his condition a thought. No wonder people fled away at the sight of him. "Is Mr. Loftus roundabout?" he asked.

"He's at Wyldes Farm," Theodosia told him, wringing bloody water out of the rag while Charity came at him with a fresh one.

"We're wintering there, going on tomorrow morning. A man named Mr. Carpenter has a society, and they've given us leave to stay in our own manner, with the barn open to us when it snows."

"*Edward* Carpenter, do you mean? The Fellowship of the New Life?"

"Aye, so they call themselves," Charity said, "although the old life suits us well enough. I can't say which Carpenter. Loftus says they've got an excess of bees in their bonnet, to be certain, but they're a peaceable lot what believes that the whole thing is the same, if you follow me, not bloody-minded bigots, as are thick among us." She looked carefully at him now and asked, "Does the missus know what's come of you?" And then, without waiting for an answer, she grabbed a small boy who just then appeared in their midst and said, "Shipton! Run out to Wyldes farm and fetch home your dad if he ain't already on the way. Tell him the Professor's come among us and is much knocked about."

The boy set out at once, scouring along like a rabbit up a moonlit path through the trees.

"I took a fall earlier today and then had a long tramp of it," St. Ives told her. "Alice doesn't know."

"Ah," Charity said. "And after your fall you took it into your mind to tramp up to Wood Pond?" She gave St. Ives a look, as if this were further evidence that his wits were addled or as if she knew that something was afoot that he didn't intend to reveal. "Was the fall accidental like?"

"Perhaps it was not," St. Ives said. "But I'd best tell the tale only once, when Mr. Loftus arrives. "I'm grateful to you for the kindness, ma'am. And this is first rate brandy, to be sure."

"Loftus's brother brought a hogshead of it across the Channel with some men in a boat that was good enough to land him and the barrel in a handy cove in Shelmerston, where we stayed for a time last spring. He shared it out, the brother did, and since then all else is 'swill' to Mr. Loftus. He must have right French brandy now that he's used to it. 'Try something new and the old won't do,' as they say truly enough. There, sir. You look less like a corpse now. Here's Mr. Loftus and Shipton, back already. Loftus will have you sorted out."

It was indeed Mr. Loftus, who took in the sight of St. Ives without a shudder, and very soon St. Ives found that there was a fresh glass of brandy in his hand and cold meat pie and cheese and bread before him on a plate, and it was only by main force that he managed to remain awake long enough to tell his tale, the details much reduced and leaving out all but a hint of an explosion. Very shortly he made his way with Loftus and Theodosia to the Spaniards Inn, a satchel of Loftus's clothing and other necessaries in his hand.

He fell wearily into bed at last, his ribs aching, listening to the nightjars calling outside on the heath and looking at the moonlight shining on the window curtains. He thought of Eddie and Cleo, tucked away safely in their beds in Scarborough, and in the few moments that it took him to fall asleep he said a silent goodnight to Alice, remembering the happy time they had spent in this very room and how easy it was to forget to be thankful for one's blessings. Some time later he awakened to the sound of rain, which made him all the more grateful to be lying abed.

EIGHTEEN

SLEEP LIKE DEATH

Finn awakened from a sound sleep in the storage room, leaning against a very comfortable flour sack against the wall. He had no memory of having drifted off, and he wondered how long he had been at it, wasting time when there was precious little time to waste. He ate his bread and cheese, stood up and stretched, and then walked out to have a look around at his prison. The cellar was large, with several storage rooms. He looked into them, finding the leather ribbons that dangled from the ceiling and that switched on the electric lights when you yanked upon them. He did so and then dropped the strap in a hurry, marveling when the glass globes switched on like the sun coming out from behind a cloud. He was leery of electricity and the buzzing it made, and had heard that it could cook a person like a Christmas goose on the instant. Gaslight was more amenable. In an adjacent, high-ceilinged room he discovered a lumber of furniture – wardrobe cabinets and dining tables and heavy, carved wooden chairs with turned legs. Some of it was quite old, the wood dark and dusty and all of it casting deep, mysterious shadows.

He made his way through it to yet another door further on, which he opened, revealing a small room with a narrow cot in it. The bed had a feather mattress, which Finn pushed on before taking a look at a case full of old books – leather-bound relics in Latin, one of which bore a date of 1712. It looked to be a hermit's room, with candle sconces on the walls, heavy tallow candles sitting on the sconces and matches in a niche by the door. He lit a match simply to see whether it was good, and the flaming tip broke off and flew away like a comet, landing on the bit of carpet on the floor and smoldering. Finn stepped on it to put it out. It seemed to him that the room hadn't been lived in for an age, but it was a comfortable cell in any event – luxurious for a hermit, say, or a highwayman.

He would occupy this room if need be, he decided, if he must spend the night in the house, or two nights, or however many days and nights passed before he could leave and take Clara with him. For he had decided that he would not leave Fell House, as he thought of it now, without Clara. Clara's fate would be his own fate. He was certain, or at least hopeful, that Beaumont would not betray him, and equally certain that no one would look into this room, if only because no one had, apparently, for a long time, given the untrodden layer of dust on the floorboards.

He returned to the storeroom and began shifting crates and boxes to see what food lay about: jars of deviled ham, it turned out, and marmalade, pickled oysters and bacon, tightly wrapped Christmas puddings and sugar-loafs. He filled an empty sack with provisions and then returned to his room. The empty sack could be packed under the door to block the light of his candles. Satisfied, he went out again, switching off the lights in the furniture room, and shutting its door and the door to the storage room, making sure that there was nothing visibly out of order – nothing that would give him away. He thought of something that Beaumont had said to him when he had asked the dwarf about finding a way out of the house. "The way you come in," had been the answer, served up without a thought.

He stood beside Narbondo's cabinet now, the Doctor looking as if he were unhappily asleep. The lift shaft stretched away overhead, and Finn saw now that it went far aloft – into the top of the house, no doubt. They could haul things to and from the storerooms if Narbondo's box was shifted, which would be easy enough, since it was on wheels and could be removed to the carriage house. A wooden ladder ascended the entire height. The shaft was illuminated, which was convenient to be sure, although he wondered whether someone climbing the ladder – himself, say – would throw a shadow.

The ladder itself was let into the wall so that the lift would slip past it without hindrance. On each floor, adjacent to the ladder, stood the wrought-iron gates that closed the shaft off from the rooms onto which it opened. For a long moment, someone climbing the ladder would be visible from within whatever room lay beyond the gate. He stood contemplating this for the space of ten seconds and then decided that there was no better time to investigate. If he was in danger of being discovered, he could climb back down easily enough, but he must know the way of things if he was to be of any use to Clara.

He ducked into the ladder niche and began climbing, very quickly rising to the level of the first gate, beyond which lay darkness. Opposite stood the double doors that let out into the carriage house. A dim light shone between the doors. He could smell horses and feed and leather, and he wondered whether the doors were locked.

From his foothold on the ladder he leapt out ape-like and grasped the lines that raised and lowered the lift, swinging straight on across to the other side, clinging one-handed to a stanchion on a narrow ledge while he pushed on each of the doors in turn. They *were* locked. The way was closed to him.

He swung back across to the ladder, grasped a rung, and climbed again toward the next floor, where a lighted room stood beyond its wrought-iron gate. He stopped to listen before he climbed any higher, but he heard nothing at all, and so he continued upward until he could see that the gate closed off a broad, illuminated hallway, empty of people. He tried the latch, discovering happily that this gate was unlocked, although clearly it mightn't remain so. Dim voices sounded now, perhaps approaching, and he hauled himself quickly upward again toward the third floor – another lighted room, quite clearly occupied, for a man's voice spoke from within with evident authority – the voice of an admiral, he thought, used to being obeyed.

Finn could see the part of the speaker's head and broad shoulders – long white hair, an old man it would seem, although if he were an old man then he was tolerably fit – his shoulders as powerful as his voice. Perhaps it was Mr. Klingheimer, who had demanded a sack with a man's head in it. Another unseen man spoke, denying that he had committed some folly that he had apparently just been accused of. In the next moment he heard Beaumont's voice – for it could be no other.

"It's as Mr. Shadwell said, your honor. We went down right deep at Deans Gate. But the deeper we went, the wider the way, so to speak, like a funnel downside up, until it was something like being sent out to find a man on the streets of London its own self. You're a-going north while mayhaps he's a-going east.

Way leads on to way, do you see?"

"I'm fully persuaded of it, Mr. Zounds. Be so kind as to return to the cellar to see that everything is ship-shape. Narbondo is visiting Dr. Peavy again tomorrow morning, so you'll be quit of him. In the meantime, you can leave the toads, as you call them, to tend to themselves. I'll look in on the heads. Your time is your own tomorrow, then – a holiday. Remain within the confines of the property, if you will, in case I have need of you."

There was the sound of a door shutting, and then the man who Finn supposed was Klingheimer said, "And so in lieu of the head of Professor St. Ives you've brought me this scrap of soiled news-print reeking of pickled onions and Smithfield ham."

"His sandwich was wrapped in it, Mr. Klingheimer. What else could it mean? It's a living man who eats a sandwich. There's a bit of crust on it."

"What of the fat man, then? Have you a theory?"

"Dead, I'd warrant."

"You'd *warrant* it? You're a confident man, Mr. Shadwell, to give me your warrant. Mind that I don't take it out of you in the form of a pound of flesh. Mightn't the fat man have eaten the sandwich, then? Among living entities, fat men are inclined to eat sandwiches above all others, or so reason leads us to believe."

"If that fool Lewis had used slow-match instead of quick, we'd have found them as we planned and had our way with them," the man named Shadwell said evasively. "He brought the roof down before they'd even set out."

"Mr. Lewis's foolishness doesn't enter into this discussion, not at this moment. I'm wondering about *your* foolishness, Mr. Shadwell. The girl Clara refuses to speak or eat, you know, and that disappoints me. My efforts haven't persuaded her, although I believe she'll come around in time. Her reticence is your doing, it seems to me."

"She's mute, sir."

"Don't you believe it, Mr. Shadwell. She's merely willful. She's also evidently terrified and believes herself to be among people who mean to harm her. We do not mean to harm her. Is that clear?"

"Yes, sir. I treated her kindly. Indeed I did."

"You were asked to enact the roll of the Metropolitan Police while in Aylesford. You were to have the girl's best interests in mind – a great help to her adoptive family, deep sympathy for all and sundry. That called for a measure of subtlety and a pleasant demeanor. What went awry?"

"That oaf Bingham set off the Laswell woman's man, by name of Kraken. He attempted to murder the both of us with a rifle, which put paid to the police ruse, and we had to turn to more persuasive methods."

"That was unfortunate. The police *ruse*, as you refer to it, should have been simple to carry out. Did Clara witness these persuasive methods?"

"We kept her well clear of it."

"Did you indeed? You and I seem to be surrounded by incompetent men on all sides: the fool Lewis, the oaf Bingham. Perhaps we need a thorough turnout, a house-cleaning. What do you think of that, sir?" Shadwell apparently didn't think much of it, for there was a long silence before Klingheimer continued. "You'll recall that I expressed my doubts about Mr. Bingham several weeks ago. You insisted that you could *keep him on the straight and narrow*. Those were your very words, I believe."

"This man Kraken is unhinged, Mr. Klingheimer. The two of them fell out when Bingham lost his patience."

"Mr. Bingham's patience was not his own to lose. His patience belonged to me, since I was his employer. I assume that you dealt with the oaf Bingham yourself, as I asked you to?"

"He's dead."

"And the Laswell woman?"

"Dead, too."

"And their ghosts won't blow back into London on the whirlwind now that you've sown the seeds of the storm in Aylesford? There were no witnesses to their deaths, I mean to say?"

"No, sir," Shadwell said without hesitation. "I hid the bodies in the woods."

"You're lying somewhere, Mr. Shadwell. Perhaps everywhere. I'm quite aware of it. But you no doubt believe that it is in your best interests to lie, and certainly it's sensible for a man to do what is in his best interests when he's sure of himself. By that same token, a man who is sure of himself must be strong enough to carry the weight of his own self opinion. It is unfortunate that this business in Aylesford was mishandled, but there's nothing ruinous in it if you've put it right – as you claim to have done. That said, I'll thank you to speak to Mr. Lewis this very day. Once again I'll ask you to practice subtlety, Mr. Shadwell, if you have any of that commodity about your person. Simply remind Mr. Lewis of his duty and of the necessity of thinking before he acts. Tell Mr. Lewis to send young Jenkins to me post-haste if there is any news at all, but, as ever, advise Mr. Lewis not to tell Jenkins anything of our affairs. And remember that we do not want Mr. Lewis to fall into a state of desperation. We want him to remain malleable. Do you understand me? Do not remove his appendages nor threaten violence against his wife. Mr. Lewis's spirit is on the wane, I fear."

"Yes, Mr. Klingheimer," Shadwell said. "I've been two days

without an hour of sleep, however, and..."

"Sleep is very like death, Mr. Shadwell. I myself make a practice of shunning it if ever I can. I'll thank you to seek out Mr. Lewis at once. Then by all means sleep if the fit is upon you. And one thing more: Alice St. Ives and her entourage have gone to ground at the Half Toad in Smithfield. Send Penny and Smythe to the inn in the guise of commercial travelers. They're to keep their eyes and ears open but are to remain out of the way – not speaking unless spoken to. Mrs. St. Ives and Frobisher's nephew are no doubt in a dangerous state of mind. Make certain that Penny and Smythe understand this. In short, if St. Ives finds his way out of the pit, then he will surely contact his wife. When he does, I must know of it. If he does not, then he has not found his way out of the pit, and you must descend once again with the dwarf to seek him out."

After a moment there was the sound of the door shutting, and silence reigned. Finn heard Mr. Klingheimer's footfalls and a chair scraping upon the floorboards. Finn contemplated what Klingheimer had said about the Professor – why he might want the Professor's head. Why, in fact, had he any interest at all in the Professor, who was apparently dead or lost underground.

There was the sound of a blackbird trilling – Beaumont's signal – and Finn was tempted to climb back down and join him. But Clara occupied a room right above him now. She was alone, mourning her poor mother, starving herself, with no idea that she had a friend nearby. He made up his mind and climbed quickly upward to the very top of the ladder. From there he looked downward and saw Beaumont far below, looking back up at him. His life was in the dwarf's hands. So be it. He waved at him by way of greeting. Beaumont waved back and then disappeared. If he meant to play Finn false, then Finn would soon find out.

He slipped the latch on the fourth-floor gate and pushed it open, entering a long hallway with several doors. At the far end stood the stairs that Beaumont had spoken of. He listened hard at the first door he came to, but there wasn't a sound, either from within the room or from roundabout him. He had an aversion to spying, but he set it aside and peered through the keyhole. There was a lamp burning in the room, and although he didn't see Clara, he saw her strangely soled shoes on the carpet near the foot of the bed.

"Clara!" he said, but keeping his voice low.

Clara's stockinged feet appeared as she swung herself off the bed and stood up. She remained quite still, however, and said nothing.

"It's Finn I've come for you." His heart swelled as he said this, and he was glad when she hurried forward now and knelt at the door. She gave out a great sigh, and he heard the sound of her weeping.

"You needn't speak unless you choose to, Clara," Finn said to the keyhole. "I've got but a moment and then I have to hide myself. We've a friend in the house, or at least I believe so. If they come for me in the next minute, then I'm betrayed, and I'll be of no help to you. If they do not come for me, then be aware that there's a bearded dwarf named Beaumont in the house who is a right good man. We must trust him. Professor St. Ives and Alice and Hasbro are in London, and I mean to get their help if I can't win the both of us free. You are not alone, I mean to say. We need a key and a way out of this place, but I'll find both. I followed your coach from Aylesford on old Ned Ludd, and I'll not return to Aylesford without you. I've promised Mother Laswell as much."

"Mother is alive?" Clara asked.

"That she is," Finn said, happy to hear her voice, which he had never heard before. Not once. It was a beautiful voice, he thought. "I came across Mother along the stream, and untied her." He realized now that Clara had begun to weep again, and the sound silenced him.

"I knew you would come," she said at last. The conviction in her voice made him happier than he had ever been. It was momentary, however, for a door shut hard, perhaps in another hallway on this very floor. Clara apparently heard it, too, for she said, "*Run*, Finn."

Finn ran quietly, down the hallway and back through the gate, which he closed before dropping down the ladder, sliding rather than putting his feet on the rungs, and slowing himself with his hands, which quickly grew hot. He dropped like a stone past Mr. Klingheimer's room; there was nothing to be gained by creeping past. Within moments he landed in the cellar. He looked upward, but saw no signs of pursuit and heard no hue and cry.

He thought about Clara, whose weeping had been happiness. She knew now that there was help at hand. She had spoken to him without hesitation, which meant something to be sure. He was glad to be here, a willing prisoner in this house, although when it came to him that he was glad that Clara was here also, he dismissed the idea as shabby, and for a moment he was confounded by such feelings.

When he pushed past Doctor Narbondo's cabinet, he looked into it and saw that the green mushrooms were glowing brightly, generating their own light. Narbondo reclined among them as if on a divan, so that the open box looked like a curiosity from one of Mr. Uffner's freak shows at Piccadilly Hall. His mouth was closed, but green bile leaked from the corners of it into his beard, which glowed faintly, as did his hair. His eyes were open now, and no longer as dull as they had been. He stared into the infinite, however, and Finn wondered whether his mind was at work or was empty. He was paralytic, to be sure. Finn held a finger as close as he dared to Narbondo's face and moved it back and forth. For a moment the man seemed not to see it, but then he blinked, and his eyes shifted toward the moving finger. Finn dropped his hand and retreated into the storeroom again, wishing that he hadn't called attention to himself.

A real weariness was descending upon him, his long nap having been a temporary respite, and he made his way past the shadowy furniture and through his own humble door, which he secured behind him, determined to eat one of Mr. Klingheimer's plum puddings and to pack his creel with another before falling asleep.

NINETEEN

THE HALF TOAD INN

A lice St. Ives sat at a table in the public room of the Half Toad Inn, Lambert Court, Smithfield, a wood fire burning in the grate, the night wind moaning beneath the eaves. The room was wainscoted in old oak, with gas-light sconces on the walls and heavily framed paintings of ships at sea. On the right-hand side of the hearth hung two etchings of old Smithfield, rendered by Hogarth a century and a half ago. Despite these homey trappings, however, there was an uneasiness in the air, or so it seemed to Alice, who had scarcely touched the glass of port sitting in front of her. She was thinking of her husband, as she had been doing almost without pause all day – where he might be, whether injured, his tenacious spirit and strength of mind. She had made an effort to shun all thoughts of his possible death: there was no reason whatsoever to assume that he was dead.

She was aware, however, that she was forcibly keeping the idea at bay, and she wondered how long her defenses would prevail. She assured herself that he had found his way out of more difficult straits a dozen times. She sipped from her glass of port now and gazed through it at the flames in the hearth.

She had seen the catastrophe on the river quite clearly, thank God. Langdon had been far down into the pit, Gilbert, poor man, not nearly so far along. She was convinced that the explosion that had precipitated the collapse had occurred near the surface, where the stone ceiling of the cavern was relatively thin. It was possible, entirely possible, that Langdon had been far enough beyond it to have survived, in which case there was no reason to suppose that he was... to come to any conclusion at all.

She regarded Miss Bracken for a moment, who sat alone at a table playing a game of Patience and cheating with abandon. Alice recalled her breathless question at the time of the collapse: "Where is my Gilbert?" There had been nothing calculating in her tone, merely heartfelt dismay. Alice thought again of the theft of the spoons, wondering whether Miss Bracken was like the crow on her astonishing hat, compelled to pick up and hoard shiny objects. Miss Bracken had been a victim of nerves this afternoon and looked destroyed now, but she seemed less grief-stricken than wary of Tubby – afraid, perhaps, that he would put her out into the windy night. It seemed unlikely, for Tubby's mind and heart were taken up with the loss of his uncle and for the unhappiness between them. Tubby was currently upstairs, overseeing the removal of Gilbert's bags from the room that Gilbert no longer required, and which had just recently been booked by two men who now sat near the fire drinking wine and waiting for the room to be tidied.

Uncannily, a newsprint broadside proclaiming the death of Gilbert Frobisher and the "famous natural scientist and explorer Langdon St. Ives" had been hawked along the embankment and elsewhere in the city within a few hours of the collapse, complete with an illustration of the sink-hole and a discussion of the explosive miasma that had almost certainly been ignited by the burning lantern. The theory was sensible – more sensible, no doubt, than Alice's suspicion of the lurking man and an infernal device – but it did nothing to restore her husband to her, and she wondered why the flash of the explosion hadn't apparently occurred in the vicinity of the lantern.

St. Ives was something of a footnote in the lurid account of the tragedy, for Gilbert Frobisher, whose wealth was inestimable, had recently brought into London a vast great Caribbean octopus that he had intended to house in a vivarium above Allhallows near the mouth of the Thames. And so he had become something of a celebrity.

Henrietta Billson, who with her husband William owned the Half Toad, was just now clearing away the remains of their supper. Gilbert had ordered the removes himself, including lamb from the Romney Marsh and giant rock oysters from Whitstable. But there had been no Gilbert to help eat the food, and even Tubby had made a pitiful job of it. Hasbro had gone out the instant that his supper was eaten, anxious to return to the sink-hole in order to discover whether anything useful had been found out.

Mrs. Billson handed an armload of plates to Lars Hopeful the tap-boy and stood staring at one of the two men by the fire, a small, oily man of perhaps forty years, muscular and veiny, with yellow, curly hair. He was coatless, and he wore blue gaiters. He looked like a racetrack tout rather than any kind of commercial traveler. His partner, a larger, heavier man with a broad face, looked up from his newspaper now and then to stare at Miss Bracken. Henrietta Billson had no use for forward men, and there was a dangerous look in her eye. Suddenly her demeanor changed, and she turned away and disappeared into the kitchen. Alice could see nothing that might have motivated her.

A moment later Mrs. Billson returned, appearing at Alice's chair with the port bottle in order to fill her glass, although Alice hadn't requested it and it didn't need refilling. In a low voice she said, "Might we speak a word to you in the kitchen, ma'am, begging your pardon for the botheration? After a minute or so has passed, if you will, just for the sake of appearances." She winked then, indicating that this was something of a conspiracy, and then she jerked her thumb toward the two men by the fire before walking away.

Alice sipped her port and attempted to read a copy of *Ally Sloper's Half Holiday*, which she had found lying on a table. Its humor was lost on her, however, and after several minutes had passed she set it down, rose from her chair, and walked into the kitchen, where the Billsons stood waiting for her.

"It's these two men, ma'am," William Billson told her. "They might be innocent as babes, or again they might not be. It's not for us to say. They come in this evening from Manchester by rail, or so they said – commercial gents – and I gave them poor Mr. Frobisher's room, which I had thought was empty. But his baggage was still in it and down they come again to wait while Tubby has gone up to fetch it. The room is next door to your own, ma'am, with a connecting door."

"The thing is," Henrietta put in, "what Bill is a-trying to say, is that one of them ain't from Manchester, and if he's a commercial gent I'll eat my hat. A cutthroat is more like it. Whether he came in on the train I can't say, and as a Christian woman I don't call him a liar, but I just now smoked him as the brother of Jack Penny."

"Jack Penny?" Alice asked.

"The leader of the Cheapside Boys, them who was murdered

this past September right here in Smithfield," Mr. Billson said. "Jack Penny was drowned in a horse trough, and seven of his mates was hacked to pieces with cleavers."

"The Snow Hill Massacre?"

Henrietta nodded gravely. "The man in there drinking our good red wine, the small man, is Jack Penny's own brother, and he's not from Manchester, not by a long chalk, and he's using a false name, because 'is own is tainted. He hails from Coldharbour right here in London, and he swindled my own cousin some years back when he was a butcher in Smithfield Market. When was that, Mr. Billson?"

"I make it four years ago, maybe five, since Penny's been gone from the market."

"He doesn't know me," said Henrietta, "but I'll never forget his face, not after what he took from Betina, and it wasn't just her money that I speak of."

"What you want us to do is what we're asking," Billson said. "I can pitch him out, but I'll need another man or two to do it right. They're likely to cut up rough. It's right strange that they put up at the Half Toad, do you see."

"It *is* strange, Mr. Billson," Alice said. "But there's no pressing need to pitch them out. They're keeping to themselves for the most part, and the last thing we want is more trouble, nor to call trouble down upon the two of you. I don't much care where they came from or whether they're lying about it or telling the truth. It's none of my business."

Billson nodded, and Henrietta said, "Still and all, I've got my eye on them, ma'am, and I've got an iron pan that weighs nigh onto two stone to lay them out with if they ask for it. That man Smythe has a roving eye. His filthy intentions are plain on his face when he looks at your Miss Bracken, although she's no newborn babe herself."

"I'll just sweep out the room upstairs, then," Billson said. And with that he went out.

Alice returned to her chair, only to discover that Miss Bracken sat with the two men now and that Smythe had his hand on her knee, although he withdrew it when Alice walked in. Miss Bracken's demeanor had grown cheerful, which wasn't a bad thing, really. Alice soon made out that the three were talking about this morning's cave-in. Jack Penny's brother listened to what Miss Bracken was telling him and shook his head sympathetically. He turned to Alice now, gave her a long, pitying look, and said, "May I express my desolation, ma'am, as regards your husband's tragedy – nay, your own tragedy? My name is Hillman, Ellis Hillman."

"No, Mr. Hillman, you may not," Alice told him, refraining from calling him "Mr. Penny." "There is as yet no tragedy to be desolated about, and I have little regard for a stranger's unaccountable desolation in any event. I'm certain you mean well, but I'd much rather speak of something else or nothing at all. Preferably nothing."

"Just so, ma'am," the man said, touching his finger to his forehead before saying, "I'll name my particular friend, Mr. Smythe."

"Charmed," Mr. Smythe said, nodding to her.

The two men returned to their wine and to Miss Bracken, and in the brief silence that followed Alice heard the rain pecking against the windows and the crackling of the fire. She had a thumping headache and a weariness that made her long for her bed. Did she owe it to Miss Bracken to keep her company? She decided that she did not. The silly woman could do as she pleased – indeed, had apparently been doing so her entire life and would continue to do so whether Alice or anyone else approved of it. Alice drank the last of her port and was just setting the glass down when Tubby Frobisher appeared on the stairs gripping his walking stick in a determined manner.

His face, Alice saw, was rigid with anger, and he strode determinedly to Miss Bracken's chair and said in a clear, even voice, "I'll ask you to return my uncle's property, ma'am, whatever your name might be. Certainly it is not Bracken."

"What's *that*?" asked Miss Bracken. "*What* bleeding property, you bag of suet?"

"Gilbert Frobisher's jewelry. The lot of it. It was in an ivory case inlaid with gold. I saw you coming out of his room earlier in the day. Deny it at your peril."

"By God I won't deny it. My gloves and scarf were in Mr. Frobisher's trunk, if you must know. I took what belonged to me."

"The jewelry box contained a diamond cravat-pin, cuff links, shirt studs, and a brooch, all with the Frobisher hedgehog crest, all solid gold, the diamonds quite valuable, as was the box itself, which was fashioned by Castellani. You have taken the box and its contents from his valise, ma'am. There's no conceivable point in denying it. You saw your opportunity this afternoon, and you took it. If you return them to me this instant and promise to be gone in the morning, I'll pay you two-hundred pounds and let the matter lie. In deference to my uncle I will not put you out onto the road on a night such as this, but if you are not gone in the morning, I'll summon the police."

Alice was stupefied, although her first inclination was to suppose that Tubby was correct in his accusation. Anger, of course, might have twisted his thinking, since Miss Bracken was his chief source of regret – the wedge that had been driven between him and Gilbert. Tubby saw her as a devil, and understandably so if it were true that she had stolen Gilbert's jewelry. But *was* it true? Again Alice considered the silver spoons, the brazen manner in which Miss Bracken had dropped them into her bag. But the spoons were comparatively trivial compared to the jewels, and mentioning them now would needlessly inflame Tubby.

"Come, madam," Tubby said. "Own up to it unless you'd rather hang."

"I take offense to your blackguarding this good woman," the man who called himself Hillman said. "What proof do you have for this accusation? The police will ask the very same question, mind you. Have you any evidence, sir? Your plain dislike for this poor woman does not constitute evidence."

"He has *nothing*," Miss Bracken said, staring Tubby down. "He has taken against me because his uncle, who was a good man, loved me more than him. This bloody whale who calls himself a man was *pissing* himself to think that I might come into a portion of the old man's money some day. But I won't have a groat now, will I? Not now. How can I when the good man is *dead*? And yet you hate me anyway, don't you, Mr. Bumfiddle? A woman with naught but a brass farthing who's been kited away from her home where she was happy. That's the truth of it. You and your mean offer of two-hundred pounds when you've just put ten millions into your pocket! What do *I* say? I say *you've* taken the jewels yourself, if there *was* any jewels. Because why? Because you want to use them against me. You're a jealous, mean pig, who can lord it over a poor, friendless woman like me. *Shame* on you. The great shame of the world!"

With that she burst into tears, hauling a kerchief out of her bodice and mopping her eyes. Tubby was struck dumb, much of his anger having drained away with her tirade.

"Here, now. You've got the two of us as friends, Miss," Mr. Smythe said to her. "Never you forget it. We'll stand by you, sure enough."

Alice realized that Henrietta Billson had come into the room carrying her cast-iron frying pan, which was broad enough to cook a Christmas goose. She looked confused, however, as if not certain whose head to flatten.

"By God, I'll sort it out this very moment," Tubby said, having recovered his wits. "But I warn you, madam, that my offer is about to evaporate. I intend to search your bags. Anyone who chooses can come along as witness."

"No one *chooses* to walk with a *turd*," Miss Bracken said to him, and blew her nose into her kerchief.

After a moment's hesitation, Tubby turned back to the stairs, and for a time the company sat in shocked silence. Alice noted that the rain had ceased, and she saw the halo of a gas-lamp outside along Fingal Street. Henrietta Billson had gone away, and Alice's weariness had completely disappeared, although her headache had not. She made up her mind that she would defend Miss Bracken if she must, if only in order to save Tubby the certain remorse of further abusing the woman whom his uncle had been fond of – the uncle who at any moment might walk in through the door, in which case Tubby would despise himself until his dying day.

Tubby reappeared on the stairs, clutching something in his hand, although it was not apparently an ivory jewel case. He looked uncertain rather than angry, and when he was several feet away from Miss Bracken he stopped short and held out his open palm on which sat the three silver spoons.

"What's *this*, then?" Hillman asked, looking hard at Tubby.

"It's three silver spoons upon which you can see the Frobisher crest, sir. I'll forgive you for asking impertinent questions, but you'd best keep silent from this point hence. I'll say again, this is none of your business."

"*Impertinent? I'm* impertinent? You accuse this poor woman of stealing valuable jewels and now you throw these three *spoons* into her face? Flash-plate spoons, if I'm any judge."

"Solid silver, and you're no judge, sir. Come, what are these doing in your possession, ma'am?"

"I pinched them is what, you fat devil. I saw my Gilbert *die* today, and one thing I knew for certain was that his bleeding nephew would put me out onto the street, as you've already threatened to do, because you're a vile piece of dog waste with the heart of a dried pea. I *loved* Mr. Frobisher, you fat pig, and I took those three spoons to remember him by, that's all. But *you've* got them now. *You* won't starve after all, now that you've got something to spoon up your swill."

"Indeed I *do* have them now. *Your* Gilbert indeed."

"Then you'd best summon the police so that I can be hanged. By God, I *long* to be hanged after speaking with the likes of you."

"What of the *jewels*?" asked Mr. Smythe.

"Still missing," Tubby began, but just then there was the scuffing of footsteps on the stairs and William Billson appeared, holding his hand out in front of him. In it lay a jewelry box made of ivory and inlaid with gold.

"I found this beneath the bed, sir, when Hopeful and I were sweeping out. It fell from Mr. Gilbert Frobisher's bag, I don't doubt."

Tubby stared at it for a long moment while Miss Bracken audibly wept. After a moment Tubby let the spoons fall to the carpet from his open hand, took the jewelry case from Billson, and moved wearily up the stairs once again, saying nothing and not looking back until Mr. Hillman said, "Hah! And *I'm* impertinent!"

Tubby turned and looked hard at him now, and for a moment there was cold murder in his eye, but he commanded himself and walked on. When Tubby was out of view, Alice rose from her chair, picked up the three spoons, and looked meaningfully at Miss Bracken, who was very quick with a lie. She set the spoons on the table atop *Allie Sloper's Half Holiday* and went away toward the stairs herself – the lamentable end of a too-long day.

"Your room is all atanto, gents," she heard Billson say as she ascended the stairs, and then she heard Smythe call for a bottle of Champagne for the lady. In her room Alice pushed the dresser in front of the door connecting her room to that of Hillman and Smythe. She prepared herself for bed and then knelt at the bedside and prayed that Langdon was alive and well. She let the prayer rest in her mind as she fell asleep.

Some time later, Alice awoke in the moonlit room, unsure of the time and of what had awakened her. Then she heard a soft knock on the door, and she slipped from the bed and walked to it, seeing when she did that the key that had been in the lock earlier lay on the floor, where it had apparently fallen out of the keyhole – a strange occurrence, but no less strange than this midnight visitor. There was another tentative knock. She picked up the key and unlocked the door, opening it a crack and peering out into the dim hallway, seeing a girl dressed in a long black skirt, with glass bangles on her wrist and an embroidered velvet cap. Recognizing her but confounded by her presence, Alice swung the door open, and the girl, holding a finger to her lips, slipped into the room.

"Theodosia Loftus!" Alice whispered. "What on earth…?" But abruptly she knew what on earth, and her heart filled with gladness. "Is he *alive*?"

"Yes, ma'am," Theodosia said, a smile on her face to be the bearer of good tidings.

Alice sat down suddenly on the edge of the bed and wept.

Theodosia put her hand on Alice's shoulder and said, "The Professor found us on the Heath, ma'am, near Wood Pond, past suppertime. He'd come up through the cellar of the old manse and out through the well on the green that's hid by a copse. He was put through some difficulties underground, in the caves as he put it – a bruised rib, like as not, and a piece torn half out of his scalp, but we patched him up straightaway, brandied and fed him, and he's put up at the Spaniards, which I believe you know. He said to say it's the *very same room*, ma'am, that you'd ken what he meant by saying so."

"The Spaniards? Indeed I do know it. I'll go there now. Just you wait for me, if you will, Theodosia." She rose from the bed, but Theodosia shook her head and took her arm.

"You mustn't, ma'am. He fears you'll be followed, and he wants to remain hid until he finds out what's what. Only you and his friends must know he's alive for the moment. No one else, for there's a danger in it, he says. You're to have patience, he says, for he'll come to this very inn at two o'clock this very afternoon, if you'll wait upon him then."

Alice nearly collapsed from the news. She sat down on the bed again. "Today, you tell me? Is it tomorrow, then? Thank God. I'll see him this very day!"

"Yes, ma'am," she said smiling. "It's well past midnight."

"Tell me, Theodosia – the older man, Mr. Frobisher, he was with the Professor?"

"No, ma'am. The Professor was alone. He mentioned the man you speak of, but they were separated and the Professor came on alone. He wants to tell you that if they were to search for Mr. Frobisher they could go down below in the same manner that he came up. And he said that he half believes that there was no accident – that it was done a-purpose – and that he means to discover who if he can. They're to think him dead, do you see?"

"Yes," Alice said, "quite right."

"And one last thing I have to say, ma'am, is that the Professor wonders can you ask the police whether the man Harry was murdered."

"Perhaps it was Harrow?"

"Indeed it must have been. That's all…"

But just then there was a low voice in the hallway – Tubby's voice.

"Peeping at keyholes, are we, Mr. Hillman?" Tubby said, clear but low, as if he was averse to awakening anyone.

Alice and Theodosia sat stock-still. Alice realized abruptly that the door key was in her hand now, and she remembered that it had been lying mysteriously on the floor. Someone – Hillman – must have pushed it from the keyhole in order to peer into the room.

"I suggest that you and I step out into the byway for a brief constitutional," Tubby said. "I admonish you not to call out. I have a proposition for you, in fact, which one man might make more use of than two, if you catch my meaning."

"I do not," Mr. Hillman said, "but I'm a man of business, and I'll listen to you. Mind your manners, however. And you catch *my* meaning, cully, or else catch my knife."

Footfalls dwindled away. Alice stood up and walked to the door, where she put the key back into the keyhole. They spoke for several minutes more, and then Alice asked, "Where is your father, Theodosia?"

"With Mr. Billson, in the kitchen."

"Do they know each other, then, Mr. Loftus and Mr. Billson?"

"No, ma'am. The Professor gave my old dad a note, you see – so that Mr. Billson would know us. We were in luck that he was still up and about, and it was easy for us to slip in quiet like. He knows some of what you know, ma'am, does Mr. Billson."

"I see. Go then, Theodosia. You and your father have a long trudge back to the Heath. I thank you with all my heart. If you see my husband give him my love ten times over, and tell him that we'll carry on at our end as best we can, including looking into Mr. Harrow's death. Tell him that I feared that something was afoot and that I saw an explosion that collapsed the embankment before he was trapped underground. He must be on his guard."

"Yes, ma'am. I'll tell him those things if I can."

"Be off now, and come visit us in Aylesford. I've framed the picture you painted and hung it in the parlor. I treasure it."

Theodosia nodded and shook Alice's hand as if they had just made a bargain. Alice unlocked the door to let her out. The hallway was empty, and she watched until Theodosia had disappeared down the stairs before she shut and re-locked the door, wound a woolen scarf tightly around the doorknob and the key, and then wedged a chair under the knob. She returned to bed and pulled the covers up to her chin, her fears swept away. She said a quick prayer of thanksgiving, shut her eyes, and found that her mind was turning on the Spaniards and on the lovely time that she and Langdon had spent there – a time of great happiness, and not the last such time, by Heaven.

When she was halfway between sleeping and waking she heard what might have been a drawn-out shriek. Now the night was silent, however. She listened to that silence until she heard footfalls passing by in the hall. A door opened and shut – Tubby's door, it seemed to her. Alice considered that he had been in a deadly mood this evening, quite at the end of his rope. She had seen him in a deadly mood before, and she wondered whether Mr. Hillman was lying incoherent in the alley. Then she discovered that she was indifferent to the fate of Mr. Hillman, and she fell asleep.

⟨⟩⟨⟩ TWENTY ⟨⟩⟨⟩
BEAUMONT IN THE MORNING

Dawn was two hours off when Beaumont crept from his room and down the stairs to the fourth floor hallway. The night watch had made his rounds, and the house was quiet. Early morning was the best time of day to be out and about in secret, Beaumont thought, too late and too early both. He knew the lay of the house by now and the habits of many of the people in it, although he could not make out the ways of Mr. Klingheimer, who might be seen coming in or out through any door at any moment, upstairs or down, day or night. Beaumont walked lightly along the hallway carpet to the picture on the wall that hid the key to the lock in Clara's door.

He took out of his pocket a double-sided, hinged key-mold filled with clay and opened it in his hand. He moved the picture aside, removed the key to Clara's room from its niche, laid it onto the bottom bed of clay and closed the hinged box, smashing the upper bed of clay around the key until the excess was forced out of the division between the two parts of the mold. He cleaned off the bead of extruded clay and pocketed it before opening the box, removing the key, cleaning it on his trousers, and putting it back into its niche. He swung the picture over it, listened for a moment to the silent house, and then, with the mold safely stowed in his coat pocket, went straightaway down the stairs. Beaumont had long been a collector of keys, and he knew a man along the river who could fashion a good brass copy as quick as you like. The man wouldn't mind being called out of bed at such an hour, either, if he was well paid for his trouble.

When Beaumont reached the bottom floor landing, he stopped again to listen, hearing quiet footfalls for a brief second and then silence again   the sound of someone crossing a short expanse of floorboards and then stepping onto a carpet. He removed his hat and peered past a newel post to have a careful look. It was Mr. Klingheimer, out and about, just then disappearing down the short hallway that led to the cellar stairs. He was going in to flap his gab at Dr. Narbondo, perhaps – a one-sided conversation, which suited Mr. Klingheimer, who was tolerably fond of his own voice. Beaumont had heard him at it before, talking away six to the dozen with great amusement, laughing even, while Narbondo watched silently through green eyes.

He hurried on his way again, around a turning and down the long hallway to the red door that led to the alley. He reviewed the lie that he would tell Mrs. Skink, but when he entered the final hallway and the red door lay ahead, she was nowhere to be seen. The curtain was drawn across her closet, and he heard the noise of her snoring. It seemed a shame to wake her, and there was no real need to make the sign of a Z on the chalk-board that meant Mr. Filby Zounds had gone out.

It was the work of a moment to step up onto the stool and

fetch the key from the pitcher in order to make another impression in a second clay mold, and then to open the Chubb lock and the padlock before returning the key to the pitcher and going out, closing the door silently behind him. He heard the lock clank, however, perhaps loud enough to awaken Mrs. Skink, and so he hurried away up the alley toward the river. Soon he was lost in the foggy early morning darkness, glad to be quit of the house, if only for a short time.

Finn woke up fast from a deep sleep, sitting bolt upright in his bed in the utter darkness, his heart racing. His mind was off kilter from a waning dream about Duffy's Circus, where he had been an acrobat for many years. It was the usual dream in which he failed to catch the rung and fell, always sure to jolt awake at the moment he hit.

He heard someone speaking, very nearby. It came to him that it was early morning and that it might be Beaumont, come down to the cellar. But surely this wasn't Beaumont's voice. Mr. Klingheimer had said that Narbondo was to be taken away this morning to the mysterious Dr. Peavy's, which might explain it – men setting out to load Narbondo's cart onto the van. It was strangely early, however, and the house was still apparently asleep. There were no kitchen noises from overhead, no sound of anyone working in the lift-shaft, nothing but silence roundabout save for the voice of one man talking, as if to himself.

Finn stood up, put on his shirt and vest and shoes, and then opened the door a crack. The furniture-filled storage room beyond was dark, but the door on the far side of it was open onto the storeroom. He picked up his creel and put on his jacket in order to carry everything with him in case he had to bolt. He went out then, closing the door to his room and following along the edge of the furniture, listening to the cheerfully animated voice – almost certainly Mr. Klingheimer. He was in the laboratory, where the machinery whirred and ratcheted. The foul smell of the mushrooms was heavy in the still air. Finn stopped beside a wardrobe cabinet. He carefully opened its door, willing the hinges to silence. He climbed in, closing the door so that he was completely hidden. Even if Klingheimer walked into this very room, he wouldn't see anything amiss. He settled in to listen.

"I am certain you would make a joyful noise if only you could, Doctor," Mr. Klingheimer was saying, "and I apologize for Dr. Peavy's very necessary experimentation. Rest assured that the man is a medical electrician of the first water and is under strict orders not to damage your... faculties, which I have need of. Now, be so kind as to blink if you understand me. A flicker of the eyelids will suffice." There was a pause, and then Mr. Klingheimer resumed: "You do not wish to blink, I see, although I believe that you can hear and see me well enough. You cast a baleful eye upon me a moment ago, an eye filled with evident distaste, and yet I am the very man who released you from your fungal servitude in the underworld.

"Rest assured that I do not mean to harm you. Quite the contrary, sir. My only desire is that you live, and with your wits intact. You and I will very soon become kindred spirits, one might say, for I mean not only to look into your mind. From that vantage point I intend to see as you see and to know as you know. You will have the same advantage of me, the salient difference being that I can choose to end our communion whereas you cannot. I will be the actor, that is to say, and you will be acted upon."

The musty cabinet was very close, and Finn was warm in the heavy jacket that he had bought from the boy on the road – a long time ago, it seemed to him. His leg was falling asleep, and so he shifted his weight, and the floor of the cabinet creaked, the sound unnaturally loud. He froze where he stood, holding his breath and listening to the silence, willing Mr. Klingheimer to carry on again.

But Mr. Klingheimer asked in a voice meant to carry, "Who is it? Who is there? Show yourself!" Finn remained still, waiting him out. "Ah well," Mr. Klingheimer said at last, "it's to be a game of hide and seek, is it? Give me a moment to complete my task, and then I'll come for you."

He started up again, speaking to Narbondo. "What I offer you, sir, is the opportunity to conjoin your mind with the minds of your fellow – I'll not say prisoners – your fellow travelers, let us say, these mounted, living heads that you see before you, maintained by fungal blood. One of them you might recognize – the one hidden by the gauze veil. He arrived just yesterday, having found his way to London after a prolonged engagement in Kent as a river deity. I have it on good authority that you and he knew each other of old. I'll draw back the veil now, so that you might look upon him and wonder."

Finn wondered whether he should run. Narbondo's box, however, was very near the door, and it would take only an instant for Mr. Klingheimer to step in his way. The man was large – too large to knock aside. Up the ladder, perhaps, if he could evade the man. Finn had quite possibly sealed Clara's fate by climbing into the wardrobe, but there was nothing he could do about it now.

"Your countenance has come quite thoroughly alive, Doctor," Mr. Klingheimer said, "and your flesh seems to be agitated, as if it were engorged with small, scurrying insects. Well, well. You don't care to look upon your stepfather's countenance, although surely it's scarcely recognizable to you. It is wonderfully preserved *beneath* the flesh, however, and the flesh, as we know, is mere stuff. The person dwells within. In a very short time you will be able to gaze into his mind, and he into yours. In that sense you'll have become as a god in your small way. As for the sputum you've vomited up, Dr. Peavy will see that it's swabbed clean. Good day to you, sir."

All was quiet for a time, and then Finn heard the disconcerting sound of footsteps drawing near, then stopping, then going on again. He could not quite tell where the man was. Then he heard a door open and close – the room, no doubt, where he had slept. The footsteps returned, stopping very close by. He should have run. He had missed his chance.

In the voice of a schoolmaster, Mr. Klingheimer said, "Come out, thief."

Finn remained silent, considering what he would do.

"No," Klingheimer said after a long silence. "Not a thief! Here is a fine opportunity to put my powers to the test. Before my mind's eye stands a boy with green stockings and a stout heart. I see… an owl. I see… a coat stained with blood. Are you a desperate rogue, I wonder, or is it the blood of an animal?"

There followed the soft scraping noise of the latch rising, and Finn threw himself hard forward, the door smashing into Klingheimer and knocking him backward over a bench, the man sprawling and grunting. Finn dodged out, Klingheimer's arm making a grab at his ankle, but missing, Klingheimer scrabbling to get up. Finn scarcely looked at Narbondo when he raced through the laboratory – had no desire to – but swarmed up the ladder with his creel over his arm, moving fast – far too fast for Klingheimer to follow.

* * *

It was early yet when Beaumont walked back toward Klingheimer's mansion through a gray fog, turning things over in his mind. He had breakfasted at Rodway's – half a pound of bacon served up on toast and enough hot coffee to drown a cat – and as he swallowed his food it had come into his mind that his stay at Klingheimer's might likely be a short one, what with Narbondo brought into the house and now the boy Finn having come to save the blind girl. And there was the heads and toads and all this upset about the sink-hole and the man underground. There was something afoot, things changing, some deviltry that he had no desire to be caught up in. Howsomever, he told himself, now that the key to the padlock on the red door lay in his pocket he could slip out when he chose to. Perhaps he could find odds and ends of things to take along with him. There was no tearing hurry.

He cut along down the Victoria Embankment, the air reeking from the smoke of the try-pots near the sink-hole melting down mineral pitch. Beyond Blackfriars Bridge a great number of men moved through the reek, laboring to fill the hole before the rest of London fell into it and was swallowed up. Barges loaded with asphalt and rubble came and went, taking full advantage of the tide. Beaumont turned up Temple Avenue and then down a narrow byway that ran along the back of several spacious old houses, relics of London's past, their courtyards invisible behind high stone walls with arched wooden carriage gates.

One of these houses he remembered quite well, because it had belonged to Dr. Ignacio Narbondo himself, and Beaumont had spent a goodly number of weeks within it, if you added the days together. He had spent some small amount of time *under* it, also, for the house had hidden passages below it that led away beneath the city and out along the river – bolt-holes, in a pinch, or for slipping in and out unseen. Narbondo, a secretive man who had been involved in many criminal undertakings, had possessed several houses in and around London, two of them deep in the rookeries, and he had shifted from one to the other so that he might seem to be nowhere and everywhere, looking out through the windows like Bo Peep but rarely seen on the street.

This house would make a snug kip for a man like Beaumont if he had to leave Mr. Klingheimer's quick-like – large enough so that no one would see lamps and candles lit in the recesses of the place, and likely wouldn't care a fig if they did. Two grapnels at either end of a length of two-inch line would do the trick to get him over the wall, the lower grapnel moored to a crate of eatables that he could pull up after.

He slowed his pace now, seeing through the fog that the carriage gate at the back of what had been Narbondo's house stood open several inches. There was the noise of workmen hard at it inside, and now the gate swung wide and two mules came out through it hauling a wagon with low sides. Beaumont stopped dead and moved out of sight behind a piece of wall. He knew the driver – a man named Wilson who worked for Mr. Klingheimer and who had gone along underground just yesterday on the search. It had been he who had found the bit of newspaper, which had perhaps saved the lot of them from Mr. Klingheimer's wrath. This work on Narbondo's house was Mr. Klingheimer's doings, that was certain. A heap of dirt and rock lay atop the bed of the wagon, which made away upriver in the direction of the sink-hole, a contribution no doubt – borrowing from Peter to pay Paul.

The gate remained open, and Beaumont made toward it now, turning his head as he passed to see what was what: an excavation, was what, much like a mine. It angled down into the ground – a sizeable hole, large enough to back the wagon straight down into it, along the edge of the house itself. The rear corner of the house was shored up with heavy beams, and more beams and boards stood in neat piles nearby, alongside a pyramid of cut stone. A stone foundation had been laid around three sides of the hole. They were building a hut, no doubt to hide the mouth of the tunnel: gatehouse meant to be the gate itself. And it was meant to be permanent, too.

A man walked up out of the tunnel now, crossed the courtyard, and began to push the broad gates shut. Beaumont looked ahead of himself and moved on, not looking back, fairly certain that he had not seen the man before and so wouldn't be recognized.

What are you about, old cock? Beaumont asked under his breath, addressing himself to an imaginary Mr. Klingheimer, but as soon as he had voiced the question, the likely answer came into his mind: Klingheimer was setting up shop in Narbondo's abandoned house and yard to bring things out of the land beneath. Deans Court was too difficult an entry, and Hampstead Heath too far away. But right here, a stone's throw from Klingheimer's own house, the man could do his rotten business behind high walls and no one the wiser. When Beaumont had worked for Narbondo, none of the passages beneath the house were so deep as to access the lower reaches of the land beneath. Something must have opened a way – the collapse of the Cathedral, perhaps, the explosion that had opened the great crack in the floor.

Did Klingheimer mean to close the other doors, the dog? Would he lock Beaumont out, the rightful potentate of the world beneath, the very man who had led Klingheimer to the toad forest where Narbondo was imprisoned? It came to him that he, Beaumont, might have sold his birthright for a handful of sovereigns – betrayed his father's secret only to bring shame upon himself out of greed and stupidity. Suddenly enraged, he made a fist and struck himself in the forehead, hard enough to dislodge his hat, although it caught around his neck by the strap and hung there. He had a mind to wrench it off and leap up and down upon it, except that he was far too fond of the hat. The hat hadn't played him false, after all. It was Klingheimer who had played him false, or was setting things in train to do so.

In fact it might be worse than that. Why would a man like Klingheimer allow Beaumont to remain alive at all once he had no need for him? Beaumont knew too much about the underworld, had seen too much of what went on in Klingheimer's cellar of living heads. A careful man would not remain at Klingheimer's house at all now that this was made clear. A careful man would take his bag of sovereigns and count himself lucky to keep his skin into the bargain. He would go underground, east to the sea, that's what he would do – to Margate, where he could enter the eastern reaches of the underworld through the sea caves and never set eyes on the likes of Mr. Klingheimer again.

When he found himself nearing the alley where stood the red door, however, he had given up any idea of immediate flight. The boy Finn and the blind girl Clara were still inside the house, after all. Beaumont had befriended the boy, who had taken no unseemly notice of Beaumont's size, and who had come into London like a hero to save his sweetheart from these low men. Klingheimer could not know that Beaumont had seen the tunnel. Beaumont knew more about his enemy than his enemy knew about him, which was a good thing. But that would soon change, and he must be gone before it did, and he must take Finn and the blind girl with him.

The fog was heavier now, although the sky was white above as if the sun was raveling the fibers of the mist. He saw someone hurrying toward him – Arthur Bates himself, waving at him.

"Avast there, Zounds," he said. "Mr. K. wants all hands to turn out for the search."

"I'm as turned out as can be," Beaumont said. "What search?"

"There's been a boy snooping in the house, a thief, most likely, and he's got out. When the old man left for Peavy's he was fit to be tied."

"What's his appearance, this boy?"

"Middling tall, roundabout fifteen years. Sandy hair. Black shirt and green stockings in his boots. He's quick, too – sneaked past old Mrs. Skink, unlocked the door, and went straight out. She never saw him, the hag. You go down along the river and look roundabout Blackfriars. I'm to search the Temple, although if he's got that far there's no finding him at all, like as not, and good riddance."

Bates turned away in the direction from which Beaumont had just come. Beaumont watched him leave, thinking things over yet again. Had Finn taken the girl with him? For it was clearly Finn who had run. If he had taken the girl, then Beaumont's work in Klingheimer's house was finished. He had no pressing reason to stay. If Finn had *not* run, then the girl was still a prisoner, and Finn was lost to her if they found him. Beaumont had no idea of searching Blackfriars, but went along toward the red door instead. It stood ajar, with old Mrs. Skink standing on the stoop, a vinegar face and her hair like the nest of an uncommonly stupid bird.

"I looked along by the river like I was told," Beaumont said to her. "No sign of the boy."

She squinted hard at him. "I didn't see you go out, Dwarf, and your mark ain't on the board."

"Then you should keep your eyes in your head and not in your pocket. Mr. Klingheimer don't want a blind woman at the gate, especially with thieves in the house. It was me who was at hand when the news broke, which is what you don't know. And the door weren't barred, because the boy had opened it. And you was no doubt asleep, with the doors standing open, so out I went as easy as nothing, just like the boy did, and now I've come back. You're an ugly, worthless, fig of a woman, Mrs. Stink, but you've got a fitting name."

He pushed past her as she began to rail at him, and he made his way upstairs toward the attic. In his head was a presentiment that things were coming apart fast. It was a bit of luck that he had left the door unbarred this morning so that Finn could get out – for that's what must have happened if the boy escaped – and another bit of luck that the unlocked red door would be blamed on Finn and not on Beaumont, although Mrs. Skink had her suspicions. He had seen that in her face. Still and all, she couldn't peach on him, since it would be plain that she wasn't at her post this morning.

He went into his room and was satisfied that all was as it should be. Narbondo would not be back from Peavy's until noon at the earliest, and in the meantime Beaumont intended to lie abed and contemplate on things. He took off his hat and set it on the table, and then removed his coat and hung it across the back of the chair before turning to the window to draw the curtain. There, framed by the casement, was Finn Conrad's face, the wind blowing his hair aside.

TWENTY-ONE

BREAKFAST

When Alice descended the stairs next morning, Tubby and Hasbro were sitting at a table drinking coffee out of a porcelain pot. Miss Bracken was nowhere to be seen, likely still in bed. Neither Mr. Hillman nor Mr. Smythe was about, either. There was a man near the fire stowing away a plate of food as quickly as possible while looking into the morning paper.

"I'll beg a cup of that coffee from you gentlemen if you can spare it," Alice said, sitting down with her two friends.

"Billson purchased the beans from a man just in from Sumatra," Tubby told her, pouring her a cup. "He parched the beans this morning and brewed this pot when he saw us on the stairs. You've never had better, I'll warrant, although it's growing cool. I must say that you seem in a jolly mood this morning. What's afoot?"

"I'll tell you what's afoot in a moment," Alice said, seeing now that Tubby's eyebrow had been split open and that there was a bit of plaster on it. Protruding from his shirt cuff was a quarter inch of bloody bandage, apparently wrapped around his wrist. "Any news, Hasbro?"

"I'm sorry to say there is not. The Board of Works is already far along with the work of filling the sink-hole. The fact that two men are still lost below makes no matter to them, nor did my protests. I sought out Mr. Bayhew as you requested, and he filed papers asking that they desist until rescue efforts had been carried out, but the Board refused. In Bayhew's opinion it's useless. The Board has an immediate responsibility to the public, we're told, and not to individuals foolhardy enough to descend into the abyss."

"Mr. Bayhew is a fine solicitor, and he performed prodigious legal wonders when we were charged with the collapse of the Cathedral," Alice said, "but if determined work on the sink-hole is already underway it would be a miracle if he prevailed over the Board of Works. It was worth an attempt, but I didn't hold out much hope."

A plate of bacon and a dozen fried eggs appeared now along with a fresh pot of coffee and slices of toast. Alice discovered that she was nearly starved. Yesterday she had had no appetite. Today it had returned in force. The man sitting near the fire put down his newspaper, paid Billson, and went out into the blustery morning, the door shutting behind him.

"Shall I tell you what it is now?" Alice asked.

"This instant. We insist," Tubby said, slathering jam on a slice of toast and engulfing half of it in his mouth.

"Langdon is alive," Alice said in a low voice. "He surfaced on Hampstead Heath last night, and wandered into the midst of a gipsy encampment where he was recognized by friends of ours – the Loftus family, who helped us with the hop harvest just a short while ago. You remember them, Hasbro. They put Langdon back together and ensconced him at the Spaniards."

Tubby gazed at her with a look of surprise on his face. "He

surfaced, do you say? That's brilliant news. What of Uncle?"

"Langdon had no knowledge of Gilbert. They were separated in the blast, which was behind them, and the force of it pitched Langdon forward into the darkness. The same was likely true for Gilbert, or so I very much hope. Langdon was injured somewhat in the fall, but he was not buried by the cave-in. He told Mr. Loftus that the world below is quite vast, especially the deep reaches. Langdon failed to find Gilbert, but he *did* find his way out, and so it stands to reason that there's hope for Gilbert as well."

"By God it *does* stand to reason," Tubby said. "I'd stake a good sum on the old man's being alive. There's no one half so game as Gilbert Frobisher. We'd best shift our gaze from the Embankment and fix it on Hampstead Heath, Hasbro. But how do you know all of this?" he asked Alice.

"Theodosia Loftus, the oldest of the Loftus children, came to my room last night."

"It was *she* who knocked upon your door!" Tubby said. "That bilge rat Hillman – not his name, by the way – was lurking in the hallway listening at the keyhole."

"I heard you accost him, Tubby," Alice said. "You went out together directly, I believe."

"Yes indeed. It dawned on me that Uncle's jewelry case had not fallen out of his bag at all, but had been removed and ineptly hidden by those two frauds when they'd gone up to the room earlier. I had a word with the alleged Mr. Hillman in the alley and discovered that the two men are mere spies, intent upon looking into our business. He admitted to the attempted theft of the jewels, by the way, and more, before I was done with him. I'm waiting for Mr. Smythe to come down to breakfast. I believe that the two of you will find our conversation amusing, although not half so wonderful as what you've been telling us."

"We're to keep it a secret," Alice said, "even from Miss Bracken, although it would give her a bit of hope, perhaps. Our enemies currently believe Langdon to be dead, and for the moment it must stay that way."

"They'll have their eye on us in any event," Hasbro said. "We haven't gone away, after all, which we would soon do if we in fact believed him dead and buried."

"Who *is* Mr. Hillman?" Alice asked Tubby. "Or rather *what* is he? I've been told his name is Penny. He's not from Manchester. I know that. The Billsons recognized him as a local man."

But before Tubby could answer, Mr. Smythe appeared on the stairs, looking out of sorts, it seemed to Alice.

"My dear Mr. Smythe!" Tubby said cheerfully, and then sopped up egg yolk with his toast and bit off a great piece, chewing like a satisfied badger.

"What is it?" Mr. Smythe asked. "I'm in something of a hurry."

Tubby swallowed the mouthful and said, "I daresay you are. The delightful Mr. Klingheimer awaits you, I don't doubt. Will you give him my *very* best wishes? Tell him that Tubby Frobisher will pay him a small visit on a particularly dark night in the near future."

Smythe stared at him, apparently struck dumb. He made an effort to compose himself, and said, "I do not take your meaning, sir."

"I believe you do," Tubby told him. "I sent a note by messenger to your Mr. Klingheimer just this morning, telling him that he had been betrayed by a Mr. Smythe and a man calling himself Hillman, although actually named Penny. Mr. Penny had no great desire to open his mind quite so completely to me about the good Mr. Klingheimer's whereabouts, but he was persuaded to do so when his ears began to fall roundabout him like autumn leaves – two of his ears, that is to say. He hadn't any others. Human beings make tolerably bare trees in that regard. He made the mistake of waving a dirk in my face after I gave him a taste of a heavy cudgel. He oughtn't to have done that, do you see? I relieved him of his weapon, ascertained that it was very sharp indeed by trying the edge on his ear joints, and admonished him to comport himself like a gentleman from this point hence."

"You're *dead*," Mr. Smythe said flatly. Then he turned around and went out through the door without another word, the wind blowing a flurry of leaves through it before it banged shut.

"You've disturbed the man deeply," Hasbro said.

"I intended to. I had an interesting conversation with Hillman-Penny."

"Please tell me that you did not actually cut his ears off, Tubby," Alice said.

"Not entirely, no, although it was necessary that I convince him that I would do so with great enthusiasm with very little persuasion. He mumbled through our conversation, unfortunately, due to his teeth being stove in, but in order to save what was left of his ears he confirmed that the Embankment collapse yesterday morning was indeed no accident. The mysterious Mr. Klingheimer ordered it done. It was quite intentional, a successful effort to close the passage to the nether world. I knew that some powerful force was behind all this, do you see? It stood to reason. And so I went to work like a terrier and worried the rat Penny until he gave up the name."

"But was the thing directed particularly against St. Ives and Mr. Frobisher," Hasbro asked, "or were they unwitting victims?"

"That I cannot tell you. Unfortunately our man bolted before I was through quizzing him, and I wasn't up to a chase."

"Did he reveal anything of substance?" Hasbro asked.

Tubby picked up the coffee pot now and filled their cups. "He revealed the location of Klingheimer's residence, very near the Temple. A wealthy man, it seems."

"Well," Alice said, "I don't intend to pay this Klingheimer a visit. And I hope that Smythe won't stir the hornet's nest up afresh when he reports to him. I would rather Mr. Klingheimer assumed that he was successful in his efforts and moved on to other crimes."

"Hasbro is quite correct in stating that the man still has his eye upon us," Tubby said. "If he were moving on to other crimes he would not have sent Smythe and Penny to spy on us. We've stepped into a nest of vipers whether we like it or not, and we cannot stand idle. We know the villain's name now and he knows ours. We can carry the battle into his camp any time we choose."

The street door opened, and the three of them looked in that direction. It was Henrietta Billson, blowing into the room on a gust of wind and bearing a great basket of eggs and another of greens. She shut the door behind her with her foot, wished everyone a good morning, and went toward the kitchen, promising to have Billson prepare a fresh pot of coffee. Before another word was spoken, the door swung open yet again, and to Alice's vast surprise, Mother Laswell, bundled in a vast shawl, came in through the doorway with Bill Kraken right behind her, his hair sculpted into a precipice by the wind and his face hard set. Abruptly it came to Alice that Clara wasn't part of their company, that they had not gone north as planned, and that beneath his cap Kraken had a bandage wrapped around his head, a bloody patch showing through.

"Thank God we've found you," Mother Laswell said to them, breathing hard and hauling off her coat. "We're here to search out Clara Wright and fetch her home."

* * *

They shifted to the great table, where there was room for the eggs and toast and rashers and beans and pudding and pots of coffee and tea that appeared from the kitchen. Tubby settled into a second breakfast, and Alice poured herself another cup of coffee, listening to Mother Laswell tell the story of the treachery at Hereafter Farm and the surprising news that Finn Conrad had followed Clara and the man Shadwell into London – that he must have arrived yesterday.

"He knew that we were staying here at the Half Toad," Alice said. "We've brought along his portmanteau, for he meant to arrive this very day. Why hasn't he come to us?"

Mother Laswell shook her head grimly. She opened a small purse and removed a wrinkled piece of paper, which she lay atop the table for everyone to see. "Finn is looking out for this address," she said. "He might have found it – discovered something there that kept him."

Alice stared unhappily at the drawing of Ignacio Narbondo, but it was Tubby who said, "Lazarus Walk, by God!"

"Do you know the street?" Alice asked.

"Yes, although... This is curious, indeed. Mr. Klingheimer resides there, as I was saying just a moment ago. The odious Penny revealed it to me, and I wondered whether he lied. It must certainly be true, however, for here's the same street, and associated with villainy into the bargain."

"Shadwell, the false policeman, carried this bit of paper – several copies," Mother Laswell said to Alice. "Finn took one along with him. What is this house, then?"

Alice related the story of the collapse of the Embankment, possibly engineered by the shadowy Mr. Klingheimer, and of the suspicious death of James Harrow, and of the land beneath London, and of St.

Ives's surfacing from that land on Hampstead Heath. She paused in her tale, thought for a moment, and said to Hasbro and Tubby, "The explosion *must* have been directed against Langdon and Gilbert then. It wasn't merely to close the passage to the underworld."

"You're in the right of it," Hasbro said. "Otherwise the coincidence beggars belief. It seems to me that Mr. Klingheimer must have engineered a far-reaching conspiracy, with his false policemen and infernal devices. But why this interest in Doctor Narbondo, who is assuredly dead?"

"Perhaps Klingheimer does not know of Narbondo's death," Tubby said.

Alice looked doubtful. "It wasn't reported in the newspapers, because there was no body and because he was a secretive man. He simply vanished, after all."

"*Is* he dead, then?" asked Mother Laswell. Her earlier determination had faded from her face, and she looked merely tired now. "He's been assuredly dead before, my son has. Has no one seen the corpse?"

"No," Alice told her. "But I myself saw him fall into the earth, and the earth close over him again."

Alice paused now, seeing that she had made a mere assumption, and Mother Laswell said, "The Professor apparently fell into a similar hole just yesterday, and yet he walked out alive."

"True, but this handbill merely makes it clear that Klingheimer is actively *seeking* Narbondo," Hasbro said. "There's no evidence at all that he's *found* him."

"Since my son ceased to be … human… and became the creature who calls himself Narbondo," Mother Laswell said, "no one has sought him out unless they were audacious villains, and most often to their own peril, as we know. This Klingheimer will

225

be no exception, I do assure you. If he has an interest in Narbondo, then he has an interest in deviltry. And now Clara and perhaps Finn have fallen into his grasp."

They sat in silence for a moment, during which Henrietta Billson carried away the dishes and brought fresh coffee. There was the sound of someone descending the stairs, and Alice looked up to see Lars Hopeful hauling Miss Bracken's bags, the woman herself coming along behind, wearing her hat. She had managed to make the crow presentable again.

"Ah," said Tubby. "It's Madame Go-Lightly herself, leaving for good and all, by the look of it, God bless her."

Miss Bracken approached the table now, looking stoic, and Alice introduced her to Bill Kraken and Mother Laswell. "Charmed," Miss Bracken said, foregoing a smile of any variety. "The boy Hopeful is seeing me into a hansom cab. I intend to stay at the Midland Grand, St. Pancras. Mr. Smythe particularly recommends it. When… When Mr. Frobisher returns – for he *will* return, mark my words – be good enough to ask him to wait upon me there."

"Are you solvent, Miss Bracken?" Tubby asked, reaching into his coat for his pocketbook. "I mean to say, could you use a ten-pound note to see you through the week? I apologize, ma'am, for having accused you of purloining my uncle's jewel case. It turns out to have been secreted away by your friends Smythe and Hillman."

"I'll take *nothing* from the likes of you," she spat, "and you can save your mealy-mouthed apologies for those who care to listen, which ain't me." Then she nodded to him with theatrical graciousness. "Your uncle is a generous man, sir – I won't say *was* – and I'll do well enough on what he gave me. If he does not return to me in a two-day's time, I mean to board ship for Kingston, where I'll once more be among friends. In that event, please tell him when you see him that I await him there where he found me, pining away for grief."

"I'll do just that," Tubby said, and then he muttered something that Alice couldn't hear, nor wanted to hear.

"If there is any news at all of Gilbert," Alice said, "we'll find you at the Midland Grand. You can depend upon it."

Miss Bracken nodded her thanks, dabbed theatrically at her eyes with a kerchief, glared one last time at Tubby, and turned toward the door, making her way out into the blustery morning with Lars Hopeful trundling along behind her.

"What an extraordinary hat that woman was wearing," Mother Laswell said.

"I rather fancy it," Alice said, "although I don't know that I'd have the courage to wear it."

"What of Finn, then?" Tubby asked, as if he were anxious to avoid any further discussion of Miss Bracken. "No doubt he found the house on Lazarus Walk, but what then? Are we certain that Clara was taken *there*?"

"No," Mother Laswell said. "We're certain of nothing. But Clara and I have a… *bond*, so to speak. We're the both of us psychical beings. I can *feel* that she's nearby. Her powers are uncommon strong. I mean to set out this morning in order to conduct a search in that neighborhood for a stronger sense of Clara's presence."

"I believe that Finn would endeavor to rescue her," Alice said. "If he still lives, he is either in that house or searching for a way in."

Mother Laswell shook her head unhappily. "The boy has saved my life twice now. Indeed he has. Now that we've filled our bellies, we'd best be about our business. I can't stand the waiting."

"Nor can I," said Tubby. "I'm off to the Heath in order to search out this tunnel below the old ruin."

"I know that house on the Heath well enough," Hasbro said. "We played among the rooms when I was a lad, growing up in Highgate. It was abandoned even then. It had a lamentable history."

"Will you help me find Uncle, then?" Tubby asked.

"Happily," Hasbro said. "Given that there's a company of us now, it would seem sensible that we divide our forces, for there's much to be done. And a crowd calls attention to itself, after all."

"Quite right," Alice said. "I expect Langdon to arrive here at the inn at two o'clock this afternoon. Theodosia tells me that he will send a message otherwise. Can we meet again at that hour?"

"With great pleasure," said Tubby. "I have much to ask him."

"In the meantime I intend to look in on the police in order to shed some light on the mystery of James Harrow's death. Langdon isn't satisfied that it was accidental, and we have reason now to agree with him."

"Not alone you ain't going nowhere, ma'am," Bill Kraken said, breaking his long silence.

"You go with her, Bill," Mother Laswell told him. "We'll walk together to Lazarus Walk, and I'll plant myself there until I discover something of Clara."

Kraken fixed his eyes on her and said, "Don't go cutting no capers, Mother. Get the lay of the land, so to say, and leave it at that. We must meet up right here in this very room for a bite of dinner and a chat with the Professor. We can all tell what we've found, and then go in together if we're a-going in."

"Go in *where*, Bill?" Mother Laswell asked him.

"Into this here goddamn Klingheimer's house and take out Clara and Finn Conrad, by God, pardon the blasphemation. And doesn't this Shadwell creature hope I don't get my hands roundabout his vitals."

TWENTY-TWO

AURA GOGGLES

The hansom cab dropped St. Ives at the Tower Gardens in the morning, making a brief stop at a tailor's shop in Hampstead in order to find more suitable clothing. Although it was monumentally unlikely that he had been followed from the Spaniards, he sat upon a bench and looked about himself for a few leisurely minutes as if enjoying the day, which in fact was just what he was doing. He felt surprisingly limber after yesterday's ordeal. The pain from the bruised rib had largely subsided, unless he forgot himself and made an awkward movement. The head wound had turned out to be nothing once the blood and muck were washed away. He put his hand into his vest pocket now and felt the piece of tissue-covered lens that had happily survived his ordeal underground. He unwrapped it and looked through it at the sky, now stained a deep purple, before putting it safely back into his pocket.

The few people roundabout him were going sensibly about their business: nannies pushing prams, the odd pedestrian, a policeman directing traffic at the intersection with a great deal of style, his arms moving almost as if he were dancing. Half a dozen ragged boys ran past on the pavement, the last of them contorting his face at St. Ives and then howling with laughter before snatching at the tail of a slouch of a dog trotting past from the other direction. The dog stopped to allow St. Ives to scratch its head before trotting away again. Aside from the boy and the dog, no one gave him a glance of any sort.

There was a brisk wind, but the sky had cleared and the sun shone, and he found that the sunlight and fresh air suited him after yesterday's sojourn through the underworld. He contemplated upon luck, which he had always considered a silly notion, rationally speaking, and yet this morning he felt lucky to be alive, and there was nothing silly about it.

The clothes he had borrowed from Mr. Loftus were slightly flamboyant but were no sort of disguise. He had decided against that – no false chin whiskers or mustaches or beggarly rags. He would go about London as a free man. He intended to seek out Dr. Pullman's friend Walter Kilner at St. Thomas's Hospital. If he learned nothing useful, he would proceed to Smithfield in order to catch up with Alice and his friends at the Half Toad.

Last night it had seemed a good idea to do some sleuthing – to look into the designs of the men who had made an effort to murder him, if in fact they had. But when he had awakened this morning he realized that he would serve his friends better if he were to lend a hand in the search for Gilbert Frobisher. Do what he might in London, he could not bring poor Sarah Wright back to life, nor did he have any desire to thwart nebulous plots that might have little or nothing to do with him. He had been a rabbit caught in a trap, as had Gilbert, because they had been in the way of that trap. He had got out of it again through sheer chance. A sensible rabbit would dust himself off, count his blessings, and return to his home beneath the hill.

He walked across Lambeth Bridge and along the Palace Road, unhappy with his easy, rabbit-like conclusions. He thought of Sarah Wright's death and the fact that Clara would carry a memory of that horror until the end of her days. He thought of Tubby, who had quite possibly lost his uncle. Gilbert had been more father than uncle to Tubby after Tubby's father had died. There was nothing of the rabbit trap in any of it. The metaphor was facetious, unworthy of his friends. He consciously took it back just as the several towers of St. Thomas's Hospital came into view with their iron scrollwork and narrow, arched windows – merely decorative, apparently, built for the scores of pigeons that flew out of them in great haste and then flew back in again.

He found his way to the Department of Electrotherapy easily enough, where he introduced himself to a forbidding-looking gray-haired dragon behind a small desk. He persuaded her that he was an associate of Dr. Lamont Pullman, who was a good friend of Dr. Kilner. Dr. Kilner was at work in his office, she told him – as usual had been there half the night. The office was close at hand. St. Ives found it, knocked on the door, which was ajar, and stepped in to introduce himself. The office was a clutter of papers and books and odd pieces of electrical machinery, the office of a man who had no leisure to neaten things up.

"Professor St. Ives! Of course," Kilner said, shaking his hand. "I know your work, or some small part of it. I read your recent paper on pipid frogs with great pleasure."

"You're a naturalist, then?" St. Ives asked.

"I cannot call myself any such thing," Kilner told him. "I'm afraid my work here takes up the bulk of my time. I'm a mere dabbler, sir, when it comes to the natural world. But what can I do for you today? You've come out from Kent on some specific errand, no doubt."

"I wanted to ask you about this extraordinary piece of tinted glass, actually." St. Ives produced the thin bit of purple lens that Dr. Pullman had found in Sarah Wright's cottage.

Dr. Kilner held it up before the light of an electric lamp and studied it. "Might I ask where you found it?"

"It was discovered by Lamont Pullman on the floor of a cottage in Kent, a cottage hidden within a woods – Boxley Woods, to be precise. A woman was murdered in that cottage, and this is a piece of mystifying evidence."

"Murdered in what fashion, sir?"

"Her head was surgically removed, the operation apparently undertaken while she was still alive. She had the reputation of being a witch, a benign witch to be certain, but a woman of profound extra-sensible powers. Pullman found this bit of glass beneath a prised-up floorboard in an out-of-the-way place. I surmise that the murderer would have recovered it himself if he'd had the leisure to search for it."

Kilner stared at St. Ives, although without any surprise or horror on his face. "There were no *goggles*, then, to go along with it? Merely this piece of broken lens?"

"Just so. If goggles existed, they were no doubt taken away. Do you recognize it, then?"

"Indeed I do. I produced it."

"So Pullman suspected. He told me of your experiments with the human aura, which two days ago would have sounded moderately fanciful to me."

"There's nothing fanciful about it. I can assure you of that. The human body produces energy in the form of invisible light.

These lenses make it possible to see that light. The quality of the light, to put it simply, reveals a great deal about the physical and mental health of the individual, or so I believe. It's my notion that any number of lenses might be contrived to distinguish various moods, shall we say: sickness and health, criminal intent, what is commonly called love, creative powers. The well is *very* deep, Professor, and I've only plumbed the surface of the waters. To say that there is much yet to learn is to understate the thing. The complexities of the human aura might easily turn out to be akin to the complexities of the human mind."

"Have you ever run across a human being who had the innate capacity to see and assess these auras? A person who would have no need for the goggles?"

"I have not, and I do not believe that any such person exists. Why do you ask?"

"The daughter of the murdered woman, a girl who is apparently otherwise blind, is alleged to see these auras and to understand what they indicate. She can… *see* in other ways also, that have no scientific explanation."

"I would very much like to meet her."

"She speaks only rarely, and only to those she particularly trusts. I was convinced that she was a mute until I was told otherwise by the one person who regularly communicates with her. She can evidently converse with animals, as whimsical as that sounds. She is also alleged to be a human hydroscope of profound powers – an exceedingly sensitive girl. She protects herself from earthly emanations by wearing lead-soled shoes."

Kilner looked hard at St. Ives now. "Are you practicing upon me, sir, with your witches and hydroscopes?"

"I am not," St. Ives said. "I have not witnessed all of these things by any means, but enough to be dumbfounded by what I have seen."

"Then I repeat that I would very much like to meet her if she's amenable to it. She might add a great deal to the little I know about the human aura."

"You've published your results, have you?" asked St. Ives.

"No, sir. The results are tentative – perhaps years away from bearing objective fruit. The lenses themselves are in a state of continual development. The chemical washes that color them are often highly toxic, the chemicals difficult to obtain. And you must understand that the study itself is of no consequence to this hospital, and so is little more than a variety of hobbyhorse. I've only recently contrived lenses that are in any way useful."

"It's a fact that someone donned a pair of the lenses in order to make use of them when he committed the murder. He seems to have questioned her first, perhaps after drugging her with henbane, and it's possible that he utilized the lenses to study his victim during the interrogation. In any event, I assume that he must either have manufactured his own lenses or have borrowed a pair from you."

"He *stole* them from me, in point of fact, although I certainly would *not* have lent him a pair, and he knew that full well. He had no right at all to put them to use."

"*He*, do you say? You know him, then?"

"Assuredly. He was once an associate of mine. He has a morbid interest in the electronic stimulation of the brain, particularly the pineal gland and various layers of the cortex including the seat of memory. He has convinced himself that the pineal gland is the center of second sight. It's often referred to as 'the third eye' in mystical teachings. To my mind he would take a keen interest in your so-called witch and in her daughter. His experimentation on the human brain is perverse, tantamount to diabolism. I cannot countenance the filthy business of trepanning the skulls of living patients merely to prod their brain tissues with electronic stimuli. He is convinced that extra-sensible powers, as you put it, are the result of brain lesions, and that electronic surgery will promote them. It is quite beyond the pale. I'll tell you plainly that it was my doing that led to his being turned away from this hospital. I regret only that I didn't have enough evidence of his illicit activities to involve Scotland Yard."

"You say that he *stole* a pair of these aura goggles? You're certain of it?"

Kilner held the piece of lens up to the light and scrutinized it. "Aye, quite certain. He stole several pairs, and of various types – different chemical washes, you see, although this particular, very deep violet wash produces the most interesting effects so far. He also stole my writings from within the desk that you see before you – those that he could put his hands on. I could not prove that he stole any of it. The lot of it simply disappeared from my office one afternoon. I was angry enough to accuse him of it, however, and he had the temerity to laugh as he admitted it, his face positively satanic. He assured me that he would henceforth deny it."

"Is he capable of murder?"

"Oh, yes. It's possible that he is incapable of *not* murdering. The man is quite depraved."

"Will you tell me his name?"

"I will, although he will confess to nothing if you press him. He operates a private hospital in Wimpole Street. He calls himself a doctor, although he is no such thing. He's a surgeon with a counterfeit degree – probably several of them, although he is quite skilled with a scalpel. His name is Benson Peavy."

TWENTY-THREE

THE TRAVAILS OF MISS BRACKEN

Miss Bracken held her hat tightly to her head as she walked down Fingal Street into the teeth of the wind. She thought about Jamaica, with its warm breezes – never a need for anything but a thin blanket on the bed at night, summer or winter – and she cursed her ill luck, thinking about what she had gained and lost in a little over a fortnight. Gilbert Frobisher was a good old bird, and had treated her kindly. No man had ever done so before, except for a boy she had played with many years ago in better times and who had died of the yellow jack when he was seven years old, leaving her friendless. Now she was friendless again, and in a cold climate.

"You're down in the dumps," she told herself resolutely. "Until you know for *certain*, you know *nothing*, and it's a fool who says elsewise." She wiped a tear from her eye, although it might have been the wind that caused it.

She realized that Lars Hopeful was no longer following her, and she looked back to see him talking to the driver of a hansom cab with a broken-down horse that was unfit for the knacker's yard. The driver had the look of an ape about him. She was no longer a rich woman, perhaps, but there was money in her purse, and she was damned if she would ride up to a posh hotel such as the Midland Grand sitting inside a moving poultry coop towed by a bag of bones. She put her fingers to her lips and whistled at Hopeful, who turned to look in her direction just as a coach reined up before her on the street. Its door opened and Mr. Smythe stepped out onto the pavement.

"Might I be of service, ma'am?" he asked, with a lavish bow. "I'll reveal to you that I left early this morning to take care of a piece of business, but now I've returned to see to your safety. I don't like the look of the fat man who cast false accusations at you last night, and I don't believe that you should be traveling alone in this city with that ruffian afoot."

"Thank you, sir," she said to him, the dregs of her unhappiness disappearing on the instant. "This north wind does get up one's gown. You! Boy!" she hollered at Hopeful, who waved her forward as he handed her trunk up onto the rack of the hansom cab.

Mr. Smythe strode down to where Hopeful was now hefting Miss Bracken's portmanteau, shouldered Hopeful out of the way, had a word with the driver, and gave him a coin. The driver tipped his cap, handed down the trunk, and set out up the road. Smythe returned, followed by Hopeful and the two pieces of luggage, and very soon Miss Bracken found herself in quite an elegant coach, driven by a stilt-legged man in a red bowler, traveling down Farringdon Street, and seated next to Mr. Smythe. She marveled for a moment about how one's luck can change on the instant.

She opened her bag, hidden by her person, and peered inside in order to have a look at her prize – the ivory jewelry case that she had taken from Tubby Frobisher's portmanteau this very morning while he sat downstairs greasing his face with rashers. The gold shone with a high polish, and she longed to look at the diamonds within, but caution advised against it. Gilbert would not have begrudged them to her. She knew that for a certainty.

She closed the bag and smiled at Mr. Smythe, who looked her up and down, and said, "You're at loose ends, then, ma'am? No friends or family in the whole of England, I believe you said."

"That's very close to being true, sir, although I believe I can count you as a friend, since you were kind enough to offer your friendship last night. I have it in my mind to stay at the Midland Grand, St. Pancras. I'm told that gold leaf adorns the walls and that there is an astonishing hydraulic lift. I intend to await Mr. Frobisher in a room with a view of the station so that I can see the trains come and go."

Mr. Smythe was silent, his face grave as he stared out through the window at the busy morning traffic. After a moment he shook his head and said, "You'll wait a tolerably long time, ma'am. Mr. Frobisher's body was found underground just this morning along with that of Professor St. Ives. Both of them were crushed. It grieves me to say so, for they were good men, especially Mr. Frobisher, who left his mark on the city. He'll be sorely missed."

Miss Bracken scarcely comprehended the words, and so said nothing as they settled into her mind. She began to sob, then, and Smythe comforted her by putting his arm around her shoulder and drawing her toward him.

"I suppose I mustn't go to the hotel as I'd thought," she said. "It's too dear by half if I'm indeed alone and hopeless. Can you suggest a small inn? I'd be happy if it were clean, but I make no other demands."

"I cannot," Smythe said, as the coach careered around onto

Fleet Street. "I won't happily allow you to remain alone in this very dangerous city. I offer you my protection, ma'am, if you'll agree to accept it."

"*Well*," she said, looking at him now. He wasn't an ugly man at all, just a trifle hard, perhaps, jowly and one eye a bit askew. In his morning coat and frilled shirt he looked very much the gentleman. She was already in his debt; it would be uncivil to spurn his offer. "I'd be happy for your protection, sir. It is my idea to return to Jamaica at the first opportunity, unless I'm persuaded otherwise."

"Then I'll do my best to persuade you."

They turned up Whitefriars Street now, and then around onto a byway that ran between a scattering of lavish homes enclosed by high walls and iron gates. The coach drew up outside one of the richest, a many-windowed mansion that might have housed ten families. There were curtains drawn across most of the windows – not a cheerful house, it seemed to Miss Bracken, although she couldn't quite say why.

"Whatever place is this?" she asked, seeing two men lounging within the dim confines of a carriage house. One of them stood up, and she was shocked to see that it was Mr. Hillman – or at least that it appeared to be, although his forehead was wrapped in a bandage.

"This is my own domicile," Mr. Smythe said. "Elegant, ain't it?"

"You told me that you were a commercial gent," she said, "in from Manchester."

Hillman came down the drive and unlatched the gate, looking in through the window of the coach with a broad smirk visible through the bandages. Two of his teeth were missing. She heard him laugh out loud.

"That was my little lark," Smythe said, grinning at her. "I'm actually a non-commercial gent from Shoreditch."

"And I dare say this is another little lark, this grand house. I'll ask you to let me out of the coach, sir. I've changed my mind and will make my way to the hotel after all."

"Will you now? And I tell you that you've come home at last. Better than any hotel. You'll find it amusing here, I dare say. Nothing is as it seems in Mr. Klingheimer's house, ma'am. Things are topsy-turvy like unless you're one of the regular crew. You'll learn to like it, I'll warrant, and you'd best believe *I* will. I'll learn the both of us to like it."

Hillman had swung the gate open and the coach began to move. Miss Bracken threw herself sideways, pushed the door open, and attempted to fling herself out of the coach, but Smythe grabbed her arm to stop her as Hillman lunged at the door and pushed it shut again. She began to scream, attempting to pull away from Smythe, seeing that the gate still stood open, although it was fast swinging closed. Smythe swarmed over her, however, smashing his hand over her mouth and hauling her back onto the seat as the coach turned sharply up the drive.

She reached up to her hat and snatched out the long hatpin that secured the crow, and with all her force she stabbed it into Smythe's stomach. It was quite sharp and it pierced his shirt before it pierced his flesh. She yanked it out and stabbed him again and again, leaning into it in order to bury it deeply, hoping to puncture his vitals. The heart was more to the point if one wanted to kill the man, but a rib would turn the pin aside or break it....

She curled forward now, making a ball of her head and shoulders so as to make herself less vulnerable as he yanked hard at her collar, cursing at her, his spittle showering her neck. He let go of her and clutched himself, gasping in pain and rage, and her final desperate thrust went into his right hand, stopping hard against bone. His mouth opened in a hoarse gasp as she began to scream again, and with his left hand he hit her hard on the side of her head, her hat flying off. His hand closed upon her neck now, pressing her head back and choking off her screams. The coach lurched to a stop, the carriage house doors closed, and as she fought to draw breath, she saw that Smythe's foot had pinned the crow to the floorboards, flattening it, and that a wad of cotton was thrust through its neck where its head had been.

TWENTY-FOUR

OUT OF THE FRYING PAN

St. Ives descended from his cab in Cavendish Square and set out along Wigmore Street considering what he might accomplish by visiting the nefarious Dr. Peavy, given that it was possible at all to do so. Speaking of anything related to Sarah Wright might be deadly, especially in Peavy's own lair, so to speak: the conversation with Kilner had made that apparent. He contemplated making his way to the Half Toad and then returning later with Tubby and Hasbro. Tubby could act the lunatic easily enough to make their visit plausible, and with two men at his back, St. Ives could be more forthright in his discussion with Peavy.

His discussion regarding *what*, exactly? Certainly he would have to be subtle. Peavy would be less inclined to reveal anything – less inclined to talk at all – if confronted by three men, whereas Peavy's apparently brazen self-assurance might betray him into an indiscretion if he were confronted by one.

He turned up Wimpole Street, walking in a leisurely fashion, crossing Queen Anne Street, and, near the corner of New Cavendish

Street, seeing the Elysium Asylum opposite, its elegant grounds deserted, its gates closed. It was an austere, squarish, three-storied structure built of stone, the heavy mullions in the iron-framed windows perhaps serving as bars. The window in the tree-shaded gatehouse stood open, and the shadow of a human head was visible in the dim interior. Surely there was no risk in chatting up the gatekeeper. St. Ives stilled any craven voices remaining within his mind, waited for a coach and a hay wagon to rattle past, and then strode purposefully across the street. He could see the face of the man inside the gatehouse now – a stout, short, balding man in spectacles who appeared to be upward of seventy years old, no sort of threat, certainly.

"Good day," St. Ives said through the window, upon which the man looked up at him and smiled agreeably.

"I'll go so far as to call it a splendid day, sir," the man said. "Indeed it is. How might I be of service to you, Mr...?"

"Broadbent," St. Ives told him.

"And why have you decided to visit Elysium, sir?"

"My wife and I are rather desperate to find a means of caring for my wife's brother. He is quite mad, do you see, although harmless. We've quartered him for a year now, thinking that it was in his best interests to be among familiar faces, so to speak – that we might improve the state of his mind. But we've grown weary of it. The thing is impossible. It's apparently not in *our* best interests to care for him, to make my meaning plain. I've lost the ability to find suitable platitudes and euphemisms, I'm afraid. We're at the end of our tether."

"That's often the way of it," the gatekeeper said. "Most people are essentially kind, I've found, but in cases such as you describe it's an ill-informed kindness, and the result is that the lunatic's inevitable descent drags those around him under. They cannot swim against the tide, alas."

"I'm quite persuaded of it."

"You would like to have a look at Elysium Asylum, then?"

"Inside and out, if you please, although I can already see that the outside illustrates the name of the hospital nicely."

"There is a serenity in the grounds, sir, without a doubt. Their salutary effect on the troubled mind is often instantaneous. I'll call for an attendant, Mr. Broadbent." He pressed the button of a doorbell, picked up a speaking tube, listened for a moment, and asked that an attendant come to the gate. A silent minute passed before a man in a white laboratory coat issued from the front door of the hospital. He shut the door behind him and strode down the walk to the gate, which he opened with an iron key that hung about his neck.

"In you go, Mr. Broadbent," the gatekeeper said pleasantly. St. Ives rather liked the man. Certainly there was nothing suspicious about him, although St. Ives had the distinct feeling that he had seen the attendant – that he had known him somewhere in the dim past.

"Have we met before?" St. Ives asked the man as he locked the gate behind him. "Your countenance is familiar to me."

"No, sir," he said, looking into St. Ives's own face. "I believe that I heard Lester say that your name was Broadbent?"

"Just so. And yours?"

"William, sir. I've never met anyone named Broadbent, although I knew a Mr. Narrows when I was a child – my tutor for a period of months, and my brother's also, until he bolted with the cook – the tutor, I mean, did the bolting. My brother is dead."

He followed a gravel path through the gardens, informing St. Ives that they had been designed by Capability Brown himself, late in life. The many trees were perfectly enormous, two gigantic beeches with yellow leaves shading the hospital roof. A number of small maples, blazing red, stood in flowerbeds among clumps of purple verbena flowers and velvet-brown helenium. A sudden gust of wind blew through, generating a fall of beech leaves and shaking the flowers on their stalks. St. Ives noted that the lawns were mostly clear of leaves, however, as if they had been raked this past half hour.

The park-like grounds were so pleasant in their beauty that St. Ives wondered whether Dr. Kilner had been altogether honest in his condemnation of Benson Peavy. There was some competitive jealousy, perhaps – bad blood that had been left to fester, if blood could be said to fester. When they strolled along the side of the house, St. Ives saw that there was a cellar to the place, the low windows mostly hidden by a wall of the same gray stone that made up the walls of the house. A heavy plume of dark smoke rose from a chimney at the rear of the house, and he could see that the chimney extended to the level of the cellar, where there was a broad iron door, no doubt leading to a vast coal scuttle. Behind the building lay a paved half-circle large enough for a coach and four to turn around on, as well as a high gate that evidently let out onto a by-way.

A van and a Berlin carriage were parked in the half-circle, the van hailing from "Waltham's Goods and Parcels" according to the sign painted on the side. The driver of the van, a man in a red bowler, sat atop the box smoking a pipe while two men unloaded parcels from the back, one of them carrying a cloth-covered dome some eighteen inches in height, a bird cage, perhaps, or the cage of a small animal. His companion closed the rear door of the van and said something to the driver, who nodded. St. Ives watched as the man with the covered cage went in through a rear door. Near it, was a heavily barred cellar window, the visible corner of which showed a light behind it. There was nothing necessarily suspicious about a cellar, and barred windows were by no means out of place in an asylum, but…

His musing was interrupted, however, as his mind once again

labored to recall where he had seen the attendant's face. It had very nearly come to him, and was hovering at the edge of his mind. Certainly he knew the man. His face was badly pock-marked, and he had small eyes looking out of his green-tinged face with a cunning look about them that might easily predispose people against him. St. Ives followed the now-silent man up the several stairs to the front entry door, which was locked. A figure appeared beyond, a man with a key, who opened the door and then stepped aside to allow St. Ives and the attendant to enter. He locked the door again, dropping the key into his coat pocket, and then sat down at a nearby desk, where a magazine lay open.

The interior of the large lobby contained chairs and tables set among potted plants and small cases of books. Landscape paintings, at least two by Richard Wilson and worth a great deal of money, hung on the walls among lesser paintings, all of them illuminated by the autumn sunlight through the windows. On the far wall, along the west-facing windows, stood a long dining table set with candles. It was lavishly set with plates, glasses, and cutlery. A number of men and women sat in the chairs, dozing, reading or affecting to read.

One man suddenly shrieked with laughter over the newspaper in his hand, and then tore it violently in half and dropped it onto the floor – a copy of the *Times*, it appeared – and then began to weep. St. Ives saw that a woman, perhaps eighty years old, played at blocks at a broad double-sided library table, a teacup and teapot precariously close to her very active elbow. She piled the blocks haphazardly and then knocked them down again, putting her hand coyly to her mouth as she watched them fall. Across from her an old gentleman clad in a well-maintained army officer's uniform shifted a phalanx of tin soldiers and miniature cannon about the tabletop, his free hand holding a pince nez to his eye.

"Hello, Major," St. Ives said. "I hope I find you well today."

"Major John English, Scarlet Lancers, sir." He looked up fiercely at St. Ives. "Sixteenth Regiment, Battle of Goojerat. Was you there?"

"A bit before my time," St. Ives said to him. "I've read about it, though. There was great glory to be had that day."

"No end of it – death and glory both." He lost interest in St. Ives and studied his artillery, his hand hovering over the horse-drawn cannon.

The people sitting roundabout paid St. Ives little mind. It might have been the lobby of a seaside hotel, full of eccentrics. The attendant moved off across the room, informing him that men lived in the south wing and women in the east, fraternizing in the lobby only when supervised. They entered a corridor of rooms – the south wing – some of them with their doors standing open and people sitting in beds or on stiff wooden chairs in the corners. In one room a man in an Egyptian hat smoked a pipe, his thumbs twiddling rapidly. A raucous scream sounded from somewhere distant, ending in a loud sobbing that dwindled away, and the twiddling man leered at St. Ives and nodded slowly with implied meaning, although what it implied was impossible to make out.

"They're allowed to smoke while lying abed?" St. Ives asked the attendant. "Isn't there some risk of their lighting the bedclothes afire?"

"They're closely watched, sir, and allowed to smoke if the door is ajar, the more problematic cases, not at all."

"Has this always been an asylum?" St. Ives asked as they walked along the corridor.

"No, sir. The house was converted to a hospital after the Lunacy Act in forty-five. There was a need for genteel quarters then, with the bad old ways gone forever and the hospitals being torn down. Dr. Peavy has had it for eight years now, and has made improvements of his own."

The doors ahead of them were closed. There was nothing more to be seen.

"We're at the end of it, Mr. Broadbent," the attendant said, his face half turned away. "This wing anyway. Would you like to have a look at the kitchen?"

"I wonder if Dr. Peavy is in?" St. Ives asked. "I'd prefer simply to speak to him. The hospital is more than adequate, actually."

"The Doctor is in if he's not indisposed," the attendant said. "We'll proceed to the kitchen and dining area, if you will, and I'll tell one of the scullery boys to inquire. Dr. Peavy is a busy man, however. It's always wise to make an appointment, sir."

Following along again, St. Ives said, "I was told by my wife's Aunt Leticia, who is well known to Dr. Peavy, that he might be available if I mentioned her name."

"Aunt Leticia it is, sir," the attendant said without turning around. On they went, into the lobby again where things were carrying on apace. It was there that the attendant's identity came to St. Ives like a cloud rolling away from the sun. His name was not William at all, but was Willis, Willis Pule. When St. Ives had last seen Pule some ten years ago on Hampstead Heath, the man had been maniacally insane, capering and shrieking. At the end of that long, unlikely evening, Pule lay comatose in a dogcart full of dead carp, the cart driven away into the night by none other than Doctor Ignacio Narbondo himself.

St. Ives's apprehension of danger heightened, and it came into his mind that he had failed to send a note to the Half Toad. He had asked Theodosia to promise Alice that he would. No one on earth knew where he was.

They entered the enormous kitchen, which smelled of cabbage and boiling potatoes. "Wait here, if you please," Pule said, and he walked away across the room to where a hulking young man labored over a heap of dirty dishes. His demeanor resembled that of an unhappy mountain gorilla. Pule said something to him, and the young man scowled at St. Ives before going out through a side door.

Pule returned, saying, "Jimmy's gone to inquire. It shouldn't take long before you have an answer." He leaned back against a long wooden table between St. Ives and the door to the lobby. A stout, grizzled man sliced up a quarter-side of beef with a long knife nearby.

Pule's face didn't reveal anything about his thoughts, and there was no real indication that the man knew him – except, thought St. Ives, that he had lied about his name. Was it coincidence that Pule had ended up in this particular madhouse? Or were Narbondo and Peavy related in some sense? Certainly they both carried out insidious medical experiments…

"You mentioned that you had a brother," St. Ives said to him, this new possibility just now entering his mind.

"Yes, sir, dead these past four years."

"I'm sorry to hear it. I ask because you look quite familiar to me, as I said. What was your brother's name, if you don't mind my asking?"

"Not at all, sir. Willis was his name. Willis Pule."

"*That* solves the mystery," St. Ives said. "I knew him, do you see. I'm sorry to hear of his death."

"Yes," Pule said. "A great tragedy to be sure. We looked much alike, although he was a year older."

The gorilla-like scullery boy appeared in the doorway, nodding and waving them forward, and they set out down a corridor lined with potted plants that ended in a stairway.

"Dr. Peavy's at work in the cellar," Pule said. "Aunt Leticia must have been the byword." At the top of the stairs, Pule said, "Stay here, Jimmy, in case the Doctor has need of you. He mentioned wanting something from the chemist not long ago."

Jimmy nodded and did as he was told. St. Ives followed Pule down a broad, well-lit stairs, looking down onto the top of his head. It appeared for all the world as if he had thread-like silver wires protruding from his scalp. Had he been victimized by Peavy? Certainly no one would be a willing participant in brain experimentation.

Then he wondered whether Pule had lied to him about having a brother – that he had recognized St. Ives from the first. If he had, of course, it might mean nothing at all. Dr. Peavy would scarcely be aware of Pule's grievances. Still... He was certain that he could dispose of Jimmy, despite his evident strength, if he made a surprising, determined rush up the stairs and simply bowled through him, then straight out the door and around to the rear, where the alley gate stood open. But he could scarcely return with his friends after doing so. This entire venture would come to nothing.

They reached the bottom landing now, and turned up another corridor that led to a bright doorway. St. Ives followed Pule into what turned out to be a large surgical theater, on the floor of which a thin man who might have been thirty-five years old manipulated a series of wires that ran into a large, glass-fronted box on wheels, something that might have transported a zoo animal. The glare of the lamps obscured whatever it was that lay beyond the glass. A jolly-looking man sat in one of the theater seats, looking very much like the brothers Cheeryble out of *Nicholas Nickleby*. He stood up and bowed ceremoniously to St. Ives, and then stepped down the several stairs and extended his hand.

"Doctor Peavy, I presume," St. Ives said, shaking it.

"Jules Klingheimer is my name, sir. Dr. Peavy is at work yonder. Do I have the pleasure of speaking to Professor Langdon St. Ives?"

"Indeed," St. Ives said.

"I've been keen to meet you for a good long time, sir. I feared that you were lost underground, however."

"I found my way out, in fact."

"I'm relieved to hear it. Were you much knocked about? Your head has taken a shrewd blow, I fear."

"That and sundry bruised ribs."

"A tolerably small butcher's bill, thank goodness. You supped well underground, I don't doubt."

St. Ives looked at the man, trying to make sense of this odd statement.

"You have the look of a man who ate a sandwich while exploring the underworld – ham and pickled onion, I'd guess, with mustard." He paused to let this take effect. "I see that I've baffled you, sir. It's merely my idea of what people commonly call 'fun.' Let me introduce you to Dr. Peavy. The man behind the glass window you know fairly well, I believe   our old friend Ignacio Narbondo, as alive as you and I, although ungrateful, alas."

St. Ives followed him, noting that the lane to the open door was clear. Pule was looking into the box on wheels, his body shadowing the glass now, so that St. Ives could see into it. St. Ives spun around without a word and sprinted toward the door, cursing himself for a fool. There was a shout, but he didn't look back. He took the stairs at a dead run, picturing Jimmy waiting at the top, and how he'd hit him. There Jimmy stood, feet planted wide, arms raised like a wrestler.

St. Ives hit him square on, running full tilt, as if no one at all blocked his way. Jimmy slammed sideways, hopping on one leg as he tried to find his balance. St. Ives spun around, his momentum diminished by the collision, and he shouldered Jimmy hard on the back, so that he flew forward, into the arms of Willis Pule, who went over backward, the two of them rolling down the stairs in a heap.

St. Ives was away again, running hard, through the kitchen door and toward the lobby. The man cutting up beef stared at him with a look of surprise on his face, and St. Ives, seeing the knife, yelled, "Fire!" at the top of his lungs. "The cellar is burning! Flee for your lives." The man gave him a stupefied look, but did nothing at all, and St. Ives snatched up a heavy wooden rolling pin and went straight past him into the lobby, his eye on the man at the desk, who was rising now, no doubt having heard the shouting in the kitchen.

St. Ives slowed to a hurried walk, nodding pleasantly. "Give me the key, sir!" he commanded, but the man dodged away, and St. Ives was forced to knock him down. He yanked the key out of the man's coat and leapt to the door, hearing the sound of a ruckus, probably in the kitchen. He stepped out and closed the door, taking a precious second to lock the door behind again, just as Pule and Jimmy rushed wildly into the lobby. He started around to the rear of a building, but saw immediately that the lanky man in the red cap – the driver of the van – was drawing the gate closed. St. Ives changed direction and walked briskly away toward the gate. The key in his pocket was half the size of the iron key that Pule had used to unlock the gate earlier. Could he scale the fence? Perhaps with a running start, although if he failed on the first attempt they would have him.

Then he saw that the gatekeeper was already unlocking the gate. He waved at St. Ives as he swung it open. St. Ives pitched his rolling pin into the verbena, wondering what had happened to Jimmy and Pule.

"Here you are again, Mr. Broadbent," the gatekeeper said as he slipped the big key into his trousers pocket. When he removed his hand it held a pistol. He pointed it at St. Ives, shutting the gate behind him without looking back at it. He gestured toward the asylum with the pistol, the smile quite gone from his face now, and St. Ives knew absolutely that the old man would shoot him if he disobeyed.

TWENTY-FIVE

BOW STREET POLICE STATION

Alice and Bill Kraken parted company from Mother Laswell on Fleet Street, the two of them bound for the newly built Metropolitan Police Station on Bow Street, Covent Garden, and Mother away down Whitefriars Street toward the river, in search of emanations in the environs of the infamous Mr. Klingheimer's house on Lazarus Walk. They would meet at the entrance to Temple Church an hour hence, and then, if they missed the appointed time, at the top of the following hour.

"You take care, Mother," Bill Kraken said. "This ain't no time for cutting capers. If you see the man Shadwell, make certain he don't see you. Lie low. That's the byword, and we'll all come home safe. I wish you had a pistol in that there bag of yours."

"I've given up pistols, Bill. You know that," Mother Laswell said to him. "I'll take particular care. As for Shadwell, he certainly believes I'm dead. You do the same, Bill. Heed your own advice." They stared at each other for a moment as if finding it difficult to part, which was something that Alice understood very well. As she watched Mother Laswell walk away, she wondered whether Hasbro's notion of dividing their forces was indeed a good idea after all. They were spread thin, as the saying went, although surely there was little danger to her and Bill, who were merely chatting up the authorities for the particulars of James Harrow's death, which should be a simple business.

They continued along the Strand now, and up Wellington Street, garnering odd glances from the people they passed. Alice was careful to walk beside Kraken, who had the habit of following behind when he accompanied Alice, as if he didn't want to presume upon their friendship. She was anxious to avoid giving anyone the idea that she was being followed by a dangerous madman. He had a resolute look on his face, his eyes squinting, his fists clenched, his mouth working, his hair wild. It was a dangerous, rope's-end look, as if he might break out at any moment into a rash act, which he very well might.

"I have a plan, Bill, for dealing with the police," she said to him as they drew in sight of Bow Street Station, newly built of stone and with a low iron fence around it. An officer stood outside the door, and there were farm barrows moving past on the street – Covent Garden market starting to clear out, most of its business done in the early morning hours.

"I'd be happy if you allow me to deal with this matter of James Harrow. It won't take but a moment for me to learn all there is to know."

"I won't lose sight of you, ma'am, not on your life. If you're a-going inside that there station, then so am I."

"It's a *police* station, Bill. I couldn't be safer. You, however, have much to lose if you run afoul of the police and were taken up. It would be the end of me if that happened. I don't know what I would do. Think of what you told Mother not ten minutes ago about lying low. I'm asking you to heed your own advice, just as she did."

After a long moment he nodded curtly and said, "I'll stand out front on the street, then, if that's orders, and watch the door for you to come out. They can't take a man up for standing in the road."

"Yes they can, Bill. They can do as they please. You'll find yourself in Newgate Prison if you don't look out. There's a coffee house down the way. You can see its sign hanging over the door. Wait for me there, if you please."

"Aye," he said, nodding again and moving away, shambling past the policeman, who looked him over with a scowl, his hand on the handle of the truncheon hanging from his belt.

"He's in my employ," Alice told the policeman cheerfully. "He's harmless."

"Yes, ma'am," the policeman said, doffing his high hat, his demeanor changing on the instant to a solicitous grin. "Just as you say."

She got that response often enough – the unearned appreciation of men who admired her appearance. She didn't find it flattering, but it was sometimes useful. She entered the building, thinking about male gallantry and female charm as she made her way to a desk with a harried-looking police sergeant sitting behind it. There were two people queued up in front of her – a distraught woman who was wringing a pair of gloves and trying to talk past a small, stout man who told her to "wait her bleeding turn," while he explained to the sergeant that a man on a horse had forced his cart into a post and broke the cart and the wheel into the bargain. "I want compensation," he said with a heavy nod of the head. "I mean to have it."

"Where is this villain?" the Sergeant asked him blandly.

"He just kept on, didn't he? Didn't look back. Not for a moment."

"Then there's nothing we can do for you, sir."

"But who's to compensate me? I have the right to compensation."

"The *right*, do you say? You have the right to be thrown into the street for being a damned ugly, slab-sided villain. *Compensation*, he says! Off with you now. Next! Yes, ma'am, step forward."

The glove-wringing woman pushed forward now and in a broken voice told the sergeant that her young son had disappeared, describing him in a way that might apply to half the boys on earth. He took down the information impatiently, and then asked, "The boy's name?"

"Charles Pickney, officer."

"Perhaps he was taken up by the police," the sergeant said, and he looked through a long list of names on sheets of foolscap before him.

"No, sir," she said. "He's not been taken up. He's a good boy."

"They're all good boys, ma'am, until they prove otherwise. As I said, his name is not on the list. That decides the matter. Move along now, my good woman," he said, waving her off. "Next!"

Alice watched the woman wander away in a state of obvious confusion and grief. Last night it had been Langdon who was missing, and she recalled her empty helplessness and despair as she lay there in the darkness thinking about it. She wondered what she might say to the woman that would help her, but nothing came to her. To the sergeant she said, "A friend of mine has gone missing, also. His name is James Harrow, and he is associated with the British Museum. He was allegedly kicked by a horse near the Swan Lane Pier, the night before last, his body taken away by the police. I'd like to verify that this is true and to discover where the body was taken. His sister has found it impossible to learn meaningful details of the event or the whereabouts of his body."

The sergeant nodded and looked at his list again – a long list. "No such name here, ma'am. Wait a moment if you will, and I'll ask Joe Matthews, who works along the river." He arose and went off, passing through a door, from which he reemerged a minute later. "Joe tells me that your man is missing, as reported by his sister in Chiswick, like you said. His wagon was burned alongside the river. His body would have been conveyed to a dead house in the immediate area."

"We were told that the body was taken away by the police. Wouldn't there be a record of it?"

"There should be, ma'am, but there is not. His body would have been conveyed to a dead house, like I said, but Joe Walton didn't hear of it."

"Where are the dead houses?" Alice asked.

"They shift about, ma'am. People aren't fond of 'em, you see. A shed back of a church, perhaps, or the basement of a boarding house that's paid a fee by the Board of Works till the tenants move out because of the stink of the bodies. The Board can tell you better nor me. That's their lookout. It's right up the way, near Admiralty Arch."

"I'll pay them a visit," Alice said. "Thank you, sir. You've been helpful."

She moved away, the line having grown to six behind her, and she heard the sergeant's, "Next!" as she pushed open the door.

She found Bill Kraken pacing on the pavement outside the coffee house, dodging pedestrians, and the two of them set out at once for the Board of Works, which was a matter of ten minutes' walk under the windy blue sky.

Kraken entered the building along with her this time and sat down in a wooden chair by the door to wait. Alice was greeted by a small and very serious woman named Mrs. Green who asked whether she wished to make an official inquiry, to which Alice asked once again after James Harrow's body, whether it had been conveyed to a dead house, probably in the City and somewhere near the river.

"We're not fond of the term 'dead house,'" Mrs. Green told her. "There are in fact three *morgues* in the general vicinity of the Swan Lane Pier, however."

At that moment a small, narrow-faced man sitting at a nearby desk interrupted, suggesting to Mrs. Green that it was more pressing that she complete the monthly roster and that he would be quite happy to reveal the location of Mr. Harrow's remains.

"Yes, Mr. Lewis," Mrs. Green said, and went away, presumably to do as he asked.

Alice looked at the man attentively enough so that he became visibly flustered. The last time she had seen him had been through a pair of opera glasses while standing on the deck of the *Hedge-pig*, moments before the collapse of the Embankment.

TWENTY-SIX
THE PRISONER

"Am I a prisoner, then?" St. Ives asked the man whose name was Klingheimer.

"No, sir. You are merely detained in this room for a brief time. I ask your pardon for Dr. Peavy's hasty actions. He is sometimes intemperate when he feels threatened."

"I threatened no one," St. Ives said.

"And yet you ran when you were confronted."

St. Ives shrugged. "It seemed to me that *I* was the one who was threatened." The man's skin was an unhealthy milky green, much like Pule's, although not so pronounced. St. Ives glanced at the several wall sconces, but none had a green shade. There was a faint stink in the air, also – the smell of the fungi, without a doubt. It came to him that Klingheimer must ingest the things, and he wondered whether there might be a narcotic quality to them.

A tiny chime sounded, and Mr. Klingheimer removed his pocketwatch from a vest pocket, glanced at it, and then showed it to St. Ives. "A Patek Philippe," he said. "It's an extravagance, but a man must sometimes satisfy his material desires. I could not resist the perpetual calendar. The watch is warranted to be running a hundred years hence."

"Someone will be happy to hear it chime in that dim age, no doubt," St. Ives said. "I'll repeat what I said a moment ago: Dr. Peavy had no reason to suspect me of wrongdoing."

"Dr. Peavy is a man who takes considerable risks. In his zeal to get at the nature of things he is unfortunately 'careless of the single life,' to quote Mr. Tennyson. I assure you that he is a savant, and the results of his experimentation more than justify his indiscretions, although they encourage a certain amount of secrecy."

St. Ives looked past him. He could see a darkening sky through a west-facing cellar window. "'Results,' as you call them," he said, "rarely justify indiscretions that are careless of the single life. Evil most often comes from that sort of indiscretion. Mr. Tennyson would be the first to agree, and to be doubtful about the abuse to his poetry."

"I have no notion of evil as such. Our widely varying notions of good and evil are the central irrationality of humankind – the antithesis of truth, a weakness."

"You sound very sure of yourself."

"I have every reason to be sure of myself. If a man cannot be sure of himself, what can he be sure of?"

"Truth, perhaps, but that's a different matter."

"No, sir. It is the *same* matter, if a man is in possession of the truth."

"Errant, despicable nonsense," St. Ives said. "My time is quite precious to me at the moment, as you can well understand. I very much want to see my wife, to put it plainly."

"I am delighted to hear you say it, and I hope to accommodate you soon. I myself am to be wed on the morrow to an extraordinary woman. Quite young, in fact, but we're perfectly… aligned in every other regard. Age, I find, is immaterial. You know the girl, I believe." Klingheimer sat back in his chair, smiling as if he were about to say something droll.

"Do I?" St. Ives asked. "What is the girl's name?"

"Clara Wright."

Klingheimer stared at him, smiling, his head cocked. "Do I amaze you, Professor?"

St. Ives had no desire to answer the question, which was rhetorical and self-serving. "You murdered her mother, then?"

"Not I, and 'murder' is a hard word. It is true that Dr. Peavy removed her head at my bidding. It is equally true that the head – the brain, the mind – is the only part of the human animal that matters in the least. The rest is a mere mechanism. It will amaze you to learn that Sarah Wright is still very much alive. You have a baffled look about you, Professor. I'll tell you something that you do not know: Clara was removed from Hereafter Farm shortly after you and your handsome wife left for London. She dwells with me now – quite safe and unmolested, I assure you. My interest in the girl has nothing of an animal quality to it. Marriage to my mind is something – something ethereal."

St. Ives nodded, affecting to take the man seriously. He glanced around the small, windowless room. Aside from the two chairs and small table, there was a narrow bed and a wooden cupboard on the wall that stood open some two inches. There were glass bottles visible in the cupboard, and St. Ives saw that they were filled with the green liquid.

"I have several questions for you," he said to Mr. Klingheimer. "Will you answer them while we wait? I am entirely in your power, after all, and I am quite curious about a number of things."

"I would like nothing better, sir. I detest secrets, especially between men of our stature. Put a question to me. I welcome an inquisition."

"What do you *want*?"

"I want for nothing. I can tell you, however, that I take a certain joy in manipulating the world to my own ends. All of us do. Even a man who sleeps in a ditch knows in which pocket his pipe resides and sees that his matches and tobacco remain dry. Disorganization constitutes madness. Without our best efforts, we're surrounded by mere chaos. I attend to such matters on a larger scale than our friends who sleep in ditches, however. My own is an ascending scale, I'm happy to say, a trek up Mount Olympus itself. I have not reached the summit by any means, but I have scaled the lesser heights, and even from those vantage points I find the view breathtaking. Clara and I will take the world upon our own shoulders; the two of us will send Atlas packing."

Klingheimer smiled broadly, and it came to St. Ives that the man was unhinged, possessed by a demented grandiosity that made him a candidate for permanent residence in this very asylum. "What put you in mind of Clara and her mother to begin with, given that they lived in obscurity?"

"Clemson Wright, Clara's father, was in my employ – a worthless man, but his coming to me was a stroke of luck in the end. When he was far gone in gin, he spoke of his daughter's clairvoyant powers and referred to his wife as a 'witch' – a term that he understood to be the literal truth. Dr. Peavy had the pleasure of opening his head. What we found therein was interesting – quite convincing – at least until the man's unfortunate death, at which point his brain matter would only have been of interest to a cannibal. In short, after I investigated his claims I determined to accomplish two things: I would wed Clara and I would possess Sarah Wright's essence on a platter. What I set out to do, I do."

St. Ives regarded Klingheimer for a moment without speaking. His matter-of-fact tone was appalling, but interesting in a clinical sense. "You knew that I carried a ham and pickled onion sandwich into the underworld," he said. "How did you know?"

"Because an inept man detonated an explosive charge that cast you and Mr. Frobisher to your doom, or so I thought. I sent a party to search for you. The world below is vast beyond belief, however, and we failed to find either you or Mr. Frobisher. What we found was a scrap of newsprint that had recently wrapped a sandwich. Certainly that's one of the lesser mysteries."

St. Ives nodded. "No sign at all of Gilbert Frobisher?"

"Alas, none. I tell you that truthfully. Some weeks earlier we had made an exploratory foray into the underworld through a little-known point of access on Hampstead Heath. Perhaps you are now familiar with it. It was then that we came upon the living corpse, if you will, of Ignacio Narbondo. I was amused at the look of surprise on your face when you saw the Doctor in his vivarium – in his fungal jungle, if you will." Mr. Klingheimer smiled broadly once again, although the smile was short lived. St. Ives wondered if his facial expressions meant anything at all, or were simply a continually shifting mask.

The door to the antechamber opened and Willis Pule walked in, carrying a silver tray with glasses, a bottle of sherry, and a half dozen cream tarts. He set the tray on the low table that separated St. Ives and Mr. Klingheimer and poured sherry into each of the glasses. St. Ives looked hard at the door and then at Pule.

"I adjure you to do nothing foolish," Klingheimer told him. "It is *utterly* unnecessary. You've come to the place of your song dream, sir. I intend to offer you a noble position in the godhead, if you will – a minor dukedom on the mountainside, but palatial."

Pule went out again. Mr. Klingheimer tasted the sherry and nodded in apparent approval. "And now a question for you, Professor. When you were finding your way out of the underworld you no doubt took an avid interest in the luminous mushrooms. You must have considered their very interesting effect on the animals they capture – a human animal in Narbondo's case. How would you describe them?"

"I would describe them as nondescript, gargantuan, vampiric, predatory, motile relatives of the common field blewit, although this last is mere guesswork. The leech like tendencies of the fungus are strangely pronounced, and they are apparently immune to the rapid growth and decay of countless species of mushroom here above. As you stated, their fluids seem to have the power to sustain life."

Mr. Klingheimer nodded. "I wonder if you can distinguish the faint green pallor to my skin?"

"I can and I have. The effect is even more pronounced in Willis Pule. The pallid green tone is consistent with that of the liquid in the fungus, of course."

"Indeed it is. Mr. Pule dines upon them, as do I. Both of us swill the luminous fluids. He was a pioneer, was Mr. Pule – a willing subject. The effect is startling – a sharpening of the senses, the diminution of age itself, the repair of the flesh. The fungal blood, I mean to say, is nothing less than the elixir of life."

"Immortality, do you mean?"

Klingheimer shrugged. "There is no such thing," he said. "There is, however, considerable ground between mortality and its opposite. One is the fate of mankind and the other the fate of the gods, all of whom have passed away in due time. How old do you take me for?"

"Old enough to have more sense and scruples than you apparently have, if either of those things in fact interest you."

"Fie, sir. Philosophical gabble. What if I told you that I was ninety-three years old? What if I revealed that small doses of the elixir have had a salutary effect upon my health? I purchased a bottle of it many years ago from a man of whom you have some knowledge, and very shortly thereafter I set out to find my own source – a great challenge, I assure you, as was the process of brewing it. It is only recently, however, that I have discovered vast fields of it, as have you, without a doubt, given your trek underground. The pressing of my first harvest yielded a small keg of refined elixir, and now I drink it in quantity."

"You mean to bottle it like wine, then? Set up as a commercial gentleman in a factory, perhaps."

"Not at all, Professor. I simply mean to possess the elixir in quantity. I mean to annex the lands in which those fields grow. I'll happily share it with my... associates – with yourself, if you'd like. I beg you to consider it."

"Your increased consumption is not due to an addictive quality in the elixir? I'm reminded of the perils of chloral hydrate or laudanum."

"Nothing of the kind, sir. It's a noxious brew at first, and it requires an act of will to consume it, even if it's diluted with spirits to cover the flavor and smell. Its result is efficacious, however, one relishes the effect and what it portends, if not the flavor of the swill itself."

St. Ives tasted his sherry. Clearly Klingheimer had manifold addictions, extreme self-opinion fueling them, and was dosing himself in order to pursue his supposed ascent to some sort of lunatic godhead. There was no means by which a mortal could reason with such a man.

"Is the wine satisfactory?" Klingheimer asked.

"The elixir of life," St. Ives said.

"Then pose me another question. I seldom get an opportunity to speak my mind."

"What do you mean to do with Narbondo now that he too has the fluids flowing in his veins? Now that he has become one of your 'associates'?"

"We've already done it, sir. We have accessed his mental faculties. Dr. Peavy has trepanned the man, and his mind has been explored. He is a receptacle of vast knowledge, which news does not surprise you, and because of the mushrooms that knowledge remains intact. He is also mentally unstable, a man driven by hatred – an emotion to be despised, as are most of what we refer to as emotions. Because of that he is destined to live out his life in his wood-and-glass prison. His life is mine to dispose of or to maintain. Would it astonish you to know that he is entirely conscious? You can speak to him, if it would amuse you."

"Nothing about the man amuses me. How does Dr. Peavy effect this 'exploration' of the mind?"

"His methods involve the electrical stimulation of the cortex and the linking of two brains, connecting them, literally, with thin silver wires across which knowledge passes in an electrical current. Willis Pule has been the medium."

"That explains the wires intermingled with the hairs on Pule's head?"

"Just so. The wires are fixed in his brain. You can see for yourself that he bears no apparent ill effects. To the contrary, Mr.

Pule has the honor of being the first explorer of the vast ocean that is the human mind. I myself am another."

"*Literally*, do you mean? You've put yourself willingly under Peavy's knife?"

"Literally, yes."

"Despite his being *careless of the single life*?"

"Even so. That unfortunate carelessness led in time to great successes. Willis Pule is an example. Narbondo another. Dr. Peavy has made other discoveries also. He has discovered the seat of paranormal powers as well as a means to enhancing them."

"You refer to this mumbo-jumbo about the pineal gland?"

"I can assure you, Professor, that 'mumbo jumbo' has nothing to do with it. It is a simple matter of effecting several small lesions with a very thin, charged wire – a matter of… opening a window, if you will." Klingheimer bowed deeply and parted the hair on the top of his head, fingering a small circular scar. "Do you see it?" he asked.

"Yes," St. Ives said. "No trepanning, then?"

"Unnecessary. Peavy spent the better part of a year finding a *route*, shall we say, to the center of the brain, where the gland lies between the hemispheres. The streets of our city and the hallways of our asylums provided subjects who, if not entirely willing, were safely persuaded to take part in Peavy's experiments. Once Peavy was sure of himself, I myself went willingly 'under the knife,' as you put it. The result was extraordinary."

"I admit to being baffled by all of this," St. Ives said. "What is your motive if not material gain?"

"I have no motive but knowledge, sir. As I said but a moment ago, I am a mountaineer. My sights are on the summit, and I use whatever means are at hand to scale…"

The door opened – Jimmy this time, who nodded and stood

by the door. He held a pistol in his hand, and he regarded St. Ives with distaste.

"Ah," said Mr. Klingheimer, "it appears that Dr. Peavy is just now completing his work. Will you follow me into the theater, Professor? I believe you'll see some prodigious wonders."

Klingheimer stood up and set out. Jimmy falling in behind St. Ives, the three of them entered the operating theater, which was stiflingly warm. St Ives saw that a large iron furnace some three feet wide by eight long was emitting a low roar, which accounted for the smoke rising from the chimney outside. A heavy stovepipe connected the furnace to the chimney.

St. Ives was distracted from the ominous furnace by the sight of Clara Wright bound into a chair. Her head hung downward as if she were etherized. A wheeled pole stood beside her. Hanging at the top of the pole was what appeared to be a pig's bladder connected by tubing to a syringe affixed to her arm. Dr. Peavy worked over her, manipulating a pump-like apparatus, drawing fluids from the bladder and forcing them onward with an injector.

"Clara and I are being wed as we speak, Professor," Klingheimer said in a low voice. "Wed in the highest sense of the word. She is appropriately clad in her matrimonial gown, as you can see, made from good, English, Macclesfield silk. You'll agree that the gown is artfully simple. There was no time to chase after superficial elegance, and of course there is nothing superficial in the girl at all."

St. Ives stared at him, looking for any facial indication of perverted humor, of irony, but he saw nothing beyond a mask of self-satisfaction.

"Our ceremony involves no clergyman, and this theater is our humble church. My blood is even now flowing into her veins, mingling with her own, and her blood with mine, a portion of fungal elixir into the mix – a *literal* marriage, do you see? Nothing symbolic. The girl has been sedated and fixed in the chair for her own good. She might do herself a mischief otherwise."

"You run the risk of murdering her," St. Ives said. "If the blood is incompatible…"

"And of murdering myself, sir. Clara and I have exchanged blood twice now, and will continue to exchange it until we are quite the same person, at least in essence. If our bloods, so to speak, were incompatible, we would be aware of it six times over by now. I depend on Dr. Peavy, you see, in these matters, just as Peavy depends upon Jules Klingheimer."

"What can you possibly hope to gain by this dangerous play, sir?"

"Clairvoyance, in a word. Second sight. It is one of my goals to expand my sensibilities, to see beyond that which ordinary mortals see. Clara, of course, is no ordinary mortal, and she will share her powers with me. I am in the act of becoming. You, sir, are in the act of *unbecoming*, which is the great human curse. Now, sir, I adjure you to silence for a brief time. I would like to commune with my bride. Please sit, Professor."

Mr. Klingheimer waited until St. Ives was seated, and then he himself found a seat where he had a clear view of Clara. He settled himself and ceased to move. St. Ives watched his now blank face, wondering what the man intended.

Clara felt the blood leaking slowly into her vein – an amount exactly equal to what they had taken from her and put into Mr. Klingheimer, or so he had told her. It was painful where the needle went in, but no worse than other things she had known in her life, and she knew by now that the pain would recede when the needle was taken out. She forced her mind away from thoughts of the tainting of her blood…

She was aware of the Professor's arrival. Finn had told her that he was in London. Had he come here to Dr. Peavy's to take her away with him? He seemed to be at odds with Mr. Klingheimer, who was enamored with the sound of his own voice, his own gabble. *You run the risk of murdering her*, the Professor had said. And yet the sharing of the blood went on. The Professor had no power here. If he did, he would stop what they were doing.

It came to her now that someone was regarding her – not from without, but from within, as if an intruder had found his way into a darkened house and was standing in silence watching the family sleep. Intruders never meant well. She began to recite "The Jumblies," which she had long used to drive interruptive thoughts from her mind when she wanted her mind ordered, or wanted it to shine a light in the darkness – a light that her mother might see:

They went to sea in a Sieve, they did,
In a Sieve they went to sea:
In spite of all their friends could say,
On a winter's morn, on a stormy day,
In a Sieve they went to sea!

Clara pictured the sieve, spinning on the surface of the sea, faster and faster, the Jumblies holding on tightly in the stormy weather.

Far and few, far and few,
Are the lands where the Jumblies live;
Their heads are green, and their hands are blue,

And they went to sea in a Sieve.

In her mind's eye the sieve spun faster and faster until it was a spinning ball, like the round head of a man – white like the moon, like the man in the moon. There was a green tinge over all, however, green like the Jumblies' heads.

> *And all night long in the moonlight pale,*
> *We sail away with a pea-green sail,*
> *In the shade of the mountains brown!*

The conversation in the room diminished to a mere droning noise like the speech of bees. She saw in her mind a bearded face, smiling an empty smile, the smile of a figure drawn in the dust with a stick. It was him – Mr. Klingheimer, who was the intruder within her mind, and he looked about him, as if to make himself at home.

> *And they bought an Owl, and a useful Cart,*
> *And a pound of Rice, and a Cranberry Tart,*
> *And a hive of Silvery Bees.*

Mr. Klingheimer's smile did not disconcert her now. She blotted out his face with the spinning sieve, which spun itself faster and faster into a silvery hive, the silvery bees holding on tightly to the hive, just as the Jumblies, not caring a fig, held onto their sieve. And then the bees let go in a wild cloud and swarmed about Mr. Klingheimer's head. Clara was abruptly aware now that her mother's mind had joined her own, and that her single-minded anger had enraged the bees. Their wings whirred mechanically, their silver, needle-like stingers plunging into Mr. Klingheimer's flesh, secreting their poisons. In her mind she saw his mouth open in a silent scream, and his hands went to his head…

…and then she was aware that the needle in her arm had been removed, and she was back in Dr. Peavy's laboratory, her mind entirely her own once again, the Jumblies and their sieve sailing away in the far distance.

I n the moments before Clara awakened, St. Ives had heard Klingheimer make a high, hollow sound in his throat, like a man in a nightmare attempting to scream. His eyes had rolled back and he had clutched his hair on the sides of his head as if in torment, quickly letting go to swat at the air roundabout him. Something had staggered him, and he was making an effort now to regain his composure.

Peavy wiped the small round wound on Clara's arm with a rag soaked in a yellow liquid, and then awakened her with a vial of smelling salts before turning to Klingheimer.

"Are you ill, sir?" Dr. Peavy asked him.

"No," Klingheimer said, affecting a smile. "A momentary discomfort, but it has quite passed away." He was attempting to catch his breath, however, and his face was suffused with blood.

Apoplexy, St. Ives thought, unfortunately not fatal. But Klingheimer had been up against it; there could be no doubt about that.

"Flinders," Klingheimer said to a stilt-like man sitting on a high stool in the corner, "transport Clara Wright and Mr. Shadwell to Lazarus Walk in the brougham. Return in exactly two hours, if you please."

Flinders took a red bowler from a nearby hook, and St. Ives recognized him as the driver of the van outside. Another man who had been sitting in the third row of seats stood up and made his way down to the floor, tipping his hat to St. Ives and winking at him. It was without a doubt the man Shadwell, the taller of the false policemen at Hereafter Farm. He helped Clara to her feet and went out through a broad door held open by the man Flinders. Through it St. Ives saw the dusky night, the dark shrubbery along the alley, the coach and the van dimmed by cloud shadow. He also saw that Jimmy still held the pistol.

"Well, well," Klingheimer said when the door closed behind them. "You were relieved, I take it, to see that Clara's infusion of blood was apparently quite safe. You'll be happy to hear that tomorrow, in order to satisfy the girl's sense of duty, she and I will undergo a more traditional wedding ceremony, suitably dressed and replete with witnesses, a clergyman, and a Champagne toast. I am happy to say that you will attend, at least to *witness* the happy event. You'll have to forego the Champagne, unfortunately. Such a ceremony is a popular fantasia, of course, but I mean for Clara to be bound to me under the law."

"The *law*?" St. Ives asked in a steady voice. "Surely you jest. The laws of man and of common decency require that you release the girl. I'm perfectly willing to offer myself as a hostage – as a replacement. I'll submit to whatever…"

Klingheimer waved him silent. "Very noble of you, Professor, but surely you misunderstand. You will *indeed* submit to whatever I ask of you, whether it is to your liking or is not, and in turn you'll become a peer of the realm, as I promised. A dukedom is granted by the King, after all. It cannot be refused."

TWENTY-SEVEN

MR. NOBEL'S INGENIOUS DYNAMITE

"I can tell you, Hasbro, that I would be happy to see the end of Miss Cecilia Bracken, except that once my uncle surfaces again it won't be the end of her at all, but the beginning, if you see what I mean."

"To my mind it would be better that Mr. Frobisher is healthy and with Miss Bracken on his arm," Hasbro said, "than that there be no arm for her to hold."

They had crossed the South Meadow on foot and now labored up a hill through the woodland beyond, the branches of the trees overhead heaving in the wind, which blew without interference at this elevation.

"I take your point," Tubby said. "But it's a difficult bolus to swallow unless a man has a cask of whiskey to wash it down with."

"I'll admit that the woman is a cipher," Hasbro said, "but I wonder whether she mightn't be something of a cipher even to her own mind. 'Know thyself,' the Greeks admonish us, and yet often enough there's something in us that seems to be a stranger.

It can take us unawares when we see ourselves in a mirror. Have you considered that Miss Bracken might be mortally confused, her motives mixed?"

"It seems to me that she has the motivation of a serpent," Tubby said, knocking a dead rodent aside with his walking stick, a short but heavy length of Brazilian ironwood with a knurled top.

"What if her desire for wealth is authentic," Hasbro asked, "and yet she also admires your uncle, also – *loves* him, even? It's quite possible that she has never been esteemed by a good man, but has associated only with bad men with base motives. To my mind it's a wonder that more women don't murder their husbands in their beds. Your uncle lacks any discernible deviousness, after all. I can think of no one with a more open and cheerful countenance, and no doubt Miss Bracken sees this same thing. On the one hand she might think of turning this to her advantage, as you fear, and yet at the same time she might also see him as her protector, who appeared out of the sea when she was very much in need. Many a rich man has made a good marriage, after all. Wealth isn't Mr. Frobisher's sole asset."

"You always were able to take the long view, Hasbro. And you might be quite correct, of course. I made up my mind that Miss Bracken was no good before we ever left Jamaica, and I've colored her in that light since. If we find Uncle, I'll have to make things right with both of them."

"It would not be a bad thing to make things right in any event," Hasbro said as they crested the hill, clear of the trees now. "You'll sleep better for it."

In the distance lay the ponds and the meadow roundabout them, although the gipsy caravan was nowhere to be seen, which was unfortunate. Speaking with them might have saved time in the search for the opening to the tunnel. There was the telltale copse, however, that Alice had referred to – the only shrubbery near the ruin that might house a secret well. The old manse itself, as Hasbro had referred to it, lay away to the right, the ruins scenic in the windy sunshine. It was an active ruin, however. A number of uniformed men were busy about the place, several on horseback. Several others were exiting the structure and moving away from it in an organized manner.

"What's this now?" Tubby asked.

"They appear to be Royal Engineers," Hasbro said. "They've set up a perimeter."

"They'd best not hinder us, by God," Tubby said, picking up the pace as they moved downhill. The perimeter was a good fifty yards from the ruin, and beyond it, in the direction of Wood Pond, stood two lorries piled high with lumber. A number of idle men stood watching, evidently waiting for something to transpire. One of the men on horseback galloped uphill toward Tubby and Hasbro now, waving his arm as if to warn them off. They continued their downward trek, however, until the horse reined up before them, physically impeding their progress.

"Good day, sir," Tubby said to the man, but before the last word was out of his mouth, a thunderous explosion rocked the green below, and the roof of the building rose piecemeal into the sky in a great billow of smoke. Splinters of wood, roof slates, shrubbery, and other heavy litter rained down upon the earth, smoke and dust whirling in the air. The stone walls of the building seemed simply to settle, as if they'd grown tired of standing. The structure had been obliterated on the instant, nothing left of it now but several low lengths of ruined wall and a heap of debris. A cheer arose from the workmen and soldiers both.

"Now *that* was very neatly done, gentlemen," the man on horseback said to them. "Note the small field of debris and the thoroughgoing destruction. No need for another charge here, I can tell you. Major Robert Cantwell, at your service."

Tubby stood gaping at the field of rubble and at the crew of workmen, who at once set about shuttling posts from the lorries and laying them out at measured intervals. Others began auguring holes into the soil in which to sink the posts. They worked with a will, as if to have a paling fence constructed by nightfall.

Ignoring Major Cantwell's introduction, Tubby asked, "*What* was very neatly done? Or rather *why*, for God's sake?"

"God had nothing to do with it, sir. All glory has to be given to Mr. Nobel's ingenious dynamite sticks and the new electronic blasting caps. And of course to the sappers who set the explosives. There's an art to that, I can tell you."

"On whose orders?" Tubby asked.

"Who are you to inquire about orders, sir?" the major asked, giving him a hard look now.

"I'm assistant director of the Bureau of Parks and Open Spaces," Tubby lied. "My name is James Hall, and this is my companion Mr. Higgins, retired. The Metropolitan Board of Works is shortly to become caretaker of the park, so this is very *much* my business. Why have I heard nothing of it?"

"Our orders came to us early this morning from the Board of Works itself. Two boys were discovered in the old well-shaft last night, their legs and necks broken. The ruin has housed criminal gangs and been the site of murders and outrages, and now these two innocent boys, who found their way in through an unlocked grate and fell to their deaths. We were ordered to act at once, and we did so, as you can see. As for the Bureau of Parks and Open

Spaces, Mr. James Hall, you must be aware that there has long been talk of razing the old ruin and building a grand pavilion and tea gardens."

"Of course I'm aware of it," Tubby said. "How could I not be? But this is a shocking acceleration of the plans, which are in preliminary stages, after all."

"Well, sir," Major Cantwell said with a laugh, "there's nothing preliminary about *this* piece of work, I can tell you that. The job needed to be done, and it's done."

"Might we be given leave to look at the result, major?" Hasbro asked. "I've an interest in demolition, and this was indeed capably carried out."

"No, sir, you may not. The Corps of Royal Engineers is taxed with hauling away the rubble and grading the site in preparation for the construction of the pavilion. Six months from now, barring inclement weather, you'll be free to stroll upon the memory of the place. Meanwhile, Mr. Hall," he said to Tubby, "as an employee of the Crown, you might consider visiting your place of employment on occasion in order to get some sense of what your work entails, rather than wandering abroad in order to put idle questions to men who very much *know* their business. Whose duty was it, I wonder, to ascertain that this apparently deadly grate was kept locked so that the void beneath it would not become a pit of dead children? *Yours* perhaps?" With that he spurred his horse around and set off down the hill again.

 TWENTY-EIGHT

MR. LEWIS AT WORK

"Mr. *Lewis*, is it?" Alice asked him.

"Yes, ma'am," he said, smiling obsequiously at her. "You inquired about a Mr. Harris, I believe?"

"Harrow, actually. James Harrow, of the British Museum. He died in an accident on the Embankment when his wagon overturned very near the Swan Pier."

"Ah, yes. Two nights ago. Just upriver of the sink-hole, I believe. We heard about the tragedy, of course, the Board of Works being in a position of some responsibility for the condition of the embankment."

"A police sergeant at Bow Street Station led me to believe that you would have some knowledge of the particular dead house to which his body had been taken."

"Yes, of course. As I recall there was no way of identifying the man at the time, although we now believe him to be James Harrow. It is conceivable that he was robbed and his pocket-book taken. I merely speculate. That is, of course, a police matter. I am told that he had a curious dead bird with him, a bird thought to be extinct but entirely preserved, although what that means I cannot say – pickled in refined brandy, perhaps. It would make a nice roast, I dare say."

He paused to laugh at this quip, but fell silent when he saw that Alice was not amused. "In any event, the body would almost certainly have been conveyed to the outhouse behind the Savoy Chapel. The Board has contracted with the Chapel to use the out-building as a morgue for the unidentified dead awaiting transportation to the Brookwood Cemetery. It's virtually certain that his body is still there, and perhaps the bird with it, although I advise you to proceed to the chapel without delay if you have any interest in either of the two."

He stopped now, removed his spectacles, and looked hard at her. "Mrs. *St. Ives*, did you say?"

"I did, sir."

"Not the wife of Professor *Langdon* St. Ives?"

"Indeed."

"Oh, my," he said, looking stricken now. For a moment he was apparently mute. "Yes, Mrs. St. Ives, almost certainly the Savoy Chapel, in the yard behind. The chapel has but the one very plain entrance at the front, and the new hotel dwarfs the place, but one can walk along an old carriageway to get to the back where the outhouse sits among the graves. It's not a pretty place, a morgue, but... May I be particularly *candid*, Mrs. St. Ives?"

"Please do be candid," she said.

He glanced around with the look of a conspirator before going on. "Work on the sink-hole – all this hurry, hurry, hurry – has progressed *very* much against my wishes. I want you to know that."

"I'm happy to hear it. It progresses against my wishes also."

"I myself flew in the face of it, and I'm happy to be able to reveal that fact to you at last. I gave an immediate order to dig away the rubble in an attempt to locate your husband and Mr. Frobisher despite the considered opinion of the Corp of Engineers, who unfortunately acted entirely against my wishes. I would like for you to know that the Board did *not* abandon your husband and Mr. Frobisher to their fate – at least Percival Lewis did not."

Alice was certain that the man was lying. He did not possess a talent for it, unlike many such men in positions of petty authority whose only authentic motivation was personal gain. There must have been something in her face that made her distrust plain, for Lewis turned his eyes and then his face away and shouted, "You there!" at a gawky boy who was just then coming into the room through a door to a hallway. "You, Jenkins!" The boy looked up sullenly. "Pardon me for a moment, ma'am," Mr. Lewis said to Alice. "This will take a short time, but I beg you to be patient."

He stepped away, waving the boy Jenkins over to his desk, where he scribbled a note onto a piece of foolscap and put it into an envelope. Alice watched as he spoke to the boy under his breath and then nodded toward the door. The boy set out at an unhurried pace, and Mr. Lewis shouted, "Be quick about it, Mr. Jenkins!" and the boy glanced back, giving Alice a quizzical look – a look that seemed to mean something, although what it meant she couldn't say. He glanced at Mr. Lewis in the next moment, and Mr. Lewis pointed at the door, through which Jenkins disappeared.

Mr. Lewis busied himself at the desk then, searching through drawers and moving objects about the surface. Alice had no patience with the man at all, despite his plea. He looked up at her finally and shook his head in a gesture of failure, and then hurried toward her, dusting his hands. "I seemed to recall having seen something regarding Harrow's death after all – had hoped to find confirmation of the whereabouts of Mr. Harrow's... remains... but I'm afraid, alas..."

When Alice saw that he was played out, she said, "You appear to be in a position of some responsibility, Mr. Lewis."

"It is one of my charges to keep the employees busy, ma'am. The boy Jenkins is as lazy as a hog if he's allowed to be. Thinks it's his duty to support the walls with the weight of his shoulders, for the most part, but I've got the measure of him."

"Thank you for being candid with me earlier, Mr. Lewis. I'll not mention what you've revealed to me about your efforts on behalf of my husband. As you are probably aware, he did not survive his ordeal, nor did Mr. Frobisher."

"I was *not* aware of that, ma'am. I'll admit that I've held onto a modicum of hope."

"A modicum of hope is as good as a feast, Mr. Lewis, and often just as transitory. There is one other thing you can be candid about, if you please."

"Your humble servant," he said, bowing to her.

"Just moments before the collapse that took the life of my husband, I witnessed a man who looked uncannily like *you* hiding among the boulders that made up the edge of the sink-hole."

"*Hiding*, ma'am? I deny it."

"So it appeared to me, Mr. Lewis. In fact, the word *skulking* comes to mind. I was no great distance away, you see, watching you through a pair of opera glasses from the deck of Mr. Frobisher's boat, which was anchored on the river. You don't deny having been there on the shore?"

He looked at her now, blinking his eyes rapidly and breathing hard, as if he had just climbed a flight of stairs. "No, indeed," he managed to say. "I deny only that I was *hiding*. It was my *duty* to be there, upon my honor."

"You're a man of duty and honor, to be sure, Mr. Lewis. I'm baffled, however. I have no knowledge of explosives, but it appeared to me that you bent over to perform some action that was coincidental with the explosion."

"You are no doubt correct, ma'am, as far as it goes. I recall that I tied my shoelace. I'm at a loss to… Are you implying that…?"

"That you are lying to me, Mr. Lewis? I wonder about it, assuredly."

"I protest, ma'am."

"Do you see that strange-looking man sitting by the door?" Alice asked him. "The very lanky man wearing the bloody bandage."

"I do, however…"

"His name is Kraken, sir, and a very appropriate name it is. He is my late husband's brother. Two years ago he tore a piece of a man's scalp from his head and compelled the man to eat it. He was adjudged mad, and my husband persuaded the court to allow him to live with us on our farm in Aylesford. My husband functioned as his keeper, and now I've got charge of him. Mr. Kraken is devoted to me, sir. If I discover that you're lying, I'll set him upon you. I guarantee that you will not enjoy it."

TWENTY-NINE
IN AT THE WINDOW

When Finn had fled from Klingheimer and found Beaumont's quarters unlocked, he had gone out through the window onto the roof, hearing the window latch behind him when it banged into place. The fog hung heavy over the rooftops and for most of an hour he was well hidden by it. But the sun and the wind dispersed the fog and for a time he was visible everywhere on the wretched roof. He had crouched in the shadow of a chimney for an age, feeling as if his life had come to a dead stop, and hoping that no one passing on the pavement below would see him and shout "thief." When at last he had seen Beaumont turn up the byway from the direction of the river, the dwarf looked very much like salvation.

"They told me you'd scarpered," Beaumont said to him after letting him in, "but I knew you wouldn't have without your Clara. Good that they think you've gone, howsomever."

"Even so," Finn said, setting down his creel, "I mean to take Clara out today, while they don't know that's what I'm about."

"How do you mean to do it?" Beaumont asked.

"I don't know. Can you help me?" Finn watched his face. He still didn't know the man, not really, and what he was asking was more than a mere favor – Beaumont's life, perhaps, if things went badly.

"Aye," Beaumont said easily. "I'm sick of this house, and the house is sick of me. The room in the cellar, did you leave it as you found it?"

Finn shook his head slowly. "The bed was slept in and food left lying about that I took from the storeroom. They'll know I was there."

"Then they'll wonder whether Beaumont knew you was there. Indeed they will." He studied the problem for a moment. "I'll play the fool, of course. It's true enough that I keep to my station and that you was hid."

There was the sound of a woman screaming just then, muffled by walls and floors rather than by distance. "Can that be Clara?" Finn asked with a rising horror.

"No," Beaumont said. "Someone's brought a woman to the house and the woman don't like it."

Finn looked away and shook his head tiredly. "What will happen to her?" he asked.

"This new woman? Like as not when they're done with her they'll give her to Peavy and he'll open her head. I was out to Peavy's second day I was here, and he had the headpiece off a lunatic as lived in his hospital, the man's eyes wide open and looking about and Peavy going after his brain with an electric wire. Smelt like roast pig."

Finn stared at Beaumont, trying to make sense of this, but then Clara returned to his mind and shut the rest out.

"Mr. Klingheimer thinks you're gone, Finn," Beaumont said. "There's a general search. But you can't stay in this here room. If they find out, they'll scrag the both of us."

"Can you put me into Clara's room, then? They won't expect that."

Beaumont seemed to be considering it. "Aye," he said, "but then there's two of you locked in."

"And you with a key."

Beaumont nodded. "For the nonce it'll work," he said. "But when it's time to run, we must run hard and not look back."

"Might we run east, to Aylesford? Clara's people will be…"

"When we get clear, we'll run where you please, Finn," the dwarf said, settling his hat atop his head and fixing the chinstrap. "It might be nip and tuck with Klingheimer, though. Word has it that he wants Clara to wed, and when he finds her gone, he'll come after her hard and fast. He has the second sight, has Mr. Klingheimer, and it'll be hot work getting out of London on the open road, for he'll have his eyeballs peeled inside and out, you can lay to that."

"Then how *will* we get out?" Finn asked.

"We'll go underground all the way to Margate, if we must, to the Vortigern Caves. That'll fox him. I know the way, better than him should he try to follow. You tell the girl Clara straightaway. She must be ready to follow, and no waiting to stuff a bag."

"I will, sir. And thank you."

Beaumont acknowledged the thanks with a curt nod of the head, and then said, "I'll just take a squint below to see what's what."

He went out directly, leaving the door ajar, but he was back within moments, tipping Finn a wink and beckoning for him to follow, the two of them creeping down the narrow stairs to the landing. Finn's heart was strangely light, he found, and he felt almost giddy by the time they reached Clara's door.

"If you hear the key in the lock, it'll likely be them," Beaumont said. "If it's me, I'll whistle like you heard before. So stow yourself and your gear out of sight. Give a knock on the ceiling if you need me, and if I'm in, I'll hear it and come." He produced a key from his pocket then and unlocked the door.

Finn slipped into the room, hearing the door close behind him and the key turn, and knowing at the same moment that Clara was gone from the house. Her things were there – her bag sat on a low table, and there was a garment spread neatly out on the bed. He saw that there was a stoneware pitcher on a dresser alongside a tumbler. He poured the tumbler full, drank it down, and then poured it full again, hefting the empty pitcher now. It was heavy, with a thick bottom so that it wouldn't easily overturn. He set it down and thought of the woman's screaming. He had spent enough time around bad men to know what they were capable of if they were given a chance. He didn't mean to give them a chance.

He listened to footfalls on the floor above – Beaumont returning to his own room – and then the sound of his door closing and the dwarf's footfalls again on the planks. *Good*, he thought. At least he would know whether Beaumont was in his room or had gone out. But it dawned on him that someone in a room below might know the same of him, and so he removed his shoes and laid them out of sight under the far side of the bed, which was high enough off the floor for him to slide beneath if he heard someone approach. They would see him as soon as they looked beneath, but perhaps they wouldn't look. He put his jacket underneath with his shoes, made sure that there was space for him along with the rest, and then sat at the desk to wait, setting his creel down in front of him, his mind turning.

He wondered what Beaumont had meant by saying that they

would "go underground" to Margate and the Vortigern Caves. The phrase conveyed no meaning to his mind, although he had seen the caves once, five years or so back. Margate was known for amusements, and Duffy's Circus had set up near what was called Dreamland, a manufactured, fabulous, mechanical world. There was little of a dream in it, however – a salt marsh, really, that was recently drained and on a hot day still stank of dead things in the mud. There were small boats fastened atop rails that one could sit in and be tossed about against the backdrop of a painted, stormy sea. People enjoyed them well enough, or at least pretended to after paying tuppence for the pleasure, but Finn preferred real boats, which he'd learned to sail when he had fished for oysters with Square Davey, a long time ago now…

He stood up, too restless to sit. If Beaumont knew a way to escape underground to Margate, then Finn was game. He heartily wished that he could get a message to the Professor and Alice at the Half Toad, if only to tell them where he and Beaumont and Clara were bound, once they escaped. When the time came to run it would be too late. He opened a tall casement window and looked down to the ground – a sheer drop of thirty feet.

The street was busy with people now, the day well underway, the wind blowing up leaves and bits of paper, white clouds moving swiftly in the sky. The tobacco shop sat cater-corner across the street, and the chemist's next to that. A man came out of the tobacconist's now and stood on the pavement loading a pipe. An old shawly woman issued from the chemist's, walking with a stick, and the man with the pipe bowed to her and lifted his hat as she moved slowly along, looking up toward the window where Finn stood. After a long moment she looked down again, her face half hidden by a large bonnet.

Finn was strongly reminded of Mother Laswell, this woman being much the same age and size, it seemed to him, although stooped and slow. He watched, however, as she stepped off the pavement at the corner of the building and moved into the shadows cast by an overhanging tree that grew in a bit of garden. She looked up at him again, standing up to reveal her full height this time and removing her bonnet, from which fell a voluminous quantity of red hair. It *was* Mother Laswell, sure enough, and the sight of her stopped his breath for a moment. A tide of relief flowed through him as he waved at her and quickly turned back to the desk. He opened his creel, which smelled of trout and waterweeds, and took out the two Christmas puddings that he'd stowed there earlier. He removed his notebook and pencil and began to write.

Mother Laswell had only the faintest sense of Clara's presence. She was gone from the house, no doubt. Seeing Finn, however, gave her hope that Clara would return. She stood along the wall of a tobacco shop in the shadow of the building and half hidden by a stand of shrubbery. Finn had just turned back into the room, in haste, it seemed to her. She held her bonnet against the very persuasive wind, listening to a bell toll the hour. She had already missed the first meeting at the Temple Church with Bill and Alice, but she would at least bear some variety of news when she found them again.

A curtain was pulled back from an open window some distance down the wall from Finn's window, but apparently on the same floor. Mother Laswell watched as a woman looked out of it. She was dressed in a peignoir, and Mother Laswell, utterly surprised, recognized her from earlier that morning at the Half Toad – the woman with the crow affixed to her hat. A man appeared beside her, looking briefly down at the street before raising his palm as if to slap her, while forcibly turning her away from the window. There was a shout, the woman's voice – angry, it seemed, from this distance, but unintelligible. The man looked out through the window again before pulling it shut.

Finn reappeared at his window, waved once again, stepped back a pace, and flung out a missile of some sort. It flew toward Mother Laswell with great speed and accuracy, and she ducked away just as it hit the wall and exploded, spraying her and the pavement with what turned out to be Christmas pudding, chunks of it glued to the paper wrapper that had enclosed it. A lump with a slip of paper thrust into it lay on the ground, and Mother picked it up, extricated the note, and read it: "Beaumont the Dwarf means for us to run underground to Margate, to the Vortigern caves *if we must*. The Professor knows Beaumont. Tell him it's the dwarf who played the organ in the Cathedral. Beaumont is a good friend, who has saved me twice, and together we are going to save Clara, who is held prisoner in this room. The three of us mean to run at the first chance, through the tunnel behind Narbondo's old house near the river. *Soon*. Finn Conrad." The "if we must" and the "soon" were heavily underlined.

"The *three* of us," she muttered, studying the note. So Clara was safe, at least for the moment.

Finn still stood at the window watching her, and Mother Laswell nodded and held up the note to show him that she had it. A richly attired carriage, its gold paint aglow, passed close by just then, cutting off her view, and she stepped back two paces to be less conspicuous. The driver took no notice of Mother Laswell.

There was another man inside the coach, however, who took particular notice – the villain Shadwell, whose mouth was agape as he apparently grappled with the strange business of seeing her there on the pavement.

Clara Wright sat across from him, and Mother Laswell was certain that she swiveled her head to look in her direction through the dark lenses of her spectacles when Shadwell's head was turned. Her elbow was raised in front of her. The girl looked forward again immediately, and it came to Mother Laswell joyfully that they were still convinced that she was utterly blind. Abruptly she realized that her bonnet was in her hand and that she was making no effort to disguise herself.

The coach was past now, slowing down and stopping before the broad gates of the house. It wasn't going in apparently, although the gate was swinging open. Mother Laswell turned and walked back past the tobacco shop and the chemist's. At the end of the block she looked back to see that Shadwell was handing Clara down from the coach, the driver holding the gate open just far enough for Clara and Shadwell to step through.

In that moment a boy dressed as if for the office dashed past Mother Laswell along the middle of the street, running like a deer. He gave a shrill whistle, and Shadwell looked back, waiting as the boy ran up alongside, disappearing from Mother Laswell's view. In the next moment she saw Shadwell climb onto the driver's seat, setting out toward the distant corner at a good clip. The driver led Clara out of sight, and the boy slouched back along the pavement, in no hurry now.

THIRTY

AT THE DEAD HOUSE

The Savoy Chapel, adjacent to Waterloo Bridge, was no great distance from the Board of Works. As Alice and Kraken made their way toward it along the Strand, Alice considered the curious Mr. Lewis. Her brazen threat to set Bill Kraken upon him had drained the blood from his face. The depth of her anger had surprised her as well, even as it was coming out of her mouth, although in some sense she meant just what she'd said. If Lewis had played them false, she would pin his ears back for him.

She wondered at his "apology," such as it was, on behalf of himself and of the Board of Works. Had he meant to curry favor with her? To what end? Surely not to persuade her to take a more favorable attitude toward the Board, which scarcely required Mr. Lewis's good word. His insistence that he was tying his shoe rather than lighting a fuse sounded like a lie to her, but in a court of law it would sound perfectly sensible. Alice was no threat to the Board of Works or to Mr. Lewis. And of course if he *had* been tying his shoe, then she had condemned him unfairly, which was regrettable.

"It's nigh onto the top of the hour," Kraken said, holding out his pocket watch. "We'd best look in on Temple Church, ma'am. We missed our tide the first time, but if we hurry we can be in port for the second meeting."

"It's not far, I believe," Alice said.

"No ma'am, though we'll have to hurry."

"You run on ahead, Bill, and bring Mother back with you. I might spend a moment alone in the chapel. I'll wait for you there and we all can walk back to the Half Toad together."

Kraken nodded. Spending a moment alone in the chapel was apparently something he understood. "You won't take no chances, ma'am? Same as you told me at Bow Street, I ain't got the fortitude to stand it if you come to harm. I couldn't face the Professor and tell him of it, not after all he's done for me."

"There's nothing to it, Bill. If they brought Harrow's body here, so be it. If they did not, they did not."

"Then I'm off," he said, and without another word he loped away up the Strand in the direction of Fleet Street and Temple Church.

Ahead of Alice lay the new Savoy Hotel, an immense structure, although only partly built, on the site where the old Savoy Hospital used to stand before it was demolished. The area had suffered great indignity in the years between, but the new hotel with its advertised electric lights and lifts and water closets in every room seemed gaudy to Alice, of little benefit, certainly, to the poor people who lived in the area, except that it might employ a few of them to wait on the well-to-do.

The Savoy Chapel, a remnant of an older London that was quickly becoming a ghost, was very humble indeed, dwarfed as it was by the structures that were rising around it. She saw the wide, cobbled path around the side of the chapel, leading to the churchyard behind, and she followed it along the edge of the building. She would look into the chapel when she had completed her work.

At the rear of the chapel sat the old cemetery, a hummocky collection of graves with tilting headstones, the enriched grass high and green from recent rains. A long, narrow out-building stood at the far side of the cemetery, affixed to a high wall.

A horse and empty wagon stood beside it, the horse cropping grass. And beside that stood a gold-painted coach, very elegant. The door to the shed was open, and a man, vigorously smoking a pipe, lounged in the doorway, no doubt preferring the reek of tobacco smoke to the smell of the charnel house. He nodded at her, and then came out to meet her when he saw that she took no interest in the graves. Despite the breeze, the air was rank with the stink of decaying corpses.

"Good day to you, sir," she said, and he nodded noncommittally and continued to smoke. "I was sent here by the Metropolitan Board of Works, in order to look into the death of a Mr. James Harrow. I'm told that his body was conveyed here after his unfortunate accident the night before last. It might not have been identified, however."

"It's just as you say, ma'am," the man said to her. "The police brought it. I'm the watchman, and I was here when he came in, dead as a stone. Kicked in the forehead by his horse, he was, his head stove right in, and soaking wet into the bargain. He'd got into the river when the horse did for him, and if there was any life left in him, the river took it. They fished him out and brought him here. He'll go out to Necropolis Cemetery at Brookwood tomorrow morning if there's naught else to do with him."

"So his body is here now?"

"Oh, aye," he said, knocking his pipe out against the sole of his shoe and then slipping it into a pocket of his vest, which was threadbare and stained. "Do you want to have a look at him? He ain't pretty, mind you."

"It's my duty to view Mr. Harrow's body, if you don't mind."

He nodded again and waved her inside. The dim room was perhaps twenty-feet long and ten-feet wide, with a wooden bench along one wall. Sunlight shone through a bank of filthy windows at either end. There were broken gravestones heaped in the corner, and sundry shovels and barrows. Cut planks, ready to be nailed together into coffins, were stacked alongside crates of nails, and there were hammers, saws, chisels, and sundry other tools hung neatly on the wall above the bench. The floor was trodden dirt, and the smell of death was enough to make Alice's eyes water. Six coffins lay upon wooden horses, all of them closed up, thank goodness, except for one that was empty, the lid leaning against it, waiting to be set into the top and nailed down. The watchman went to one of the closed boxes, removed the top and set it aside, and then stepped away and motioned Alice forward.

She peered into it, holding her breath. Within lay a long-dead corpse, a man's corpse, its flesh withered, its eyes staring, its lips shrunk back so that its teeth and gums seemed to stand out. Obviously this could not be Harrow's corpse. There was no sign of a wound in the forehead. The corpse's coat gave a small twitch now, and a rat leapt out from beneath the arm, sailing with a loud squeak out onto the floor and running out through a hole in the wall.

Alice trod backward, her mouth opening to speak but unable to make a sound. The watchman, standing at her back, threw his arms around her shoulders, and another hand snaked around and covered her mouth with a cloth smelling of a sweet chemical. She held her breath, struggling to free herself, but she couldn't move – another man obviously having joined the first, his free hand clutching her hair. She gasped for air finally, drawing the chemical into her lungs, and within moments she felt her hands tingling. She began to fall but was held upright, and she knew that she was beyond fighting. She thought of Mr. Lewis, his sending her here, sending the boy Jenkins out with an urgent message. In the next instant the world went dark, and her mind fell silent.

Bill Kraken found Mother Laswell at the door of Temple Church, and without wasting a moment they hurried back along Fleet Street and onto the Strand, Mother telling the story of seeing Finn Conrad at the window, the note that he pitched at her, about the woman called Miss Bracken at another window, and about Clara in the coach with Shadwell, and no harm done to her, except Miss Bracken was being misused.

"So he *seen* you?" Kraken asked unhappily.

"He did, Bill. He might not have known me. I can't be sure."

"It's much of a muchness whether he did or did not, Mother. If he did and he wanted to catch you, he would have done it." Bill took her by the hand now and picked up the pace, so that Mother had to hurry to keep up.

"This is *good* news, Bill," Mother said to the back of his head. "They're all safe, it seems, except that poor woman from the inn."

"It'll be good nowo when we get them out. There's the church across the way, Mother. Alice was to wait for us in the chapel."

They crossed the road and opened the chapel door. Mother uttered a small, surprised, "Oh," when she looked up at the coffered ceiling, painted in shades of deep blue and decorated with gold stars. Several people sat at the pews, but Alice was not among them, and Kraken immediately turned around and went out, muttering the words, "Damnation hell."

Mother Laswell followed him, around the side of the chapel and into the lonesome churchyard behind. Again, Alice was nowhere to be seen, only a solitary man smoking a pipe in the open doorway of a shed. A horse and wagon with a coffin on the bed stood nearby. The man took the pipe from his mouth and gestured with it, nodding at the two in greeting.

Kraken hurried toward him, speaking out in a loud voice. "We're a-looking for a woman who was just hereabouts."

"The dark-haired beauty, you mean? She was here indeed. Not fifteen minutes past. I'm to tell you that she went on to the King's Head, on Maiden Lane, across the road and take the left turning. She'd been walking all morning, she said, and needed something cool to drink."

Bill shouldered past him, into the shed, and the man followed him, Mother Laswell at his heels.

"She's gone on," the man said, "as I told you. It couldn't have been but a few minutes since."

"If you're a-lying," Bill told him, "and you're thick with this piss-ant Klingheimer…"

"There's no call for that tone, Bill," Mother said, taking him by the elbow. "We'll just nip around to the King's Head, like this man says. If she's not there, and they haven't seen her, then we'll come back here for another chat." She looked at the man, whose face was blank, and said, "Do you hear me, sir? We'll take you at your word, but it will go ill with you if you've lied."

"The lot of you is stark crazy," he said, "coming in here and blackguarding a man. 'Another *chat*,' by God. If I see you again *I'll* take it ill."

"Then you'll eat a blue pill, you hell-bent snipe," Kraken said.

"Now, *Bill!*" Mother said, leading him out through the door. "We'd best find Alice and get on about our business. We've got trouble enough without making more for ourselves."

Bill pulled his arm away, but went along with her, looking back twice before they were around the corner and walking up along the chapel again.

"You shouldn't have uttered Klingheimer's name. It's not *safe,*" Mother said.

"This here pipe-smoking, brazen-faced shite, he's got a liar's eyes, and I can't abide a liar."

"Don't *dwell* on it, Bill. Here's Maiden Lane, just as he said, and there's the public house yonder, a nice enough place, it seems to me. We can have a pint of something ourselves when we've found Alice. Catch your breath, Bill."

They went in through the door, the pub half empty and no sign of Alice. "I'll inquire of her, Bill," Mother said in a small voice. "If the publican hasn't seen her we'll go back to the chapel straightaway."

"She'd be here if…" Kraken started to say, but Mother stepped up to the bar and began to speak to the publican. When she turned back a moment later, her face stark, Kraken said, "You'd best wait in the chapel, Mother, whilst I parlay with that bugg… that scoundrel."

She followed him out the door and up Maiden Lane again. "No, Bill," she said. "Two is better than one. I wish I *did* have a pistol."

"Pistols is noisy, Mother. Did you see the tools a-hanging on the wall? A man don't like the look of a sharp saw, not if it's lying over his throat."

They had just crossed the road, nearing the chapel, when the horse and casket-bearing wagon that had stood in the churchyard issued from the cobbled path. The man driving the wagon saw the two of them and whipped up the horses, out into the traffic on the Strand, making away in the direction of Charing Cross, where he nearly ran down a trio of old men.

"Shadwell!" Kraken shouted. He gave chase, running at a loose-limbed gallop, dodging between carts and carriages, caroming off a chaise, the driver slashing the whip at him.

Mother Laswell stood helplessly on the pavement, watching him disappear and feeling utterly empty. She knew beyond doubt that it was Alice who had been borne away in the coffin on the wagon. She strode up and down, looking in the direction that Bill had taken, and at last she saw him hurrying back. He was evidently tuckered out, and he came along with a limp, his trousers torn open along his bloody leg.

"What have you done to your leg?" she asked.

"Nothing," he said. "Caught the hub of a wagon on my shin. It was that Shadwell, and no doubt, and Alice in the box, or I'm a Dutchman."

"It *was* her, Bill," Mother said. "I sensed her clear as I've ever sensed anyone, although it wasn't so when we were in the reek of the dead house. She's *alive*, Bill. They're taking her somewhere. If they wanted her dead, she'd be dead already."

"Let's have a word with Mr. Pipe," Bill said. "Put me right, Mother."

She straightened his hair, wiped blood from his chin with spit and a kerchief, and took up the flap of torn cloth from his trousers and simply glued it to his bloody leg.

"We won't fool that man for more than a moment," she said. "We must take him unawares."

Kraken jerked his head in agreement, and the two of them strode around to the back and across the graves toward the empty doorway. They saw the pipe smoker at the bench, turned away from them. Bill rushed silently upon him, his hands gripped tightly together overhead. He clubbed the man hard, striking him to the ground, his pipe flying from his mouth. He rose to his knees, and Kraken knocked him sideways with a second heavy blow, the man lying stupefied, his wits addled. Mother had closed the shed door and latched it.

Kraken fetched a piece of rope from beneath the bench and whipped it around the man's ankles, tying them tight, and taking the loose end and doing the same to his wrists. He put a foot on the man's stomach now and hauled the rope upward, hanging it between the open jaws of a bench vise, so that the man dangled there like dead game, his lower back just touching the ground.

Mother brought Bill a saw, handing it across to him just as the man opened his eyes and stared around himself, stupefied. "*Bluff*," she whispered, "Or it'll be you that's looking at a rope, Bill. Hear me now."

Kraken gave a curt nod, took the saw by the handle, and ran his finger along the blade to test it, immediately drawing a line of blood that he showed to the man as an illustration.

"What the bloody hell?" the man croaked.

"Hell is just the word for it," Mother Laswell said, leaning over him and looking into his face. "My companion wants very badly to saw your head off."

The man stared up at her face, which was set like a stone mask, and she reached down and pinched him hard on the ear. "That's meant to clear your mind," she said. "Alice St. Ives – is she alive? Mind that you tell us the truth this time, as you value your neck."

He managed to nod.

"I'm a-going to saw out his vocals," Bill said. "He's murdered Alice. It's nothing but lies with the likes of these here by-God cutthroats." Then he laughed aloud. "Did you catch that, Mother? A 'cutthroat' I called him!"

"That's wit for you," Mother said, as Bill laid the saw across the man's throat, allowing gravity to bear it down so that small pinpricks of blood rose beneath the teeth of the saw. The man lay deadly still, breathing hard and making small sounds in his throat.

"No, sir!" he gasped out. "She's *alive*, by God. She ain't dead. He didn't want her dead."

"*Who* didn't want her dead?" Mother Laswell asked. "Who is this 'he'? The truth now!"

"Shadwell! Him who drove off in the wagon."

"Where to?" Mother asked.

"I don't know!"

Bill pressed lightly on the saw, letting the weight of the instrument make his argument for him.

"It's a place over near Harley Street, and now I'm a dead man for saying it."

"Give us an address, and we'll set you free."

"Wimpole Street, top end, number fourteen, with a gatehouse on the street. Elysium Asylum, it's called, run by a man named Peavy. That's God's truth. It ain't the first time they've done it, neither."

"With your *help*, they did it," Mother Laswell said. "Cut him down, Bill, and we'll heave him into one of these coffins and nail down the lid. If he's lied to us, he'll have time to consider his ways, as the Bible recommends. If he's told the truth, we'll come back and set him free."

Bill sliced the rope with his clasp knife, and the man slammed to the ground.

"*You won't put me in no box!*" he shouted.

"On the contrary, that's just what we'll do," Mother Laswell told him, "as you did to our friend."

Bill hauled an empty coffin beside the trussed up prisoner, who tried desperately to roll beneath the bench, but managed simply to jam his shoulder under it, his face in the dirt. Kraken tilted the coffin on its side, and he and Mother Laswell rolled the man easily into it and then heaved the box upright. Bill picked up the lid, at the sight of which the man jack-knifed upward, and Mother Laswell slapped him hard across the face. He slumped downward, startled by the blow, and Kraken put his foot on his neck.

"Here's the thing, cully," Bill said. "You lie still, and I'll put some holes into the box so's you won't smothercate. If you're a-lying, you won't never see us again. Mayhaps you can shout the lid open. If we find Mrs. St. Ives, and she's fit, we'll send word to the chapel, and you ain't dead after all."

"You have our word on that, sir," Mother Laswell said, and the man looked from one to the other of them, still shaking his head.

Kraken fitted the lid onto the top of the casket and pounded a half dozen nails into it. Then he drilled two holes through the lid with a heavy auger, cast the tools aside, and the two of them went straight out into the windy afternoon. The graves were cast in cloud shadow now, the wind blowing the high grass. Mother Laswell put the padlock through the hasp and locked the door. They heard a wooden thumping from within the shed now, along with a muffled shouting, although from ten feet away it was scarcely audible.

The hansom cab carrying Hasbro and Tubby Frobisher rattled along, returning them to the Half Toad in Smithfield. The morning had been a waste, and Tubby stared bleakly out the window. "Dead boys, forsooth," he said. "Klingheimer is shutting us out is what he's doing, and the Board of Works is abetting him. If boys were discovered with legs and necks broken, they were certainly pitched into the pit a-purpose to bring this to pass, although I'd bet a fiver there were no boys at all."

"Certainly the thing was contrived," Hasbro said, "but unless I'm mistaken, Major Cantwell is doing his duty as he sees it."

"And I must do my duty to Uncle Gilbert. If Klingheimer has closed this passage, then there's a passage that he has *not* closed. I don't for a moment believe that he has shut *himself* out of the underworld. I want to know where it is, this other passage. I'm incapable of cooling my heels at the Half Toad when the answer to the mystery lies with Klingheimer and his minions."

"Wait until St. Ives joins us and we can reconnoiter," Hasbro said.

"You have a duty to St. Ives and Alice," Tubby told him. "My duty is to my uncle. Every hour that passes lessens the odds of finding him alive, or so I fear."

They turned up Fingal Street now, and the cabby reined in the horses outside the inn. Hasbro opened the door and climbed down onto the street, and Tubby leaned across to speak through the door. "I won't play the fool," he said, although he had a hard, desperate look about him. "If there's nothing to be discovered, I'll return straightaway. Leave word with Billson if the lot of you go out again, and I'll follow."

Hasbro nodded curtly, gave the driver further instructions, and shut the door as the coach moved out into the traffic.

THIRTY-ONE

THREE SEVERED HEADS

The portable vivarium had been rolled out of the way, but Narbondo sat in it as ever, looking out like an ape in a tree, his eyes open and filled with unmistakable loathing. The box sat on a wheeled cart, and Dr. Peavy ordered Pule to take it out the back now and load it into the van, not forgetting to lock the van door afterward. He would want it again later, but in the meantime Narbondo could sit in the darkness, Peavy said, rather than foul the air in the surgery with his dirty looks.

The surgical theater was scrupulously clean and neatly arranged, most of the equipment on wheels, which would make it easier to scrub the floors and walls. The floor was constructed of large marble tiles, each some three-feet square and snowy white. St. Ives had been in a number of surgeries in his time, both privately and publicly funded, but he had never seen such extravagance. There were drops of blood on the floor where Clara had sat, but otherwise the floor was pristine. Even as this came into his mind, Peavy himself wiped away the blood with the same cloth that he had used to clean Clara's arm, and then without speaking a word he went out through the door, leaving St. Ives alone with Jimmy, Pule, and Klingheimer.

Electric lamps behind red shades went on as if by magic along the wall to St. Ives's right. The red glow illuminated a confusion of bubbling apparatus – bladders, aerators, India-rubber tubing, enormous glass bottles full of the green fluid – much of it resting atop a long wooden bench. He was startled to see that three human heads sat on barbers' basins on that same bench, the green fungal elixir running from their mouths and nostrils. The severed necks were fixed upon thick cross-sections of luminous mushroom stem, each stem apparently regenerating a cap – becoming whole again – so that the heads seemed to wear collars.

The heads were in various states of preservation, two men and a woman. There were two other basins, empty of heads, although with a piece of stem mounted in each, a plinth waiting for a statue, and the fluids bathing them. Hanging from pendant rings nearby were three empty, wire bird-cages each of which might have held a large parrot, but without perches and with broad doors. Evidently they were used to transport the barbers' basins, and were the same that he had seen being unloaded from the van earlier.

"I told you that you would see wonders, Professor," Klingheimer said. He had obviously regained his self-possession, and he appeared to be gratified by the unhappy scowl that was fixed on St. Ives's face. Klingheimer produced a pair of aura goggles from within his coat and put them on, gazing for a moment at a nearby lamp. "I'll introduce you to our charges, although I see now that one of them has expired. With the aid of these very interesting goggles I can tell you that his inner light has quite gone out."

He gestured at the first of the heads – a woman's head. The

flesh, with its telltale green tone, was remarkably preserved, and the eyes were shut. Although he had never seen her – or at least her face – St. Ives had no doubt that it was Sarah Wright. There was nothing of the death mask about her features, however. Clearly a semblance of life was preserved by the fluids.

"I see that you know the woman, sir – Sarah Wright, as you have ascertained. I also see that after your initial distaste you reacted with intellectual interest. It is a marvel, is it not? The gentleman in the middle is James Harrow, dead beyond recovery, as I said. You recognize him, no doubt."

"Of course I do," St. Ives said. "I expected as much."

"There was too little life left in him when Peavy removed his head, and the fungi have apparently failed to revive him."

St. Ives said nothing.

"He had a first-rate mind, or at least an excellent memory. I was anxious to look into it, perhaps to engage with it, although I have little interest in natural philosophy, except as a means to an end. The third head is a terrible creature, once married to your friend Harriet Laswell and stepfather to our mutual friend Narbondo – one Maurice De Salles. His is a long and interesting history. Would you like to hear it?"

"I'm well aware of it," said St. Ives.

"I'd wager a small sum that your knowledge is trifling. Suffice it to say that Clara Wright, who has magnificent hydroscopic powers, found De Salles's head buried several feet beneath the sandy bottom of a riverbed in your small corner of the Empire. The head had been preserved by Sarah Wright in a cunning manner – his life, that is, his faculties. Ironically, it would have been better for her to incinerate the head, if indeed the intention was to eradicate the man's spirit. That puts me in mind again of poor Harrow, who will soon begin to stink, I'm afraid."

He picked up the head of James Harrow, clutching it by the ears, and carried it to the furnace, where Willis Pule raised a hatch in the iron lid, his hand encased in an asbestos-lined glove. Klingheimer dropped the head into the red glow, flames leapt upward with a great roar, and Pule dropped the hatch into place.

"This oven attains a heat in excess of a thousand degrees centigrade," Klingheimer said. "It was built at no small expense by the factory that produced the Woking Crematorium. I fully expected that they would inquire as to its use, that they would be in some sense curious. But they were not curious. They fixed a price, and all of us were happy. I like a clear, single-minded motive, Professor. Indeed I do."

He gestured at the third head now, which had long, lank hair and eyes that might have belonged to Satan himself. The eyes twitched sporadically, as if something in the brain was overactive. Even so they had a demonic cast to them. "I like to refer to Maurice De Salles as 'the wizard,'" Klingheimer said. "He had quite a reputation among the cognoscenti. I was aware of his work at a very young age, and I had the pleasure of seeing him murder a boy with no other instrument than his mind. It was from De Salles that I bought the bottle of elixir I spoke of earlier, to my great good fortune."

"You had the *pleasure* of seeing him murder a boy? Finally you reveal yourself," said St. Ives.

"By 'pleasure' I meant a purely scientific satisfaction, of course. I took no *emotional* pleasure in the boy's death, nor did I feel any particular aversion. Death is the fate that awaits the lot of us, after all, unless we take steps to avert it. De Salles was a prodigy of arcane learning, to say the least. I have high hopes that he will recover his wits in time. His being a blood relative to Ignacio Narbondo might lead to interesting results were the two linked. But of course he cannot speak except in thought, which you are deaf to. His thoughts are primitive – distilled anger, eager hatred. Some would call it idiocy, which it might very well be. I communed with him only once, and his mind was… a force, and little more. But it was a force that I could… access. An accelerant, as it were, very like turpentine poured onto a fire. Listen! The wizard attempts speech!"

De Salles's mouth worked, bubbling out green fluid, his lips making a distinct flapping sound. Everything that Mother Laswell had told St. Ives about her dead husband was quite evidently true. It was written plainly on his face, even in its wizened, desiccated condition. If ever a head wanted badly to be cast into the furnace, it was the head of Maurice De Salles.

"Come, Professor," Mr. Klingheimer said, gesturing at the viewing seats, "I believe that you'll have a first-rate view in the second row. Take the seat two rows in front of Jimmy, if you will. Yes, directly in front of him, where he can put a bullet through your heart if the need arises. Pule, do us the favor of fetching Mr. Fez. Be quick about it. I'll reveal to you, Professor, that I intend to undertake a small experiment while Dr. Peavy is busy performing his duties as a mad doctor. I can assure you that the patient whose mind I intend to probe will not come to any harm. I beg you not to interfere. If Jimmy is compelled to shoot you, Alice will find your head in Mr. Harrow's basin, I'm afraid. We all wish for a happier outcome."

And then, to Jimmy, Klingheimer said, "It is my direct order that you shoot Professor St. Ives in the back if he endeavors any heroics, any at all. I need not tell you, however, that we must preserve the head."

St. Ives calculated the odds of taking Jimmy by surprise, liberating the pistol, and blowing Klingheimer to kingdom come.

The odds weren't at all good. The act would necessitate standing, turning, and scrambling over seats, which would give Jimmy adequate time to murder him or simply to knock him down with the butt of the pistol.

The door into the hallway opened, and Pule ushered the man wearing the Egyptian hat into the room. He looked about himself furtively. His head jerked uncontrollably, and he was attempting to speak, but could do little more than make noises in his throat. He hadn't been nearly so agitated when St. Ives had seen him previously. Pule guided him to the chair that Clara had recently vacated, put his hands on the man's shoulders, and compelled him to sit. Immediately he strapped his wrists and ankles and belted him into the chair at the waist and around the forehead.

"This fellow's name is Kairn," Mr. Klingheimer said to St. Ives. "Dr. Peavy tells me that his bill is paid promptly on the first day of the year by an unknown party – a bank draft. No one has visited the poor fellow in eight years now, alas. No one would know, in other words, whether he was alive or dead, or, if dead, how he died. He has a great fear of rats, has Mr. Kairn. Dr. Peavy put him to the test, do you see? Locked him into his room with a half dozen of the creatures. The result was extraordinary. It cost the poor man his tongue, which he chewed off in his fear. The rats were quite docile, actually – in no way did they threaten the man. They would have been content to build a nest in Mr. Kairn's hat. There was nothing in their behavior, in other words, to provoke the fear. It is entirely self-invented, as are the great majority of our fears, alas. I am curious to see whether I can bring him to such a pass merely by mental suggestion."

Klingheimer took a seat in a part of the theater that was out of Kairn's sight. He put on the aura goggles and held himself quite still, leaning forward now in evident concentration. Kairn had fallen silent, and he gripped the wooden arms so tightly that his knuckles were white. Nothing at all happened for the space of two or three minutes. Klingheimer's mouth was partly open, and he scarcely seemed to breathe, as if he had fallen into a self-induced trance.

Kairn's body abruptly went rigid. His eyes opened widely, and his head jittered rapidly up and down as if an electric current were running through him. He made a high, keening noise in his throat, and rocked his body erratically, the keening turning into a high-pitched shriek.

The wild idea came into St. Ives's head that he must break the spell, and he stood up and began to sing "God Save the Queen," as loudly as he could, but he got no farther than "Send her victorious…" before Klingheimer held up his palm and gave him a withering look. He shook his head at Jimmy, who was also standing now, the pistol aimed at St. Ives. Kairn had either fainted or died, although his head was held upright by the various restraints. He stirred now, and opened his eyes, looking around in apparent terror. Pule cast Kairn loose and supported the now-sobbing man out of the room.

"Well, well," Klingheimer said to St. Ives, a forced smile contorting his face, "if you will do me the favor of sitting in the chair recently vacated by Mr. Kairn, we will do what must be done."

St. Ives felt the muzzle of the pistol pressed against his back below his right shoulder blade, and when Jimmy grasped his collar in order to haul him to his feet, he stood up of his own accord. St. Ives decided that he would rather walk to the chair with some modicum of dignity and with his wits intact than be compelled by Jimmy. Pule reappeared after a minute and set about strapping St. Ives into the chair. St. Ives, for his part, set his mind to the task of thwarting Klingheimer's attempts overcome his mind, for surely that was what the man intended to do.

Klingheimer, however, crossed the room to a collection of machinery and drew out a wheeled cart. Whatever lay on top of the cart was hidden beneath a cloth. As he rolled the cart toward the center of the theater, Dr. Peavy returned and without a word began to wash his hands at a sink. Klingheimer maneuvered the cart to a position in front of St. Ives, before pulling the cloth away with the flourish of his hand.

Beneath the cloth lay a device that was at first unidentifiable. In the center of it, suspended in the air, was a metal cylinder of sufficient diameter to settle over a man's head, and below that was a wooden apparatus with supports that were obviously meant to lie on the shoulders of the victim.

"What you see before you is an electronic decapitator," Klingheimer said to St. Ives. He had regained his composure, and looked almost jolly. "It was built by Dr. Peavy, whose talents never fail to astonish me." He bowed in Peavy's direction, nodding in appreciation. Peavy dried his hands on a towel. "It is a great improvement on the guillotine, which can splinter bone and which compels itself through flesh by mere gravitational force.

"You are not situated in such a way as to see the intricacies of the circular blade, Professor, so I'll tell you about it. Electrical power causes the blade to spin, and as it spins, the circumference of the blade diminishes, the blade closing in upon itself. The blade is a simple spring, do you see, serrated and uncannily sharp, which maintains its shape as it is compressed. The compression of the blade is not absolute, however, and the last quarter inch of vertebra must be severed with a surgical saw. The decapitation is swift and clean, however, and the blade springs free of the incision when the electrical power ceases. The cylinder is raised an inch or two, Dr.

Peavy wields the bone saw, and *hey presto!*, the man in the chair has lost his head, although the head remains supported by the cylinder, ready for the plucking. What do you say to *that*, sir? Not a great deal, I take it. No pretty speeches? Another stanza of 'God Save the Queen,' perhaps, falsetto instead of tenor? Ha, ha! Now then, you'll note that the floor is clear in a radius of ten feet roundabout it. The saw makes for a regular Catherine wheel, but blood rather than sparks – quite an image, I dare say."

The door that led out onto the alley opened now, and Shadwell walked in. "She's here," he said to Klingheimer, and then he grinned at St. Ives.

"Excellent news!" Klingheimer said, rubbing his hands together. "*Really* first rate. Escort the lady in, if you will."

He turned to look at St. Ives now, and said, "I'm happy to say, Professor, that you'll be reunited with your own dear Alice without further ado."

THIRTY-TWO

FINN AND CLARA

Beaumont unlocked the door to the cellar and went in, groping with his hand to find the ribbon overhead that switched on the electric lamp, and knowing at once that all had changed since yesterday evening when he had last been here. The cellar was utterly silent, the machinery quiet. The stink of the toads was diminished, mixed with the smell of lye now. When the lights buzzed and brightened he saw that Narbondo's box was missing, although it was well past noon and should have returned from Peavy's by now.

The lot of it was gone – the heads, the machinery, the barrels of toad fluid – all of it cleared out, nothing left. The room had been swabbed down. They had shifted wholesale to Peavy's, giving Beaumont no part in it. They must have been at it all morning while the others were searching for Finn. He shifted his knapsack on his back, his coat hiding it somewhat – nothing left in the garret that was worth taking.

He stood for a moment calculating. He was out of a situation, and no doubt about it. Klingheimer had given him the day's holiday because Klingheimer no longer had any use for Beaumont. How much time did he have, he wondered, before Klingheimer returned from Peavy's and sent for him in order to have a squint at him through the spectacles, or simply to have him hit on the head with a lead pipe?

He was certain that Klingheimer hadn't returned from Peavy's yet. The house was in too much of a taking. Klingheimer's influence in the house was absent, and had been since he'd turned his mind to Clara. There was a brutish air about the place, as if it was coming apart, everyone seeing to himself.

He turned in through the door of the storage room and switched on the light there. Plucking an empty flour sack from the heap, he set about loading it up with food. Drink they would find easily enough underground, but they'd get precious sick of eating dried meat if they couldn't bring down a pig or a goat. He thanked God that he had stowed the rifle and plenty of cartridge in the hovel. When Klingheimer came for them, which he surely would, he wouldn't expect the rifle.

He looked up and down the hallway before going out – empty in both directions – and he headed toward the stairs carrying the sack. On the second floor the hallway was again empty, although he heard a sneeze and then a blasphemy from within the card room, which had broad double doors, standing open now. There was low talk from within, and they would see him carrying the bag if he passed. Also, he wanted to have a look into the room, where there were odds and ends that he could nick. He stepped into a handy alcove and waited.

"My ear's just about severed," someone in the card room said. "God-*damn* that fat pig."

"You should have murdered him straightaway when you got into the alley. That's what I'd have done. Leave him for the dustman to find." Beaumont recognized Smythe's voice, and knew that the other must be Joe Penny, the two of them being pals, and Smythe having brought in the woman.

"He was on me like a shite-bird. I had no time to murder anyone. Now you've come home with the Bracken piece and I've got nothing but a bloody ear and two teeth knocked into the dirt."

"And I've been skewered in three places, the whore," Smythe said. "I mean to teach her a lesson, is what. No woman treats me so and lives to gloat, I can tell you that."

"Gag her. She'll raise the house otherwise."

"His majesty is out for the day. To hell with the house. In any case a woman can't shriek once her throat is slit."

"Well, I mean to look in on the blind girl," Penny said. "You ain't having all the fun."

"You're a stupid sod, Joseph Penny. The girl's marked for his majesty. You're worried about raising the house, and now *this* caper?"

"She can't speak nor see. Don't you know that? It's no kind of secret."

"It's coming it pretty high, is what it is."

"Well, I'm sick of this place," Penny said. "I shouldn't have come back this morning. If that fat bastard from the inn shows up and fronts Klingheimer like he said he would, it's over for me. I might as leave have my way with the girl now, while I've got the chance."

"It's your funeral, then," Smythe said. "We're wasting our breath sitting here, though."

There was the sound of the two men moving. Beaumont stayed where he was, well hidden, the two men going away toward the stairs to the upper floors. He peered past the doorjamb and saw their backs, and he took the chance of darting around into the now empty card room, where he plucked up six nice scrimshaw pieces on the mantelshelf, all of them carved in the last century if he was any judge, which he was. He looked around for something else, seeing a pair of silver candlesticks. He pitched the candles into the coalscuttle and put the silver into the sack before peering down the hallway again – empty. He returned to the hearth for the fireplace poker, heavy iron, and then trotted along to the stairs, seeing that they were clear before going up.

Finn watched the brougham drive past on the street. He hoped that Clara was inside, although the angle was too steep for him to know. Mother Laswell hurried away in the direction of the Temple, carrying his message. He went to the desk and shoveled everything back into the creel, looked about to make certain nothing was amiss, and then slid beneath the bed, in among his things, nearly sneezing with the dust that lifted from the floorboards. He waited, listening hard, the time crawling past. When the key turned in the lock, the sound surprised him, and he held his breath, ready to move fast if he had to. Someone sat on the bed, however. The door closed and the key turned.

"Finn, is it you?" Clara asked, and Finn, elated, pushed out from under the bed and stood up.

"Yes, it's me, Clara," he said. "Are you... safe? Were you at Peavy's? You're dressed very elegant."

"Yes, mostly. Klingheimer means to marry me, and tells me that this is my wedding dress. I'd rather be dead."

"Don't say so, Clara. It's bad luck."

"Professor St. Ives was there, Finn. They've captured him. I don't know what they mean to do to him."

Finn was silenced by this. "Was the Professor hurt?" he asked finally.

"No. Not that I saw. Mr. Klingheimer was talking away to him six to the dozen, telling him things, like he does. He's full of himself, is Mr. Klingheimer. He's a terrible man, Finn."

"I believe you," Finn said. "He nearly had me this morning, but I bolted. I found my friend Beaumont, and he let me into this room to hide me. I've been here for a time, wondering if you were coming back."

"And I wondered whether you would be here when I returned. When we drew nigh to the house, I was sure that you would be. That's why I said your name when I came into the room."

"Tell me, Clara, Mr. Klingheimer must still be there? He's not here? Not in the house?"

"Yes, he's still there, lording it over them. I was brought home by the man they call Flinders. There's great activity at Dr. Peavy's. He sent me back to rest, but he means to come for me again tonight. I don't know if…"

In the pause that followed, Finn heard footsteps in the hallway. "I'll hide beneath the bed," he whispered to Clara, and very quietly he slipped out of sight again. There was the sound of laughter from down the hall – men's laughter – and then of a door banging open, and a woman's voice saying something coarse. Laughter again, and the door closing, and then a moment's silence before the metallic clinking of a key in their own door lock. Perhaps it was a plate of food being brought in…

There was the sound of someone entering, saying nothing, and of the door closing behind and locking. Finn saw boots moving, the man who wore them standing silently over the bed. "You've been waiting for me like a good lass," he said quietly. "If you can't hear, then I'm wasting my breath, but if you can hear, then you listen to me. If you call out, you're dead. There's no Mr. Klingheimer here to save you. Them that's left in the house might come, but they're worse than me. Do you understand me, girl?"

Silence followed, and then the man said. "It makes no matter, does it? You'll understand well enough in a moment."

Finn saw his trousers slide to the floor, then, and he yanked them off over his shoes. The bed slumped and creaked under his weight, and Finn very carefully slid out from under again, not making a sound, pulling himself around to the footboard. He stood up, grasped the handle of the water pitcher, and without hesitation, clubbed the man hard on the side of the head. The handle broke free, blood flew, and the pitcher thumped down on the bedside table with a loud bang. The blow had snapped the man's head aside, and he slumped sideways off the bed now, falling onto the floor where he lay unconscious.

A fter an hour of loitering, and despite seeing several men going in and out of Klingheimer's carriage house – neither Smythe not Penny among them – Tubby had learned nothing useful except that he was prodigiously hungry despite having consumed two breakfasts this morning. He had spent an empty half hour looking over the wares in the nearby tobacco shop, while surreptitiously watching through the window, and had bought an envelope of headache powder from the chemist before going out into the wind to complete his third pass. He walked slowly now, taking an obvious interest in the great house beyond the wall. If Penny or Smythe saw him, his very presence on the pavement would dare them to come out. But neither Penny nor Smythe appeared, and it had begun to look as if he had sent himself on a fool's errand. His anger and determination had quite drained out of him, leaving him with the unhappy dregs of defeat.

He walked past the mouth of the narrow, shrub-lined alley that led along the side of the house, determined to make his way back to the Half Toad. On impulse he turned down toward the river, however, passing a red-painted door in the wall of the house. He glanced fore and aft, seeing no one, and tried the door, which of course was locked. It came into his mind to knock, and then to simply burst in when the door opened, but doing so would be a rash act, quite likely fatal, and so he walked on.

A man appeared ahead of him, Tubby nodding to him as they passed, receiving a scowl in return. At the end of the alley Tubby looked back, seeing that the man was just then going in through the door, the house swallowing him up. On impulse Tubby retraced his steps, seeing ahead of him an opening in the shrubbery wide enough to hide him.

Holding the pitcher handle, Finn stood listening in the sudden silence. It was quite possible that someone had heard. The man's head and elbow had both knocked on the floorboards, and the noise of the pitcher had been loud. He looked at the man who lay there, blood pooling around his head. Finn was shocked by the quantity of blood. Was he dead? Abruptly the man made a rattling sound in his throat, gasping for air. Finn set the pitcher handle next to the water glass, went around to the side of the bed, and slid out his things. "Did he hurt you, Clara?" he asked as he pulled on his shoes.

"No. He didn't touch me. He hadn't time. Listen, Finn. The house is stirring. Can we get out?"

There was a tumult of some sort in a room down the hall – the screaming woman fighting back, perhaps. And now once again there was the sound of a key turning in the lock. Finn snatched open the creel, yanked his knife from its sheath, and leapt toward the door as it swung open.

Beaumont slipped through, pulling the door shut after him and shifting his bag in front of him when he saw the knife in Finn's hand and the man who lay bleeding on the floor. He carried a fireplace poker. "I heard the ruckus coming up," he said.

"This is Miss Clara," Finn said. "Clara, it's Beaumont, who I told you about. Are we running?"

"Aye," the dwarf said. "This clatter will bring Smythe, who's with the woman." He nodded at the man on the floor. "That there's Joe Penny, with his trousers around his feet," he said. "Is he dead? Best if he is."

"I don't know," Finn said.

Beaumont glanced at Clara, who was up and gathering the few possessions that she had carried from Hereafter Farm. Beaumont knelt down and put the iron bar of the fireplace poker across Penny's throat, but before he pressed any remaining life out of him, the door flew open and a heavy man in a frilled shirt and stocking feet stepped in. He looked down at Penny bleeding on the floor and at Beaumont, who had stood up now. In that moment a female voice cried out, "You're mine now, Bucko!" and a short, stout woman with wild hair appeared behind Smythe and began beating him across the back of the head with the broken-off leg of a chair, swinging her weapon with shocking force, driving Smythe's head downward with each blow.

Finn moved Clara behind him and backed away toward the far corner of the room as Smythe turned on the woman with a roar. She struck him again in the forehead, and the chair leg broke in two. Beaumont, who leapt to his feet as Smythe turned away, was already swinging the iron poker, cracking it against Smythe's wrist, which was trailing behind him. The woman fled away down the hall, Beaumont and Smythe moving out of the room after her.

"Stay here," Finn said to Clara, and he ran after them, gripping his knife, but there was no opening for him to lunge in. Beaumont wielded the poker like a saber, thrusting and parrying, gouging the man with the point of the thing and then hammering him, the poker whistling as he swung it. The woman reappeared, carrying the broken chair in its entirety, then smashing it wholesale over Smythe's head, she and Beaumont beating the man to the ground together. Beaumont stepped away, breathing hard, but the woman, dressed in a peignoir, but with her coat over it and her boots on her feet, calmly stepped on Smythe's face with the heel of her boot and leaned her weight on it.

"You've done good work, ma'am," Beaumont said, gasping, "but I'll ask you to let me finish it quick."

"Charmed, sir," she said, stepping back.

"In the room with him," Beaumont said to Finn, and the two of them grabbed Smythe's feet and hauled him through the doorway, laying him alongside Joe Penny.

Finn took Clara out into the hall, saying to the woman, "You must trust us, ma'am. Get what things you need. We're running."

"I'm with you," she said, already hurrying away.

Finn drew the door shut, having no real idea what Clara could see or could not see. Hearing was bad enough, and he led her farther from the door, which opened again a bare moment later. Beaumont stepped out, his face giving nothing away, and a moment later the woman rejoined them, fully dressed now and carrying her bag.

"My name is Cecilia Bracken," she said to them.

"Finn and Clara," Finn said, "and this is Beaumont."

"There's gallantry for you," she said, taking Beaumont's hand and kissing it, which seemed to stupefy the dwarf, who made a bow before turning away to lock the two corpses inside the room.

Then the lot of them hurried away along the hall, Miss Bracken taking Clara by the arm now and nodding to Finn as if giving him leave to do what he must. He wished that she had brought one of the remaining chair legs.

Down the stairs they went, Finn and Beaumont ahead and the women behind.

Into the lion's den, Finn thought. Then he saw the shadows of two men ascending, followed by the men themselves, looking upward, coming along in a rush. Finn bent at the knees and launched himself from the edge of a stair tread, rolling himself into a ball and striking both men at once and bowling them over. The three of them tumbled downward in a tangle, Finn's creel smashing to bits beneath him.

Finn rolled out onto the landing and onto his feet. His carved owl caromed off the wainscot, and Finn snatched it up and pocketed it just as Beaumont ranged in among them, swinging his poker, his face strangely calm. Miss Bracken helped Clara past the sprawled men, and they were off again, down the last set of stairs to the ground floor, where a strange-looking, skeletal woman in an old green gown shouted incoherencies.

"Shut your gob, Mrs. Skink," Beaumont yelled at her.

Miss Bracken stepped past him, leaving Clara behind, and ran forward and struck Mrs. Skink hard on the side of the head with her fist, then pushed her over backward onto a wooden settle. She bent down and picked up the front of the settle and flung it over backward again, Mrs. Skink shouting "Oh! Oh! Oh!" as she rolled into the wall, the settle lying atop her.

Again they were running, Finn holding Clara's hand, Miss Bracken following. They were in a long hallway now, nothing to trip them up, a door at the far end – freedom if they could open it! He heard the sounds of pursuit from somewhere behind and a muffled shouting from Mrs. Skink. Finn saw that the door was barred, and with a heavy lock for good measure. A man looked out of a door on the left-hand side of the hallway, and then disappeared back into whatever room lay there. Beaumont, running swiftly on his short legs and waving his fireplace poker over his head, dipped into his pocket and came up with a key that he tossed at Finn before turning into the open doorway where the man had vanished.

Finn snatched the flying key, left Clara with Miss Bracken again, and opened the lock as quickly as he could, then yanked the bar out of its place, snapped open the Chubb lock, and flung back the door onto blessed daylight. He stepped aside so that Miss Bracken could haul Clara out past him. From the corner of his eye Finn saw Beaumont coming back toward him. Behind the dwarf a man pushed himself to his feet, a bloody gash on his chin.

Now there were three more men – four – coming on hard behind, pouring into the hallway in a rout. "Out! Out!" Beaumont shouted, pushing Finn from behind, and out they went, Beaumont pulling the door shut. Finn heard the Chubb lock engage with a metallic clank. He also heard Mrs. Bracken wheezing to catch her breath, Clara holding tightly to her; neither was moving. Then Finn saw a man, very heavy and powerful, step half out of the bushes several yards along the alley. He stood waiting in the shadows, holding a cudgel – the end of things, Finn thought.

Except that it wasn't the end of things. It was Tubby Frobisher, like an angel come from the sky. "Tubby!" Finn shouted, following Miss Bracken down the three stairs, Beaumont at his heels.

Tubby stepped aside and waved them past, the surprise on his face equal, surely, to Finn's own. "Go on, then!" Tubby cried.

Finn looked back to see Tubby wading toward the men just then coming through the door, a two-handed grip on his stick.

It was an escape, and no doubt about it, Tubby thought as he stepped aside to let the four pass, immensely surprised that it was Cecilia Bracken who leapt past him, her hatless hair flying about her head, and she holding the hand of an apparently blind girl wearing smoked glasses – certainly the girl Clara, Mother Laswell's charge. Finn Conrad plunged past, followed by the strangest dwarf Tubby had ever seen. He was carrying a flour sack in one hand and holding tight to an enormous beaver hat with the other, a hat big enough to contain a severed head as well as the dwarf's own.

Four men bowled out from within the house now, two of them turning away – up toward Lazarus Walk – and the other two running straight at Tubby, obviously pursuing those who had fled. The men slowed at the sight of him, but then came on again, running hard.

THIRTY-THREE
FLIGHT

Finn and his three companions rounded the corner, Clara running flat-footed but gamely in her lead-soled shoes, her gown hiked up to her knees. Finn held onto her hand now, and she showed no hesitation, but trusted him utterly. Beaumont had run on ahead, but Finn, determined to leave no one behind, had no intention of outpacing Miss Bracken. They dodged the traffic and pedestrians on the Embankment, hurried beneath the leafless trees, and descended a set of stone stairs to the river, where a man in a rowing boat was just shipping his oars as another man stepped out onto a small pier and tied a line to a bollard. Finn tipped his cap, and the two men nodded back at him, giving him a curious look. The four of them were well worth staring at, Finn thought, which was problematic.

Beaumont led the way beneath Blackfriars Rail Bridge, turning uphill in the shadow of the bridge toward the Embankment again. He drew to a halt between two heavy stanchions, further hidden by the darkness. For a time no one spoke, but merely breathed. Miss Bracken bent forward and placed her hands on her knees, her wind whooshing in and out of her lungs. The mud bank smell of the Thames was strong, and in the gloomy half-light Finn could see the rubbish cast up by the river. Despite the dimness, Finn felt exposed. They were a curious group, to be sure, with no possibility of disguising themselves.

The problem of Ned Ludd sprang into Finn's mind – a further complication. He wished that he had included Ned's whereabouts in the note that he had heaved at Mother Laswell. If worse came to worst, she could fetch Ned herself. But it hadn't come to that yet. The George Inn wasn't far away, although how they were going to get there without imperiling themselves, Finn couldn't say. The afternoon was already darkening, however, with clouds in the west hiding the sun. With luck, night would come early.

"Dear me," Miss Bracken said after her bout of hard breathing, "I believe I'll live after all. If we intend to hide beneath this bridge for any length of time, we might as well make ourselves better known to each other."

"This is Miss Clara," Finn said, thinking that it was unlikely that Clara would speak for herself, although he was equally worried about being too forward. Clara curtsied but said nothing, and he went on: "I'm Finn Conrad, and we both of us come from Aylesford."

"And you knew Tubby Frobisher, the fat man in the lane?" she said.

"Yes," said Finn. "Do you, too, then?"

"Indeed I do. I'm betrothed to that man's uncle."

"To *Gilbert Frobisher*?" Finn asked, astonished to hear this.

"Indeed. The poor man is lost below ground."

"He might still be alive," Beaumont said. "We found the newspaper what wrapped his sandwich, if it was his and not the other's – Professor St. Ives."

A train clattered along overhead now, making speaking impossible for a time. Boats spun past beneath the bridge, the river running fast and high through the narrows.

"I know nothing of a sandwich," said Miss Bracken when the train moved on. "Gilbert and the Professor descended together. Neither returned. But I won't say that either of them is lost until there's proof. *Show me the body*. I shall say just those words until my dying day. And what is your name, my small friend?"

"Beaumont the Dwarf, ma'am, although some call me Zounds."

"How did you come to be in the house?" Finn asked Miss Bracken.

"I was taken off the street by the villain Smythe, who tricked me with a falsehood. I should have seen through him, for I've met his type often enough. But I very much wanted to believe he was doing me a kindness. My heart got in the way of my sense, I'm afraid."

"Aye, that's the way with hearts," Beaumont said. "Smythe won't bother you again. The worms already have him by the toe. Now that we're all mates I'll say that we must lie low until after dark and then go back the way we've come. It's dangerous above ground with Klingheimer's men looking out for us. They've got urchin boys, you see, who they'll put to the search for a shilling or two. The sooner we're down below, the better."

"We mean to go underground to Aylesford," Finn said, by way of explanation, although he scarcely understood it himself.

"Where my own Gilbert disappeared?" Miss Bracken asked.

"Just so," Beaumont told her.

"That's good. That's *very* good. We'll search for him. We'll find my Gilbert and bring him out with us. That's just what we'll do."

"When it's dark we can go below," Beaumont said. "I know a way. But for now we've got to lay up somewhere out of the way like."

"Before we go under we've got to fetch Ned Ludd, Clara's mule," Finn said. "I rode into London on his back, and I won't leave him behind. I made him a promise. We'll take him along below with us."

"A *mule*?" Beaumont asked.

"Yes," said Finn. "He's in Southwark, at the George Inn. Close by." Clara squeezed his hand, for which Finn was thankful.

Beaumont stood contemplating and then said, "The mule might be the death of us."

"Or the life of us," Finn said. "He can carry two of us if the way below is hard. And the mule speaks to Clara. Ned Ludd is more alive than the heads on the plates, and he's a Christian mule. It was Balaam's donkey that spoke out loud when the Angel of the Lord was blocking the way, and he was let into heaven for it."

Beaumont considered this. "My uncle had a mule as could ring the Pancake Bell upon Shrove Tuesday," he said. "We give him a pan of grease for it."

"There you have it then," Miss Bracken said. "You can't argue with the pancake bell."

"Then we'll cross the river in the boat these two men just left a-lying there," Beaumont said. "But coming back to this side, even after night fall?" He shook his head. "And leading a *mule*? It won't hardly answer."

"Shush," Clara said suddenly, and Beaumont fell quiet. There were footsteps approaching, and the four of them moved farther up the shingle, deeper into the shadows. A man appeared, stepping out of the sunlight and into the darkness beneath the bridge, and then standing still while his eyes found their way. Finn let go of Clara's hand, ready to fight if he had to. If he was quick, he could rush the man and knock him into the river where it ran swiftly beneath the arch. The current would sweep him downriver long enough for them to run. The man looked roundabout himself carefully, seeing them now.

"Zounds!" he said, bending over to look harder at them. "Here you are then, with the boy and the women, a-standing about like statuary. It's your infernal hat that caught my eye, Zounds. A man can't hide in such a rig as that. They're a-looking for you up and down. They found Penny and Smythe beaten and choked out, and they think it's you what done it. Klingheimer will murder the lot of us for letting it happen when he comes back from Peavy's."

"This here is Arthur Bates," Beaumont said, gesturing in the man's direction. "I'm glad it's you, Bates. You'll not give us up. Klingheimer can go to the devil, and Peavy with him."

"That's right. But the word's gone out for a reward if you're taken, Zounds, so every boy in the street is looking out. London Bridge ain't safe, nor Queen Street nor Blackfriars neither. Shadwell knows the girl's from Aylesford, and they're watching the roads east."

"What of the house where they've been a-digging?" Beaumont asked. "Near Temple. You know the one, mayhaps, though they kept it from me."

"Nothing. What of it?"

"Is there a lookout, I mean."

"Not that I know. But I ain't been there, Zounds, not recent. Why would they watch it?"

"It ain't *why* would they watch it, Bates; it's *if they ain't* a-watching it."

"Well they *mayn't be* is as good as I can say. I've got to be on my way now. I won't peach on you, Zounds, but that hat..." He shook his head.

"He is quite correct," Miss Bracken said. "This disreputable hat doesn't show your features to advantage. Not at all. You're not a man who is difficult to look at when you haven't got this egg upon your head."

Beaumont blinked at her, apparently having nothing to say to this.

"And you, Mr. Bates," Miss Bracken said. "Won't you quit that dreadful place? You don't belong in that house, a good man like you."

"I'm owed nigh onto twenty pound, ma'am, and I mean to have it before I scarper," Bates said, nodding a goodbye to them while already walking away.

They watched him out of sight and then turned toward the boat – the sooner across the river the better. The men who had arrived in it were nowhere to be seen. They were well heeled, it seemed to Finn, and could afford to lose their little boat, if that was what came of their borrowing it. Beaumont went straight to it and untied the dock line as if the boat were his. They climbed in, and within moments were skimming along downriver on the tide, Beaumont pulling hard and steadily through the shipping toward the opposite shore, all of them looking studiously at the water that sloshed across the planking in the bottom.

Tubby stepped aside as he had been commanded to do, his back in the shrubbery, gripping his stick with both hands. As the first man rushed past, he swung the knurled end into the man's face, a vicious, chopping blow that caught him on the bridge of his nose. His head flew back, and he fell into the arms of the second man, whose eyes shot open in surprise. Tubby's bowler flew off as he speared the stick over the head of the first man, throwing his considerable weight into the blow and ramming the brass tip into the second man's forehead, the two men falling in a heap together.

It came to Tubby that he might have killed the man with the broken nose, and in fact he appeared to have no nose at all, just a bloody pulp where it had been. It was time to retreat, perhaps. The second man tried to roll clear of his companion, however, and Tubby had no choice but to hit him a second time, catching him on the shoulder, and in that moment, yet another man, dressed in an apron, issued from the door carrying a bent iron poker. Without a second's pause the new man saw what was what and pitched the poker hard at Tubby, who had time to turn his face aside and throw an arm up. He felt it carve a deep furrow over his ear, although he sensed no pain at all. His man was weaponless now, and so Tubby roared at him, gripping his stick and swinging it back over his shoulder – just enough room in the alley for a roundhouse blow. But his adversary was having none of it. He turned around and jumped back in through the open door, Tubby at his heels.

Tubby stopped himself at the threshold, however, and shouted, "Tell your master that Tubby Frobisher has come for him!"

There was an answering shout from nearby: "The *pistol*, Mrs. Skink!" and Tubby made away down the alley at a heavy run, snatching up his bowler and heading toward the Embankment. He had no desire to face down a man with a pistol in a narrow alley, and it occurred to him that with every passing moment there was more of a chance that his way would be blocked by the two men who had gone out into the street and might easily have come around behind, searching for Finn and his lot.

He felt his own blood running freely down his neck, seeping in under his collar. He probed the patch of scalp that hung loose, gingerly pressing it closed before placing the brim of his bowler along the wound and then painfully tugging the hat down until it secured the injury – perhaps the first hat-band bandage on record. He came out at Temple Avenue, seeing the open cistern that had stood there for a decade and hurrying down toward it, blessing the Cattle Trough Association for putting it there. The gray water was floating with horsehair, but he swept it clear and splashed it onto his neck by the handful, wiping the blood away, rinsing his hand in the trough and swabbing it again. *Clean enough*, he thought, heading down toward the cab-stand at King's Bench.

"Half Toad, Smithfield!" he said to the cabby, and he slumped gratefully onto the seat and closed the door against the wind that blew cold against his wet clothing. Two of Klingheimer's men trotted past, the one's blue shirt giving him away as one of the first two that had come out through the door. Good – they were still searching. Tubby slumped lower in the seat, holding tightly to his cudgel, coming up again when his coach had rounded the corner and was moving away at a fair pace.

The afternoon was wearing on, and he wondered whether his companions were gone from the Half Toad, and whether they would have left him a message. He had stirred up a hornet's nest for certain, against Alice and Hasbro's wishes, not to mention being truant from the dinner meeting. But there was virtue in it. He had forestalled whatever fate had lain in store for Finn Conrad and his odd companions, and he knew beyond doubt that Finn and Clara were safe, at least for the moment.

The wound on the side of his head throbbed, the pain pulsing from temple to temple, but the bleeding had stopped, his hat-band doing its job. He thought about his luck – three against one, and he had lain out two of them and sent the third packing: a satisfactory rout. The coach headed up Old Bailey now, Newgate Prison off to the right, and within minutes Fingal Street and Lambert Court came into view ahead, and he saw the great wooden toad that looked out from over the door of the inn. A wave of relief swept through him, and it came to him that a roast chicken and a glass of beer would set him up admirably. Uncle Gilbert would scarcely deny him the pleasure.

THIRTY-FOUR

THE CALM BEFORE

"It's time, Finn. Pull in the anchor," Beaumont said, taking his pipe from his mouth and knocking the burning tobacco over the side. They sat in their borrowed rowing boat near the Bankside shore, with its tumbledown riverside buildings, the people picking their way across the mud that lay stinking along the water's edge, searching for whatever might have been left by the falling tide. The four in the boat had spent the past hour out of the wind on the lee side of a schooner that also sheltered them from the view from Southwark Bridge, mostly from people crossing from the Queen Street side, which meant Klingheimer's men. The schooner's bow shouldered the current around the rowing boat, making for an easy anchorage. Blackfriars Bridge lay upriver, distant enough so that they were safe from lookouts, unless the lookout had a telescope. Night was fast falling, however, and with it came a modicum of safety, if they looked sharp and wasted no time.

Finn hauled in the anchor, the iron flukes dripping water on his shoes, while Beaumont was already pulling away. They moved along beneath Southwark Bridge toward London Bridge and the steps just beyond. When they were out of the shelter of the schooner, the wind grew sharp, but at least there was no rain falling from the heavy clouds. The ships riding at anchor in the Pool of London were dark silhouettes dotted with lamplight.

"I like your idea, Finn," Beaumont said. "It'll work. You trust the ostler, then, at the George?"

"He's a friend. I've known him from old."

"It seems bad luck to travel in a hearse before one's time," Miss Bracken said.

"Worse luck to be caught on the bridge by Mr. Shadwell or one of his men," Beaumont told her. "They'll be quaking like a baby, thinking of Mr. Klingheimer asking for a reckoning, and they'll cop it for sure if we don't cop it first."

"I don't know the man Shadwell. Is he worse than Mr. Smythe?" Miss Bracken asked.

"Smythe is royalty compared to Shadwell. But Shadwell won't look twice at a hearse, and he don't know your mule. We'll fox him yet."

The boat bumped up against the stairs, and Finn tied it up tightly. He didn't hold with theft, but he held even less with being caught for theft. The boat was brightly painted, an odd green color that couldn't be mistaken, and was easily visible by anyone crossing the bridge in daylight. They climbed the steps, walking amidst the crowds crossing London Bridge. Beaumont went on ahead of them, being the most visible even though he was small. Finn and Clara followed, and Miss Bracken walked along behind, carrying Beaumont's hat as if it were a large purse.

Beaumont angled into the shadows alongside the darkened interior of the Borough Market now. Finn followed, looking back over his shoulder to see that Miss Bracken was still in sight. All were aware of their destination, although Miss Bracken, being new to London, knew it only by description, and Clara was blind, except for her sighted elbow, which was as useful in the dark as in full daylight. Still and all, Finn would rather die than drop her hand. There was St. Thomas Street opposite, and Beaumont crossing the High Street now, the George Inn just ahead. Finn listened for the shouting and the rush of feet that would herald their end, but there were none. He glanced back again, surprised to see Miss Bracken directly behind them now.

He put his arm through Clara's, holding tightly. They walked around into the courtyard – its galleries lit, the fire burning in the center of the yard within its stone enclosure, and, to his vast relief, Arwyn holding a pair of black horses steady while two people climbed into the coach that the horses would pull.

Finn waved at him, Arwyn nodded, and within minutes they were within the shelter of the stables, Finn laying out his plan.

The Half Toad was quiet but for the sounds of supper preparations in the kitchen. The late afternoon lay gloomy and prematurely dark beyond the bullseye glass of the windows, where quavering images passed up and down the Fingal Street pavement. "I can't *stand* the waiting," Bill Kraken said to Hasbro and Mother Laswell, the three of them sitting at their customary table, talking low so as not to be overheard. "I say we go a-looking for Tubby or go on to Peavy's without him."

"And two minutes after you'd gone out looking, he'd walk in through the door, and then someone would have to go out looking for *you*," Mother Laswell told him. "We've agreed to wait until the clock strikes four, twenty minutes from now."

Henrietta Billson came out of the kitchen just then with the dinner they'd put off because of Tubby's absence. She laid it out on the table next to Finn's Christmas pudding message. Dinner was a four-decker sea pie, with strata of mushrooms, onions, peas, carrots, and sage smothered with pork and chicken in gravy, each layer laid over with a crust of flour, steam ascending from blowholes in the crusty brown top. There were no fish in the pie, despite its oceanic name.

Kraken squinted at the food. "My guts is pinched shut," he said. "I can't eat. The Professor's late by nigh on to two hours. Never was there a man more timely than the Professor. He said he'd send word if he weren't coming, but there *ain't been no word*, which there *would* be could he have sent it. Did they take the Professor, too, is what I'm asking."

"Just you try this pie, Mr. Kraken," Henrietta said. "You'll be happy for it an hour from now, and I'll hear nothing to the contrary. Food in the stomach is foundational. There can be no life without it." She took a vast wide spoon out of her apron and heaped pie onto their several plates.

In the middle of the heaping, the inn door opened and Tubby strode in, nodding at his companions and looking around at the other patrons, of which there were three – a man and a woman near the fire and an old gentleman nodding over his newspaper.

Mother Laswell looked hard at Tubby, who was in a state of advanced gore. "God help us," she said when he arrived at the table.

"Sound as a bell, my friends," he said, patting his bowler gingerly. "My apologies for my tardiness. Give me a moment to wash up, and I'm your man."

"But what news, Tubby?" Kraken asked him.

"Good news, Bill," he said. "Finn and Clara and their lot are free of Klingheimer's house. A knot of villains was chasing them, but I put paid to their capers. Two notches on my stick, and a third man sent packing. A good afternoon's work, although I learned nothing of Klingheimer, nothing at all. It was dumb luck that I came along when I did."

With that, Tubby turned away and mounted the stairs, keeping his head judiciously turned away from the patrons, who in fact paid him no mind.

In the silence that followed, Hasbro considered what Kraken and Mother Laswell had told him about the dead house, about Shadwell driving the cart away with a coffin in the back, about the man nailed into what might be his own coffin if he weren't set free, and his freedom dependent upon his honesty. "We must assume that they *have* taken St. Ives," he said, looking at Kraken, who still hadn't touched his food.

"Or maybe this Klingheimer means to draw all of us into his web now that we know enough to be a danger to him," Mother put in.

"Possibly," Hasbro said to her, "but we must find out in any event. There is no choice. What do you know of Wimpole Street, Bill? I can picture the surgeries and the general lay of things. Most of the buildings are fenced – a broad, open street, as I recall."

He watched as Kraken rubbed his chin with his fingers and stared into his ale glass. Bill Kraken had lived on the streets of London for years, and he knew every inch of it. He fairly loathed the city, however, for what it had done to him – driven him mad for a time.

"Posh houses out that way," he said after thinking for a moment, "and the medicos, like you spoke. There's an alley runs along behind it, the back way into doctors' houses, deliveries and such. All sorts coming and going, early and late. Corpses in and out, greengrocers and fishmongers...."

Tubby reappeared wearing a fresh shirt and vest, his face washed clean. His hat still stood atop his head, pulled down tightly. "By God this is food to set a person up," he said, plunging his fork into his portion of pie and hacking up the crust. In a lower voice, he said, "Here's the way of it: Finn and his lot came out of a door in Klingheimer's house and made away toward the river. Miss Bracken was with them, along with a dwarf in a beaver hat."

"Lord have mercy," Mother Laswell said. "I saw the Bracken woman through a high window, and I knew it was no good that she was there – a prisoner, I thought. It's a blessing she's out."

"What manner of dwarf?" Kraken asked, narrowing his eyes.

"Smallish," Tubby told him, "but a game dwarf. He gave me a fierce look as he passed me. If Finn had not called out my name, I'm certain the dwarf would have savaged me. Pardon me if I don't remove my bowler, Mother. It's currently holding my head together."

"You'll want a doctor," Mother Laswell said.

"To the contrary, I want nothing more than my share of this capital pie, two glasses of ale, and to know what's up. Where are Alice and St. Ives?"

"Missing," said Hasbro. "The both of them."

"*Neither returned?*"

"No, sir," Kraken said.

While they ate, making a job of it but wasting no time, they caught each other up. Kraken told what happened to Alice, and Mother showed Tubby the missive from Finn – welcome evidence that they might yet find a way into the underworld to search for Gilbert.

"Now that we're all assembled," Hasbro said, "I can think of no better plan than to proceed to Wimpole Street, Bill leading the way. Tubby and I will approach from the street, and Mother and Bill from the alley – front and back, and no hullabaloo. Whoever succeeds first will let the others in. And mark me, the asylum is full of innocents. We cannot be careless."

"And yet we must assume that no one is innocent," Tubby said. "Klingheimer's house is full of cutthroats. The same must be true of Peavy's."

"I'll attend to the boarders," Mother Laswell said. "Hereafter Farm has seen its share of those who have been touched. It's them who first called me mother, aside from my own sons. I have a way with them."

"Well then," Tubby said. "Death or glory, I say. More notches for my stick, if my luck is in."

"I counsel a quiet glory," Hasbro said. "Our friends are in a precarious way. These men mustn't know of our existence until we're upon them."

"Agreed," Tubby said, "but they'll know of it then, by God."

THIRTY-FIVE

THE MADHOUSE

So this is how it ends, St. Ives thought, and it came into his mind that he had never in his life done anything more suicidally foolish than he had today – looking into the asylum alone, betting his life on the kindly demeanor of the old gatekeeper. When Pule had locked the gate, trapping him inside, the tale had been told, all but the epilogue.

But was that true, or was there a larger, more damning truth? He thought about the murder of Sarah Wright and his saying that he would "look into it." He had visited Pullman and learned the details of the woman's death. He had visited the icehouse and had his suspicions verified, or something near to that. He had passed the false policemen on the road, and he had known that there was something wrong with them. He had been happy with the notion that Clara's problem could be solved by whisking her away to Yorkshire, and had left for London without a backward glance in order to take a scientific ramble that had come to nothing beyond ruination. Klingheimer was forthright in his self-regard and his contemptible undertakings, but St. Ives had believed in himself no less – in his own rationalizations – and not in the apparent truth.

The squeaking of wheels interrupted his thinking. He could see nothing of what was transpiring behind him, although he knew that the door was still open – could smell the fresh air blowing in. He was unable to turn his head, however. Then a rolling table came into view, followed by Shadwell, who was pushing it, Klingheimer following. On top of the table lay a simple wooden coffin.

St. Ives's mind went dark with fear. He had no doubt, no doubt at all, that Alice lay in the coffin, but whether alive or dead...

"Your face tells the tale, Professor," Klingheimer said. "You assume correctly. I told you that you would soon be reunited with Alice, and I have kept my promise. She is perfectly well, however. I am told that chloroform often makes the head ache when the effects of the drug diminish, but the pain passes away quickly."

"Open it," St. Ives said in a voice that cracked.

"In the fullness of time, sir. We will open it when she stirs. I am told that she was very gallant in her efforts on your behalf, Professor. She put the wind up our man Lewis at the Board of Works. She brazenly accused him of blowing up the entrance to the sink-hole in an attempt to murder you and Mr. Frobisher, which was near enough to the mark to paralyze Mr. Lewis with fear. I can assure you that Mr. Lewis was guilty of stupidity, however, rather than attempted murder. I care nothing for Gilbert Frobisher, dead or alive, but I was positively elated when you appeared here at the asylum today, demanding to see Dr. Peavy. If *you* had died in the explosion, I would have been compelled to dispose of Mr. Lewis. But the man has redeemed himself by contriving to send Alice to me."

There was a rustling in the coffin now and a knocking against the side. Klingheimer nodded to Shadwell, who prised off the lid with a crowbar and then carried it out of sight.

"She's a great beauty, sir," Klingheimer said, gazing into the box. "I congratulate you on the several years that the two of you shared."

Alice sat up, holding her head and looking about her, mystified. Her eyes focused on St. Ives, and after a moment of evident confusion, a look of horror crossed her features, followed by something more calculating. Shadwell returned then and stood nearby.

St. Ives shook his head slightly. Peavy's was a madhouse in every sense of the word, and Alice was in mortal danger – something that she appeared to be increasingly aware of. She mustn't do anything rash, or even think of doing so. She was staring past St. Ives now – at the heads in the basins, no doubt. She looked at him again, at the device that encircled his neck. Shadwell placed his hands upon her shoulders. If he had the power to murder the man, St. Ives would have done so in an instant, but he willed himself to keep his composure – to watch for his chance, although he knew he had no chance at all.

"Be at ease, ma'am," Klingheimer said. "You are powerless here. You wonder where you are, no doubt, and I can tell you. You have made your way to the center of a grand experiment in the science of human ascension."

Hasbro and Tubby crossed Wimpole Street just up from the gatehouse, not showing any undue haste. The window shutter slid along a track, and was half closed against the wind. There was an old gentleman within the lamplit interior, his magazine turned toward the light, his spectacles reflecting the glare. The door in the side of the gatehouse stood open three or four inches, and Tubby planted himself very near it, ready to step inside in order to beard the old man in his den. Through the open door Tubby saw that a drawer stood open near the man's left hand, a small pistol lying within.

Hasbro rapped twice on the shutter, leaned his head into the hut, and said, "I am Detective Newnes of Scotland Yard."

"A pleasure to meet you, sir," the old man said, making no move toward the pistol. "How can I accommodate you?"

"I have a warrant for the arrest of Dr. Peavy on the charge of kidnapping and murder. You can accommodate me by opening the gate."

"Might I see the warrant, sir? My job requires it."

"Not any longer, it doesn't," Tubby said, pushing the door fully open and stepping into the hut. "Your job requires that you keep your hand away from that pistol." Tubby watched the man's face as he reached into the drawer for the weapon, and put it into his pocket. "Now, the gate key, sir. If you cry out or make an attempt to warn your employer of his impending doom, you doom yourself into the bargain. In short, I mean to break both your kneecaps with my stick if I'm required to do so. It'll take several blows, no doubt, but I'll put my weight into it. Do you understand me?"

"Completely, sir," the man said, looking at Tubby over the top of his spectacles. "There is no need for violence, no need at all. I had no idea of.."

"Of wasting our time while your cohorts escape? Quick now, the gate key."

"I have no *cohorts*, sir. I'm a mere…"

"You're a mumping villain," Tubby said, seeing a ring of keys hanging upon a hook. He plucked it down and handed it to Hasbro, who set out at once to try them.

"I was just going to say so. If you had given me another ten seconds…"

"*Success*," Hasbro said in a low voice.

"Listen here," Tubby said to the old man. "You must cross the street at a steady pace, turn left at the end of the block, and disappear. If you hesitate or call out, I guarantee that you will crawl away carrying your head in your pocket. And that, sir, will be your condition when Scotland Yard picks you up out of the street. Here – take your coat with you. The wind is chill."

Tubby opened the door wide and stepped out, bowing and gesturing at the street. The old man set out straightaway, pulling his coat on as he walked. He dodged a coach by a narrow margin, stepped up onto the far pavement, and hurried toward the corner, not looking back. By the time Tubby and Hasbro ascended the stairs to the entry doors of the asylum, he was gone.

Through the glass, Tubby could see a man sitting at a desk just inside, clearly asleep, his chin on his hand. Some distance away a number of people, the more well-behaved inmates perhaps, sat at a long table in a far room eating their candle-lit supper. Hasbro rapped on the glass, and the man at the desk jerked awake and turned toward them, a look of puzzlement on his face. He stood up but made no move to open the door. Tubby smashed out a leaded glass pane, reached inside, and turned the key in the lock. Hasbro pushed the door open and collared the attendant as he was turning away, Tubby following him into the interior, pistol in hand.

K lingheimer looked away when the cellar door open yet again. A voice shouted, "Sir! Sir!" followed by the appearance of Flinders, out of breath, holding his hat in his hand.

"What is it?" Klingheimer asked him, evidently unhappy with the interruption.

"The girl Clara is run, sir."

"*Clara*, do you say? How can that be?"

"The dwarf murdered Penny and Smythe. They were in the girl's room, no one knows why, knocked about, their throats cut. The girl bolted with a cutthroat boy, mayhaps the very boy as was in the house this morning. The dwarf must have hidden him. Smythe's woman is with 'em. Brooks and Pinwinnie gave chase but were beaten by a fat man in the alley. All hands have been out searching, but there's no sign of them."

"*What* fat man?"

"Frobisher," he said, "who assaulted Penny at the inn."

"God *damn* my eyes! When did this occur?"

"An hour ago, or suchlike."

"*Suchlike!*" He struck Flinders in the face with the back of his hand now, knocking him sideways. "I'll give you suchlike! Why wasn't someone sent to me *immediately*?"

"It seemed right to search for the girl first, in daylight. We all went out, but they foxed us."

"Peavy!" Klingheimer shouted, riding right over Flinders' excuse. "You, Pule! Keep watch."

"Shall we take his head?" Pule asked anxiously.

"Yes. But do so with particular care. The woman will fly out at you, however. Lock her into the back room. Do not underestimate either her physical strength or the strength of her mind. You have your truncheon about you?"

"Yes."

"Keep it by, but do *not* harm her. She'll fetch a good price if she can be tamed. She is more valuable to me than you are. *Dr.*

Peavy! Do you hear me, sir?"

"I'm not *deaf*," Peavy said, having come in from the hallway carrying a teacup.

"Set up the camera. I want a record of the beheading and the activity of the fungi when they are offered a particularly fresh head. Jimmy, you have the pistol, I see. Use it *only* in the extremity of danger. Mr. Shadwell, put the wizard's head into his cage and bring it along. Mr. Flinders, you will drive the coach. You'd best pray that we find the girl."

Trees moved in the dark backyards behind the fences that lined the deserted alley behind Elysium Asylum. The night was full of the noise of leaves and twigs skittering along the pavement. A dog howled somewhere nearby, which set other dogs to howling and barking. The moon floated clear of the clouds, and the night was illuminated. Bill Kraken drew Mother Laswell into the shadows. A piece of newsprint flailed toward them, fixing itself to her ankle, and Bill bent down to detach it.

"I wish that the lot of us were drinking punch at the Half Toad," Mother Laswell said in a whisper. But whatever Bill started to say in return was lost in an eruption of loud, angry talk from nearby. Kraken pulled Mother Laswell further into the shadows. Horses' hooves clattered, and out through the open gate of the asylum came a carriage, already moving out, the driver plying his whip, the headlights dark.

"It's Shadwell!" Kraken shouted as the coach swept past, and without another word he let go of Mother Laswell's arm and ran hard down the alley in the wake of the coach, shouting imprecations at the top of his lungs and waving his fist in the air. A second man within the coach turned in his seat to look back through the window, the moonlight showing his bearded face clearly. Even at a distance Mother Laswell could see that his face was seething with anger, and it came to her with uncanny clarity who the man must be. She was glad that Clara had somehow escaped his clutches. She saw a brick lying in the dust against the wall, and she picked it up and dropped it into her tapestry bag. With the brick inside, it swung like a heavy pendulum.

Tubby crammed the pistol into the midsection of the helpless attendant and said, simply, "Where is Dr. Peavy? Hesitate and you're a dead man."

There was no hesitation. The man jerked his head toward the back of the building and said, "Through the kitchen and down the stairs," and in the same moment shrugged out of his coat, spun around, and went straight out through the door, running through the gate in his shirtsleeves. Tubby and Hasbro wasted not a moment on him, but pushed on through the sparsely populated lobby. The inmates continued to eat their supper at a long table. They seemed strangely nonplussed – used to strange carrying-on, perhaps.

"A jolly good evening to the lot of you," Tubby said, saluting an old soldier in a red uniform, who looked back at him skeptically.

In the kitchen, three men worked, cleaning up. "Scotland Yard!" Hasbro said to them, and none of them offered to interfere, possibly persuaded by the pistol in Tubby's grasp as well as by Hasbro's admonition. They passed between the long counters and steaming sinks, Tubby covering the three men with the pistol, until they arrived at the top of the broad stairs. All three men cut and ran then, bound for freedom, pitching aprons and towels aside as they went.

It was a den of iniquity, and no doubt about it, Tubby thought, but without any loyalty to Dr. Peavy, apparently.

For the sake of silence they slowed as they descended the stairs, hiding for a moment behind the doorframe at the bottom landing. Tubby took in the underground chamber at a glance: Alice visible within the coffin, a thin, pockmarked man standing near her; St. Ives strapped into the heavy chair, with an odd yoke-like device resting on his shoulders; and yet another man – Peavy the mad doctor, Tubby guessed – setting up a camera tripod. The pockmarked man who stood near Alice saw Tubby and Hasbro now, his eyes widening in surprise. Strangely, he remained mute, putting a finger to his lips and drawing a black truncheon from his pocket. He crossed silently and casually to where Peavy was just then mounting the heavy camera to the tripod, and he clubbed Peavy hard over the back of the head with the truncheon.

Tubby and Hasbro stepped into the room now, Tubby seeing a movement near a rear door – a heavy youth who looked at them stupidly for a moment before raising the pistol in his hand. Tubby fired a round from his own, failing to aim it in his haste, and the youth flung the door open and ducked out into the darkness, slamming the door behind him.

Mother Laswell took Bill's arm when he returned from his futile chase. He was breathing heavily and muttering under his breath. She pulled him in through the gate, heading past a wagon with two skittish horses and an enclosed van with something painted on the side of it. She heard a shot, just then, fired from within the hospital. The back door of the asylum swung open, and a man issued from the doorway, his arm bent at the elbow, a pistol visible in his hand. Kraken jerked free of Mother Laswell's grip and ran like a hare across the grass, flinging himself at the man's knees, which buckled, the man sitting down hard on Kraken's shoulders with a look of wild surprise on his face, his pistol flying away into the darkness, clattering down behind the stone wall that half-hid the cellar windows.

The two men rolled across the lawn, Bill battering the other with his fists and being battered in kind. Mother Laswell hovered around them, looking for a way to help, swinging her brick-laden purse in case she could get a blow in. Bill's foe was heavier and much younger, and he heaved himself up now and cocked his arm back, and in that moment Mother Laswell swung her purse at his head. He grunted, rolling free and clambering heavily to his hands and knees, staring at the leafy grass, obviously stunned. He was even younger than she had thought, with heavy, ape-like arms, criminal eyes, and a lowering forehead.

She strode toward him, her face set. "It's done," she said. "They're closing the asylum tonight. Peavy will hang."

He gave her a long look, evidently thinking hard, and then he turned without a word and loped out into the alley. She watched him go, her brick-laden bag at the ready in case he changed his mind. Bill appeared by her side. His head wound was bleeding through its bandage and his eye was swollen.

"He'd have shot one of us with that gun if you hadn't clipped him," she said. With that she removed the brick from her purse and tossed it away. Tubby was just then coming out, bent low and holding a pistol of his own.

"It's finished," Tubby told them, herding them away from the door and around the side of the house. "Alice and St. Ives are safe, thank God." Leaves swirled roundabout them, and the night was dark once again, the moon behind clouds, stars visible in the east. Inside they found a troupe of patients milling about in the lobby.

"Hello, friends," Mother Laswell said in a hearty voice, falling straight into her role. "Are there any among you who can lend a hand? There's been trouble, as you know, and so we have to rally round...."

Alice entered just then, disheveled but apparently fit, and so Tubby left them to it, hurrying downstairs again, where he found St. Ives in conversation with the pockmarked man, whose name, apparently, was Willis Pule.

Tubby got a more expansive look at the place now. It was scrupulously clean and well lit, but there was the stink of a horse stable on the air and a severed head in a basin upon a nearby table. Scientists were a strange crowd, Tubby thought, discounting St. Ives out of loyalty. He saw that Dr. Peavy had been strapped into the heavy chair, although the wooden yoke that had been placed over St. Ives's head was set aside, the wicked-looking, ring-shaped saw blade visible now. Peavy's face held a look of intense loathing, and his eyes were unfocused, no doubt from the truncheon blow.

"Dr. Peavy should not have *used* me so," Pule was just then saying to St. Ives, his voice at a high pitch. "Close onto ten years I've been tortured in this house. I won free three years ago, but he found me and brought me back. That's when he put a drill into my head and inserted the wires. He has a machine that sends out waves so that my mind goes dark and I scarce know who I am. He threatens me with the saw, saying he'll have my head off and pitch it into the fire. You don't know what all he's done to me, sir."

Pule wept now, a pitiable creature, great heaving sobs that rattled his frame. St. Ives looked at Tubby and shook his head.

"Get your things, Willis," St. Ives said to Pule. "Hurry. The authorities will be here soon and we must be gone before they arrive."

As Pule hurried away, Tubby asked, "Is that wise? Setting the man free?"

"Wisdom is a great mystery to me at the moment. I thank you, however, for saving our lives here – Alice's as well as my own. Another few minutes and…" He shook his head. "Here's what we're about. I've sent Hasbro to Devonshire Hospital to report the trouble here. He will reveal just enough to bring them running. The hospital is in the old Buxton stable block not two hundred yards distant, so we cannot tarry. We'll get away in the wagon parked behind the building – the only conveyance that will hold the lot of us. Hasbro will alert the hospital in a quarter hour's time and then wait for us at the top of the street."

St. Ives stepped across to the basins, which gurgled away as ever. He considered Sarah Wright's head, the only one of the three remaining. There could be no leaving it behind, hooked up to the percolating fungal juices, which would cease to percolate shortly after the authorities arrived. Better to take her along. Mother Laswell would have some idea what to do with it. He disengaged Sarah Wright's basin from its tubing and slid it into one of the cages, securing the cage door and covering it with a drape. "I'll just see if everything is running smoothly in the lobby," he said and hurried out.

Tubby was left alone with the head and Dr. Peavy. Tubby looked closely into Peavy's face, which was disfigured with loathsome emotions, his eyes twitching, and his very active, mustached upper lip looking overmuch like a vile sort of sea creature. Tubby knew nothing of Peavy, although Pule's testimony and the severed head on the table made the man's character evident.

"Quite comfortable, are you, Doctor?" Tubby asked him. "Everything to your liking?"

Without looking up, Peavy spat at him, most of the spittle landing on Peavy's own leg, but a dribble spotting Tubby's lapel. Tubby heard laughter from the distant lobby, and then a number of voices rising in song – the "Old Hundredth," sung with a will and a certain amount of high-pitched hooting.

"I wonder what sort of head you'd make, were you on a plate," Tubby said cheerfully. "A formidably *ugly* head, I don't doubt." He fixed the forehead strap around Peavy's head, yanked it tight, and then picked up the decapitator, settling the yoke on the man's shoulders. "I'm no scientist, mind you, but I'd imagine that the electric fluid that drives this machine is conveyed through this cord. Can you tell me how one activates it? A switch, perhaps? A lever?"

There was no response except for inhuman noises in Peavy's throat.

"I'll ape the scientist, then, and experiment with it," Tubby said, picking up the electrical cord that led away toward the apparatus behind him. Peavy began to struggle in the chair, making further noises in his throat. After a moment Tubby stepped quietly up behind him and shouted, "Boo!" into his ear, and Peavy let out a wild cry.

Tubby, seeing St. Ives coming back in through the door now, said, "What ho, the lunatics?"

"Major John English of the Scarlet Lancers has formed them up as a choir," St. Ives said. "Our lot went out through the front and are loading into the wagon as we speak." He noticed that the saw now encircled Peavy's neck, and he gave Tubby a startled look.

"An experiment in human fear and regret," Tubby said, "unfinished, alas."

"He'll hang, Tubby. Better that someone else releases the trap, so to speak. You don't want it in your dreams."

Tubby shrugged and followed St. Ives toward the door, St. Ives carrying the cage with the head of Sarah Wright in it. Willis Pule had come into the room and was apparently regarding the back of Peavy's head. He glanced back at Tubby with a wild glint in his eye. Tubby gave him an indifferent shrug and then stepped out through the door and pulled it closed.

Kraken sat on the bench of the wagon, the reins in his hand. Tubby clambered up onto the bed, aided by Mother Laswell and Alice. St. Ives handed up the cage, saying, "Keep it level if you can," and Tubby took it from him, setting it on the floorboards as St. Ives boosted himself up and onto the bed. Hasbro would ride on the box with Kraken. At last they were moving, past the covered van, its patient horses out of the wind, the high wall sheltering them. Their wagon wheeled around the circle and away up the alley toward Devonshire Street and the waiting Hasbro.

Tubby looked back at Elysium Asylum. The heavy smoke ascending from the chimney seemed to be writhing with demons as the wind tore it. It came to him that he could make out the droning noise of the saw now, and he heard wild screaming rise in volume for a brief moment before it diminished again, obliterated by distance and the clattering of the wagon. On the instant he knew what Pule had done, and that there was no undoing it.

"There he stands!" St. Ives said, pointing at the figure of Hasbro, who hurried down the alley toward them now. Kraken stopped the wagon, and Hasbro climbed onto the bench. They were off again, although in the moment that they turned out of the alley and onto Devonshire Street, Tubby looked back and saw the dry goods van enter the alley, Willis Pule at the reins. Tubby tapped St. Ives on the shoulder and gestured at the fleeing Pule, who made away in the direction of the river, carrying Dr. Narbondo in his vivarium.

THIRTY-SIX

NARBONDO'S ALLEY

The sky was full of broken, fleeing clouds when Finn climbed out of the hearse in the alley behind Narbondo's abandoned house, the night dark for a moment and then brightly lit when the moon appeared. There was the smell of pending rain on the wind. No one was in sight either up or down, just a gray cat running into the nearby shadows. The headlights of a coach crossed the alley far down the way, and Finn could hear the clanging of a ship's bell and the night sounds from the river. He put his head in at the door and said to Miss Bracken and Clara, "The wind is chill. Best to stay inside the coach until I open the gate and the way is clear."

He closed the door and climbed atop the hearse. From that height he could see that there was nothing along the top of the wall but a broad coping – no glass or metal shards to deter burglars. Nothing stirring in the alley yet, either. The gray cat sat on the limb of a tree in the yard opposite, watching him. Finn leapt across to the wall, grabbing the coping and using the momentum of the leap to catapult him to the top, dropping straightaway to the other side.

He put his back to the wall immediately and looked around, but nothing moved, and the place had a deserted air. Moonlight shone on a great pile of excavated dirt and stone – the mouth of the tunnel that Beaumont had spoken of. The digging had undermined the foundation of a single-story stone room at the corner of the house, the room's many windows giving it the look of a conservatory. The weight of the room rested temporarily on posts and beams. There was a half-built arched wall rising toward the exposed foundation. With another day or two of work, the wall would be made to support the corner of the house, a door would fill the arch, and it would appear to open onto a cellar, or perhaps a tool shed.

The broad tunnel that led away beneath was pitch black – no lamplight inside, although certainly there must be lamps somewhere, since there would be no working below ground without them. He saw a canvas-covered pile against the wall, with a lean-to roof over it to keep out the weather. He hurried to it, casting the canvas back and finding a wealth of tools, as well as a dozen or more lanterns and cans of lamp oil. There was a heavy, iron crowbar in among the tools. He had it out in a trice and ran to the gate, where he jammed the crowbar beneath the bolt and threw his weight against it. The heavy screws held for a moment and then tore loose with enough force to throw him down onto his breech. Already he could hear the hearse rattling away, and Beaumont at the gate, pushing it open.

His three companions came straight into the yard, Beaumont leading Ned Ludd. As the gate was swinging shut again, Finn looked up and down the alley. A dog slouched along in the distance, and his friend the cat was still at its post, but there wasn't a human animal to be seen. It was good luck, without a doubt, and he was emboldened to say so to Beaumont. "Have we duped them, then?"

Beaumont shrugged. "Klingheimer might know I'll go under. He's a rare old bird for knowing. Let's fetch some stones, Finn, to brace this gate shut." Together they hauled two or three hundredweight of stone from the debris pile and heaped it against the gate – good for nothing if Klingheimer's men came in through the front of the house, but it was the work of only a few minutes. While they hurried the stones across, Miss Bracken slit the side of Clara's dress with Finn's knife to make it less cumbersome, and then cut off the bottom two feet of her own dress.

They picked up a coil of rope, two of the lanterns, and a can of oil. Beaumont lit the lanterns, and then they all walked in through the half-built arch of the supporting wall and into the tunnel. Finn was anxious to be away – far enough and deep enough where their lantern light couldn't be seen by pursuers. He calculated the distance to Margate in his mind – too far to go without food or sleep – but they could be miles from London before they were forced to stop and rest, at least if the way was easy.

He realized now that Beaumont wasn't following, and he saw that the dwarf stood contemplating the pilings that held up the foundation of the conservatory.

"We'll take it down," Beaumont said.

"Take what down?" Miss Bracken asked.

"Them two posts what are holding things up top."

"Block the tunnel, you mean?" Finn asked.

"Just so. That there post isn't fixed, do you see? It's just the weight above that's holding it." He tied a quick loop in the end of the line. "Fix this around the pommel," he said, handing the line to Finn. "Ned Ludd's going to pull down Jericho's wall, just like in the Good Book."

"It's a lot of weight," Finn said.

"We'll pull along with him," Beaumont said. "He'll follow Clara. I know he will."

"Yes," Clara said, and she held onto the bit in Ned's mouth while Beaumont tied the rope to the base of the post that held the bulk of the weight. He tied a second loop into it twenty feet farther along and slipped it over his head so that it wrapped over his chest and under his arms.

Beaumont walked forward to tighten the line as Clara led the mule farther down the tunnel. Finn took the line over his shoulders and put his back into the pulling, and Miss Bracken set the lanterns and Beaumont's beaver hat on the floor and stepped in between Finn and Beaumont. "I'm no weakling," she said, putting both hands on the rope.

The lot of them set out, heaving away as Ned strained forward, Clara speaking into his ear, and then suddenly sprang forward as the post gave way with a roar of falling debris. Beaumont was flung to the ground, and Finn caught Miss Bracken's weight as she slammed into his back, the two of them staggering forward. A blast of windy dust flew past them, and the debris continued to fall, until there was a walled heap of stone and timbers where the tunnel mouth had been, the new wall with its arch completely buried.

Finn heard a low, creaking sound, and for a moment he thought the roof was coming down upon them. Then he realized that it was simply Beaumont laughing as he cast off the rope and began to coil it, his chest heaving up and down with the exertion.

"There's one in your eye," he muttered, no doubt meaning Klingheimer's eye. Then, taking his hat from Miss Bracken, he said, "You don't lack for bottom, Miss, by which I mean fundament, or some such. If we find your sweetheart, then he's in luck. If we don't, then I mean to try my hand at wooing you. I tell you that plainly."

Miss Bracken smiled and nodded, and then whispered to Finn as he helped Clara up onto Ned's saddle, "I believe that Mr. Beaumont proposed to me."

"I believe he did, ma'am. I *thought* he was sweet on you."

"He's a good man, despite his awful hat. He killed Smythe, and for that I'm grateful – grateful to be alive, I mean. I abhor violence, of course, unless the dirty pig deserves it, which men so often do. I don't include you, Finn, nor Mr. Beaumont."

Clara sat easily atop Ned Ludd, her hand curled in Ned's short mane. Beaumont slung the flour sack, knapsack, and the can of lamp oil over the back of the saddle, and Finn moved straightaway down along the tunnel into the darkness, holding Ned's reins and carrying one of the lanterns, Beaumont coming along behind with the second lantern. Miss Bracken, carrying her bag, walked beside Beaumont when the trail was wide enough.

Some fifty feet farther along and thirty feet below ground, they came to a door set into the rock, cleated with iron. There was a heavy wooden bar leaning beside it. A ribbon of iron ran along the top and bottom sides of the bar. "Now that the tunnel's blocked," Beaumont said, "they'll come from inside Narbondo's house, through this here door, like they *been* doing, given it ain't barred." With that he picked up the bar and settled it squarely into iron brackets on either side. "That'll thwart them for a time, the reptiles."

They went on, Beaumont and Miss Bracken chatting amiably in low voices, Miss Bracken quizzing the dwarf, and he growing more and more voluble. They traveled into the depths, the steep trail zigzagging for a time, passing the first small fields of luminous fungi, which amazed Miss Bracken, who said cheerfully that the smell reminded her of her dead husband, after he'd begun to stink. Finn heard Beaumont mutter something and then laugh, to which Miss Bracken giggled and then said, "Oh, you are a *wag*, sir!"

A dark shape the size of a moderate pig moved across one of the green fields, going away from them at a good pace, its shadowy form vanishing the instant it moved out of the green toad light, as Beaumont called it. They paused to listen from time to time, but there was no sound of pursuit, no sound at all, for that matter. Finn began to feel at ease for the first time that day, and he considered putting his hand on Clara's hand where she held onto Ned's mane. He made up his mind to do it, and laid his hand on hers, squeezing it lightly. "We're going to be all right," he said.

"Yes," she said, and patted his hand in return.

Beaumont told them of a fine great pig he had shot below ground some years back, that he had butchered and hauled to the surface on his back, selling it in Smithfield, but leaving much of it below, the pig being so hugeous, with tusks ten inches long. Miss Bracken said that it was a stupendous tusk to be sure, and that she had heard that men of Beaumont's persuasion, dwarfs that is to say, often had tusks of a similar length.

Finn didn't attend to Beaumont's reply, but said to Clara, "I brought you a gift. Not rightly a gift, but you gave me *Black Bess*, and… Hold your hand out, if you will." He fetched the carved owl out of his pocket. "Here." She took it from him and ran her fingers over it. "Do you know what it is?" he asked.

"Yes," she said. "It's an owl. And very real seeming, too. I can make out the shapes of things, you know."

"How does that work – your elbow? Do you know?"

"I do not. I don't use it much at all, only when there's need. Do you know how your eyes work?"

"No, they just do," Finn said. "When they're open."

"Yes. That's the way of it with me. I could see, you know, when I was a girl, and I remember colors and light. There's no more color or light, just shapes. Light doesn't matter to me. Night and day are the same. This is a good owl, Finn."

"I'll take you to see him, the real owl, he and his mate, when we're home. Would you like that?"

Clara said nothing, but sat very still now, her face blank.

"I didn't mean *see*," he told her, thinking that he had blundered – perhaps he was too forward. "I meant…"

"*He's coming*," she said aloud. "Mr. Klingheimer is at the gate. Along with others."

"Is he?" Beaumont said, not questioning Clara's knowledge. "Can you say how many?"

After a moment she said, "Four."

"So *soon*," Beaumont said. "And it was me who told Klingheimer that I knew the way below ground to Margate. A man's mouth is best off closed lest there's something to eat or drink."

"What's to do?" Finn asked. "We can't fight. Can we outrun him?"

"No. I have a hut down below that my old dad built. There's food and a rifle. It's backed against a cliff, so they can't get around behind us."

The path ahead angled sharply downward, zigzagging again. Finn kept up a steady pace; glancing back he saw that Miss Bracken was coming along at an easy gait, holding on to Ned Ludd's tail. Finn strained to hear any sounds of their followers, but aside from their shuffling and the clopping of Ned's hooves, there was still nothing but the close, silent darkness surrounding them. The trail turned again, between walls of stone that rose precipitously on either side. The air was cool and smelled of water now, and Finn thought he could hear the sound of it not far off – an underground river, perhaps.

"How did you know that Klingheimer had followed us?" he asked Clara. "There was no sound of it."

She was silent for so long that Finn wondered whether she was simply declining to speak, but at long last she said, "Dr. Peavy put Mr. Klingheimer's blood into me, and mine into him. He meant for us to be married. That's what he said."

She fell silent again, unable to continue, perhaps. Finn reminded himself that she was given to silence, and he let her be. After a moment she said, "I'll die before I'll go back."

"I won't let them take you back," Finn said, hoping when he said it that it wasn't just bluff. He heard her weeping quietly now – thinking of her mother, perhaps, and of being torn away from Hereafter Farm, and of the way Klingheimer had used her – putting his blood into her. Finn could think of nothing further to say, and so he once again put his hand upon hers where she held Ned's bridle, and let it lie there.

As if from a great distance now came a sound like a kettledrum being beaten. The sound seemed to be tumbling down toward them from above – a low, "boom… boom… boom…" at measured intervals.

"They'll be through the door quick," Beaumont said. "Step out hearty now."

The wall at their left side fell away now, and the sound of falling water was very loud, although the lantern light wasn't strong enough to show it. Far below them lay a cloud of green light, like a meadow – masses of toadstools, no doubt, with dark geometric shapes among them. How far off it lay, Finn couldn't tell, and there was nothing for it but to go on. The lantern showed a flat place ahead, and then the first of what appeared to be stone stairs leading ever downward.

THIRTY-SEVEN

THE CHASE

They went by way of Lazarus Walk, St. Ives anxious to see what Klingheimer's lair looked like, and also on the off chance that something was afoot. It could be that Finn and his comrades had been apprehended. In that case they would have to act immediately, possibly violently. But the house was largely dark, and there was nothing stirring.

Alice and Mother Laswell had summarily dismissed St. Ives's suggestion a few minutes back that the two of them retire to the Half Toad in order to be out of the way of danger. "You want watching," Alice said to him. "It is unbelievable to me that you walked straight into this Doctor Peavy's hospital and begged him to cut off your head."

His parry was to say that she oughtn't to have walked into the dead house without Kraken at her side, but she dismissed that also. She had no notion that Mr. Lewis had sent her into danger. This was spoken as if in good humor, both of them loathing a public squabble, but St. Ives knew that for Alice this was no laughing matter, although it had turned out well so far, thank God.

He held the cage that housed the head of Sarah Wright, which was covered with a cloth through which its handle protruded. It didn't bear looking at. What he intended to do with it, he didn't know. Klingheimer understood the head to be alive, and although St. Ives for the most part had no regard for what Klingheimer claimed to understand, he himself had seen the eyes and mouth move. St. Ives had to suppose that the head was alive in some sense of the word. When he took it out of Peavy's asylum, he had committed himself to keeping it so. It was a cumbersome thing to carry, and now that it was disconnected from the dripping elixir, there might come a time when it – when she – must be allowed to expire.

The wagon drew up to the back of Narbondo's house. Again, all was quiet, the gate shut. Hasbro made a back for Bill Kraken, who stepped up and scaled the wall. There was the sound of Bill dropping to the ground, and then, as the rest of them climbed down out of the wagon, St. Ives heard him say something about "these here stones," followed by the thumping sound of heavy objects being pitched aside. The gate swung inward now, and they went through in a body, Hasbro driving the wagon in behind them.

St. Ives saw that Klingheimer's carriage stood in the yard, moonlight shining on the glossy coats of the horses, and that a heavy crowbar lay beside the wall, and the lock on the gate had been pried off. Klingheimer would not have needed to pry off the lock in order to get in. It stood to reason that Finn had got into the yard before Klingheimer did, and that the lot of them were underground. They pushed the gate shut and secured it with stones once again. St. Ives dusted his hands and then picked up the cage, seeing that Mother Laswell was giving him a significant look.

"I'll carry her, Professor," she said to him. "Sarah Wright was my friend, and her business is my own and no one else's. You're correct in supposing her to be alive, or something close to it. I can feel her mind turning. She's searching for Clara, I believe, and might well be a lodestone in the underworld. In any event, I won't abandon her. Good or ill, what happens to her will be my doing." She looked steadily at St. Ives, evidently meaning what she said, and he handed the cage to her with a sense of relief.

He took in the heap of rubble where Klingheimer was evidently opening a passage to the underworld, and he wondered who had collapsed the corner of the house in order to block it. Unless it was accidental, it was no doubt Finn's work, he and the dwarf.

"There ain't no time to dig through that there rubble," Kraken said. "Them others knew it and didn't try, for there stands their coach, and them villains ain't a-standing with it. There's another way in, and they took it."

"Yes," Alice said. "There are secret passages in the house. The dwarf took Eddie and me through them, under the road and up again into the Cathedral from behind. The passages are quite deep. I counted twenty-six steps downward before we arrived at a landing."

"Fetch out three of those lanterns from that tool pile, Bill, if you would," St. Ives said, "and anything that might make a useful weapon." St. Ives rescued a pole some two-meters long from the debris pile that would be useful as a walking staff and weapon both. He stepped up the several stairs and tried the rear door of the house, which was locked tight.

"Stand aside," Tubby told him. He carried the crowbar now, which he jammed in beside the door, leaning hard into it. There sounded a sudden creaking and rending, and the door tore open and banged back on its hinges. In they went, Alice and Hasbro

carrying lanterns. Kraken held a small sledge-hammer of the sort
that Thor might have carried. It wouldn't be easy to wield – quickly
tiring – but it would only require a single blow to crush a man's
head. Tubby carried his cudgel. Mother Laswell dug the pistol from
out of her bag and gave it to Hasbro, who was the deadliest shot
among them.

"Five rounds in the cylinder," he said to St. Ives.

They lit the lanterns, pulled the door closed behind them,
and followed Alice through several rooms into the center of the
house, where a broad stairway ascended toward the second story.
Despite the Turkey carpets and ancient furniture, the shuttered
house had the air of a mausoleum about it. The back of the
stairway was paneled with age-darkened oak, and there was no
sign at all of a hidden door until Alice pushed on the edge of a
panel midway along it. The panel shifted inward, and Alice slid
it fully open.

St. Ives wondered at the secret panel having been shut. Why
hadn't Klingheimer left it open, given that he would return
this same way? He was clearly wary of being followed, and so
they must be equally wary. They descended the long stairway,
Hasbro going along ahead, his pistol at the ready. They arrived
at the landing, the stairs taking a right turning and disappearing
downward. On the left-hand side, however, stood a ruined door.
It sagged on broken hinges, having been smashed to pieces, the
jamb torn free along with the door.

"Was this door here before – when you descended?" St. Ives
whispered to Alice, who shook her head.

Hasbro held up a restraining hand, crouched down, and
peered past it into the darkness, looking and listening for a long
moment. "Nothing," he said.

"Would they be at all likely to wait for us?" Tubby asked. "Simply in order to waylay us?"

"Perhaps," St. Ives said. "Klingheimer means to retrieve Clara, however, and he can scarcely be certain that anyone is following him. He'll suppose that we *might* be, of course, and he'll murder us if he has the opportunity, but he'll waste no time on us until he has overtaken Clara."

"Neither he nor his men will give us any quarter," Alice said, her statement surprising St. Ives, who was used to her advising restraint. "He'll be bloody-minded given how things have gone for him today."

"Then we sail under a black flag," Tubby said. "We'll strike first or we'll be a pack of dead fools."

"If we're pressed," Hasbro said, "stay out of the way of the pistol so that I can have a clear shot at them."

The went on now, single file, quickly deciding that the lanterns would be beacons, alerting their enemies below. And yet there was no going on in the pitch darkness without a glimmer of light. "Let's shade the lanterns," St. Ives said, and they did so, using Mother Laswell's winter shawl and Hasbro and St. Ives's coats.

Perhaps they would have the advantage of Klingheimer, St. Ives thought – perhaps they would see Klingheimer's lanterns before he saw theirs.

THIRTY-EIGHT
THE PAINTED BOX

Mr. Klingheimer had never been fond of the darkness, and he kept the lamps in the house on Lazarus Walk perpetually lit. Now, in the gloomy lantern light, he was surprised to see that his skin glowed – that he himself was in essence a walking lamp, which had a fine metaphorical ring to it. Since he had begun to harvest the fungus in quantity, he had increased his consumption of the elixir, which no doubt explained it, as well as explaining his renewed vigor, as if age and time had been set in reverse.

It was a savory thought that he was the one man alive who could travel in the underworld without a lantern or a torch to light his way. He would be a tolerably easy mark if the darkness were complete, of course – no hiding from his enemies, although it would not come to that in any event, he being the hunter and not the hunted. There were three armed men with him, however. The boy Jenkins was at his back, carrying the head of Maurice de Salles. He had a ready need for money, his mother being ill and his manifold brothers and sisters as skinny and malnourished as he.

Jenkins, however, could have little idea what they were about, and he could not be counted upon absolutely. He might run if there was trouble. Flinders, carrying a rifle, came along behind Jenkins. Shadwell, also armed, strode ahead with a lantern. Except for Mrs. Skink, the rest of the house had been out beating the bushes – a reprehensible crowd of nitwits who had allowed four easily identifiable people to elude them. Perhaps he should have rounded up more men and left Jenkins behind, but in the meantime Clara would have been ever more distant.

He considered his likely enemies as he paced along. The women were of no account. Clara was blind, easily frightened, and now shared his blood. She would yield to him, under compulsion if necessary. The other woman, whoever she was, would not have the pluck to stand up against men carrying rifles. That left the dwarf and the boy. The boy was enterprising: he had hidden from the men searching for him and then had fought his way out of the house. It would be more difficult for him to elude a bullet, however. The dwarf played the fool as if he was born for the stage, but he was no fool, and he knew the underworld well. Quite likely he would vanish into the darkness and never be seen again, for he owed nobody anything and had no notion of loyalty. In that regard he was the most dangerous of the lot.

Who might be coming along in back of them, then? It had been Mother Laswell's man Kraken capering in the alley behind Peavy's this evening, obviously unhinged. That meant that the voluminous woman who had stood in the shadows must be Mother Laswell herself, whom Shadwell had allegedly disposed of in Aylesford. Had there been unseen others?

St. Ives had been secured in the decapitator, and Peavy had but to trip the switch to remove his head from his body. Jimmy was armed with a pistol, and Willis Pule was looking after Alice St. Ives, who was a perfect hostage. Surely nothing could have gone awry. And even if it had, it was unlikely that any of these interlopers knew of the tunnel or knew that the others had descended into the underworld.

He stilled the chatter in his mind and compelled himself to seek the mental disposition that allowed him to open the lens of his third eye. He was practiced at the art of it by now, well on his way to becoming an adept. He began now at the beginning: breathing evenly and carefully picturing the hinged lid of a wooden box slowly opening – the very same wooden box that he'd had as a boy, the box in which he stowed the things of his childhood. There was a picture painted upon it of green mountains with a waterfall tumbling down the slope. Birds flew in the blue sky. The painting was something that he had believed in when he was a boy, and he had longed to discover where those mountains stood – somewhere in Wales his father had told him, although even then he knew that it was probably a ready lie. Now he knew that the painting was a shabby bit of sentiment, but picturing the box came naturally and instantaneously to him, quickly focusing his mind.

He compelled himself to gaze upon the box until it lay squarely behind his eyes, which looked inward now. The lid rose silently on its hinges, allowing him to slip into the dark interior like a wraith. Once inside and out of the world, he was able to range forth into what seemed a vast nothingness. Very soon his mind began to ascertain its surroundings and the nothingness took on dimension. He made out mysterious but evident horizons in the far distance, and he observed other questing minds, perceiving them as psychical scents and their thoughts as whispers in the dark vastness.

He was well aware that he was walking – felt the ground beneath his feet, heard the footfalls of his companions – but his essential mind was afloat in the dark, immeasurable night. Incorporeal shapes flitted past like the shadows of birds and insects. Some passed ghostlike through him, and he felt momentary, detached sensations of misery or ecstasy or fear or longing. These emotions, such as they were, passed quickly away, having no connection to Jules Klingheimer.

When Clara's essence – the perfume-like quality of her mind and memory – passed through him he recognized it instantly. *She* could not simply flee away. Clara and he were one under the flesh. She would be aware that he was near, and she would know that he had come for her.

His reverie was jangled by a sudden recollection of the silver bees that had attacked him when he had communed with her at Peavy's. That had been a peculiar business indeed. As a child he had dislodged a wasps' nest from where it hung in a barn, and he hadn't been able to run fast enough to outdistance them. Perhaps the silver bees had been the playing out of a nightmare that had lain hidden in his mind all these years – nothing but an effaced memory. He considered whether it had been Clara who was responsible for the incident, or, more dangerously, whether it had been the work of Sarah Wright. Either way, he would know it if it came again – or anything of the same sort – and he would be prepared to overcome it by a force of will, just as one compelled oneself to awaken from a nightmare.

THIRTY-NINE

COMMODORE NUTT

How long they had traveled, Finn couldn't say. For the last ten minutes they had traversed a downward-sloping field of stones, with occasional monoliths, the upper parts of which were invisible in the darkness overhead. They had left the long stairway and the sound of the river far behind.

"Is he come?" Finn asked Clara.

Clara answered, "Closer," as she had answered the last time he had asked. "His mind found my own some time back, but I did not engage him. Now that he's found me, I can find him quite easily, and I hope to keep him at a distance. Will you put these somewhere?" she asked, and she took off her lead-soled shoes and gave them to him. "They'll do nothing but hinder me if I wear them." There seemed to be no point in asking why, so Finn silently stowed them in Beaumont's flour sack.

Some minutes later they came out onto level ground among small fields of toads that were cut with a winding stream. Their path, a dark, meandering ribbon, passed illuminated pools of water and would have been very nearly cheerful if it weren't for the stink, which was powerful now. Although Beaumont had told them where they were bound, Finn was astonished to see a stone hut standing a short distance away, built against a sheer, black wall. The roof was thatched, and lantern light shone from two small windows. They drew to a halt and Beaumont asked, "Who the devil is this now?"

"A man," Clara answered. Finn could see only a shadow moving on the wall within, but he had no reason to doubt her.

"Aye," Beaumont said, "a man who has no business in Beaumont's hut, the thief, nor hunting pig in my territory. I'll brace him."

Beaumont set out forthrightly toward the hut. When he was several paces from the door, however, a round-shaped man stepped out, his head bald but for tufts of hair on either side. He held a lantern at head height and peered into the gloom, the light falling on his face, which looked as if he had been in a bloody battle. "Who goes there?" he asked.

It was Gilbert Frobisher, and the sight of him confounded Finn, just as it did Miss Bracken, who cried, "God in heaven!" and ran forward. "Don't strike him!" she shouted. "You mustn't harm that man! It's Gilbert Frobisher, and a glad day!"

"Is the man known to us, then?" Clara asked Finn, as they moved along toward the hut now. "I sense that his wits are sadly scattered."

"He *is* known to us," Finn said. "It's Tubby Frobisher's uncle." Miss Bracken had spoken of him when they had taken shelter under the rail bridge, but Finn had no idea that she meant this *particular* Gilbert, or how she had come to know him.

"*Tubby*, did you say?" Clara asked. "I don't recall a Tubby."

"The two of them are the Professor's great good friends."

The old man looked from one to the other of them in a

befuddled way. "I do declare," he said, bowing, "I'm certain that I behold Blind Justice aboard a mule – Lady Themis herself, no doubt. And you, my small friend," he said to Beaumont, "I believe that I have the pleasure of addressing Commodore Nutt. How very good of you to visit me here in this hellish place."

"Who is Commodore Nutt?" Clara whispered to Finn.

"A circus midget," Finn said. "I met him once, and Tom Thumb along with him, when I was in Duffy's Circus, near Edinburgh. That was ten years back. Commodore Nutt has been dead these five years now."

"The poor man," Clara said. Finn didn't know whether she meant Commodore Nutt or Gilbert Frobisher.

"My *own* Gilbert," Miss Bracken said breathlessly, stepping past Beaumont now and taking Gilbert by the arm. He gazed upon her with no recognition at all. Then he looked hard at Finn with the same result.

"Do I know you, my good woman?" he asked, patting Miss Bracken's hand.

She gawked at him. "Tell me, sir, do you know who *you* are?"

"I… That is to say, not entirely. I found myself in this dark land, apparently having fallen into a pit, and I wandered until I came upon this rude dwelling, which has become my home. Come in, my friends. Come inside."

"Aye," Beaumont said. "Everyone in, the mule as well. We'll want stone walls roundabout us before we're through. We must sit, or we'll be naught but targets. They'll be armed when they come. Take care if you go a-gawking out the windows."

Clara climbed down from Ned's back and led the mule in, everyone else following. The floor of the hut was covered with pieces of carpet, so that it was comfortably padded, and there was a stuffed tick against the wall where Gilbert had obviously been sleeping, for a woolen blanket was folded at the foot. A heap of oilcloth lay in the corner, with a rifle standing upon it, leaning against the wall. A box of cartridge sat alongside. The hut was crowded, but there was enough room to sit comfortably, with Clara and Miss Bracken sitting on the bed and Gilbert perched on a small stool. Finn fetched out Clara's leaden shoes and set them neatly on the floor beside her. Beaumont stood. He seemed to be considering things in a restless manner, as if he was uncertain what to do.

"I'm afraid I'm a poor host," Gilbert said. "I can offer you hard-tack and dried meat – edible, I believe, but scarcely food to *dine* on, so to say – food for the belly but not for the soul. I cannot recommend that you consume the fish that swim in these ponds. They taste of filth, although the water is safe to drink if one holds one's nose. I have a capital bottle of rum, however, and I can offer you a tot, although I've only the one glass to drink from. Would you condescend to drink a glass, my dear?"

He said this to Miss Bracken, who nodded politely and said that if ever she had need of a tipple, it was now. She threw back the rum in a single swallow and then said forthrightly: "Now, Gilbert, listen to what I say. I am *your* Miss Bracken, *Cecilia* Bracken. Don't you know me, sir? Recollect now, with all your powers."

He closed his eyes, evidently recollecting, but shook his head unhappily and said, "I cannot say that I've had the pleasure of meeting you before now – a lamentable fact."

"Have you lost your mind, then?" she asked him.

"I very much suspect that I have. My mind seems to have been holed with roundshot, a veritable Swiss cheese. I recall having known a Miss Bracken once – although she would be a woman twice your age. Alas, that was in another country, and

I've been told that the wench is dead."

"*Lord have mercy,*" Miss Bracken said. "The man has gone off his chump." As no one else was interested in the rum, she allowed Gilbert to pour her another dram, which she drank off before wiping the glass out with the hem of her dress.

"Harkee, sir," Beaumont said to Gilbert. "There's villains a-coming for us. A bad lot. Very. They mean to take Clara."

"Not while I draw breath, by God," Gilbert said. "There stands a rifle, Commodore. You have a reputation for being able to use such an item."

"*He's coming now,*" Clara said, with a sharp intake of breath. "Two of them now. They'll soon be upon us – Mr. Klingheimer and the man Shadwell."

"Just those two, do you say?" Beaumont asked. "Were you sure of the four earlier on?"

"Quite sure."

"Then two turned back," Beaumont said. "Why? Because Klinghcimer wonders were they followed, that's why."

"My mother has come for me," Clara said abruptly. Her eyes were shut, and she seemed scarcely to be breathing.

"Mother Laswell?" Finn asked. "That's good news. I passed her a message and told her that we were going underground for Margate. She'll have given it to the Professor and Hasbro."

"No," Clara said. "I mean my own mother."

Finn had nothing to say to this. He had seen Sarah Wright's head sitting in a barber's basin.

Beaumont asked, "What's this *message*, Finn? Do you mean these others know where we are?"

"Leastways they knew where we meant to *go,*" Finn said. "They would follow if they could."

Beaumont apparently considered this for a moment and then, gesturing with his thumb, he said, "I'll tell you the plain truth. There's treasure in a sack buried in yon corner, what I've collected since I was a boy." He stood up and walked the three steps to the far corner of the carpet, pulled it back, and began shoveling stones away from beneath with his hand. Within moments he drew out a leather bag that might have held a large and lumpy pomelo. "Will you take me, ma'am?" he asked Miss Bracken, holding his treasure aloft and gazing at her intently.

She stared at Gilbert for another moment, and he stared blandly back at her. And then to Beaumont she said, "If you consent to parting with that terrible hat, I *will* take you."

Beaumont nodded once, removed the hat, and pitched it into the dug-up corner before running his hands through his hair. He opened the leather bag, held it under the light, and said to Miss Bracken, "Take a look within, then."

Miss Bracken arose and looked into the bag. She gasped and put her hand over her mouth in surprise.

"He's come!" Clara said.

"Listen now," Beaumont told them. "They dursn't shoot into the hut. Mr. Klingheimer is come for Clara – the *living* girl, do you see? He wouldn't have come else. You must stay inside, for he'll shoot you dead if he sees his chance. I'll see what I can do to help, but I'd be a fool to die here now that I'm to be wed." He grasped Miss Bracken by the wrist, and said, "You're a good lad, Finn. Mayhaps we'll meet along the way." The two of them went out through the open door, Miss Bracken carrying the flour sack, passing the window at a brisk pace, and very soon gone into the darkness.

FORTY

THE BLACK FLAG

"If I might have a word, Professor," Mother Laswell said as they descended, her voice just above a whisper.

In the low light of the darkened lamps, St. Ives saw her as a mere shadow. "Assuredly," he said. They had come a good distance from the upper world by now and had long since passed the first patches of fungus. There was the sound of rushing water, although dim, and it seemed to St. Ives that they might soon encounter the long stairway.

"Sarah Wright is woefully uneasy," Mother Laswell told him. "She is aware of my presence, I believe, but her mind wants order. I cannot *speak* with her, if you follow me. I cannot penetrate the chaos of her psychical being. I know only that she is sadly agitated, whereas when I first took her from you her mind was very nearly at ease."

"Perhaps the increasing air pressure as we descend is the cause."

"It might be, now that you say it, but even if that is so, her will is *very* powerful, possibly because of the violence of her death.

I believe that we are nearing our destination and that she senses Clara's mind. Much was left unsettled between them when Sarah was murdered. And Clara, of course, is in grave danger. The sense of pending danger is very nearly primal, Professor. I myself am uneasy within my mind, although whether from premonition or plain fear I cannot say."

"How can I be of service? I could carry the burden again, if you'd like. I'd certainly be less sensible of Sarah's... emanations."

"No, sir. What I mean to say is that if something comes amiss – trouble of any sort – I intend to go on as quickly as ever I can. Bill will not leave my side, of course, and so we won't stop to parlay first. And if something happens to me and I *cannot* go on, someone must carry Sarah downward at once if we're to succeed. She *must* be brought as close to Clara as possible. I do not for a moment believe that Clara will return to the surface with this Klingheimer. Clara will be in need of an ally when she does battle with the man, and none of us is more suited to the task than Sarah Wright, her own mother."

"I'm with you completely," St. Ives said. "When it comes to matters of this arcane nature, I'm far out of my depth."

It was only moments later that Kraken said, "Douse the glim. They're a-coming up."

"Hoist the black flag, shipmates," Tubby muttered. "Both sides of the path, then."

St. Ives saw Tubby and Hasbro disappear into the complete darkness on the left hand. He and Alice followed Mother and Bill Kraken several steps aside on the right hand. They were in an area of long, narrow walls of rock, much like standing stones, lying on their sides. St. Ives felt his way to the edge of the one that sheltered them, and at once he made out two men ascending, perhaps fifty yards below. They had also veiled their lanterns, although carelessly.

There was enough of a glow to see that both carried rifles.

The footsteps of the two men grew audible. St. Ives heard the cocking of Hasbro's pistol, and he heard Alice's breathing. He could neither see nor hear Mother Laswell and Kraken, and it came to him that they might already have gone on, creeping downhill in the shadows of the rocks in order to get below the men who were coming up.

He gripped Alice's hand, and in the next moment the downward glow of the first man's dark lantern swung into view on the path. St. Ives saw Hasbro's silhouette in the dim light, the pistol outstretched, and then he saw the flash of the muzzle and heard the immensely loud *bang,* followed close on by a second report. This second shot, however, was not from Hasbro's pistol, which flew from his hand as he pitched over backward.

Mother Laswell and Bill Kraken had made good time at risk of life and limb in the darkness, but then had been slowed by an interminable stairs. They were at the bottom now, Mother catching her breath. Away to their left stretched an extensive, luminous plane on which was built a veritable city of low stone huts. She wondered who had lived there, so deep within the ground. Troglodytes of some variety, long gone away, for the huts had the look of having been abandoned for eons. The two of them went on, through another field of great, upward-tilting stones, the path winding among them.

Abruptly they came out onto level ground, with a broad view, and in that moment Mother Laswell felt a tightening of her forehead, and a crushing pain in her temples that nearly staggered her. A feeling of despair settled over her, and she had the sensation that an evil presence was very near. She felt a similar agitation in Sarah's mind, and she wondered what accounted for it. She realized that Bill held her by the upper arm now, and was endeavoring to draw her into the shadows.

Ahead of them, at a distance of perhaps a hundred yards, crouched a tall, heavily built old gentleman – Klingheimer without a doubt – and the villain Shadwell, who held a rifle. One of the covered cages sat on the trail between them. Mother Laswell stared at the object, knowing that the cage contained the head of her late husband. There could be no doubt that Klingheimer meant to use it against Clara. It seemed very like madness, however, for the man to bring the head along with him, and she wondered at the extent of Klingheimer's powers – whether they were a long enough spoon to protect him, so to speak, when he supped with the devil.

Both Klingheimer and Shadwell looked ahead, apparently studying a hut very like those of the troglodyte village away to the left, but roofed, and with lamps burning. There were people within – their shadows revealing their presence. One of them was Clara, of that Mother Laswell had no doubt, and surely Finn was with her.

"Shadwell won't shoot because he's got no target," Bill whispered. "That's plain." He lifted his blacksmith's hammer and dropped the head of it into his open palm with a light smacking sound. "How's Sarah Wright in her mind?" he asked.

"Troubled, despite the nearness of Clara. But there's something worse. Much worse. I must tell you that the cage between the two men holds the head of my dead husband, Maurice de Salles. He was an evil man, Bill. He is the source of Sarah's agitation, and my own."

"All right, then," Bill said. "We'll go back up to high ground. I'll come back down with Sarah Wright alone."

"No, Bill. I must see this through. It's my destiny to do so."

He stared at her, his face set, dropping the head of the hammer into his palm. "What are you thinking on?" Mother asked him.

"I'm thinking on taking that there rifle away from Shadwell."

"Don't be hasty, Bill."

"If I take that rifle, Klingheimer's ours, do you see? I'll feed him this hammer as a choke pear, and then I'll beat that cage flat with the head inside. We'll be done with them all, and can go home peaceful like."

"Don't speak so terribly, for heaven's sake."

"Heaven's heard worse," he said. "You stay low, behind this here rock, and settle in with Sarah Wright. I aim to stop this here and now. I don't hold with hocus pocus, nor with the filth like this crowd is mixed up in it. Here's what I say. If they catch sight of me, I'll take to the rocks and come back around to you. They won't have time to shoot me. If you see trouble, douse this here lantern, slip back a nip, and wait for me. I won't leave you alone." He winked at her and started forward in a crouch without waiting for a response, creeping through the shadows from rock to rock.

Mother Laswell said a prayer for them all and watched him go. But he hadn't covered sixty feet before there was a movement in the window of the hut – Finn Conrad's face looking out, but keeping well down. Quick as a snake, Shadwell brought up the rifle, having a target at last, and Mother Laswell nearly cried out a warning to Finn and to Bill both. In that moment, however, she heard the report of yet another rifle, and she saw Shadwell jerk sideways before crumpling to the ground, a gout of blood spurting from his neck, dousing Klingheimer as if from a hose. Klingheimer staggered aside, crouched behind a handy rock, and stared down at Shadwell's shuddering form for a long moment. Abruptly he darted out, snatched up the fallen rifle and the head of Maurice de Salles, and fled away into the field of standing stones.

Mother Laswell, filled with both horror and relief at seeing Shadwell dead, looked behind her up the path, thinking that the Professor and the others might have come down behind and shot Shadwell from a distance. There was no sign of them, however. Bill had turned back now, coming along quickly and crouching beside her, both of them well hidden, but with a good view of what lay below.

Within moments two people came into sight, crouched and running across the front of the hut and away along a narrow trail toward the troglodyte village. One of them was a dwarf, carrying a rifle. Incredibly, he held the hand of Miss Bracken. There was once again the sound of a rifle firing – Klingheimer, she thought, endeavoring to shoot the two runaways. Very soon they were hidden among the ruins, however, and he had missed his chance. She saw the two reappear after a moment, heading downward along a stream that sparkled with green light. They walked easily now, like a mismatched couple out of a fairytale taking a ramble. It appeared to her that the dwarf was playing a flute, and there was the high, thready sound of "Bobby Shafto's Gone to Sea" clearly discernible on the still air.

"It were a *dwarf*," Bill said now in a surprised and unhappy voice. "Shadwell was *mine*, by God, and then a *dwarf* what plays a flute up and shoots him through the neck. Did you *see* it?"

"Indeed I did, Bill."

"I'm to be deprived of killing Shadwell my own self, then."

"Perhaps it was God's will – a way to preserve you from taking a man's life in a state of pique. That would be a lot to account for on the Day of Judgment."

"But God went ahead and let the *dwarf* shoot him? *That* just don't seem right."

"Who knows what's right, Bill, when you're a mile underground in the darkness? We'll make our stand here, come what may. Here's what you must do: If I slip away – trance-like, I mean – watch over me. Maybe I won't, but I must do my part. I'll come back to you when it's done, and we'll go home."

S t. Ives moved toward Hasbro, looking back down the trail as Tubby pushed past, growling like a beast. He took in the sight in a moment – the fallen lantern and the flaming lamp oil revealing a lanky boy who knelt on the trail behind a dead man, the dead man's face blasted half away, a red bowler hat lying nearby. The boy looked downward and held his own rifle out with both hands, like an offering.

Hasbro had been shot through the thigh, St. Ives quickly discovered. He was also unconscious, his breathing labored. There was very little bleeding where he had hit his head – perhaps a depressed fracture.

"It's Mr. Jenkins!" St. Ives heard Alice say, apparently to Tubby. Tubby asked, "Do you *know* this villain, ma'am?"

"Yes. Club him only if he threatens to run," she said, "and please refrain from cutting his ears off." She turned and knelt next to St. Ives.

"Press steadily against my kerchief here over the wound," St. Ives said to her. "The bullet went through, but there's a mort of bleeding. That's right – hard as you can. You won't hurt him."

He removed the laces from Hasbro's boots now, twisted them

together, and wrapped them around the thigh above the bleeding wound. "Lend me your sheath-knife, Tubby," he said. "And your coat, also, if you don't mind. It'll be less of a coat when we're done, but we must get Hasbro topside and we'll want a stretcher. The boy's coat also. Three should do it."

Tubby, keeping an eye on Jenkins, passed St. Ives his knife, which he used, sheath and all, to twist the tourniquet tight around Hasbro's leg, hooking it back through the lace to hold it. "We must loosen it from time to time," he said to Alice, "or we'll damage the leg." He looked at Hasbro's head again, moving his hair aside. "Nothing to do here," he said, "except get him to hospital. We'll make a stretcher of the coats – frap together the rifle barrels for the second stave. My stick will work for the other. It'll take the lot of us to carry it, and it means that we must abandon our friends."

"It's a matter of practicality, surely," Alice said.

"*Practicality*, yes," he said. "It sounds like damnation, but of course you're correct. We haven't a choice. Who is this boy, then? Can he be trusted?"

"This is Mr. Jenkins, an employee at the Metropolitan Board of Works," Alice said, standing up and looking at Jenkins, who was in a state of advanced fear, regarding Tubby warily. "He's an associate of Mr. Lewis at the Board of Works, who I am quite certain set off the bomb that nearly murdered you in the second collapse."

"I'm no friend to Lewis!" Jenkins said. "I did what he and the others told me to do, or they said my family would cop it. I haven't held a rifle except to shoot hare and suchlike, not till today when Mr. Klingheimer said I must come along with him underground."

"When you and I first saw each other, Mr. Jenkins, did you know what was afoot? That Mr. Lewis was sending me into danger? The truth now."

"*Danger?* No, ma'am. Not that. I give you a look. Do you remember? I didn't know what more to do, so I done what I was told, which was to tell them you were going down to…"

"I believe you, Mr. Jenkins. You have a chance to redeem yourself now, sir. We'll want your jacket, your outer shirt, and braces, if you will."

"Bootlaces, too," Tubby said.

"But do you remember the look I give you, ma'am? I didn't mean for…" He began weeping now, mopping his eyes with the side of his forearm as he fumbled with his braces and jacket.

Tubby was at work on the stretcher. He threaded the staff and the rifles through the sleeves of his coat, which he buttoned over the top, and then set about strapping the rifles together along the overlapped barrels, yanking Jenkins's coat over the other end, the two coats neck to neck.

"I *do* remember the look," Alice said, "lucky for you. I should have heeded it. Here's the ribbon from my hat, Tubby."

"And if I might borrow the hat-pin, also. I'll want to tie these jackets shut, but I must pierce the fabric to do so. The buttons alone won't hold."

St. Ives loosened the tourniquet for a moment and peered under Hasbro's eyelids. After securing the tourniquet again, the four of them picked Hasbro up and laid him on the makeshift stretcher.

"Fall in line, Mr. Jenkins," St. Ives said. "Put a hand under the frapping, there, so as to support it. And Tubby, you also, if you don't mind. We cannot afford to drop him. God help us – this is a jury-rig if ever there was one. I'll carry the lantern. Lift now! All together!" And away upward they went at a shuffling, steady gait, Hasbro's weight shared among them.

FORTY-ONE
THE BATTLE

Jules Klingheimer sat in a limestone alcove, illuminated by his own phosphorescent flesh. The head of Maurice de Salles sat in its cage, which also emitted the green light. It emitted other things as well. There was something disturbing about the head, a mental decay that was almost like an odor. The man had been evil incarnate in his day, brilliantly so, but the emanations from within de Salles's mind now were essentially idiotic, and more essentially evil because of it – a bestial insanity that was appalling even to Klingheimer, perhaps uncontrollable. *But why should it be?* he thought. The head was a mere *thing* – a force, yes, but one that could be hammered into a jelly with a stone. Jules Klingheimer, being a living man, had the choice not to be disturbed by it. It was as simple as that. He gave the cage a kick with his foot.

By shifting just a bit he had a clear view of the hut in which the boy and Clara sheltered. He had seen another face within, that of a man who must be Gilbert Frobisher. None of them could leave without Klingheimer knowing of it, and he was fully prepared to follow them – to shoot the two males if he had the chance. He would rather wait until Flinders and Jenkins returned, however, so that he would not have blood on his own hands, if only in deference to Clara, who had innocent sensibilities.

The side of his face, unfortunately, was sticky with Shadwell's blood, which very nearly sickened him, since he put a high value on personal cleanliness. His irritation, however, was offset by his happiness that the man was dead. Shadwell's failures were the cause of the day's distractions, and certainly of these unnecessary difficulties with Clara. Shadwell had instilled a deep fear within her instead of a trust that could be increased and played to advantage. Shadwell had been weak – a nasty-minded, mean-spirited bumbler when all was said and done, with only a passing usefulness.

It was because of Shadwell's ineptitude that they were here now, far beneath London rather than seeing to the preparations for tomorrow's wedding. Women had a high regard for ceremony, especially a country girl like Clara. It would be strange if she did not come around once she allowed him to show her the way, which for Klingheimer proceeded ever upward.

Even now he did not know her true mind. It was entirely possible that she had been spirited away by Zounds and this renegade boy against her own wishes. Klingheimer had seen Zounds flee into the stone village with the woman alleged to belong to Smythe, carrying the rifle that Zounds had used to kill Shadwell. Carnality no doubt explained the dwarf's desire to possess the woman. It was a motive that was easily as profound as greed. The human animal was far too often a repugnant creature. Clara must be convinced of this: that Jules Klingheimer had no base motives whatsoever, but wanted simply to rise to a more elevated plane.

Leaning his back against the wall now, he made himself

as comfortable as a man could be who sat in a stone chair. He endeavored to cast a veil over his surroundings now by looking inward, silencing the mind chatter and allowing himself to drift. He pictured the wooden box of his childhood where it dwelt in the void, contemplating it until the mountain scene painted upon the front panel grew clear in the smallest detail. He saw the grain of the wood and the small cracks in the boards and the black iron latch, flecked with rust. The lid opened slowly now, circumscribing an arc as it rose and then descended backward, opening a window into the spirit world. He allowed his own spirit to drift upward above his sitting form, and he hovered over the box for a moment before descending into it. After a time he perceived the bat-like shadows of the spirits flitting roundabout him. In the distances lay the deeper darkness of the distant sea that he suspected was consciousness itself. It heaved and shifted like an actual sea, and he wondered whether one might sail upon it, perhaps descend within it – what varieties of monsters dwelt beneath.

With that thought came an awareness of two things – the odious presence of the deformed spirit of Maurice de Salles, and the nearness of Clara, whose mind was quite composed. He experienced a flickering vision of her face, of her closed eyes and becalmed features. She was lying upon a mattress in the stone hovel, her mind seeking his, or wary of it. *Yes*, he thought, and he settled his own mind nearby, very like a shepherd settling himself near a sleeping lamb.

A sound like air escaping from a dead and bloated animal issued from de Salles's cage, bringing him partially out of his reverie, and in that brief, unhinged moment, Sarah Wright's visage floated an inch from his own face. It sat upon its fungal stem, its dribbling mouth partially open, its animate eyes staring into his with a look in them of stark loathing. She blinked, and his mind jerked away instinctively, as if it were a fish on a hook. The image began to draw away, retreating toward the distant sea, growing smaller until it floated in the darkness like a green-tinted moon.

He forced his mind to compose itself again, although it was hampered by the thought that Sarah Wright had evidently looked in upon him. Certainly it was possible – he suspected that her mind had been active at Peavy's – but such a thing was unlikely given the depth of stone that separated them. It was more likely a nasty trick of the imagination, an errant mental photograph and nothing more. A mind astray was a weak mind, he warned himself, and by and by he drifted downward once again.

Clara's mind awaited him there, remarkably steady and focused. He searched for a means to enter it, and he welcomed her into his own mind, anxious to reveal his dreams and desires…

…and on the instant he felt a swelling within his head, a cacophony of mental noise like the drumming of dry bones on tin plates. A fog arose around him that his vision could not pierce. Now a wind began to blow, a wind that he saw rather than felt as it opened windows in the fog. Loathsome images appeared within these voids like objects in museum cases – murdered children, flayed animals, human body parts black with flies. In one he saw his own mother and himself as a child, his mother croaking out noises, grasping his wrist and dragging him toward the glowing coal that she held in an iron tongs in her other hand, a demented smile on her face. The images spun around him as if he were fixed at the center of a carousel. He remained still, not daring to move lest he step bodily into one nightmare or another.

The terrible pressure pulsated in his head, pushing at the back of his eyeballs as if another mind was shoving its way into the confines of his skull. He lurched forward, crying out and flailing with his hands in a wild effort to encounter the solidity of something actual. The back of his left hand cracked against limestone, and he found himself on his knees, his heart laboring, his knuckles running with blood. He clutched his temples and sat down again, breathing heavily and forcing down the gorge that had risen in his throat.

Where had the images come from? Clara had not generated them. She was incapable of imagining such things. But she had invited him to open his mind, and when he had, these things had rushed in, just as the silver bees had rushed into his mind at Peavy's. He had descended into the dark inner core of his own mind, its doorway having been held forcibly open. It had been a masculine presence that had engaged him; he had seen enough of the horrors to know that. He staggered to his feet, picked up de Salles's cage, and pitched it out through the door to the alcove in which he sat, watching as it bounced twice and then lay still – closer than he would have wished.

This… intrusion would not, could not, happen again. He had not wanted to use his own mind against Clara as he had used it against the lunatic Bates, but Clara's willfulness left him no choice.

Clara lay on the mattress, pretending to sleep. She had no wish to talk, even to Finn, for talk was a distraction that she could not afford, and Mr. Klingheimer might return at any moment. There had been fear and anger in him, along with a measure of bewilderment. She knew very well what had caused it – the odious presence of the thing that she had found for them on the riverbottom. The monster's head was here in the land beneath, which could mean only that Mr. Klingheimer had brought it with him, thinking that it might be of use to him. It might as easily destroy him. Certainly it would not be a willing ally.

She had been aware of her mother's presence for the past half hour. In Mr. Klingheimer's first attempt, Clara had done little else but guard the doorway, to trick him into thinking that she was open to his entreaties. It had been her mother who had unshuttered his mind and kept it so. Her mother's thoughts were disordered – not thoughts at all, actually, but unexpressed essences of love and sorrow, loss and regret, and of a deep and chaotic fury at the men who had taken so much from her and now were trying to take it from Clara.

She became aware that Mr. Klingheimer's mind was ranging out once again, that he was seeking her own. As her mother had taught her, she envisioned her childhood in Boxley Woods: the black cat Larceny, whom she loved and who would take things that weren't his and hide them in her wardrobe closet when the door was left open; the white chickens in the yard and the yellow chicks that grew too quickly; the color of the leaves in autumn and the green of summer; the clear stream and the animals that lived along its banks....

The pain was sharp, concentrated behind her eyes, when he made his second effort to enter. She compelled herself to lie still, watching the stream bubbling over the rocks, running into a clear pool. She began to utter "The Jumblies," visualizing the words as they floated downward on the stream, the words and sentences passing out of sight around the swerve of the sandy bank. She knew that the stream would turn back onto itself on a neverending current – "They went to sea in a Sieve, they did, in a sieve they went to sea," – and at once she felt her mother's watchful presence as she herself envisioned the circulating stream and the sieve and the Jumblies not caring a fig.

Klingheimer was puzzled by the placidity of Clara's mind and his utter inability to see into it, to communicate with her. He cast out pleasant thoughts and imprecations, beseeching her to understand who Jules Klingheimer was in fact, and what he offered her: wealth, of course, beyond measure. More than that, however, he offered her a father and husband at one in the same time, a superior man quite unlike her own drunken oaf of a father, whom Mr. Klingheimer himself had removed from the world. He offered her insight rather than power, and he contemplated their mutual ascent toward a vista that looked down on all other creatures, an Avalon where the two of them dwelt as one in utter and complete unanimity. The logical sense of his offerings was impeccable, of that there could be no doubt.

He could discover no response, however. Instead, he had a growing consciousness of the sound of running water, of a swift flowing brook passing over stones. Beneath this sound a voice intoned verse – a repetitive, sing-song meter, the words and the rhythms and the ceaseless flow of water going round and round Clara like a moat. He listened for a time, mesmerized by the revolutions of sound. Then he caught himself and closed his ears to it, abruptly certain that it was more of Clara's willfulness. She had never been taught to listen, never taught to obey. By learning to obey, he thought, she would free herself from the whimsies and vagaries of her own mind.

It came to him that he might use Sarah Wright herself to

overcome the girl's defenses – an earthquake to bring down the barricade. It would horrify the girl, but out of that horror might come reason. He set about picturing Sarah Wright's head as he had first seen it, lying in a layered box within walls of bloody ice, the utter terror in the eyes: a terror that revealed the panic of someone who sees very clearly how she must die, who imagines the pain of the flesh parting around the blade, the nerves shrieking, the life blood flowing out. He envisioned the head in its cage: the horror of being alive in death, the grasping teeth of the fungal stem seizing on to the trailing flesh, the green fluids circulating, leaking out of her mouth and nose.

She was a hideous specter, and he focused on her with all the acuity that he could summon – saw her with particular clarity, every detail sharp in his vision, the wizened flesh, the scraggle of hair. He had always kept joy at a distance – a foolish emotion that opened the mind to distracting sentiment – but he found something very much like joy in what he saw within the cage that held Sarah Wright: elation in the stupendous fact that *he* had brought it into being. He had given a dead thing life, or some semblance of it, and it was within his power to grant it life as long as he chose to do so.

He felt Clara's mind waver, as if struck by a blow, and he redoubled his energies. Without hesitation he thought now of the way in which her own father had used her, picturing it with invented clarity, but not far from the truth, for he had probed Clemson Wright's mind and was familiar with the man's misdeeds. He considered them quite specifically now, and again he was swept with a sharp elation. Spittle dripped from the corners of his mouth, and a laugh arose unbidden in his throat.

The sound of it checked him momentarily, but he considered that she had brought the unhappiness upon herself, and like a child she was resolutely clinging to childish notions, refusing to see, rejecting intellect for mere mawkishness. Again he assumed the persona of Clemson Wright, the pace of his dumbshow slowing as it increased in detail. He envisioned a summer afternoon, coming upon Clara in a forest glade, his intentions written upon his face. In his vision, the girl became aware of him, and her eyes revealed the loathing, the childish bewilderment, the knowledge of what was to be.

He had descended to a level of base lust that surprised him but also compelled him. He spoke to her in what he imagined was a fatherly way – base trickery, to be sure, for he knew exactly what he meant to do. She turned away toward the stream along which she had played since she could remember, but her escape was blocked by a thorny entanglement of vines. He felt a heightening pleasure as he moved toward her, hearing the sound of the water bounding over the stones.

But somewhere beneath the surface of that water there sounded the low murmur of a voice intoning rhymes – Clara's voice – and it came to him in the midst of his increasing euphoria that the only audience for the theater playing out in his mind was himself, and without willing it he beheld Clara standing safely beyond the entanglement of thorns. Her mother stood with her, looking as she did in life, the sound of water and verse spinning around them.

Klingheimer was thrust bodily backward now, as if compelled by a heavy, concentrated gust of fetid air, and his head cracked into the limestone wall with such force that his skull rang and his eyes flew open. Gasping for breath, he peered around in misty darkness, the only illumination radiating from the strange moon that was the head of Sarah Wright. He had the sensation that insects crawled within the confines of his brain, pressing upon his skull, and it came to him that something – somebody – had entered him, that he *invited* it to enter – the demented spirit of Maurice de Salles. Unwillingly he pictured the decomposed face, and it seemed to him now to become his own face. In his mind he denied that such a thing could be, and he frantically willed it away in an effort to reclaim himself.

Instead of reclaiming anything, however, he recalled in vivid detail the day that he was hanged. He knew that he was enacting a role that wasn't his own, and yet he saw the gibbet before him in utter clarity as he climbed the several stairs, saw the grain of the wood and the black iron hinges, flecked with rust, that were affixed to the trap upon which he was compelled to stand, a rough hand pushing him forward. He felt the noose tighten, heard the trap open with a ratcheting sound as he fell into the void, his breath choked off as he swung out over the crowd of people who had come to watch him die – to celebrate his death.

A foul smell came into his nostrils, and he heard a high, keening noise arising from his throat. His hands twitched and scrabbled in the darkness, plucking at the cloth of his trousers and slapping the rough limestone floor. He fought to awaken, to return to the world of the sun and moon and stars, but to no avail. His teeth clacked together, and warm blood gurgled out of his ears and mouth, choking him into a silent death, his last thoughts a chaotic idiocy of incomprehension.

Bill Kraken raised the lantern over Klingheimer's body. Mother had told him that the man was dead, that his brain might have exploded, but he had not expected to see the yellow matter that leaked out of his ears and nose like bloody custard. He prodded Klingheimer with the toe of his boot. He had seen a number of dead men in his life, but no one deader than this. He picked up the rifle that leaned against the stone – Klingheimer had no further use for it – and he stepped out into the open again and made his way along the narrow trail toward the cabin where Mother and Clara waited for him, along with Finn Conrad and the old man.

He and Mother Laswell had buried Sarah Wright in her wire coffin, the cloth draped over it – only the head. He himself had removed the toadstool that gripped her. She lay now in a hole near the village of stone huts, a cairn of heavy stones covering it. Mother had said a prayer over it and had wept, but a load of trouble and sorrow had passed out of her face when the thing was done. It came into Kraken's mind that they were to be married at Christmas, only weeks away. He thought about his good fortune – where he had gone in his life and come back from, and where he was bound.

He heard a snuffling sound away to his right, and he saw the silhouettes of two pigs standing together, one of them waist high and the other slightly smaller, back-lit by the light of the toadstools. Pigs could smell death better than any other animal, and they were overly fond of human flesh, especially feral pigs. No doubt they smelt Klingheimer, and were anxious to look in on him. He walked the remaining fifty feet to the cabin door before he looked back. It took a moment, but he made out the pigs' shadows moving along the narrow trail that led toward Klingheimer's resting place, if a man like that would ever have any rest.

* * *

The five of them set out toward the surface after putting out the lantern in Beaumont's hut and securing the door. Beaumont had left his hat behind, which Finn saw as a change in the dwarf, a nod to his high regard for Miss Bracken. Kraken strode on ahead, carrying the rifle, and Clara rode atop Ned Ludd again, Mother Laswell walking alongside, the two of them speaking in low voices. As they trudged upward Finn attempted to explain to Gilbert Frobisher what had happened over the past two days – that which he knew, which wasn't much. Gilbert responded by asking what had happened to Commodore Nutt and the astonishing woman he had gone off with. The whole thing was a sad confusion to him.

Within the half hour of their upward trek, however, a light appeared on the trail above. Finn let out a cheer, for it was Tubby Frobisher who bore the lantern. Seeing them, Tubby raised his cudgel in the air and hailed his uncle with a wild shout of happy relief.

"Tubby, by God!" Gilbert shouted back at him, and Finn looked away when he saw that the old man was openly weeping.

FORTY-TWO

THE PENULTIMATE ENDING

Alice, St. Ives, Tubby, and Gilbert had eaten a late supper at the Half Toad, and now the port decanter made another circuit, along with a mountain of Stilton cheese and a plate of biscuits. Alice felt sleep settling over her mind, and Langdon had dozed off twice in the last ten minutes and was making an effort to attend to what Tubby was saying to Gilbert. Mother Laswell, Bill Kraken, Clara, and Finn Conrad had elected to return to Aylesford, although it meant traveling most of the night and arriving in the early morning. Within minutes of ascending the stairway in Narbondo's abandoned house they had rattled away in Mr. Klingheimer's Berlin carriage, Finn Conrad driving and Ned Ludd trotting along behind. Mr. Klingheimer had no more need of a carriage then he'd had need of a rifle, Bill Kraken had explained to Tubby with impeccable logic, whereas Hereafter Farm had need aplenty. Possession, as every right-minded person knew, was nine-tenths of the law.

"It was the most astonishing thing," Gilbert said now, looking at the fire in the hearth through the ruby liquid in his port glass. "When I saw Tubby shaking his cudgel at us from the heights, and I heard him hailing us, my memory was restored – entirely and on the instant."

"That was almost certainly a result of post-traumatic amnesia, or so a medical man would tell us," St. Ives said. "You had taken a shrewd knock on the head, which resulted in a concussion. Do you have a clear memory of the time you spent in the stone hut?"

"It's tolerably vague," Gilbert said. "No day or night down below, you know. My stomach was my only clock – far more accurate than my mind. It astonishes me that it was so short a time, however. Would you be so kind as to pass that plate of cheese, Tubby?"

The cheese crossed the table, and Gilbert spooned up a mountain of it and dumped it on his plate. "I do recall Miss Bracken going off with this dwarf, however, who passed himself off as Commodore Nutt, which is errant nonsense, of course. I was quite unaffected by her leaving, aside from finding it strange. The dwarf had dug up a fat bag of treasure from under some rocks, do you see, and had enticed her with it. I don't harbor any ill will toward her, nor him neither. I was a mere walking halfwit. There was nothing I could offer her, and she could have no notion that I would recover the lost half of my wit any time soon. It seems to me now that Tubby was correct – that she was not whom she claimed to be. I wanted badly to think otherwise."

"Still and all," Tubby said, "I behaved shamefully. Love should be above suspicion, after all. You, on the other hand, behaved gallantly, Uncle. It was I who was in the wrong."

"Don't talk nonsense out of a mistaken sense of duty, Tubby," Gilbert told him, piling a heap of Stilton onto a biscuit with great care and wolfing it down.

"There's nothing nonsensical about it," Tubby said, following his uncle's example with the cheese. "Desiring to be in the right of something is one of the great human weaknesses. It's true that I did not believe her to be any sort of Miss Bracken, as she claimed, but that mattered little. 'What's in a name?' as the poet asked. The woman was a rose of some variety, or a fern, and if her name was not Bracken, why then it was something else."

"That's a remarkably philosophical statement," Alice said, before Gilbert could contradict him. "And here's a happy thought for you, Gilbert. If our Miss Bracken was indeed *not* the authentic Miss Bracken's daughter, then what she told you about the death of her mother was no doubt false. The Miss Bracken of your youth might still await you somewhere in the world."

"A toast to you, Alice," Gilbert said, winking heartily at her, and Alice drank off the rest of her port. She pushed the empty glass away from her and waved Tubby off when he offered to refill it.

"I have something not quite so pleasant to relate, Uncle," Tubby said, setting down the decanter. "To put it succinctly, your jewel box was stolen with the jewels inside it. It had been in my portmanteau, but it is not there now."

"The Castellani box?" the old man asked.

"Yes, sir." Tubby glanced at Alice, who was observing him closely, and said, "Apparently it was stolen by two of Klingheimer's cut-throats, named Penny and Smythe, not to put too fine a point on it. Both are dead. Finn Conrad told me that the dwarf murdered them for attempting to have their way with Clara and Miss Bracken."

"By God I'm developing a high regard for that dwarf," Gilbert said. "Castellani is dead these past twenty years, of course, but I have a passing acquaintance with his son Augosto, whom I met in Rome some time ago. I'll have another box fashioned and the trinkets reproduced. Think nothing of it, Tubby. We've got out of a tight spot with our skins intact, save for sundry wounds that people like us don't give a damn for. Hasbro, of course, is another matter, but the medicos tell us that he'll live to fight another day. Our enemies, on the other hand, are routed, beaten, destroyed, or have run off in terror. The rest doesn't matter, Tubby — neither stolen jewels nor stolen women." He looked sheepishly at Alice, as if thinking that he might have phrased this last bit more carefully.

"You're right," Alice said to him. "But what matters to me at the moment is sleep." She stood up and went around the table to St. Ives, who was dozing in his chair again. She put her hands on his shoulders to awaken him, and the two of them said goodnight to Tubby and Gilbert. As Alice ascended the stairs, she looked back with fondness at the two men, who remained at the table in an atmosphere of great good will, the decanter and the cheese and biscuits between them, both of them with stories left to tell.

EPILOGUE
THE FIRST SNOWFALL

St. Ives and Alice sat in the dining room at The Spaniards, a log fire roaring in the brick fireplace, casting a yellow glow on the paneled walls, the air cheerfully warm. "I'm just saying that I feel as if I failed Mother Laswell," St. Ives said. "I misjudged things, do you see?"

A short waiter with bowed legs and with a red bow as a tie brought a small decanter of cognac to the table, along with a plate of toasted cheese. "Vittles is up shortly," he said, setting down the plate and decanter, and then he went away again. It was Alice who picked up the decanter and poured a healthy dram into their glasses.

"To us," she said.

And then St. Ives said, "May our family prosper."

They both said, "Cheers" before they tasted it. It was entirely up to the standard set by Loftus's half keg, St. Ives was happy to find – a perfect stimulant to precede the roast beef and potatoes that were being prepared in the kitchen. There were onions, too, sautéed in butter in the French style, and mushrooms braised in broth.

"I admit that I have a rather violent compulsion to twist your nose when you condemn yourself," Alice said, "except that you would tell me that it was nothing more than you deserve, and then I'd be compelled to twist it in the other direction. Humility is sometimes of limited value, as is guilt. I'll ask you this: why regret not doing what you *didn't know* you should do?"

"I'm simply saying that this was a test in… in morality, if you will, and that I failed it. I would that it weren't so, but there you have it."

"You utterly overlook the fact that your friends are safe. Even Sarah Wright was able to take her revenge upon that monster. I'll remind you that brandy is efficacious against the blue devils," she said, nodding at his glass.

Their table was very near a window alcove, and from outside now they heard the high-pitched voice of a young boy shout, "Horror on Wimpole Street!" and they watched him sell his last newspaper to an old gentleman who stood beside the tollhouse across the road, sheltered from the sharp wind.

"I feel as if I sold my soul against the promise of seeing a preserved auk."

"Have you considered that your failing to *protect* Clara put Clara in the way of protecting herself? Of becoming the heroine of her own tale? Mother Laswell came to us for help, and she found a way to help herself and Clara and Sarah Wright into the bargain. Finn Conrad was called upon to do his part, and he did it well. Clara is quite happy about that, by the way. All's well that ends well, I say."

St. Ives smiled at her. "You've always been formidably persuasive," he said.

"Then eat your toasted cheese before I snatch it out of your hand and eat it myself."

Alice was as beautiful as he had ever seen her, and he marveled at her ability to step away from the horrors of the preceding days as if through a door, which she had apparently closed behind her. But of course it wasn't as easy as that; she was simply a stoical creature, not looking back, as the saying went. His mind moved to the night ahead of them, but he reminded himself that it was equally wrong to look forward and miss what was before one's eyes in the present moment.

"*Wimpole Street*," Alice said flatly. "I'll avoid that address for the rest of my days. Have you any desire to read about what they found there?"

"None whatsoever," St. Ives said. It came into his mind that he would very much like to know the fate of Ignacio Narbondo, however – whether Willis Pule would find a way to release him from the grip of the mushrooms or would keep him as a zoo specimen. Ideally the latter.

They sipped their brandy and watched through the window. It was the tail end of the dark afternoon and the leafless trees shook in the wind. Now it began to snow, the flakes blowing against the window glass and melting. The old man across the road hurried away in the gathering gloom and was soon out of sight. The newsboy blew into his cupped hands and then shoved them into his pockets, walking away downhill in the opposite direction. The toasted cheese tasted particularly well, the night outside giving it a certain relish. Very soon the ground beyond the window was white in the glow of the lamps, and snow had begun to build up on the mullions of the windows.

The soup arrived now: *bisque de homard*, the shelled lobster claws floating in the red-gold broth. They clicked their spoons together – an old habit – and set in with a will, not having eaten anything since the morning's breakfast at the Half Toad, where they had said goodbye to Tubby and Gilbert and went off to visit Hasbro, who, thank goodness, would walk only temporarily with a cane.

The evening wound on as they ate and chatted, logs going to the fire at regular intervals, the soft snow falling in the lamplight, and the food appearing and disappearing, right through the treacle pudding with lemon sauce.

"I might never eat again," Alice said, "at least until breakfast." She looked lazy and happy, and the sight of her made St. Ives smile.

Together they rose from the table and walked arm-in-arm to the stairs where they ascended to their room – "the very same room." Here too a fire burned in the grate, and they lay in bed cheerfully for a time, listening to the logs pop and fizz. Alice pointed out that Eddy and Cleo would be home from Grandmother Tippett's house in Scarborough in three days' time. St. Ives realized that he looked forward to it – the family together in Aylesford, sitting around a fire in their own hearth, Alice reading something aloud before bedtime, and St. Ives carrying Cleo to bed, she having fallen asleep in the middle of the reading.

But there was tonight to think of. The wick of the lamp was low, scarcely enough light to read by, if reading had been on their minds. Whirling snow still fell beyond the window in the rising breeze, light shone from under the door, and someone's jolly laughter sounded from below. St. Ives cupped his hand over the shade of the lamp and blew out the flame.

ACKNOWLEDGMENTS

I'd like to thank several people who helped out when I was writing this novel: Tim Powers, Paul Buchanan, John Berlyne, and, for patient editing, proofreading, and invaluable suggestions, my wife Viki.

ABOUT THE AUTHOR

James Paul Blaylock was born in Long Beach, California in 1950, and attended California State University, where he received an MA. He was befriended and mentored by Philip K. Dick, along with his contemporaries K.W. Jeter and Tim Powers, and is regarded – along with Powers and Jeter – as one of the founding fathers of the steampunk movement. Winner of two World Fantasy Awards and the Philip K. Dick Award, he is currently director of the Creative Writing Conservatory at the Orange County High School of the Arts, where Tim Powers is Writer in Residence. Blaylock lives in Orange CA with his wife; they have two sons.